IN EVERY WAY

A CHOOSE YOUR OWN ADVENTURE ROMANCE

DANI MCLEAN

SET THE MOOD PUBLISHING

IN EVERY WAY

www.danimclean.com

hello@danimclean.com

First edition: December 2025

Editor: Jovana Shirley, Unforeseen Editing, www.unforeseenediting.com

Cover Designer: Sam at Ink & Laurel, www.inkandlaurel.com

Photographer: Dani McLean

For the young at heart and filthy of mind.

AUTHOR'S NOTE

This book has been a labor of love.

It takes place in the fictional location of Chance, which is a city where anything can—and frequently does—happen. Characters don't always treat these situations as commonplace, nor do they find them overwhelmingly strange.

This is an MMF why-choose romance. That means that Mia, our protagonist, has two love interests—Lachlan and Sterling—and her happily ever after is with both of them.

Lastly, if you enjoy this book, I'd love to hear about it! Tell me which ending you got first, which path or ending was your favorite, and any moments you enjoyed. I want to hear it all.

Dani x

CONTENT WARNINGS

While this story is a lighthearted contemporary romance, there are elements that may be difficult for some readers.

This book contains:

- explicit language
- explicit sexual content with multiple partners. **Where a choice involves sexual content, it will be denoted by the asterisk symbol (*).** You will be given the option to read or skip the intimate scene and continue.
- parental death (off-page)
- hostage situation during a robbery (police appear off-page)

The protection of your safety and mental health is crucial to me. Please do what you need to look after yourself.

Welcome

Before you proceed, know this: this is a choose-your-own-path book, which means at the end of each node, you'll get a choice—you'll either decide what you will do next, go back if you've changed your mind, or start over if it's the end.

Each option will be followed by a page number, taking you directly to where you want to be.

You're in control. The story unfolds in the way you wish it to.

Live one life or many. Read once or as many times as you'd like.

Most importantly, have fun.

Ready? Let's go! (**turn to page 15**)

THIS ISN'T A REGULAR BOOK. You can't read it by simply turning the page! This time, follow the instruction below, and there won't be any issues.

Got it?

Okay, let's try this again.

I've got it this time (**turn to page 15**)

Um ...

I don't know how to tell you this, but it happened again. But it's okay! It's never too late to learn. I believe in you. Third time's the charm?

I'm REALLY ready now (**turn to page 15**)

1

It would be easy to hate a city like Chance. Loud as a tantrum and just as demanding. *I* should hate it here. People walk too fast, crash into you with prejudice, stare on the subway, and after two years, I still can't find a good cinnamon roll.

A fresh-from-the-oven, melt-in-my-mouth cinnamon roll.

For two years, living in Chance has been like signing up for the Olympics in a sport I never trained in.

That's exactly why I love it.

There's a thriving pulse to this city, filled to the brim with more people than I could've imagined when I was back home in Ferntree. Heck, my parents still live in the house their parents grew up in. By the time I was six, I knew that cows would find a hole in a fence quicker than you could catch 'em, the best place for your boots was by the door, and just because you were short didn't mean you had to let everyone look down at you.

Now I'm more adept at dodging commuters than hens.

Chance is wonderful—as long as you look past a little noise and a lot of attitude. It tests me, but I'm hardly about to let a little thing like pessimism get in my way, even today, where it's as heavy as the clouds overhead.

"Morning, Red."

I smile. Celine never calls me Mia.

She raises an amused brow at me from her perch on the side-walk. "Their coffee might be nice and all, but it's not going to do you any good from out here." Gone is the moth-eaten blanket from last week, replaced with a bright blue sleeping bag. "Trust me, I've spent a lot of time looking."

"I'm late," I explain, trying to rub warmth back into my frozen fingers.

Four alarms are usually enough, but in the two months since Huey moved out and winter laid siege on the city, getting out of bed has only gotten harder. An extra five minutes snowballed into ten, then twenty, and now I'm seriously close to being late.

And I *need* caffeine.

"Can't relate," she says, a twinkle in her eyes. She's old enough to be my ma's ma—bless her—but her tongue is as sharp as the easterly that blew in overnight.

Right now, she's the only friend I have left in this city.

"What's with the skirt? Did you forget it was winter or something?"

I tuck a lock of red hair behind my ear. Celine is never without an opinion on my outfits. Or anything else for that matter.

"You don't like it? I thought it brought out my eyes." Maybe forest-green faux leather isn't fashionable, but it keeps me warm, and I like it. I'd rather look silly in style that's my own than blend into a crowd of clones.

"Your eyes pop regardless," she says. "But you're young; you'll figure it out eventually."

"I'm twenty-seven."

"I've worn shoes older than you," she teases. There's more color in her face today, a brightness in her eyes that is a relief to see.

"How was your night?"

Finding room in a shelter has only gotten harder and harder with budget cuts, but Mayor Jackson's speech last week gave the impression he actually cared about improving support for the homeless, and I want to believe him.

I want a lot of things for this city.

Fanning the flames of hope in Chance is a hard task, but it's exactly why I packed up my entire life and moved here.

"Steve snored all night again. Kept half of us awake, until someone rolled him over. It's fine. Can't do much about it even if it wasn't."

She says that a lot. "Is what it is," and, "What are you gonna do about it?"

It makes me sad that she expects the worst, that people have let her down enough times that it doesn't faze her.

She once said it was hard for her to hold on to good things because getting attached only made losing them harder.

I'm inclined to agree with her.

Celine smooths her long white hair over her shoulders. It gleams in the early morning light. Silky and smooth, a point of pride for her. "You want me to put in a good word for you now that the bobblehead of a boyfriend left you high and dry?"

The wind picks up as it curls around the street corner. I wiggle my knees to shake off the chill seeping under my coat.

She's not wrong. Huey left me—went and fell in love with someone who wasn't me, which was pretty rude after ten years together—but I'm still swimming.

After months of putting it off, I finally packed up his shit. My best friend, Alice, offered to come all the way from Ferntree to help, but she's got her hands full with her bakery, and I couldn't ask her to up and leave like that. Instead, she kept me company over the phone, all while detailing the ways she'd remove his junk if he even thought about walking into her store.

"Hold that thought," I say. "I have until Saturday to be out of my place, but that's plenty of time to collect the keys for my new apartment."

There's also the small issue of signing the paperwork to ensure it's official, but I'm sure the realtor is busy. I'll hear from him soon.

Hopefully.

"Plenty of time for something to go wrong too."

I shake my head. This city really needs an infusion of optimism.

The lime-green door of the coffee shop opens and closes once more. A woman, wrapped up in more fleece than a sheep show, pushes her way out of the crowd and into the cold. Inside is busy for a Tuesday. Not a good sign.

Faintly, I feel a clock ticking, each second of indecision pressing down on me. Monica's always looking for mistakes, but I've never once been late to work. Not in two years.

"Have you made your decision yet?" Celine asks.

It's now or never.

Make Your Choice:

stop for coffee (**turn to page 19**)
go to work (**turn to page 23**)

2

I HAVE to stop for coffee. I can't survive without it.

"Your usual?" I ask Celine.

She nods. "Bacon, cheese, un—"

"Untoasted—I remember. Anything else?"

"I have no need for your liquid addiction."

I tuck my smile into my collar as I walk to the door.

Heat blasts me as soon as I enter, a clammy perspiration already clinging to my skin before I get in line. Ma's old wool coat is perfect when the wind picks up, but right now, it's stifling.

The coffeehouse is packed. A line of people blocks the register, with more at my back. The armchair I usually claim on weekends is currently filled by a small child. Dwarfed in the worn paisley seat, he swings his feet back and forth happily while his mother types on her phone one-handed, brow creased with stress.

I know if she looked over, she'd see the same expression on me, except my stress takes the form of my hard-as-nails boss.

I really hope the barista works quickly this morning.

The new year is meant to be the dawning of a fresh start. Clean slates, all problems left behind. Even the song playing overhead says so.

Performed by the latest top 40 teen star I've never heard of, it's a surprisingly haunting tune about loneliness and love lost. It's been following me for days. Fate sure has a funny sense of humor.

Eventually, there's only one customer left in front of me—a

tall guy with a man bun and a thick black sweater over expensive distressed jeans.

Please let him be an Americano kind of guy. Straight in, straight out.

He's not.

As soon as he steps up to the counter, Sarah looks up from the register and beams.

I remember smiling like that once. These days, I'm learning to fold my feelings neatly away, keeping them safe until I can let loose on my best friend. For a city stuffed with people like they're packing peanuts, Chance doesn't handle vulnerability well.

Can you tell I've heard the word *naive* a lot since moving here?

"Lucky, hey! This is early for you." Sarah's ponytail bounces as she leans across the counter to kiss him on the cheek.

His name is Lucky? School kids must have been ruthless.

"Couldn't sleep, or you haven't gone to bed yet?"

"You know I don't kiss and tell," he says with a smooth, accented voice.

My chances of ordering soon fade away like a beautiful dream. So close and yet so far. Jeez. I never used to be impatient. Ask anyone. The only person I know who is more patient than me is my older brother, Louis, and he's so gentle that we're not entirely sure he's not adopted.

Two years in Chance really changes a person.

"This is the first time I've seen you before lunchtime, so … I'm going to guess whoever's name you forgot last night kicked you out."

"All right, go easy." He laughs. "Honestly, I woke up early and saw what a beautiful day it was. Thought I'd explore the city a bit. I do exist outside of midnight, you know." He's British, but there's something else there, something bouncy and lyrical.

Birmingham maybe? I'm not sure.

As he leans against the counter, I take in the rest of him. Easily six feet, with a trim waist and wired with enough muscle that he could probably push a tractor out of a ditch with his bare hands. The silver around his neck and wrists is thick and flashy, so whatever he does, he does it well.

"Only you would see rain and think it's a beautiful day," Sarah jokes.

There isn't another decent coffee place near the office unless I walk two blocks in the wrong direction. Sure, we have a machine in the break room, but that coffee tastes of old socks and recycled rubber. I like the coffee here. It'll be super inconvenient if I blow up at this guy for taking too long and get banned from coming back.

"Well, whatever the reason, I'm jealous," Sarah adds. "These exams are destroying my life. It'll be a miracle if I see the outside before next year."

Lucky is in no rush, tapping along with the music and still not ordering anything. Did he simply come by to flirt?

"You work too hard," he says.

My gaze catches on his back as his muscles flex. Someone isn't skipping the gym.

"A break isn't going to kill you, you know."

Something about him scratches like a bad tag under my shirt. I know his type.

Everything from the too-tight-to-be-an-accident knitwear to the I-bet-you-want-me attitude. He expects life to go his way. Everything falls into place for him, no effort required.

He'd probably tell me I'm chasing a fantasy by staying in Chance and ask why I am so hell-bent on becoming a reporter anyway.

Okay, that last one is only Huey.

He always left the heavy lifting to me. I chose to move here. I picked the takeout. I made plans and had to remind him about them. To him, I was a walking day planner/GPS/assistant.

He never made a single decision in our entire relationship. Well, he finally made one, and it was a doozy.

Lucky and Sarah are still talking.

"Easy for you to say. When was the last time you worked full-time?"

"Being talented *is* a full-time job," he jokes.

Maybe that's why I don't have room for Chad 2.0's leisurely attitude this morning. Does he not notice how busy this place is? Or is it that he doesn't value anyone else's time?

Do they even have Chads in over there in England?

Taking a deep breath helps. Okay, I might be letting stress get to me. It's not this guy's fault I'm late after all.

I still need him to hurry it up though. Maybe it's time to push this along ...

Make Your Choice:

wait (**turn to page 33**)
interrupt (**turn to page 43**)

3

I DECIDE NOT to risk it.

The Observer building is a relic of glass and steel, the upper floors groaning anytime the wind picks up. One of the original icons of this city's long history. The paper has proudly filled the top three floors since its inception. Production moved off-site some years ago, but the heart of the paper remains.

I rush into the elevator when it opens, following a man inside. Thanks to booking it here, I won't be late. I'm sweaty and cranky without my coffee, but at least I made it on time.

Even better, the button for my floor is already lit up.

I wonder who I ... oh no.

The doors close.

In a hundred years of publication, there have been many good journalists signed to *The Observer*, but no one stands out like Sterling Ross. He's imposing in prose and in person, towering over everyone in strong black suits and an even sterner disposition. Only eight years separate us, but the lines by his eyes speak of stories that took parts of him to tell, truths that have been carved into or out of him.

Sterling is more than a byline; he's a movement.

He's also the reason I'm here.

Ever since I read his exposé on doctors who were misdiagnosing patients on purpose to generate more appointments, I've known I wanted to follow in his footsteps.

I'm surprised. This is late for him. Usually, he starts hours before anyone. First in, last out, holed up behind his desk with his brow furrowed over his glasses like he's solving world peace.

He probably is.

Meanwhile, I'm working late, responding to social media comments on an absolutely crucial post about "Where to Eat after 10 p.m.: Chance's Best Late-Night Eats."

My sigh echoes in the silence as the elevator rises.

Sterling Ross is a tour de force. Formidable, with a sharp mind and unerring dedication to ethical journalism.

He's also more attractive than any person should be. Six foot three, with the upper body of a god. Big enough to overpower anyone he wants, but he outsmarts people instead. For a body like that—and it's a damn fine body—he must spend half his life in a gym. I don't know when he sleeps. Maybe never.

He can make me blush by walking by.

I'm not alone in feeling that way either. Rooms hush when he enters, falling silent in awe of his looks, his Pulitzer, or both.

"I loved your piece last week." The words slip from me eagerly in the confined space. "The way you referenced the allegations without outright stating she was lying while still countering every point with evidence was amazing."

For the barest second, his gaze shifts from the elevator doors to meet my own, and his response is a gruff, "Thank you."

I shouldn't take it personally. He's always polite, but there's no one in the office he's friendly with. Then again, there's no one in the office who warrants friendliness. Sterling's silence is kinder to me than their competitiveness and insults, hidden as jokes.

My bag shifts on my shoulder, and I grip the handle like a lifeline. "Monica's making me include one particular brand in my skin care recommendations that's been proven to cause breakouts. I'm under strict instructions that it can't look like an ad—which, of course, it is."

His long lashes brush his cheeks as he blinks, but there's no change in his expression.

"But now I'm going to use your trick to hint at the allergy complaints."

"Be careful with that," he says, surprising me. "It's a fine line to walk, and the brand will have final approval over copy."

"Oh, right," I stumble. "Maybe you could take a look over it later today? Make sure I'm not about to risk my career for a subpar moisturizer." I chuckle—a nervous habit I've had for as long as I can remember.

His nostrils flare, and I'm drawn to the way his taut chest rises under his black button-up with each breath.

Seconds pass in silence, the floor counter ticking up slowly. Five, six, seven. I'm starting to think he'll never answer, letting the question linger in the air between us, awkward and limp, while I watch the muscles under his jaw tic.

Finally, the quiet gets to me. "I'm sure you're busy though, so—"

"I'll look over it."

The blue in his eyes is unnaturally bright under the fluorescents and piercing in its unyielding stare.

I'm too stunned to speak, but that doesn't stop a flush from rising to my cheeks.

"Wow, um, yes—I mean, thanks."

Shit. No wonder he offered to help. He probably thinks I can't string two sentences together. He'll take one look at my draft and storm into Monica's office, demanding she fire me.

Is it too late to take it back?

"Obviously, it won't be up to your level," I add. "But any advice you can give me is appreciated." The pad of my thumb hurts from where I'm rubbing it nervously against the strap of my bag.

It means so much to be here, at *The Observer*, with him. How many people get the chance to meet their idol? And I get to work next to mine. Or on the same floor at least.

One day, it'll be my desk beside his. My byline on the front page.

My articles inspiring others.

"You know," I start—and if not now, when?—"you're the reason I wanted to become a journalist. Ever since the series you did on selective biotech research, I knew I had to work here. Follow in your footsteps. Not that I'm ..."

Oh God, he looks like this is physically hurting him to listen to.

"Anyway, Monica says no every time I submit in-depth pieces, so maybe it's a good thing I'm only writing about antiaging creams."

In truth, she threatens to fire me, but telling Sterling that feels like whining.

"Are you always in the habit of diminishing your skills?" he asks, shutting me the hell up.

"Um," I say, then stop—because honestly? Yes.

Sterling, of course, doesn't miss a beat. "I've read your work, Mia," he says, stalling my brain in its tracks, then sending it into overdrive.

Wait. He has? Voluntarily? I have so many questions.

"Stop doubting yourself."

The command settles on my skin, then slips under, electrifying every inch of my nervous system, as though he has it on speed dial.

Yes, my body says, jumping at the chance to follow his lead. *Please, more.*

Not trusting myself to keep remotely professional if I open my mouth, I nod, blissfully thankful when the elevator opens.

I peel off toward my desk, half hoping he'll follow me even though he has no reason to, burying my disappointment when he stalks to his own desk instead. Of course he wasn't going to follow me. It was a single conversation. Just because he knows my name and has read my work—which posts, and why?—doesn't mean we're friends.

I urge my pulse to calm down while I log in, and it's almost back to normal when Sterling barges into Monica's office and slams the door. It's kind of a useless gesture—the glass hides nothing. As soon as she raises her voice, we'll all hear it, and she likes that.

It keeps us in line.

The only person she's never yelled at is Sterling. If he's called in—and I can count the times I've seen it on one hand—you can't hear a word. I've never met a man so attached to keeping his cards close.

Which is why the whole office jumps when the shouting starts.

"This is a business," Monica says. "Not your personal playground. Whatever crush you're harboring—"

"I wasn't asking." Sterling casts an impressive shadow from where he looms over her desk. An immovable object.

Monica rises to the challenge, her palms pressed to her desk. "I don't care who you want. Pick someone else."

"No," he responds. Short. Sharp. "If you want this story, this is what I need. It's nonnegotiable."

"You don't control me, Sterling. If you don't like my decisions, you know where the door is."

"How long do you think you'll keep your job after I walk?"

Silence fills the office as Monica stares him down.

"One mistake, and she's fired. Do you understand?"

Sterling opens the door and storms out without answering her. It hits the reset button, and the rest of us scramble to pretend like we weren't glued to every word.

I risk a look into her office and freeze.

Monica's gaze is ice cold, twin pools of disdain pinning me to my chair. I quickly turn back to my computer.

The ache behind my eyes is building. I really wish I hadn't skipped coffee, but at least I don't have to face Monica. My skin care piece is due to her by the end of the day, and I need to get a jump start on my weekend assignment at the opening of Zero, this new bar downtown.

My head throbs a little harder when my phone rings, and I stare down at the empty mug in my hands. So close. I could ignore it, but what if it's my folks? Or Alice? Maybe I won a competition I don't remember entering, and not answering could mean passing up a brand-new car or a trip to the Seychelles.

I fish my phone out of my pocket, and it's even better than a free trip; it's a whole new chapter of my life.

"Hi, Mia. It's Bryan from New Realty. I'm glad I caught you. I wanted to let you know that everything is ready for you to sign."

I bite back a squeal of delight.

In the corner of my eye, I can see Bianca is trying to eavesdrop, but she's intercepted by Andy, who is probably trying to pawn off his proofing again. She shoves her bowl of mints at him and scowls when he doesn't take one.

"When can I pick up the keys?"

I need to be out before Saturday, so the sooner, the better. I'll have to move my stuff late at night, after I'm done here, but it'll be worth it.

"Once we confirm payment of the deposit, you can collect the keys."

"I'll send it right now."

Yes, this is perfect. I needed some good news.

I jot down the address and barely get a thank-you out before he hangs up. I guess manners aren't as important as his next commission.

Alice picks up so fast that I have to hide my smile.

"You'll never guess who I saw today," she says, always mid-conversation. I can picture her—her apron dusted in flour, curls piled high on her head in a riotous bun, phone on speaker while she keeps her hands busy kneading. "*Hot Bod*. He picked up a special order earlier. For his mom," she emphasizes.

"Oh."

The last time Alice said those words, it was because her date still relied on his ma to buy his underwear.

"No, no, it's a good thing. She's setting up a book club, and he wanted to make sure their first meeting started off right."

Gosh, that's sweet. "Please tell me you asked for his number this time."

Outside, the sky is awash in gray. I hope it rains soon. I miss the thrill of lightning. It reminds me of home.

"I chickened out," she admits. "I don't know. It just seems creepy to hit on a customer when I'm working."

"It's not creepy. It's romantic. This is what, the third time you've run into each other?"

"Fourth. He actually made a joke that we should make plans in advance next time, and I was so flustered that I handed over the business card for the bakery." She groans and turns off the oven timer that started beeping. Her voice gets more distant. "It was so embarrassing."

"He's clearly into you. He'll be back."

She sighs. "I hope so. So, is it good news? Did you get the apartment?"

There's no hiding the smile now. "Yep."

Alice lets out the squeal I can't. "Video chat next week? I miss talking to your face."

"I miss talking to yours. I've gotta go, but please promise me you'll flirt with Hot Bod next time he comes in, or I'm jumping on a plane and making you."

"Don't threaten me with a good time," she jokes. "Oh, the buns are ready. Love you."

"You too."

Fate is a lovely concept. Destiny? Soulmates?

Bad people facing karmic retribution, balancing out the evils committed in the world, while good people live long, happy lives.

A wonderful idea.

If only real life worked that way.

If Fate exists, she's fickle and unpredictable. Maybe Cupid ghosted her one too many times or told her that he didn't really want a commitment right now, all the while speed-matching on a dating app as he sat beside her.

Maybe she's sick of doing all the work while we do nothing.

I don't hold it against her.

I, Mia Finnegan, will create the change I want to see in the world, and I want to live in a world where strangers will do the same for me.

Let Fate take a day off. She's earned it.

Sterling's response arrives fifteen minutes after I convinced myself to press Send, and what the hell does that mean? Did he even read it? It's only 1,600 words, but certainly, he's got more important things to do than read about eczema treatments. Or maybe not. Maybe he's so offended by my terrible writing that he took one look and couldn't stomach the rest.

Maybe I'll open his comments and find the entire draft redlined and a single note to quit while I'm behind.

"I told you to stop that."

I shiver at the deep tone of Sterling's voice.

A faded *Observer* mug is placed in front of me, branded with

The Observer's original motto—*Small print, big difference.* There's a chip over the *V*. It's been run through the dishwasher so much that it's got varicose veins. I've seen it many times before on Sterling's desk.

I follow the offering up a well-defined arm to the man in question. Sterling blinks down at me, tall enough to block out the overhead lamps.

"I guarantee it tastes terrible, but the caffeine works."

He brought me coffee? Am I dreaming?

For a second, all I can do is stare. The coffee here is notoriously bad—bitter and burnt. There's not a single redeeming feature about it.

I cup the mug in both hands. You couldn't tear it from me.

"So, is this a prank or an undercover-boss sort of situation?"

Sterling slides one hand into his pants pocket and ignores the question. "How busy are you?"

That certainly isn't what I was expecting. "Um ..." Is he digging? "A little."

He continues, checking his phone when it beeps, "The article I'm working on has become a little more complicated than I originally planned. I need a second pair of eyes to dig through the data."

He doesn't usually need an assistant. I wonder what the piece is.

"Will it take long?" I've seen the stacks of research that go along with Sterling's investigations, the long hours he submits himself to. I'm still not convinced he sleeps.

Rest will be a distant memory if I agree, especially since I need to do my actual job as well.

"This isn't something that can be rushed, Mia." There's a rough edge to the way he says my name that raises the hair on the back of my neck. "It's extremely important, and it can't be taken lightly."

I swallow.

Why me? We're not a huge company anymore, but there are still plenty of options for help, and I know at least half the office would jump at his command. But he's not asking them; he's asking me.

And he brought coffee.

I make the mistake of checking Monica's office. She's staring, and she's livid.

"I don't know ..."

The look Sterling levels at me is serious. "Yes or no, Mia."

This is everything I've been waiting for, but like all wishes, it comes with a cost.

If I say yes, I already know Monica will use it against me.

But if I say no, I'll miss out on the opportunity to work with the man who inspired me to apply here in the first place.

What do I do?

Make Your Choice:

assist Sterling (**turn to page 38**)
turn him down (**turn to page 50**)

4

I WAIT.

Back in Ferntree, waiting is enjoyable, the everyone-knows-everyone icing on every cake. Neighbors are friends, and friends are family.

I miss it deeply, along with my parents and Alice and the best rocky road fudge ice cream I've ever tasted, but this city called to my heart from the moment I learned of the world beyond the highway.

Growing up in a small town taught me the beauty of community. The value in people working together, sharing space and caring for each other. I'm determined to bring that to Chance in whatever way I can.

One day, the byline *by Mia Finnegan* will be proof I've done some good in the world, not just three words that sit under a post for "17 Succulent Meals to Keep You Warm This Winter."

I learned great reporting from the brave and brilliant minds of Sterling Ross, Ruslan Seitov, and Aubriella Noelle. Sterling is still in his prime—he's only eight years older than me—but he kick-started his career with an explosive piece at twenty-two, which is five years younger than I am now.

Hopefully, I'm not too late to follow in his footsteps.

As soon as I discovered he lived and worked right here in Chance, at *The Observer*, I knew where I wanted to be.

Huey said I forced him to move here. Maybe I did. I'd been so set on our big, bright future together that I hadn't wanted to see any other option. He'd always been hesitant to change, always looking for the trap door in every decision. I thought he was just nervous. Heck, so was I. But I wanted to realize my dream more than I was afraid.

I still do.

"Anyway, I'll get out of your hair now."

Finally.

Lucky—and I'm still not over that—turns, giving me a wide smile. It is, of course, gorgeous and hugely distracting. His hair looks satin soft, as dark as his trimmed beard and equally well cared for. Then there are the tattoos.

"Floor's all yours, love."

Great. On top of it all, he has to be one of the sexiest men I've ever met.

I step forward, meeting Sarah's smile with my own.

"A caramel latte and a fresh bacon and cheese sandwich to go." I wince. "Please." This is the end then. I'm finally rushed enough to forget my manners.

It's all downhill from here.

Speaking of handsome strangers who I don't have time for ... he's stepped to the side, but we're close enough that I can count every freckle.

I stand a little taller, fighting the urge to hunch my shoulders, hiding my chest, which is another bad habit I've gained recently. You would, too, after a dozen different men stared at your breasts while telling you to smile more. As if they'd even notice from that viewpoint ...

Sarah takes my money and returns with the sandwich. As I move away from the counter to wait for my coffee, Lucky joins me.

"You're too tense."

From this distance, I catch the notes of his woodsy cologne. It suits him.

"You're too friendly," I retort. "Your girlfriend could have served half of the line by now if you hadn't been so selfish."

His eyebrows climb up his forehead before he grimaces. "Sarah's my cousin actually, but I'll take that jealousy as a compliment."

"You shouldn't," I say, trying to cover the flush of attraction and embarrassment flooding through me. This is why I don't talk before coffee.

"My apologies." But it doesn't sound like he's sorry at all. "Let me make it up to you." He pulls a hundred-dollar bill from his pocket, casual, like they appear for him out of thin air. Maybe they do. "For your coffee."

His face is angular, with pink lips under sharp cheekbones, and his smile moves like the tide, smooth and enticing. I take the money from him and ignore the spark I feel when our fingers touch. He might be able to treat money like it's nothing, but I know a much more deserving recipient.

"Thank you."

The bill folds easily into a napkin, which I place alongside Celine's sandwich.

"I'm Lachlan," he adds. "But you can call me Lucky."

"Do I have to?"

Lucky's laugh is loud and boisterous. The butterflies in my stomach jump and flutter like a puppy among fallen leaves.

"Love, you can call me anything you'd like."

Oh God, I might be blushing.

Is he really flirting with me?

It's hard to tell since I haven't flirted with anyone since ... hmm. Too long.

It's not something I'm good at. Banter takes wit and a silky sort of seduction I've never understood, let alone had. Lucky has it coming out of his perfect pores.

"Mia," I say, holding my hand out.

The calluses on his fingers graze my skin when we shake, and a million questions flare to life. Who is this guy who wanders the streets on a Tuesday morning just because he can?

Why can't I take my eyes off him?

"You're right," he says, keeping my hand in his.

He turns it over with a look of concentration, and I have the ridiculous idea that he's about to kiss it. The sharp tang of anticipation stings my throat.

"Coffee isn't nearly enough to apologize. Have dinner with me."

In shock, I pull my hand free. He doesn't look upset about it.

"But you don't know anything about me."

"That's what dinner is for."

Unbelievable. "Have you always been this presumptuous, or did money make you that way?"

It's an educated guess that must hit close to home because he sobers.

"It's nice to have, but I don't see any reason to put material shit on a pedestal. There are far better things to covet."

His eyes don't leave mine, and I can feel myself flushing all the way to my toes.

"Clean air, equal rights, taxing the rich?" I guess. It's what I want.

"Sure," he says, leaning in. Everything about him is intoxicating. "There's also art, food, and sex."

I could set a match to my clothes and not feel the fire burn as brightly as his words do.

Thankfully, as he opens his mouth to say more, the barista calls out my order.

About time!

take your drink (**turn to page 47**)

5

"OKAY," I say, "where do we start?"

Sterling clears off the desk behind mine, which is being used as a tech graveyard. In one long sweep of his arm, he corrals everything into an empty box and sets it on the floor. It's a smooth move. Powerful.

He could do that to my desk, easily. In a fit of passion, throwing everything to the floor, then grabbing me and ...

I turn to hide the fierce blush that rushes to my cheeks.

Then he's back, sitting *right there*, inches away from me, with his laptop and a terrifying stack of financial records. It makes a resounding thump as it's set in front of me.

"I've already highlighted what I'm looking for on the first few pages. I need you to look through the rest and let me know if anything else jumps out at you."

I open my mouth to follow up, but his attention is gone, all gates closed as he types.

Okay ...

There's no reason I should feel anxious right now—except, actually, there is because the man I've looked up to since I discovered his writing has just asked for my help, and I'm going to do it, even if it risks me losing what little I have here.

I look over my shoulder and catch him quickly turning away. "When do you need it done by?"

Sterling doesn't take his eyes off his screen, his eyes narrowed and focused. "Monday."

"That's six days away."

He hums an acknowledgment. I get nothing else.

So much for working together.

The highlights don't reveal much—an account number that recurs every other page and some red marks beside any transfer over fifty thousand dollars. These records go back at least six months, and I'm going to have to sleep here if I want any chance of finishing it before next week.

"So ..." I start, ignoring his silence. I might be a small-town girl, but I can be just as stubborn as he is. "What's the story?"

His hand twitches. There's a stack of blue Post-its sitting by a mug spilling over with hotel pens, and when he reaches for them, I wonder how we're going to work together if he refuses to talk to me. Maybe we'll work exclusively by note.

A small glimmer of hope appears when he cocks his head in my direction, lips parting and closing again. God, I never watch anyone this closely, but with Sterling, every detail is one more piece to a puzzle I'm desperate to solve.

My gut churns. The urge to fill the silence with words is almost indescribable; it itches under my skin, stretching and pulling at my patience as the seconds tick over.

Is it some sort of power play? Use me as an errand girl while he dangles the promise of a real story in front of me? How did he even know that's what I wanted? Does he have lunch with Monica and laugh over how naive I am?

My stomach flips over.

Eventually, I accept my fate, slip my headphones on, and let Hayley Williams keep me company as I work.

I collect the keys to my new place that night and find a letter slipped under my door.

Welcome to the building, neighbor! I'm 704, down the hall. Shout if you need anything or if the music's too loud. Text if I can't hear you. Thanks, Lucky

There's a badly scrawled phone number underneath. I can't tell if it's a scam, but I'd rather be safe than sorry, so I crumple the paper up and throw it in the trash.

Sterling isn't making it easy to ignore him.

Anyone would think he's a spy, not a journalist, tailored in all black, his collarbone exposed by the open collar of his shirt.

How am I meant to work like this? It's completely distracting.

"Maybe you shouldn't be in the office if you're having trouble concentrating."

I tear my eyes away from his throat to find him peering down at me. Huh?

"You're staring." His voice, deep and final, does not make room for a question.

I flush all the way to my toes.

He noticed. Of course he noticed. Details are his job. Still, I can't help the zip of a thrill that runs down my spine.

"I skipped breakfast," I lie.

As Sterling checks his phone, a crease forms between his brows. I've spent a lot of time staring at him, trying to work out what that crease means and how I can make it go away.

"Bad news?" I can't help but ask.

His eyes flick up to mine. They're so, so blue. Fall skies, clear and cool. My favorite.

"Nothing I can't handle." *Not your business,* he means.

Right. We're not friends. Sterling doesn't have work friends.

In college, I dreamed of working here, near—and hopefully with—the famed Sterling Ross, cutting through the PR schemes that covered the asses of the rich and powerful, exposing the underhanded motives they used to stretch the class divide even further.

Now I'm questioning why I ever wanted to be near the man.

This is why you should never meet your heroes.

My neck gave up an hour ago and is now protesting loudly. I push my laptop away, rolling the aching muscles but it doesn't help.

Everyone else left hours ago, leaving only Sterling and me. It's quiet enough that I can count his even breaths. I'd almost think he was asleep.

I glance over and find him watching me.

He keeps doing that.

He reaches over to replenish his stack of papers, and my gaze snags on his hands—strong, with long fingers and no freckles. A clean canvas, highlighting the rippling of veins under his skin. I want them on me.

His sleeves are rolled up, and I stare at the now-bare skin of his forearms. There's a fine layer of dark hair there. My pulse spikes. I bet his calves look the same. Mature. Rugged. This newfound fact coalesces into my image of him, morphing it into something gruffer to match the deep furrow of his brow and rough growl of his voice.

It's dangerously sexy territory, not that I've ever needed an excuse to think he was sexy before.

A sneeze tickles my nose, and I rush to cut it off, but a soft, muffled snort escapes me. "Excuse me," I say when I'm sure there won't be another.

Sterling reaches across his desk, pulling a Kleenex from the box and thrusting it toward me, but that's not what stops my breath. Poking out above the cuff of his shirt is a black four-leaf clover.

"Oh, I didn't know you had a tattoo."

Immediately, I know it's the wrong thing to say.

Sterling stills, drops the tissue on my desk, and rolls down his sleeves. "I don't let most people see it."

Disappointment flashes cold against my skin. I guess I'm most people.

It's late. The sun went down hours ago, and I can't remember if I ate lunch. My stomach grumbles, and my back is screaming, but there's at least a hundred pages to still get through. If I knew what I was really looking for, I could work faster. Any detail at all would help, but Sterling's been nothing but vague. Does he think I'm going to steal the story from under his nose?

This is ridiculous.

Is this really what he wanted me for? To sit pretty and shut up?

Once again, I've let his reputation intimidate me. If I can't hold a conversation with a colleague, how can I expect to ever hold my own against Fortune 500 assholes?

I'm better than this.

Make Your Choice:

say something to him (**turn to page 64**)
let it go (**turn to page 86**)

6

"EXCUSE ME," I say in my calmest voice. "Can I get—"

"Just one second," Sarah says, smiling over Lucky's shoulder.

My jaw clenches as I smile back. "It's just that there are a lot of people waiting, and—"

The man in front of me turns. He is one of the most attractive men I've ever seen, second only to Sterling. Rye-whiskey eyes, five-o'clock shadow, and a wicked smile. He's dressed for comfort. Either he rolled out of someone's bed or he's ready to roll into one.

I stand taller, fighting the urge to hunch and hide my chest. It's a beacon of attention—wanted or not.

And I do want it.

He speaks over his shoulder, gaze never leaving mine, his eyes glimmering with bright amusement. "It's all right, Sarah. I'll let you get back to work. Just wanted to come and say hey."

As he pushes off the counter, I fill the empty space, but he stays close, and now all I can think about is his body heat and the scent of leather and smoke. It's intoxicating—rebellious and decadent in the way all bad decisions are—and I need to get my coffee before I do something embarrassing, like fall into his arms.

"A caramel latte and a fresh bacon and cheese sandwich to go."

A hand shoots out when I go for my wallet. Lucky holds a

crisp bill out across the counter. It's a hundred. A tactic to impress me? Or does he just have enough money to not care?

"Let me," he says. "An apology for holding you up."

I push it away. "I can pay for myself."

"I'm sure you can." He nods to Sarah. "Make it two."

"Sure thing." Sarah smiles, taking his money.

I step aside to wait, and Lucky comes with me.

There are fine lines at the corners of his eyes that crinkle when he smiles. I suspect he never stops.

"Thank you," I say.

You can take the girl off the farm, but the manners stick like glue.

"Having a bad day?"

"Only when someone thinks the morning rush is the perfect time to flirt," I counter. "News flash: not every person you meet thinks you're as amazing as you obviously do."

He's close. Temptingly so. If my body is a compass, he's north, pulling my attention, begging me to turn my head. A shiver runs through me.

I can't stop myself. I look over to find him watching me, his eyes shining. Why is it always the hot ones who are the most trouble?

"I don't always," he says, as if that's meant to mean something to me.

"Excuse me?"

"Flirt. Only when I meet someone interesting."

Did that really work for him?

"You could have chosen a better time to do it. I'm pretty sure she'll be here all day."

He looks confused, tiny lines collecting between his brows before they climb sky high. "Wait, Sarah? She's my cousin."

Oh.

"But she doesn't have an accent," I blurt.

He steps toward me as someone passes behind him, and he doesn't move back after they're gone. My hand brushes his sweater. It's so damn soft, I could cry. "Mum moved to Manchester when she met my dad, but the rest of the fam lives over here."

His voice is husky and rich and has no right to sound as good as it does. No right at all. Perspiration starts to collect at my temples, the back of my neck. I pull on the sleeves of my coat and take a deep breath. How long does a coffee and sandwich take?

"Is that why you're named after a dog?"

His surprise gives way to a boisterous laugh, as free and easy as the rest of him, and my traitorous lips curl in response. A few heads turn in our direction.

"It's a nickname. Name's Lachlan." He holds his hand out, thick black ink curling over his skin. "But my friends call me Lucky."

This is a grown man. A man who's older and more experienced than me. It should intimidate me. God knows there are enough guys in this city who have tried.

But all it makes me want to do is grind my boot into the ground and be the one to put him on his knees.

I'd bet he wouldn't even mind.

It's such a horrible, no-good, perfect approximation of all the things that get me going. I can practically feel Alice nudging me to get closer.

Though I make no move to shake his hand, Lucky isn't deterred. "Are you always this chatty in the mornings?"

I square my shoulders and look up at him.

Go on, I hear Alice saying. *You're hot and single. What have you got to lose*?

"Sometimes. On a really good morning, my mouth is preoccupied." I flush as I say it. I love sex—I miss it—but saying it out loud? That's a different story. It's the kind of thing that can make people uncomfortable.

But from the way Lucky's gaze darkens and zeroes in on my lips, he's nowhere near uncomfortable. Discomfort might as well be on the other side of the moon for how far away it is. Something electric tingles down my spine.

He slips a hand into his pocket and slowly, deliberately lifts his gaze to meet mine. Completely at ease and definitely interested.

"Whoever's sharing your bed had better be giving as good as they're getting."

A kid clutching his backpack squeezes in behind me, pushing me closer to Lucky. His elbow brushes against my nipple, which jumps at his touch.

It's definitely time to go.

Thankfully, as he opens his mouth to say more, the barista calls out our orders.

Finally.

take your drink (**turn to page 47**)

7

Blindly, I reach for the closest cup on the counter. If I'm lucky —*ha*—then maybe I can sneak into the office without Monica noticing. I don't place my chances very high, but there's always hope.

A rogue shoulder catches me in the back when I turn, knocking the cup I'm holding to the floor. Panic spears through me in a thousand tiny cuts as I prepare for the splash of scalding hot liquid, but then I feel it. Ice.

Something shockingly cold and sticky seeps into my ankle boots.

That wasn't my coffee.

Shit.

To his credit, Lucky looks as shocked as I am. Okay, maybe not as shocked. More like stunned with a strong helping of amusement.

I assess the damage. My skirt has been spared, but my shoes are soaked, and my socks are damp. I can feel my toes squelching as I wiggle them.

Gross.

Lucky catches my gaze, ducking down to do it since I'm staring, unmoving, at the mess on the floor. "Just an accident. It'll be okay."

He's wrong. I can't show up to work like this. "It won't. My boss already hates me. Do you know how long I dreamed about working at *The Observer*? Two years of being on my best behavior in hopes that they'll finally give me a real shot at my dream job, and the first day I'm ever running late, this happens."

I'll have to go home. I can't spend the day in wet socks. I just can't.

"You work at *The Observer*?"

Lucky isn't smiling anymore.

"It's the third-largest national publication," I say because I don't care what this guy thinks. I'm proud of working there. "But maybe current affairs are too much to expect from a man who woke up on the wrong side of a barstool."

Lucky laughs, which is the opposite of the reaction I was going for. The man is relentless.

"Are you worried about where I'm sleeping at night, gorgeous?"

"Definitely not."

He smiles wider. "And if I was to acquaint myself with this prestigious and pretentious publication, where would I find you?"

I straighten, a little embarrassed. "In the Lifestyle section, and don't you dare call it vapid." Don't get me wrong; I have issues with my assignment, but highlighting the best parts of this city isn't one of them.

"I wouldn't dare. I happen to love going out."

I'm sure he does.

"And it's not pretentious," I add. "Sterling Ross is one of the most acclaimed journalists of our generation."

Lucky's smile looks strained. It's not a frown, but there's definitely something complicated going on behind his eyes. "I'm sure he thinks so."

My jaw drops, but between one blink and the next, his expression clears, hidden while he takes a stack of napkins and kneels, cleaning the floor at my feet.

I'll take this as my cue to leave.

Immediately, I turn to face the guy behind me, whose drink I accidentally dumped on myself. "I'm so sorry." I quickly hand over enough cash to cover it, too mortified to say anything else.

I can't get out fast enough. I make my way to the door, ready to forget about sexy Englishmen with perfect hair and biceps that beg for love bites.

Before it closes, I hear his voice calling out, "Don't worry; it'll all work out."

His life must be a wonderful dream.

I leave the luckily unharmed sandwich with Celine, then race back home.

It's every nightmare I had during exams. Waking up in a cold sweat because I'd slept in or gotten everything mixed up. But I don't get to wake up and realize this is all a horrible dream.

There's no time to save my shoes, so I throw them and my socks into the sink, dry off the sticky feeling from my feet, and throw on my favorite sneakers. They're scuffed, and the laces are frayed, but hopefully, Monica will be too distracted by how late I am to criticize my fashion choices.

It's only when I lock my door that it hits me ... I left my coffee behind.

Today really can't get any worse.

The only thing left to do is...

get to work (**turn to page 59**)

8

Yes sits so heavily on my tongue that I have to swallow before I speak. "I …"

A few desks behind him, Bianca is now pretending to sort paper clips. If there's one thing I've learned from working in journalism, it's that there are ears everywhere.

"I can't," I say, dropping my eyes to my desk, avoiding the frustration I know must be on Sterling's face right now.

He lingers, silent, and guilt settles across my shoulders, pressing inward. I've spent a year promising myself that I'd take the opportunity if it arose, and here I am, turning it down.

I miss how vast and exciting the world felt when I was in school, when the future was so full of opportunities that I was almost sick with it.

Maybe everyone is right to call me naive.

"Be certain what kind of career you want, Mia."

Sterling's reprimand sets my shoulders back. I know exactly what I want. How dare he!

"It won't be gifted to you. If you're unwilling to pursue what is difficult—"

"I'm not unwilling."

Nerves jump across my stomach as he pins me with his gaze, the air sizzling between us.

Prove it, that looks says.

Oh, how I want to.

Caution overrides my instinct as I dart my eyes over to Monica's office again. It's empty, the door left ajar. Panic seizes the reins, and I shake my head, avoiding Sterling's eyes, certain there will be nothing but disappointment now. If there isn't, I don't want to know. He should be; I'm disappointed in myself.

"I can't," I repeat. "I'm sorry."

There's the quiet shuffle of Sterling's polished shoes, a sigh that echoes through the growing frustration in my chest, and then he's gone.

The rest of the day passes without issue. I send the article, Monica shoots back a response to *ensure more weight is given to the affiliate links next time*, Sterling broods at his desk, and Bianca tells Andy off for cooking fish in the microwave again.

It's a regular day.

The only difference is that every time I look over at Sterling's desk, he's looking right back. He's probably masterminding my downfall; it'll be an excellent footnote to my journalism career.

At least I'll have a memento—the printout of my article is stashed in my bag, marked up with Sterling's notes.

Our first collaboration.

Scratch that. Our last collaboration.

"Did he say you couldn't change your mind?" Alice asks me that night.

My phone is propped up against a stack of books, and I'm going a little out of my mind because I promised myself I'd take every opportunity I could, and when push came to shove, I turned it down.

"No, but he did put the fear of the unknown into me."

"You've built him up too much. He's just a guy. I don't know why you're so afraid of him."

Everyone's afraid of him.

"He's the most decorated journalist of his age. He's spoken with presidents, celebrities, killers. My first week, Andy complained that the women's league uniforms weren't sexy enough, and Sterling stormed over and made him apologize. He almost got fired." It was then I understood the leverage Sterling had. "I can't just walk up and ask him how his night was."

"Why not?"

Because I want him to like me too much. "Because I want his respect as a professional."

"Then ask about work."

I almost laugh. One doesn't just chitchat with Sterling Ross.

"Tell me you had a good day at least."

She scowls, brushing hair out of her eyes. It leaves a white streak of flour across her forehead. "I was. Then I stopped at the post office, and *he* was there."

Ah. "It was bound to happen at some point."

"He broke your heart. He doesn't deserve to be smiling and buying stamps."

Maybe. "That's the thing though; my heart doesn't feel broken. Just bruised." Aching for a love that lasts. Something real.

In the end, we weren't a couple; we were two ghosts, haunting the same house. We ate together, slept together, breathed the same air ... but there was no life left between us.

"He's still a shithead," she says.

Alice loves Ferntree; she'll never leave. We talk as often as we're able—texts and voice memos and video calls—and it's great. Truly. I'm blessed to have a wonderful best friend; I know how lucky I am. But it's not the same.

There's no comfortable coexisting in the same room. No in-the-moment jokes about silly things that you just had to be there for. It's recaps and follow-ups and check-ins. It's *I miss you*s and *I wish you were here*s.

I miss her. It's lonely here, on my own.

"I appreciate you."

"I've got your back, babe, always."

The thing about growing up in a place where everyone knows you or of you is that you never feel alone. There's a familiar, if not friendly, face around every corner.

There are few familiar faces in Chance.

Even less now.

Okay, now I'm convinced someone is pranking me.

I set my alarm twenty minutes early this morning, made it into work on time, coffee in hand, only to find one already on my desk.

A caramel latte with an extra shot. There's a Post-it attached, in Sterling's impeccable handwriting.

Sterling knows my coffee order?

A reminder, it says.

A reminder of what?

Underneath the coffee is a printout, a short piece with a familiar title—

Oh.

I'm glad it's too early for Bianca to be here because it's impossible to keep my head from snapping toward Sterling's desk. He isn't there.

I stare back down at the article in my hand. My article, from college. The one I submitted with my application. How did he get this?

My heart races as the elevator opens, the chime calling out

across the rarely quiet floor. Tim saunters out, yawning large and loud as he complains about the time. Missy is behind him, rolling her eyes behind his back even though her headphones are blaring her usual angry rock—some variation of a band no one's ever heard of.

I slip the article into my bag. I trust my coworkers about as much as Andy enjoys women's sports. He really is the most disappointing cliché.

My twin coffees stare back at me while I boot up my laptop. Tasting the one Sterling got me, I have to bite back a moan. It's incredible.

His desk is still empty. There aren't many hiding places on the floor, so I take an educated guess and make my way into the break room with his gift.

Even surrounded by printed reminders to *Wash Your Own Dishes!* and *Take Your Tupperware Home or Lose It Forever*, Sterling is impressive.

I wonder if he owns anything that isn't black. He looks fantastic, those shoulders and his thighs—sorry, he looks very professional and not at all like someone I want backing me into a dark corner, kissing me until I can't breathe.

Either. Both. I'm not choosy.

I clear my throat, and he turns his head, acknowledging me.

"Good morning, Mia."

I think my heart just stopped.

"Morning," I manage, and it sounds as breathless as I feel. Remembering Alice's advice, I step farther into the room. "How is your research coming along? You were still here when I left last night."

He's standing by the coffee machine, confusing me—because didn't he stop for coffee when he picked up mine? I watch his gaze drop to the cup I'm grasping in both hands, and maybe I'm imagining it, but I think he's smiling.

Sterling Ross.

Smiling.

I'm definitely being pranked.

Sterling sighs over the grind of the machine. "It's frustrating. I'm finding what I want, but not what I need, if that makes sense."

Not really, but I'm still shocked he's talking to me, so I nod.

"Look, I want to apologize for yesterday—"

"Oh, you don't have to do that—"

"Yes, I do. I shouldn't have pressured you—"

"Pressured me? What? No, you didn't—"

"Mia." His commanding use of my name shuts me up. "I'm sorry."

It's clear this means a lot to him. Sterling is a man of his word. Words he has used to great effect. Words he is now blessing me with.

I've never had an apology give me goose bumps before. "You're forgiven."

Seconds pass while I try to think of something, anything, else to say. I've never been here before; I can ask him anything, and he's actually going to answer me.

Suddenly, everything I want to know seems trite and childish.

"There's a trick I use on my uncle's farm," I say, taking another step closer. There's only one floor tile separating us. I'm not sure why I'm noticing that, but it's true. "His hens are pretty ruthless, and the best way to handle it is to grab a net and go after the meanest one first. Everything gets easier after that."

Dimples appear in his cheeks. Holy shit. "Narrow my focus in the short term, and worry about the rest later?"

Wow, he actually understood that. "I don't know if it applies with your story, but yeah."

He thinks it over, finally pouring himself a cup and adding sugar and cream. "I'm not in the habit of going in unprepared, but there's an angle that might work if I can back up my hunch. I'm working against the clock on this one, so it limits my options."

Oh. That explains why he wanted help with the research.

My heart sinks.

His hand comes down on my shoulder, warm and reassuring. "But it's good to know I have a professional wrangler on hand if my chickens come home to roost."

"I'm at your service," I say automatically, my mouth going dry when his eyes darken.

"Are you?" he asks low.

The sharp sound of angry footsteps interrupts us, and I step back.

The room ices over as Monica enters. She doesn't even pretend to need anything—why would she? It's clear this is about me. Even when I choose to do the right thing, it's still wrong in her eyes.

"I shouldn't have to remind you that your commitment to work should always come first," she says, not even addressing Sterling. "I don't want your move to get in the way of your assignment this weekend."

"Not at all. I'll be there."

"Good." Her narrowed eyes pass between Sterling and me one more time before she leaves.

An uncomfortable silence fills the space in her wake. I should go.

I've barely taken a step when Sterling's voice stops me.

"You're moving?" His voice is cold.

"Um, yes?" The high, uncertain echo of my answer taunts me to try again. "My new apartment is ready, which is actually saving my life right now because I cannot afford my current place on a single income. I guess I should thank my ex for cheating on me before we signed the lease."

It'll be nice to wake up somewhere I'm not reliving our failed relationship.

Sterling is quiet. I've said too much again.

"And you didn't think to mention that?"

I'm so confused, and, yeah, you know what? Angry. "I didn't think you'd care."

He grunts, and apologies spring to life on my tongue, tumbling over themselves in an effort to get out.

But why should I apologize?

Up until yesterday, I was sure he hated me.

I set my coffee on the counter with a thud. "You know, you used to be my hero." He still is. "The great Sterling Ross, the man who can't be moved. The day I signed my contract, I spent my last forty bucks on a bottle of champagne, thinking I'd gotten my dream job. Work for *The Observer*, learn from the best."

He shifts beside me, but I can't look at him. I'm furious. If he wants to kick me out after this, let him. I'm sure Monica will throw a party.

"I've spent two years writing thinly veiled advertising copy and being too scared to talk to you because you're, well, kind of terrifying. You work constantly, you never talk about your personal life, there's the whole intense-stare situation you've got going on. You'd do well to open up to people every once in a while."

His glasses do nothing to hide the intensity of his gaze. I can only hold it for a few seconds, until my heart is beating too fast and everything gets a little too warm. It doesn't help that he always smells amazing. Like coming home to your favorite meal.

Head-turning. Rewarding. Delicious.

"Can I help?"

I can feel my face contorting in confusion. "With what?"

"The move," he says as though it were obvious.

Oh. "Um ..."

Do I want that? *Yes, obviously.* But do I?

"Do you have a quota of good deeds you need to complete each day?"

"Only where you're involved."

There's no escaping my blush and no chance it isn't a hundred percent obvious to Sterling right now.

I've already turned him down once. Can I do it again?

Make Your Choice:

let Sterling help you move (**turn to page 66**)

decline his offer (**turn to page 91**)

9

My lungs burn as I speed-walk to the office. I really need to start using the gym in my building. I've stopped promising myself that I'll go; it halves the shame, but not the guilt, although running myself in circles to meet Monica's demands should really count as cardio.

By the time I finally arrive, I'm sweating. The back of my neck, between my thighs, under my breasts.

Any calm I once had lies shredded at my feet, ripped apart by the angry badger of panic I fought the whole way here.

Monica is in her office, her razor-sharp brow lowered in disappointment when she spots me through the glass. Her lips are set in a tight, thin line, and I can imagine the sound she's making.

Everyone else is busy at work, and I pick up speed as I cross the floor, almost barreling into Sterling on the way.

"Careful," he says, his voice rough and low. It reminds me of morning sex.

Power radiates off Sterling. Black hair, black suits, strong jaw. A gaze that could pierce through steel. He looks at me as if he already knows what I'm thinking but he's going to make me say it anyway and I'll enjoy every second of it.

Sure, he's packed with enough muscle to put you anywhere he wants you, but something tells me he'd rather use his words.

As always, I smile and say, "Good morning," in hopes that today will be the day he says something, anything, back.

A muscle in his jaw twitches, but he only nods, his close-set eyes shifting between blue and green with the ease of water before he walks away.

I should stop trying. He's never said it back. In fact, since I started here, we've swapped maybe a handful of words. I'm confident he hates me. Sterling seems to hate everyone.

Slipping my bag under my desk, I wince at the time. No wonder Monica is pissed.

Nearby, Tim barks at IT over the phone. They're going to hate coming up here if he's locked out of his computer again. His desk is in danger of collapsing under the weight of every note he's ever written in thirty-odd years of journalism. That is, if he still has a desk under all that mess. It's difficult to tell.

The Observer is loud and brash and waits for no one. If you work here, you chose to get thrown into the fire with no protection. Those who can't keep up weed themselves out. It's cruel and stressful, and sometimes, at night, when silence descends and it's only Sterling and me left under the unforgiving fluorescents, I plot how I'll turn it around someday.

Return *The Observer* to the beacon of excellence that led me here.

Despite the dozen desks separating us across the bullpen, I have a clear view of Sterling. It's impossible not to take advantage of that, watching as he works, head down in a shroud of concentration, his sleek black suit as imposing as the man wearing it.

Sterling Ross. Tall, dark-haired, and dangerous—at least to my self-control.

I've lost count of the number of times I've willed myself to walk over and ask what he's working on. Hoping he'll want my insight or that there's a lead I can chase for him.

Anything to get my foot in the door.

I've never wanted to work in Lifestyle, unless it was to investigate shady practices of skin care companies who promised fountain-of-youth-level rejuvenation while rebranding harsh chemicals as "newfound minerals" your body was deficient in.

Meanwhile, the only consistent thing people are deficient in is the money these unscrupulous organizations will lie to take from you.

Two years on, and I'm not sure I've achieved anything.

It would be easy to let it stop me, but I refuse to back down. There are too many tales of corruption, too much greed smothering the world in shades of gray. I won't stop until I've restored color.

"Mia!" Monica's voice stills the entire floor. My heart jumps into my throat. "My office—now."

Monica doesn't do courtesy or hand-holding. She expects you to know what she wants, when she wants it, which means I need to have my butt in that chair ASAP.

It makes her a great editor, but a brutal boss.

Andy smirks from his desk in the corner as I cross the floor to her office, smiling with the glint of a man who is seconds away from offering unsolicited advice. God, he loves it when he's not the one in the firing line.

I make a point of staring him down as I close the glass door behind me. He looks away first.

It's the little things really.

Monica taps her foot, and I turn around.

"Sit."

I do.

"How are you?"

I freeze. Monica never asks how anyone is. Monica doesn't care about our personal lives.

Anxiety eats away at my empty stomach, pinching the nerves behind my eyes. I'm going to get a stress headache—I'm sure of it.

Why did I have to stop for coffee? If it hadn't been for Lucky and his damn smile, I would have been here, and Monica wouldn't be asking me *how I am*.

I don't bother with excuses. She never has any time for them.

"I can't apologize enough for being late today. There's no excuse; it was unprofessional, and I'll do better."

Her blonde hair is gelled back in a tight bun. My head throbs with sympathy pains while she pins me with her small, cold eyes. "How would you say you're performing here?"

I straighten and tuck my feet further under my chair, out of her view. "Well?" Shit, that shouldn't be a question. "I've always submitted work thoroughly proofed and on time, and I've never turned down any assignment you gave me." Including many I wish I had. "I've also never taken leave or asked to be reimbursed over the limit of what I'm allowed to spend, even if an article required it."

Monica's lips purse. That doesn't have to be a bad sign. It's no secret she isn't my biggest fan; she's always the first to remind me of how young and inexperienced I am.

It's a wonder she hired me, to be honest.

I start to squirm under her assessing gaze. If she ever needed a career change, she could take up interrogation. Those icy-blue eyes could pry war crimes out of a dictator.

Clearing my throat, I add, "I also had a suggestion. Um, I thought now would be a good time to promote local charities, and I could even speak with the new mayor to get an endorsement."

"No." The word falls between us like a gavel.

"It doesn't need to run this week. I know it's short notice to fit it into the schedule, but if I—"

"You're not going to write it at all. You write a Lifestyle column, Mia. It's not your job to cover the election, and even if anyone could be convinced to care about charity now that the holidays are over, we aren't in the business of goodwill."

We should be.

I'm left staring at her desk, the floor, the view. Something worse is coming—I can feel it.

It's quiet beyond her office. The glass behind me does nothing to buffer sound, in or out, so that'll make for a fun walk back to my desk. Despite the way it started, it's another day in the office. I'll walk out of here with a warning, but nothing else will change.

"Okay." This isn't the first debate we've had over my work. I'm not giving up. I simply need to try again another day.

She hums, sour-faced. It pairs nicely with her navy blouse. "You were an hour late this morning," she says. "I might have made an exception if you'd given me notice or provided an explanation."

"I really am sorry. It won't happen again."

"You're right; it won't."

Worry creeps in at the edges of my hope, easily stomping over the fragile ground.

"It won't happen because you're fired."

Time stops.

No, no, no, no. Anything but this.

Months of promises, overtime, and working through period pain, the flu, stress headaches, or three hours of sleep. After all of that ... she's firing me?

Monica smiles.

Make Your Choice:

give Monica a piece of your mind (**turn to page 77**)
hold your tongue (**turn to page 99**)

10

I THROW the highlighter down and spin his chair to face me. The jump of his eyebrows is satisfying.

"I'm going to say this, and you're not going to interrupt me, okay?"

He nods and settles back in his chair, arms crossed, all of his focus on me.

His biceps are huge ...

It's everything I've wanted; he's finally taking me seriously, finally ready to listen. I feel important, more than I ever have before, because Sterling Ross is paying attention to me.

"I didn't have to agree to help you, but I said yes because I believe in this job, in the impact you have. You inspire people; you inspire me—or at least you used to."

He has the grace to look contrite.

"The world needs more than one of you, and no matter what you think of me, I plan on becoming that good. Better even. You should want that. You should be teaching me, but you're intent on keeping all that wisdom in a tower, aren't you? No one but you in there, looking down over the rest of us—over me, and all I'm trying to do is help you."

"You're right; I'm sorry."

Honestly, *sorry* is nice, but it isn't good enough.

"If you're serious about working together, the cold shoulder and the silent treatment stop—right now." Oh God, I sound like my ma. "Agreed?"

"Yes, ma'am."

Fuck, that really shouldn't turn me on.

"Good." My cheeks heat like the sun in the middle of July.

I make the mistake of looking at him, and my mouth goes dry. He's smiling in that small, secret way he does.

I clear my throat. "Now, can we get back to work, please?"

Sterling stands, stretching his back and shoulders. He stripped out of his jacket an hour ago, so there's nothing hiding how his shirt sticks and clings to his muscles as they pull taut.

"Hungry?"

"Um ..." I'm starving, but this feels like a trap.

"It's not a threat, Mia. If you don't want food, we can take a walk. But I have to get out of this chair before I become fused to it."

I know what he means.

Make Your Choice:

food sounds good (**turn to page 105**)
I'd rather get fresh air (**turn to page 110**)

11

I STARE in disbelief at the truck Sterling rented. "At least let me buy you dinner as a thank-you." If the offer sounds like a date, I'm okay with that.

"That won't be necessary," he says, sliding my bedside table into position and taking the box of books I'm holding with ease.

"Don't be ridiculous. I'm going to find a way to make it up to you."

He closes the door with a satisfying clang and palms the keys. It's strange, seeing Sterling outside of the office. He's wearing jeans. They stretch over his thighs in the most obscene way. I'm already obsessed with them.

"If you feel that strongly about it, I can't refuse."

"Good. Dinner then." I'm not sure where I find the confidence to say it, but I can't take it back now.

He stops before me. "That eager to get me alone?" His hair is a mess from where he's run his hand through it. Being this attractive should be a crime.

Heat sparks to life in my belly, spreading out like wildfire. "Maybe I want to interview you."

I swear there's amusement sparking behind his eyes.

"Do I get to ask a few questions in return?"

"Only if you're willing to put your money where your mouth is."

"That depends on where you want my mouth."

Holy shit. Sterling Ross is … flirting.

The man who rations his responses in the office to limit any and all interactions is suddenly a Chatty Cathy on a charm offensive.

I'm not prepared for this, but since when have I ever let that stop me?

"We've worked together for two years, and I don't know anything about you that I haven't learned from the internet."

He walks me to the passenger side of the truck, supporting me as I pull myself up into the seat.

"What would you like to know?"

Oh, wow. Just like that?

"Um …" I didn't think this far ahead.

He closes the door and walks around the front. The leather jacket he's wearing stops at his waist and gives me direct eye contact with his ass. Does the man own a single pair of pants that makes him look bad?

How am I supposed to function in these conditions?

He hops in, and the truck roars to life. "Ready?"

"As I'll ever be."

"I read a lot of comics, growing up—manga especially—and fell in love with the way it merged complex stories with beautiful artistry. I always wanted to be able to draw, but sadly, the most I'm qualified for are stick figures."

"Manga? Really?"

"Not pretentious enough?"

I laugh, and he joins me.

The world always seems to hang heavy on his shoulders, hunching them. I've always wondered what he might look like, free from it. It's nice. More than nice. Fantastic. I like him without the permanent furrow. His smile smooths out the tanned skin into something softer, sweeter.

He's beautiful.

"No, it's much too interesting," I tease. "You're a mystery to everyone. All we see are scowls and silence. Half of the office is convinced you're secretly a vampire, sleeping in a coffin. The other half is scared you have blackmail on us all."

"Which half are you?"

"Doesn't matter. I've got nothing to hide."

"Clever girl."

The back of my neck starts to perspire. I crack open the window and let the blast of frozen air from outside cool me off. "If I'd known how different you were outside of work, I'd have ..."

"What?" He shifts gears, and I stare at the vein running along the back of his hand. His fingers are long, thick. "How did you imagine me? Am I waiting in a dark corner, teeth bared, desperate to taste you?"

Fuck. That question is dangerous. I'm not about to tell him how many times I've seen him take off his jacket and thought of him stripping his tie off, his shirt, his pants ...

I clear my throat. "I don't know." I'm stalling. "The same way you are at work, you know? Powerful." Shit, I didn't mean to say that. "Or, um ... commanding."

"Do I intimidate you?"

Yes, but I like it. "Not in a bad way."

"You like it."

Oh God. I'm starting to sweat.

"Your watch is an antique," I say, changing the subject before I catch on fire. I've been admiring the thick chronograph on his wrist. I've never seen him without it. "A family heirloom?"

"Yes, my great-grandfather's. Passed down from father to son, and now it's with me."

Everyone knows what happened with his parents. A drunk driver ran through a red light. Head-on collision. No survivors.

Sterling was sixteen.

"Ma says if you can't pass down good habits, at least pass down good gifts." She used a different word, but I'm not sure I can handle swearing in front of Sterling.

The corner of his mouth curls up, a hint of dimple at the edge, like he knows what I didn't say. "I'd say she did pretty well on the first part."

I crack the window down a little further, and he parks the truck in the loading bay of the complex.

We've done well, if I say so myself. Not that we had to move much in the end. A dresser, a television, a box of kitchen goods, the second half of my wardrobe.

My bed is all that's left.

The sight of Sterling handling my mattress stirs warmth under my skin. The brand of his fingertips will remain under my pillow when I lie down tonight—the closest I'll get to feeling his touch.

He's walking backward with his hands full; we're saved from having to navigate the entrance by one of the residents, who opens the door for us.

"Thank you," I say, my mouth going dry when I get a good look at him.

Jaw-length hair, trimmed stubble, a flirtatious sparkle in his eyes ...

He's gorgeous, seeking eye contact the way only the most confident people do—eagerly—but smiling with a softness that is instantly disarming. Add in the tight pants and tattoos, and I'm already hoping to bump into him again.

"Happy to help, love. It's all part of being a good neighbor."

The bed jolts as Sterling adjusts his grip. "Hello, Lachlan."

Lachlan licks his lips, then settles into a smile that's hungrier than before. "I thought I recognized those thighs ... among other things. You look good."

"So do you. I like the hair; it suits you."

Lachlan runs a hand through it, preening. "I know."

It's difficult to hide when I'm fighting to grip the other end of the mattress, but Sterling isn't moving, and this beautiful stranger, who he clearly has history with, is looking between us like we're the answer to a riddle that's been bothering him for years.

"Moving in? Please say yes."

"Mia is."

Both men turn to look at me, setting off a series of fireworks in my belly. I have the ridiculous urge to wave.

"Even better," Lachlan says. "Let me be the first to welcome you to the building. If there's anything you need, anything at all, I'm Lucky, in 704."

"Is that a name or a promise?"

Lucky's laugh fills the foyer, stirring up butterflies under my skin. "Why not both?"

A muscle in Sterling's jaw twitches.

The weight of the tension between them is heavier than the mattress I'm struggling with. "It's nice to meet you," I say.

"I have to get to the studio; otherwise, I'd help. Don't be a stranger," Lucky says, eyeing us both. "Either of you." He winks on his way out.

Curiosity burns through me as we take the mattress upstairs, but I'm not sure how to ask. Sterling's a private person. Until today, I've never imagined having a conversation with him, and all morning, he's been loose and talkative.

It's completely destroying any chance I have of getting over him.

"You were right," I say. "Making the bed was a great idea."

Sterling pushes my mattress onto the frame with his thigh, sheets and all. It slides into place perfectly, and I have to count to five while my brain shorts out at the inherent power he's casually throwing around. Christ.

I want to wrap myself around him like a vine.

"Good. Rest is important." He steps closer, sliding his hands into his pockets.

God, his *arms*. I'm going out of my mind.

"I wouldn't be able to leave without knowing you're satisfied."

Fuck me.

"I'm going to get some water. Would you like some?"

He nods and follows me into the kitchen. Half the boxes sit open on the counter, waiting for me to decide where everything will go. If only it was that easy to know what to do with Sterling.

Okay, I know what I want to do, but I need a few answers first. I fill a glass and turn to him. "Lucky seems nice."

Sterling takes the water and gulps it back quickly. He places it on the counter with a dull thud, raising a hand to rough his hair up.

At work, it's shaped and styled. It fits in with everything else about him—the clean shave, the fitted suits. He cares for the details. Which is why I'm so taken by the way his fringe is fighting gravity right now, sticking out of place from the careful style, like a meerkat on recon.

It makes him human. Touchable.

"You don't have to tell me; it's none of my business."

Sterling rubs his jaw, as though it's absorbed all the stress from today. Probably longer. I'm not good at patience—never have been. Act first, think later. It's mostly worked out for me. But that's not going to work here.

So, I wait.

He drops his hand. "We went to university together, in Manchester. Lachlan was the only person who wouldn't let how big of an asshole I was stop us from being friends. But I sabotaged it, and we haven't spoken since."

"From the way he spoke to you, I wondered if he was your ex."

"He is."

Oh.

"You can ask," he adds.

And it doesn't surprise me that he knows me so well. Sterling Ross is the smartest man in every room.

"It's just that … you never seem to date, so I wondered if maybe you were …"

"Pining?"

God, Ma would be so disappointed in me for asking, but I saw the way he looked at Lucky, and it's so painfully obvious that Lucky misses him too. How could anyone see that and not want to nudge a little bit?

I can't help but want to help. It's one of my best traits.

"Are you?"

"It's complicated."

That's a yes then. I fight hard to not let my disappointment show.

"I'd like to believe in soulmates," I admit, flopping onto the sofa. "When my ex and I survived college without breaking up, I really thought it was fate. High school sweethearts, destined for more. I think our love was coasting on who we wanted to be rather than who we were. We let it live in the clouds and had nothing to grab on to when the storm came."

Sterling takes the seat beside me. Outwardly, his expression is calm, but now that I know where to look, I can see the cracks—slivers of pain peeking through. It's all in the eyes.

"For a long time, the only friend I had was loss. Then I met Lucky. He was everything I wasn't—confident, optimistic"—he knocks my knee with his—"friendly. Being near him was like standing under a sun lamp. Falling for him was easy; everyone who knows Lucky falls for him sooner or later. It's part of his charm. It damn near killed me to leave, and I haven't let myself get close to anyone new in a very long time."

I stare at the point where his knee rests on mine. I want to reach out, but I'm scared to break the moment by doing the wrong thing.

"If you could go back, would you change anything?"

"No," he says, more certain than I expected, and my pulse jumps when he places his hand on my knee—the very thing I've been too scared to do. "I regret hurting him, but I can't regret making the choice I did. It's what led me here."

Look at us, two lonely hearts with trust issues. What a pair we make. I cover his hand with mine, trying for any small bridge across the vast ocean we're both swimming in.

Two days later, time stops.

It's on every single news channel: *Armed robbery at Chance's Reserve Bank. Eight assailants, over fifty hostages, including* The Observer*'s own Sterling Ross.*

I'm in the elevator before Monica can yell at me. If she finds out I used department records to find Sterling's address, I'll be out on my ass so fast that I'll reverse the clocks.

I'm stunned when Sterling opens the door. There's dried blood on his shirt and a bandage over a cut on his cheek.

"Oh my God, are you okay?"

He guides me inside and closes the door. "I'm fine, physically."

I balk. This is fine?

With his hand on my elbow, he leads me farther into his apartment. It's a lot smaller than I expected. I pictured big windows overlooking the city, where he'd sip whiskey and grumble about the state of corruption.

Instead, it's plain and a little cramped and absolutely overrun with books. There's one left open on the sofa, a collection of poetry, titled *Love Poems and Death Threats.* The pages are dog-eared and well loved. This isn't his first read of it.

"Picked it up while on assignment in Australia," he says.

"I've never left the country before, but I'd like to. Do you miss traveling?"

When I first started reading his work, I loved discovering all the new cities he'd visited. It was the closest I ever got to exploring.

"No. I'm where I want to be. There's as much work to do here at home than anywhere else, and if I want to eat takeout in an empty room, I have my apartment for that."

I take a second look. It's a little sparse, but there are signs of history everywhere. Foreign language titles and a bouquet of dried flowers in an intricately painted vase.

"It doesn't look empty to me."

"It isn't—now that you're here."

He hasn't looked away from me since I walked in, and, sure, he's always been intense, but there's something else going on.

"Are you sure you're okay?"

He lets out a sharp exhale. "I'm more annoyed that I missed out on the story. Cox will surely move his money now, and I'll lose the one good lead I had."

"Nothing more important than the story, huh?" I ask, not expecting the tortured look he gives me.

"No, there's one thing more important."

He cups my cheek with his palm, and I'm so distracted by the heat of him that I don't realize we're kissing until his tongue grazes my bottom lip.

It's electric, and I surge into him, convinced this is a trick my mind is playing on me. How else can I explain the feel of his fingers in my hair? The heady taste of him on my tongue?

The way he's pulled me close, tilting my jaw with his thumb, kissing me longer, deeper.

I reel back.

"It's the shock." It's got to be.

"It's not. I've been unfair to you by keeping my distance. I thought it was for the best—for both of us. I had no idea when I convinced Monica to hire you that she'd take it out on you, and I thought if she knew how much I favored you, it would make things worse, but I was wrong."

"How long have you felt this way?"

"A little over a year."

A year? He didn't simply hide it well; he buried it.

He continues, "It was close to midnight, the latest I'd ever seen you work, and you were curating a care package from the PR you'd been sent."

I remember.

"Before each item went in, you added a date on a label to note when they'd expire. It was a small detail I don't think many would consider. For a month after, you pitched partnerships with brands that all had one thing in common."

Monica was confused by my apparent turnabout, but didn't put the pieces together. But Sterling did.

"Did the shelter give you a list of what they needed, or did you put it together yourself?"

I'm proud of what I did, proud of sneaking it past Monica's nose, proud of being able to use my work to help people, and I've kept that pride to myself—until now.

"Myself," I say. "I interviewed everyone there who agreed to it and went from there."

"That's why," he says, stepping closer. "You're incredible."

"What about Lucky?"

Sterling's palms are warm against my cheeks. "I won't lie; I miss him, but what we had is in the past. When you arrived, wide-eyed and impassioned, I couldn't take my eyes off you. I'd already fallen for your writing, and here you were, this beautiful comet, ready to take on everything. I had to keep it professional; I wanted to make sure you had the best chance to succeed without making it about me."

"It's always been about you."

"God, I've been so stubborn. I'm sorry."

I pull him into another kiss. "You're forgiven."

THAT WAS LOVELY.

Wait! I want an epilogue (**turn to page 417**)

12

She can't honestly be serious. This is a cruel joke, and everyone knows she doesn't have a sense of humor.

"You're not even going to give me a warning? You're just going to fire me? That's ridiculous."

Still smirking, she stares at me with the shrewd gaze of a woman who always knows when you clock out one minute early and keeps a record of it—one of many mental tabs she has open of what the world owes her. "No, what's ridiculous is how long I've let this charade go on. I didn't even want to hire you in the first place."

Well, that explains a lot.

"If I hadn't been talked into it by—" She cuts herself off, huffing. "It doesn't matter now, does it? He was wrong about you, and I'll happily let him know."

I've reached my limit. *Sorry, Dad, you'll have to forgive me for losing my patience this time.*

The chair pushes back with a squeal as I stand. "You know what? I'm glad you're firing me." I don't give her a chance to respond. "Two years of pushing affiliate links so the owner can get kickbacks and promoting his buddies' restaurants is not what I studied journalism for."

Monica leans back in her chair. She's completely unbothered, which only turns the burner up on my anger.

My dreams of *The Observer* being a beacon of truth and

integrity have been holding on by a thread, and in this moment, they shatter, leaving me pierced by the shards of what's broken.

"Find some other desperate graduate to be your puppet because I'm done. Have the day you deserve."

Fate, if you're there, please, please, make sure her sheets are always a little bit damp—no, worse, that there's always a hair stuck on her tongue she can never get rid of.

I know I'm burning this bridge down to its studs, but I can't find it in me to care. Two years of waiting, and working, and hoping, and for what?

She was never going to give me a chance.

I can't breathe properly until I've slammed her door closed behind me. The glass rattles, but doesn't break, and I shove the disappointment down.

With that, I'm done. Box packed and led to the elevator without a second thought. My only regret is that I won't see Sterling again.

As I exit the elevator into the foyer, I'm once again faced with tattoos and chains. Lucky beams at me when I exit, and I'm starting to wonder if anything fazes this guy.

"Fancy bumping into you twice in one day," I say, then nod at the coffee cup in his hand. "Are you here for payback? Because I think I have room for one more disaster."

Heck, I have all the time in the world now that I don't have a job anymore.

He looks at the box in my arms with concern. "What the hell happened up there?"

"How far back should I start? My ex ran off with another

woman, I just got fired for being late, and to top it off, I probably nuked my career by yelling at my boss."

Lucky holds the cup out to me, along with a small paper bag that smells like cinnamon. His eyes are kinder than I deserve, but I soak up the attention anyway.

"I know it's not much, but I hear coffee and sugar go a long way in the healing process."

I can't help it; I laugh. He's still wearing that beautiful smile from earlier, and I feel the tension inside me pop and release in an instant. I bet he never has to worry about anything.

"Rejection must wash off you like water on a duck's back," I say, letting him take the box from my hands and swapping it for the treats he brought me.

I'm shocked when his smile falls.

"Some, not all."

Shit. I've made the world's first human Labrador sad. Today is truly stacking up to be a crowning achievement in my list of shortcomings.

"Sorry, growing up with an older brother made me a little prickly."

Lucky holds the door open for me. "Nothing to be sorry about."

I doubt that, but it's sweet of him to say. We spill out onto the street, and for a lack of anywhere else to go, I start walking home. Lucky follows.

My parents would have a hundred things to say about me leading a strange man back to my apartment—Alice would have a hundred more to say in favor of it—but the company is nice.

"What brings you here anyway?" I ask, moaning when I taste the coffee and find it rich and sweet. He remembered my order.

"I owed you one. Two now. Look, I'm really sorry you lost your job. You can yell at me if you'd like; it'll make you feel better."

"I think I've done enough yelling today, but thanks for the offer. Don't you have a job to be getting to? What do you do anyway? Apart from showing up unannounced at people's offices."

"I write pop songs. Perform a bit every now and then, but my rock-star days are behind me."

"You certainly have the look for it."

"Dead sexy?"

Yes. "Something like that." Facts are facts, and Lucky is gorgeous.

My phone starts to ring, and I struggle with the paper bag in my hand before Lucky shifts the box and takes it from me. I smile a thank-you and answer before I check the caller ID.

"Hello?"

"Miss Finnegan, I'm glad I caught you; it's Bryan from New Realty. I wanted to let you know your lease is ready to sign."

Relief washes over me. Moving into my new apartment is the last good news I have left.

"Unfortunately," he continues.

Oh no.

"We just heard from your employer that you were terminated, and as such, the owners have decided to deny your application."

My steps falter. "Um, okay. Thank you for letting me know."

"Have a nice day."

The sun is struggling to poke through the heavy clouds, its light cracking and splintering off the towering high-rises. Broken, like my hopes of ever getting this apartment.

Maybe this is a sign.

Maybe I've won the lottery for bad days.

In a single day, I've lost my job and home. In five days, my current lease will run out, and what then?

Move back to Ferntree?

I stand on the sidewalk, dazed. Then, with hysteria bubbling in the back of my throat, like an excited kid in a pet store, I start to laugh.

"You okay?" Lucky asks.

"No," I answer shakily. "I'm officially having the worst day ever."

"If it is the worst day, it can only go up from here."

Gosh, he's actually sweet. Despite it all, I smile at him.

He smiles back, and I almost stumble forward from the force of it.

"Hey, do you wanna get a drink?" I ask.

"Sure, but we might have a hard time finding an open bar."

"Lucky for us," I say, flushing at the heat in Lucky's gaze, "I have a bottle I've been saving for the occasion."

"Lead the way."

The pop of the champagne cork echoes off the walls of my apartment. My cupboard and counters are bare, boxes litter the floor, and it's hard not to feel like my whole life is packed up and ready to leave me behind.

I rip the tape off a box in the kitchen to find something to drink out of, staring at mugs and dish towels, but no glasses.

"How particular are you?"

Lucky looks over my shoulder into the box, our elbows brushing. It's indecent how good he smells. Bringing him here might be the best idea I've ever had.

"I grew up on a council estate, love. If you want, we can drink it straight out of the bottle."

He takes two mugs out of my hands and is already pouring wine halfway to the top before I can protest.

If he keeps this up, I'm really going to fall for him.

"Cheers," he says, lifting his cup to mine. There are little yellow bows on it. "To new beginnings."

I snort. Here I am, my life packed up in boxes, dumped, unemployed, and about to be homeless. This hardly feels like a beginning. More like a toast to my crumbling life.

The wine is bright and tart, and the alcohol does its job, buffering the sharp edge off of today.

"I was saving this for the first night in the new place," I say, skipping the sofa to sit on the floor. Lucky copies me, our knees touching. "But I guess my last day in the office also counts." Not having to deal with Monica anymore is something to celebrate.

"What are you going to do now?" he asks.

"That ... is a great question. Maybe you should be the reporter."

Lucky laughs. It's delightful. "Nah, I prefer talking about myself too much. I'll stick to writing hit songs."

"A self-aware musician? I didn't think those existed." These bubbles are wonderful. All my bones have liquefied, and there's no more annoying pain in my head anymore.

"I'm also gorgeous and talented, with a thick—"

I cover his mouth with my hand, and it stops whatever he was about to say, but it doesn't do a thing to stop my brain from filling in the long, pulsating blank.

The warm, wet touch of his tongue along my palm shocks me into pulling back. I'm blushing all the way to my belly.

"The smart thing to do would be to count my losses and go home. My parents would put me up in a heartbeat, and my old boss always said my job was waiting for me if I ever returned."

"But you're not going to do that," Lucky guesses.

"No, I'm not."

Huey never understood my determination to stay, but then he'd err so far into caution that he would quit halfway through an idea.

"I love where I'm from, but I'm not supposed to be there. Ferntree's the kind of place where people root themselves into the ground, their whole life a steady state of doing exactly what's expected of them and nothing else. I want more. Or maybe that's the champagne talking."

"It's saying all the right things." Lucky tops off my mug. "You said it was your dream job earlier. Why lie?"

He's so solid that I give in to the urge to lean on him, stretching my legs out and staring at my beat-up sneakers.

"It's silly, but every time I told someone what I did—lifestyle reporting—they'd make this face. Like, *Oh, she has no brain because she likes to wear makeup and go out*. Which was garbage. It might not be the job I wanted or ever saw myself in, but I worked damn hard. It's just ... I'd made myself a promised when I left home that I would stick it out in Chance until I became the reporter I knew I could be, and somehow, I've messed it all up."

"Bullshit. Sounds to me like you gave it your all, and now you're free to do what you really want."

"You really think so?"

"I know so." He slips his hand in mine and turns it over. Gently, he starts tracing the lines across my palm, every drag of his finger sending goose bumps through me. "Dreams are beautiful, delicate things, and they need to be treated with care. Just like their owners."

It's rare that I'm aware of a memory as I'm making it.

"What do you dream about?" I ask.

All of his focus is on the point where he's touching me. I want to burrow into him, press myself into his skin, the way I feel him being stitched into mine.

"Love," he says and punctuates the word by kissing my palm.

My hand feels heavier, as though he placed a piece of his heart there, along with his lips.

I have the wild urge to press my own mouth to it when he releases me.

Lucky picks up his mug and swallows what's left in one gulp. "You remind me a lot of the ex I had in college. He also wanted to change the world."

There's so much sadness in his eyes; I have to ask, "Did he succeed?"

"Yeah. Left everything behind to do it, but he did."

I suspect that everything includes Lucky.

I reach over him for the half-finished bottle and refill his drink. "Do you think your friend is happy?"

"Maybe? I don't know." He rolls his head to look at me. He really is gorgeous. The amber in his eyes glows when the light hits it just right. "Anyway, you worked with the big shot. Would you say he's happy?"

I can't imagine who he's referring to, unless he means ...

Oh my God. "Sterling Ross is your ex?"

He nods.

"Wow. I mean, I knew he was bi, but he's always been so tight-lipped about his private life. I've never really thought about the people he dates." Shit, that sounds like an insult now that I say it out loud.

Surprisingly, Lucky chuckles. "If Mac is anything like he used to be, he doesn't date. He cloaks himself in so much broodiness that no one can get close while secretly wishing someone would crash through his defenses."

"Mac?" I ask.

"Mackenzie. It's his middle name. Don't tell him I told you."

Yeah, there's about zero chance of that ever happening.

Lucky pulls the elastic from his hair, running a hand through the now-free strands. It's sexy and effortless, like everything else he does. Like he can't help but express himself fully in every moment.

I bet he's mesmerizing onstage.

"He wrote me after he ran off, but I was angry. We haven't talked since."

"I'm sorry."

Lucky waves off my apology, putting his arm around my shoulders and pulling me tighter against him. "We were stubborn young assholes. It happens."

I really misjudged him.

All that swagger, and there's a level of insight underneath I didn't expect. It's humbling. I know better than to judge first, and I let myself get lost in the swell of my anger, my sense swept out by the tide of Monica's hurtful words.

"Does that make you a stubborn old asshole now?"

His smile could warm the coldest nights. "Thirty-five is not old."

"So, yes," I tease.

He's so close, so beautiful; all I would have to do is move and do something about it. And why not? I've got nothing to lose.

Make Your Choice:

what are you waiting for? kiss him (**turn to page 114**)

it's too soon. I want a slow burn (**turn to page 133**)

13

"HE'S INFURIATING. I don't know what I ever saw in him." I'm out of breath, on my third trip from my old place to my new one, and I'm so exhausted that I could fall asleep in this lobby.

It wouldn't be so bad; this bag of clothes would make a pretty good pillow.

"He's a jerk," Alice says. "You're a thousand times better than Sterling Ross."

The elevator opens, and I push my suitcase ahead of me with my foot, watching it roll in and promptly fall over. I manage to hit the button with my elbow and sag against the wall. I'm ready to lie down.

If only my mattress wasn't still at my old apartment.

"I'd better go," I tell her. "If I wake up early enough, I can finish this research and go back to never talking to him."

"I'm telling you, I'm more than happy to fly out there and remove his balls for you. Some cultures consider them a delicacy—"

"Goodbye." I hang up, still laughing.

A hand shoots through the elevator doors before they close, and a man I've never seen before steps on. Soft brown hair, pink lips, and wired with enough muscle that I'm having trouble remembering my own name. He's wearing a guitar strapped to his back and a smile that could weaken the knees of the coldest fish.

Heck, he'd probably make Sterling swoon.

“Let me help,” he says, kneeling down to right my suitcase. The chain around his neck jangles as he stands back up. “I’m Lucky, by the way.”

You’re gorgeous, is what I want to say back.

“Birmingham?” I ask instead, curious about his accent.

“No, but that’s the best anyone’s guessed before. Manchester.”

Ah. “Sorry, that was rude of me. I’m Mia.”

The elevator opens on seven, and we both step out, but when Lucky stops beside me, I realize he’s waiting for me to take him to my door. “Oh, um, I should probably take that myself. It’s not that I don’t trust you. It’s only that—”

“I’m a strange old man?” He chuckles as he pushes his hair out of his face.

“You can’t be more than what, thirty-five?”

“You’re good at this.”

I shrug, but, yes, I am. It feels good to impress him. “I’m a reporter. It’s my job to notice things.”

Lucky passes me my suitcase, stealing a kiss on the cheek that lights up my nervous system. “Well, if you want to not be strangers, come by sometime. I’m in 704.”

“I’ll do that.”

I watch him leave, a little sway in his hips that I know he’s doing on purpose.

No, we definitely won’t be strangers.

I miss my assignment on Saturday. Monica is going to be livid, but I can string together something from the videos circulating on social media.

I’ll have to, if I want to keep my job.

It takes me all weekend, but I finish Sterling's research. I could have done a better job if he'd worked with me, but I did the best I could on four shots of espresso and five hours of sleep.

I even wrote a note and left it all in a neat pile on his desk.

His old desk.

Job done. I'll miss our titillating conversations. Mia

Sterling sees it as soon as he's off the elevator. Of course he does; he doesn't miss anything.

Without stopping, he crosses the bullpen, towering over me. It might as well be a week ago. If only I could go back and tell myself to say no when he asked.

"That's it?"

I stare up at him. We're both in the office early today. There's no one else here. Nothing to distract me from those big blue eyes.

"That's all you asked for. So, unless you want more from me, I have a job to do."

The silence is so loud; it feels like a third person filling the space between us. Frustratingly, Sterling looks ... impressed?

"If that's how you feel, then I guess I have no choice."

But he doesn't move, and the longer we stare at each other, the warmer I feel. I wonder how many confessions he's lured from people with only a look. How many desires.

He gives so little away; I'd love to meet the person who can affect him.

"I want to start by saying thank you."

It should be too little, too late, but it's nice to hear, and it's *him*.

So, I pin back my shoulders and hold his gaze. "You're welcome, Sterling."

Using his first name feels powerful, like a promise.

I wait, expecting him to walk away. Aren't we done? This is already more than he's said before. Maybe I should have said something sooner.

Or maybe not ...

"Would you like to get a drink?"

Oh, um ...

"Sure," I say, stepping away from my desk. "Is your cup in the break room already or ..."

I jolt as his hand curls around my elbow, heat rushing through me. He's never touched me before. I keep expecting Monica or Andy to burst out of the elevator and ruin this moment, but there's no one.

Only me and Sterling.

"I didn't mean ..." He trails off.

Of course he's changed his mind. What was I thinking? One assignment, and we'd be friends?

"That's okay," I say, shoving my disappointment into a box and throwing it into a mental trash compactor. It's where the rest of my feelings for him go, crushed into tiny cubes to save space.

"Mia ..."

And, oh, he's still holding me, his palm warm on my skin. I'm so glad I chose this shirt; there's nothing to get in the way of his thumb stroking the inside of my arm. It goes straight to my head, weightless and joyful, like the third mimosa before brunch.

"Mmhmm?"

He's staring. He's ... smiling? Gosh, his eyes are the prettiest shade of blue I've ever seen.

"Fuck," he whispers, and has any word ever sounded so good? "You don't even know what you do to me, do you?"

No, I don't. My mind has gone soft and mellow, my whole body ready to melt into him. Is this going to happen every time he touches me?

"Have dinner with me."

Wait, is he ...

"Yes." Date or not, there's no other answer.

His lips curl deeper into a smile. Fuck, he has dimples. "Mia," he repeats. I'm going to need him to keep saying it. "I'm going to kiss you now."

Oh good.

He leans closer, his lips brushing against mine. "Say yes, Mia."

"Yes."

THE END

14

I STARE at the pink concoction before me with concern. I may be a little wet behind the ears, but even I know what a margarita looks like. This isn't it.

"Sorry."

The only sign the bartender has heard me is a slight turn of their head in my direction.

"I didn't order this."

A man slides into the seat beside me. "That's from me, love."

Oh boy.

I'm here on assignment. The club scene in Chance isn't usually worth a piece in *The Observer*, but the owner has powerful friends, and those friends wanted a showpiece, so ... here I am. An hour before opening and being accosted by—*fuck*—the hottest man I've ever seen.

Blue denim, black leather boots, the body of a Greek god ... and just enough scruff that I want to sink my claws in and feel the scratch of it against every inch of my skin.

"I'm Lucky."

I bet he is.

Even without the black eyeliner and sheer shirt, I'd recognize him from the press release.

I hold out my hand. "Mia Finnegan."

His hand is soft and warm. "From the paper, right?" He nods

as I do. "Figured if you're stuck here to watch us set up, you should at least try the best they have to offer."

The lilt in his accent spins the flirtation into smooth silk.

There's an ease to it, a gentle persuasion, that could be dangerous in the wrong hands. His hands though are lovely. Inked and strong. I can almost feel the rough edges caressing my skin as he looks me over.

I curl my fingers around the cool glass, already damp from perspiration. "This is the best, is it?"

"Won't know until you get a taste, will you?"

Giving in to him would be dangerous. Lucky's rye-whiskey eyes and inviting smile would slip in as easy as a knife, all the better to rip your heart out.

I should say no.

I won't, but I should.

I'm no slouch; I've done my research.

Lachlan Williams, thirty-five, born in Stretford, raised in Manchester. Goes by Lucky. Played lead in the independent rock band Red Dragon, who saw minor success in the UK before he left to focus on writing at twenty-three. The following year saw five of his songs hit the top 100, and he got his first platinum record with *Half Measures*.

I take a sip. It's sweet—I can taste pineapple and raspberry—but there's an undercurrent of spice beneath it. It's every bit as good as promised, and, boy, does he look pleased about that.

"You must miss being onstage."

He picks at the label of his beer. "Not even a little. Half the reason I quit was getting up there. Got sick before every show. Shit scared I'd mess it up or forget the words to my own damn songs. Never did, mind you, but it still freaks me out."

"So, you're human after all," I tease.

Goose bumps flood my skin as he leans in. Close enough that

I can practically taste the salt of his skin. "I can give you a hands-on demonstration if you'd like."

It must be a wonder to walk around with all that self-assuredness. Most days, I don't trust myself to wake up on time, and here Lucky is, bold as anything, trusting I won't throw this drink in his face.

Though that would be a pretty effective way to get his shirt off …

"Tempting," I admit, distracted by his mouth. Now that I'm looking, I can't stop—full pink lips that constantly move, curling around his words, always ending in a smile, so expressive, so eager.

"Please tell me you know how lovely you are." His beautiful, perfect mouth ghosts my ear, his voice cascading over me in a purr, and my pulse spikes.

It's waking up something inside of me I didn't even know was asleep.

"Let me take you out."

"We're already having a drink together."

"Dinner then. Breakfast. I'll cook."

I want to say yes. It would be easy, I think—to fall into something with him, fun and comforting—so much easier than with, say, Sterling.

I've hesitated for too long.

"Ah," Lucky says, reading into the pause. "There's someone else. Shame you can't have two boyfriends."

I laugh. If only. "The only way I'd want that is if all three of us were boyfriends." Wait, that didn't sound right. I'm already tipsy. "I mean—"

"I know what you meant, love." Lucky taps my glass with his. "And I like where your head's at."

"But …" And I do feel the need to clarify because there is a gorgeous man hitting on me and I'm turning him down for what? The totally unattainable man—equally gorgeous, for sure—I can't have? "The other guy—he isn't—we're not ..." I take another sip, a breath; hopefully, the alcohol will save me. "I need to get over him. We work together, and it's"—an ache every time I see him—"awkward. He doesn't even know."

"He's an idiot then." He pauses, chewing over his thoughts.

I force myself to wait, see what it is that's meaty enough that he needs to think it over first. The house lights are all the way up; his shirt is like liquid silver over the rise and fall of his muscles, and, God, it'll be a thousand times better under a spotlight. Seductive. Enticing. Impossible to look away.

"Big paper, *The Observer*. That's the one Sterling Ross works for, yeah?"

It's a coincidence—that's all. Sterling is the biggest name there; it's no surprise Lucky knows his name. No reason to think he plucked it from the secret hiding place in my heart.

"Yes," I choke out, staring down at the blossom floating in my drink.

The answering silence says volumes, and something tells me Lucky doesn't believe in coincidences at all.

"Some things never change," he says, knocking his bottle against my glass in solidarity. "Welcome to the club."

And, *oh*, I could laugh.

"How long?"

"Too long. We stopped talking after uni. I hated him for a long time, but I never stopped loving him. It's why I'm here, if you can believe it, because I can't seem to stop chasing the bastard."

This time, I do laugh. Of all the people in Chance, how many moved here because of the same man?

"He's always been a dark horse, huh?"

"Oh, yeah." Lucky chuckles into his beer. "Moody. Didn't party, didn't drink. Didn't seem to have any fun at all. Closed off and so bloody beautiful that it hurt. So fucking smart that he could have taught half the classes we took."

"What happened?"

"Oh, you know ..." he says, his tone light. "Turns out, being in love with your best mate doesn't end well. Wasn't even gonna tell him, but he figured it out. He had a gig in Australia straight after graduation; he'd be gone for three months, chasing a nonprofit, and we talked about meeting up after. Coming here. I didn't think anything would change, you know?" He takes a pull of his beer. "Night before he left, he kissed me, and, fuck, it was everything I'd wanted. Next thing I know, he's on his knees, and —" He cuts himself off. "Anyway, it didn't matter that he wanted me back; he still left."

He hides it well—pain behind playfulness—but it's there if you look.

I'm looking.

Reaching over, I place my hand on his. "I'm sorry."

Lucky intertwines our fingers, squeezes. "I'm not. Heartbreak gave me my first Grammy." His smile is strained at the edges. "Besides, I'm a right hypocrite. If he walked in right now, I'd forgive him. Take him back in a heartbeat."

Light flickers around us as the door opens, closes. One of the staff pushes through the front, hands laden with a box, cords spilling overtop.

"His loss is my gain."

Lucky's grin shifts my nervous system into overdrive. "Yours and mine."

Oh, he *is* dangerous.

Lucky is incredible onstage. Sexy, passionate, a true performer. It's only because I'm looking for it that I can see the tense line of his shoulders, how often he avoids looking at the crowd for too long, how quickly he gets offstage when he's done, chest flushed and dripping sweat.

He doesn't stop until he finds me, nursing a water by the edge of the dance floor. Heat pours off him. Our fingers touch as he takes the glass from my hand, throwing it back in big gulps. My gaze catches on his mouth, wet now, and doesn't leave.

Lucky reaches past me to set the glass down, bringing our hips together, and doesn't move back. "Dance with me."

I should call it a night. I've got all I need for the article, not that it matters. It's a fluff piece; I'm contractually obligated to say nice things. I could have stayed in and written it with my eyes closed, but I wouldn't have met Lucky if I'd done that.

Fuck it.

The music is everywhere, replacing every sense with the snap of the snare, the thump of the bass. I sink into it, giving my hips over to the rhythm until I'm only an extension of the song, endless as it morphs into the next and the next and the next.

He grabs my hips, pulling me closer, dragging his body against mine in slow circles, a tease and a promise. His skin is damp through his shirt, hard and hot. I love the way his muscles move under my touch, find myself pressing and pulling, closer, closer. I want to blanket myself in him.

I don't hesitate, shifting until his thigh slips between my legs, letting my skirt ride up as I rock against him, lifting my head to search for that devastating mouth.

Oh, this is what I've been missing. He kisses with his whole body, and there'll be no getting over this—the slide and pull of his lips; his tongue, perfect and tender, so much softer than I imagined.

I've lost track of the music, of anything that isn't him. The rough pads of his fingers. The perfect friction of his thigh grinding against my pussy. Each swipe of his tongue.

I can taste the bitter edge of the beer he drank earlier, salt and sweat and something deliciously *him.* I chase his mouth when he pulls back, not ready to stop, and get to taste his smile as he slides his hands up my back, my shoulders, where my hands are tangled in his hair.

He steps back, licking his lips. Tasting. Then he pulls me toward the restrooms.

I don't know this club. I have never done anything like this before, but I don't stop to think about it. I just hold tight and follow him down the corridor.

It's dark, near black without the strobe lights, and he's walking ahead, so I can't see his expression, can't see what stops us, but the restroom door opens, and the light catches on an all-too-familiar face.

Either I'm drunk off of one cocktail or that's Sterling Ross standing there, gaze darting between us and sticking on where our hands are gripped tightly together.

Lucky recovers first. "Mac. I'm surprised to see you here," he says. "This isn't really your kind of place."

"A club?"

"Outside."

It's hard to see in the dark, but I think Sterling is smiling. "I came to see you. I'm glad I did. Hi, Mia."

The weight of his attention falls on me, the touch of it as strong as Lucky's hand. "Hi, yourself."

"You looked good out there. Both of you."

He saw that?

The person behind me recognizes that we're loitering, not waiting, and pushes past us to the restroom. This surely isn't the best place to have a reunion, but neither of them seems inclined to change that. It'll be up to me then.

“We should move somewhere quieter.” In truth, I only mean to find somewhere for them; they’re the ones with history after all.

“She’s right,” Lucky says, eyes locked with Sterling’s. “My gear’s in the office back here; no one will bother us.”

He leads us to the end of the corridor, where he unlocks the door and waves us both inside. Sterling follows him in.

I’m not sure what to do.

Make Your Choice:

follow them* (**turn to page 430**)
let them work it out alone (**turn to page 395**)

15

In the end, I say nothing, swallowing down the bitterness that's burning the back of my throat.

It wouldn't matter anyway; Monica's made her mind up.

"Thank you for the opportunity," I force out because my parents raised me right.

In a final act of disrespect, she says nothing, already turned back to her computer, her French acrylics hitting the keys sharply as she types.

Andy smiles smugly as I walk back to my desk. The weight of everyone's attention pokes and prods at me as I move.

No one says a word as I box up my stuff.

Sterling isn't even at his desk.

He likely won't even notice I'm gone.

As soon as the elevator doors close, I change my mind.

I should have said something. What kind of a hard-hitting reporter am I if I can't even stand up for myself to my own boss? Maybe this is a sign that I'm not suited for this after all.

When I reach the foyer, I'm greeted by a familiar grin.

"Are you stalking me now?" I shift the box in my hands as I

pushed past Lucky into the foyer. "Don't tell me; your brother works here."

He laughs, causing something traitorous in my chest to chime like a bell. I grind my teeth to ward it off.

I will not like him, no matter how chipper he is. And cute. So, so cute.

"Nah, they're back home. All five of them. But I've got a cousin who runs a bar downtown."

"Of course you do." I walk past him.

"Hey," Lucky says, popping up on my right. He's holding out a coffee and a takeout bag. "How about we swap?"

I pull the box away. I'm mad. At Monica, at Lucky, at myself. "Thanks, but you've done enough helping today. How did you even find me?"

"I felt bad about this morning, so I brought you the coffee you'd missed and a doughnut as a peace offering."

I do love doughnuts.

"I have a soft spot for the classics," he adds, following me like a puppy that's eager to play. Doesn't anything faze him? "Hopefully, you like sprinkles."

Dammit. My favorite.

I grip my box tighter.

"Thank you, but no. Today has already gone about as bad as it possibly could. I don't think a single doughnut is going to fix the fact that I got fired for being late."

"Do you want to yell at me? It might make you feel better."

I level my best stare at him.

His smile remains. "Hey, maybe it's a blessing in disguise. Come on. A bit of caffeine and sugar, and you'll feel better."

I snort. "Are you always this disgustingly optimistic?"

He cocks a brow. "Are you always this hopelessly cynical?"

Cynical? How about pushed to my limit?

"That's pretty rich, coming from a guy who gave away a

hundred dollars like it's nothing. How about you take all that money and persistence and do something good with it? Then we can talk."

I blow past him. It isn't easy to get through the revolving doors with my hands full, but I can't stop. I need to get out of this building, away from the crushing sense of disappointment that's eating away at my gut.

The wind outside is harsh, the chill snapping my brain into focus. Okay, so *The Observer* didn't work out, but there's more than one paper in this city, and I'm as qualified as anyone else.

Getting a reference will be difficult. Monica is out, and who else could I even ask? Andy would lie to spite me, Bianca doesn't answer calls she doesn't recognize, and Sterling doesn't even know my name.

I jump when my phone rings.

It's a juggle to pull it from my pocket, but at least it's good news.

"Bryan, hi. You've got great timing; I was about to call you to see when I could come by your office to pick up the keys."

There's a sigh down the line. No, no ... not this too.

"I'm sorry, Mia. I received a call from your employer, and I'm afraid we've had to deny your application for the apartment."

I come to a stop on the sidewalk, the last of my hope draining onto the pavement, trampled beneath the feet of the jostling crowd. Someone curses me as they pass by.

"Please, my lease runs out this week. I need this apartment. I'll pay two months up front, whatever you want."

"I'm sorry. We've already rescheduled a viewing for Thursday. Unless you can regain steady employment in the next two days, there's nothing I can do for you. Have a nice day."

That's it then.

They say losses come in threes, right? Boyfriend, job, apartment. I've lost it all. Do I win a prize now?

Maybe I should hang it all up. Move back home, go back to the *Ferntree Gazette*. Start again.

As I start walking, I've no goal in mind. I have nowhere to be.

It doesn't surprise me when Lucky appears at my side. "I've been told I'm a pretty good listener, you know, and if sugar's not your thing, there's still time for breakfast. My treat."

I must really look pathetic if he is willing to subject himself to breakfast after I yelled at him. Twice.

He bumps my elbow with his. "I'm going to guess you skipped breakfast this morning, so you have to be hungry, and I know the right spot for something hot and filling."

I bet he does.

No.

No sexing the Englishman.

"Why do you even care?" I ask. "You don't even know me."

The kindness in his eyes is too much. Soft and compassionate.

Too close to pity.

It's a stark reminder of everyone who said I shouldn't move here, that I couldn't make it, that this city would chew me up and spit me out. It's the knowing looks I'll get when I slink back home, proving them all right.

I can't do this right now.

A crew cut in a suit is stalking toward us, on a mission somewhere. Lucky steps out of their way, bringing him toward me quicker than I can process, seemingly between one blink and the next. My heart thunders in my chest.

On instinct, I step backward, the scent and heat of him intense up close, my nerves sparking and jolting in a way I haven't felt in a long, long time. It's too much and not enough.

There's something behind me, something knee-high that barks, and I startle. The world shifts, tipping sideways, and I know I'm falling the wrong way. Not onto the sidewalk, where all

I'd have to worry about were people trampling me, but to the road.

Ahead, a bike messenger barrels toward me, and there's not enough time to stop him.

Lucky's hands grip my arms as he pulls me upright, out of the way.

My stomach is in my throat. My eyes feel like they are pulsating, or maybe I'm blinking too much. I can't breathe. My fingers are clawed in Lucky's shirt. I can see them, but I can't feel anything. There's nothing but noise.

"You're okay. Breathe."

Jesus, he smells good. Or is that the doughnut? Knowing my luck—ha, luck. Like Lucky. Okay, maybe I'm delirious. He probably smells like this all the time. Just walks around, smelling amazing, like some sort of English Pied Piper with rock-hard pecs and kissable lips. I bet they'd be soft. They look soft.

Vaguely, I register his voice, gentle and low, but I'm distracted by the way he's running his hands up and down my arms. He hasn't even tried to pry my fingers out of his shirt yet.

Oh, I dropped my box.

His lips look delicious. Is that sugar? I want to taste him.

Oh God, how long have we been standing like this?

"T-thank you." It comes out shaky, shakier than I'd like, but I can't feel my knees right now. A light breeze is likely to knock me over.

His grip tightens. It's nice. Solid. Strong. It's the only thing keeping me together.

"That's good. In and out. I've got you."

He does, so I focus on his words. His voice is sweet. I like the accent, like the way he's still calm. Steady. Like his chest. I press harder, chasing the *pa-dum* of his heart under his sweater.

I don't think about work or the apartment. I don't need to think about anything other than breathing in and out and the searing heat of him. I used to make Ma bury me in a pile of steaming clothes, straight from the dryer. I'd curl up underneath and soak in the warmth. I'd like to drape Lucky over me sometime.

There's noise around us, people probably, but all I can see is him.

It helps.

Slowly, the rest of the world comes into focus. Cars, people, my feet on the ground. How closely we're standing together. Intimately. A tingle runs up my spine.

He smiles. "Come on. I know a spot."

I let go and step back, blinking up at him.

Make Your Choice:

go with lucky (**turn to page 144**)
go home alone (**turn to page 117**)

16

"I COULD EAT," I say.

"Great." He slips his jacket back on. "I know just the place."

We end up at a hole-in-the-wall ramen spot down an alley I've never seen. Tables are stuffed into every corner, and the air is thick with the most delicious spices.

Sterling pulls out a chair for me. "I practically lived here when I first started at the paper."

An older gentleman with thinning hair and kind eyes drops his hands onto Sterling's shoulders. "He fell asleep in this booth so many times that I almost brought in a mattress."

Sterling pulls him into a hug, and his smile is so bright that I feel like I'm trespassing.

"Do you want your usual?"

Sterling sits, his knees brushing mine. Have we ever touched before? I can't seem to remember, and I can't stop being aware of it.

"Can you give us a few minutes to look over the menu, Leo?"

"Of course."

Leo smiles at me. I want to tell him this isn't what he thinks—that Sterling can't stomach a conversation with me, let alone a date—but I know he won't believe me.

"Take your time, but I recommend the champon."

"Let's do it then," I say, ready to trust whoever is responsible for that incredible smell.

"I'll be right back," Sterling says, standing and making his way over to the bar.

I watch in awe as he talks with easy familiarity to the server. I've never seen him look at home. It's a good look on him.

Sterling returns with a bottle of still water and two glasses. "I'll get sparkling if you prefer—"

"Still's fine."

Once the water is poured, there's nothing left to do except wait. Wait for the food, wait for Sterling to explain why he brought me here, wait for the other shoe to drop.

"Why did you ask me to help you?" I have to ask. I have to *know.*

It doesn't make any sense. He's not the kind of man to give out favors. There has to be something else, some other reason why he requested me specifically. My gut is telling me there's more.

He unrolls his napkin, smooths it out, places his chopsticks neatly on top. Controlled. Precise. "I know what it's like, chasing that first opportunity. You deserve a chance. Your work in college, especially ousting the department head for covering up assault charges, was impressive stuff."

"You read that?"

"I've read all your work. There was a line last month I particularly liked—now, what was it?"

My breath stops because I cannot imagine Sterling Ross reading, *The best rooftop bars to day drink at*, and, *Diaper cream: the latest skin care miracle?*

"That's right." He says, reciting it by memory, "*When the end of the world is nigh, why not face the gates with a little pizzazz?*"

Heat rises to my cheeks.

Monica hated that line, but I fought for it, probably more than I should have, but in the end, she let it through. To know that it's lived an extended life in Sterling's mind—when his words have lived on in my own—means more than I can say.

And it was only there because it made me smile.

He's still watching me. "Why do you love this job so much?"

There are a hundred reasons. I could talk about the people I meet—Celine at the shelter, the small business owners who are so incredibly grateful for the exposure.

I could mention the thrill I get from writing a really good piece, the satisfaction that comes from seeing my byline, or finding the hook no one else can.

I could be honest and tell him that walking into *The Observer* and seeing him every day, knowing we're colleagues, still makes me pinch myself.

But the truth is ...

"I can't do anything else. I won't. The crappy reality is that not everyone gets a voice, and they should. There is truth to be told, and I want to help tell it. I'm not going to wait until it affects someone close to me to care. I can't sit by and watch while people take advantage of others with lies and money."

I'm aware of how idealistic it is, but I'm sick of debating my reasons with people. If Sterling wants to call me naive, ... well, fine.

"You're a good person, Mia."

God, I love how he says my name.

"And that's a bad thing?"

There's a smile pulling at the corner of his mouth as he shakes his head and rolls up his sleeves. There's the tattoo again. My breath catches in my throat.

"Not at all, but the people you're chasing will see that as a weakness and do everything in their power to crush you if you don't protect yourself. Success isn't a buffer; it's a megaphone."

"Okay, so teach me how to do it right." I'm not backing down on this. "I'm not going to give up my optimism because you or anyone else thinks cynicism makes you smarter. I'd rather learn how to get out of trouble than avoid it."

He's silent, staring me down. So intense, like everything he pursues.

"Well then ..." He pauses, clears his throat. "I'll show you what I can, but you don't want me as a mentor."

Has he always been this frustrating?

"Why the hell not? You're the best there is."

"I've made plenty of mistakes."

And I haven't?

"Then tell me what they are, and I won't make them."

A muscle in his jaw tics. "Are you saying you'll do what I tell you?"

As though my body has heard the magic words, it flares to life, tingles flaring out like fireworks. *Pop-pop-pop.*

"Yes."

He licks his lips, holding my gaze, but says nothing.

Our food arrives, and Leo looks especially pleased to have interrupted ... whatever the hell that was. Maybe he can fill me in.

The meal is even better than promised, and I order seconds to take home for dinner tomorrow.

"You're as bad as him," Leo says before running back to the kitchen.

"I feel like I've learned a secret," I say.

"About my terrible eating habits?"

"That you have friends." I'm a little afraid of how it'll land. Sterling is having an actual conversation with me—over dinner even—and here I am, pushing a little bit further. "It's nice. Everyone deserves to be happy."

"Even the miserable black hole with an inflated ego?"

God, I could kill Andy.

I shift in my seat, pressing my knee into his. A gesture and an apology.

"Especially him."

Make Your Choice:

let's get back to work (**turn to page 119**)
I'm in a rush. Give me the CliffsNotes (**turn to page 138**)

17

"A WALK SOUNDS NICE."

We step out of the building into the night. The air is humid, thick with the anticipation of rain. The roads glisten like oil spills, slick under the dinner rush. Traffic sits at a standstill, voicing its anger with horns and complaints.

Another night in the city.

"Must be a big change from back home," Sterling says. He shoves his hands deep in his pockets, the collar of his coat turned up.

"It's not so different," I say. "Especially when the cicadas arrive. I get more peace here than I ever did on the farm."

More so now that I live alone. Sometimes, it's like the whole world is shut off, and it's too much, too lonely, too ... empty. Like I've finally run farther than anyone could find me and I don't know my way back.

Sometimes, the only sound that keeps me company is Sterling typing from ten desks away.

Sometimes, I like to imagine he's as lonely as I am.

"I'm curious," he says. "Two years is a long time to write about local events and beauty trends when your heart is set elsewhere. When you could be helping in a more meaningful way."

It hurts, even if I've made the same complaint to Alice before, but having Sterling see me like that ... well, maybe it's proof I'm not cut out for the job I really want.

Maybe I don't have the stomach or the heart for it.

But I haven't stopped trying yet, and I'm not about to let anyone—even the great Sterling Ross—talk me out of it.

"I do help people," I say.

We turn a corner and blend into the crowd. Food is nearby, a block away at most. Restaurants spill out onto the sidewalk, their rich aromas beckoning us forward.

"Maybe not in the way I really want to, but you can't dismiss the help because it's not geared toward you or doesn't look like you think it should."

People huddle tightly together as they wait for a table. The cold won't turn them away. This city is made of harder stuff than that.

"You're right; I apologize."

I think about all the nights I've watched him work, silent in his vigilance, always pushing further. What does he do to unwind? Where does he find joy?

Or does he avoid it as ruthlessly as he does everything else?

"Look around us. This is what makes this city beautiful. It's us, life. All the ways we're constantly seeking it, come rain or shine or money or exhaustion. It's complimenting a stranger's outfit, tipping the waiter, joining in when a restaurant sings 'Happy Birthday.' It's lending someone your umbrella or giving them directions or stepping in when the creep at the bar gets too close. It's kindness and support, not as performance, but as an act of peace."

We pause at the intersection, pressed close, and his sigh is loud enough for me to hear it.

"I've seen a lot, doing this job, talked to men who hate the world and would leech it dry simply so no one else could have it. Any day that I can get in their way, slow them down, or—if I'm really lucky—stop them is a great day. Because people like you," he says, staring down at me, "good people—deserve it. If what you're writing makes you happy, that's all that matters."

His eyes look black out here, the blue swallowed up. It makes his sincerity too intense, his focus a laser cutting straight through me.

I have to look away.

Across the street, a shop catches my eye. As black as the road, as alluring as the korma calling my name. *Chance's Curious Creations*, the sign reads.

Something tugs, and my feet follow.

A bell jingles as we enter. A strange feeling washes over me, buoyant and bubbling.

It's nothing like I expected from the outside, organized and modern, with neat racks of pouches and potions lining the walls, the room stretching forward like a question—*Do you dare answer?*

Curious, I continue. Sterling hovers close behind me, his coat brushing mine, the heat of his hand at my back.

A young woman with bright pink hair smiles from behind the counter as we pass by, her gaze crossing between Sterling and me. She says nothing.

Items change from bottles to books to jewelry.

"Do you smell that?" I whisper to Sterling once we're deep in the back, far from the shopkeeper's ears.

Memories crash over me, unbidden: Alice testing recipes, flushed pink and wild-eyed, the kitchen a sweet haven of cookies and muffins and cakes. Sunday mornings, Louis drowning waffles in syrup, Ma dancing to the radio, Pa stuck in the paper.

"I've never ..." Sterling whispers, the pallor of his face stark and gray under the harsh overhead light. "It can't be."

His voice is ghostly, and the feeling inside me flares, pulling at the corners of my mind, stretching me out thin. Before and after. Once and again.

Beside him, a heavy stone set into gold hangs from a hook.

It's glowing.

I reach out. Sterling lifts his hand to cover mine. To stop me?

My fingertips skim the stone ...

Make Your Choice:

something magical happens (**turn to page 139**)

nothing happens (**turn to page 151**)

18

I LEAN IN.

His lips part around mine, and, gosh, they're just as soft as I imagined they would be, smooth relief within the light scratch of his beard. Easy to sink into.

It's a slow, gentle fall, not at all what I was expecting from him, but all the more consuming. Everything gets magnified—the press of his mouth, firm and hot; his breath against my cheek; the swipe of his tongue on my top lip, then bottom; the promise of something rougher with the graze of his teeth.

It's like nothing I've ever felt.

Tingles spread through to my hands and toes, racing like my pulse, as though I were diving headfirst into the bottle we were drinking from.

No one has kissed me like this.

Never.

Lucky pulls away. "Not like this," he says and stands up.

Everything hot goes cold inside me. But I thought ...

I sigh and follow Lucky to the kitchen. It doesn't matter what I thought because he pulled away, and that's clear enough for me.

I don't meet his gaze as he hands me a glass of water.

"Are you hungry? I'll make something."

I nod, feeling embarrassment fill up the spaces left empty by his touch.

He finds his way around easily, pulling together a meal more naturally than I ever have. I love food, but I think I'm allergic to cooking. Lucky definitely doesn't have that issue. He doesn't even comment on the lack of ingredients, humming while he works, deft hands making us both a grilled cheese while he wears a smile that only makes it harder to not storm over there and kiss him again.

Who knew cooking could be so sexy?

"You should move in with me," Lucky says, stealing my attention away from how good his ass looks in those jeans.

I'm staring, but I can't stop.

"What?" I think my brain is still scrambled from that kiss.

"Move in with me."

Yes. Definitely scrambled.

"It's not quantum physics, Mia." Lucky slides a plate over. It smells amazing. "You need a place to stay, and I have a spare room."

This is ridiculous—or it should be. I'm actually considering moving in with a man I just met. He could be anyone. He could be the first hitmaker turned serial killer, luring me in with smiles and food, like a hot villain from a fairy tale.

What the hell did they put in that champagne?

I want to say yes. Is that silly?

What would my parents think? Actually, Ma would love him, all that spirit and sass.

Lucky watches me, one hip cocked against the counter, looking like a temptation.

I trust my instincts, and they're telling me to say yes, but I'm torn.

Make Your Choice:

let's do it. Move in with Lucky (**turn to page 181**)

shouldn't you think about this? (**turn to page 165**)

19

THIS MUST BE what defeat feels like.

When Huey left, he went on and on about this city chewing him up and spitting him out, how he was like gum thrown into the gutter—disliked and discarded.

I'm sorry to say I pitied him. Don't get me wrong; I'm still mad as hell that he cheated on me and dumped me via a voice message, but a small part of me cheered. I'd proven that I was stronger than him because I'd stayed. He couldn't hack it here, but maybe I could.

I was hacking it.

Until today.

Alone in my apartment, surrounded by packing boxes, I don't feel triumphant.

Unemployed and soon-to-be homeless, I have a choice to make.

I think about Lucky's easy grin and the perfection of his dimples, offset with a single snaggletooth that only adds to his bad-boy image. How much his devil-may-care attitude reminded me of ... well, me, when I moved here. So sure of myself, of my future. Ready to take on the world.

Maybe that's why we're drawn to each other.

I think about Sterling and how much I still admire him—a storm cloud of determination and courage. He surely hates me, barely uttered as much as a *good morning*, yet I believe in his work and will forever want to follow in his footsteps. I've always hoped for his advice, for him to be a mentor, if not a friend.

Leaving will deny me a chance with either man.

Most of me wants to stay, a soul-deep drive to continue what I came here for—a mission stitched into my bones that feels bigger than me. I'm meant to be here—at least, I thought I was.

Do I really want to pack it all up and go home?

DON'T LOOK AT ME, THIS WAS YOUR CHOICE.

move back home (**turn to page 135**)

20

"Have you heard of Montgomery Cox?" Sterling asks.

Who hasn't? The second-richest man in the state and CEO of SME Industries—a tech company with a strong mission to protect sustainable manufacturing. Cox is extremely popular and very charming. A born businessman.

"He was the cover man for last month's *Time*," I say.

Sterling nods. He's clean-shaven; I can smell the lingering scent of shaving cream and soap, and it's a heady mix when I'm this close to him. I'm so used to the pasture's worth of distance he usually keeps around himself that sitting beside him is a little overwhelming.

"He's also funding election fraud."

Holy shit. I scoot my chair closer, my elbow brushing Sterling's. He jolts. Oh, right. Personal space. Sometimes, I get so excited that I forget.

As subtly as I can, I pull away and see his hand flex on the desk before stilling.

Sterling peers out over the bullpen, eyes tracking our coworkers' movements, but I know for a fact that Bianca is trying to beat today's crossword and Andy is too involved in his fantasy draft to care what we're talking about.

"These are campaign donation records," I realize, looking at them with fresh eyes. "How did you get these?"

"That's right," he says, evading my question. "Cox gave over sixty million of his own money, which he's been obnoxiously loud about, but he's a master of nesting shell companies within other shell companies, making it impossible to keep track of his private donations." He pauses. "Almost impossible."

He's so pleased with himself. It's wildly attractive.

"But that's why I also have these," he says, shuffling through a second stack of papers he's attacked with a red pen.

Jeez, it's like looking at my old Economics homework. Sterling lays them in front of me, our shoulders brushing as he leans in.

I sway closer. He smells divine.

"This is a list of offshoot companies I can prove are his. I believe he's shuffling the money around so that no one will notice it's missing. I want to add up all the incoming donations tied to these companies. Getting a judge to grant discovery access to a hundred small companies would be a red-tape nightmare, but if we can narrow it down to a few big ones, I might be able to pull in some favors."

My heart is beating really fast.

"I'll still need someone willing to go on the record; otherwise, he'll hide behind his lawyers and bury everything that points back to him." He rubs a hand over his jaw. "It's clear he's been very careful, and I'm close, but there's still something missing. A pattern. I can tell something is off, but I can't pinpoint it yet."

"What made you suspect him?"

"When you've done this as long as I have, you learn to trust your instincts."

It's not the only thing he's picked up. Sterling speaks with a confidence that is bone deep, subtle enough that I might dismiss it as humble if it wasn't for how unequivocally he knew his own worth. I would kill to borrow that feeling for a day. I'd be able to move mountains.

I turn it all over in my head. The money, I get. All roads lead there, especially where corruption is concerned, and using the shell companies as a basis is smart, but ...

"Even if you can prove he made significant private donations, how are you so sure it's for election fraud?"

He leans back in his chair, eyes the papers as though the answer might divine itself from them.

Either he's guessing or he doesn't want to tell me.

"I don't trust him," he finally says. "Cox has a history of friends in low places. Now he's changed his tune and shaking hands with a progressive? It doesn't add up. He's not addressing any of his past either, always giving vague answers to sway the conversation in a new direction or using charm and Mayor Jackson's positive following to shield himself from criticism. I'm afraid he's trying to tarnish a good man's reputation by aligning with him or else he's playing a more dangerous long game."

"You'd undo all the good Jackson will do because he's following the same playbook the bad guys do?"

He stands, two palms on the table, pushing his chair back. The indecision is gone. This is a Sterling that is in full command. Determined.

Gorgeous.

My breath catches in my throat.

"And when Cox decides he wants to switch sides? Bankroll the other guys? Changing the rules to suit your cause is exactly what put us in this situation. Let's say this turnaround convinces you to give him a second chance. Maybe he's changed; shouldn't we want that? In a few years, he gets to piggyback off that goodwill into a political position of his own. Maybe he even spends the first year following through on positive change. Then things start to shift. Suddenly, his talking points start sounding a little too familiar. He's protecting the rich, sabotaging his new friends in favor of his old ones."

He's right. I hate it, but he is.

"You're right, but I won't make good people pay the price because one asshole wants to play dictator. Catching Cox won't stop anyone else from doing the exact same thing, but it will be a loss for this city."

"So, he just gets away with it," he huffs, dropping back into his seat. He groans into his hands. "These fucking assholes. Cut off one head ..."

"Two more take its place."

He pulls his glasses off and rubs his eyes. I stare at his long fingers and think absolutely nothing.

Nothing I'll admit to anyway.

"What if Jackson has no idea? You'll destroy his reputation."

"And if he does know and willingly went along with it?"

I can't believe that.

"Just because he's saying what you want to hear doesn't mean we shouldn't look a little deeper."

We.

My heart skitters around that single syllable for a few beats.

"I hate having to second-guess everyone," I admit.

Good people face the kind of scrutiny no one looks flawless under while bad players get praised for doing what we expect of them.

"You're right. You know what? Don't listen to me."

I look up, surprised.

"Hold on to that hope. It's important. Incredible things are achieved through hope."

"And a lot of bad people have been ripped from the shadows through cynicism."

He laughs—a throaty, deep sound I want to press my cheek to, feel it work through his chest and into my bones. "Glad to know I'm still useful." His eyes shine with contained joy, even as his smile becomes something smaller, deeper, settling over me like a conviction. "You're good at this, Mia. Don't forget that."

Speechless, I hold the words close, tuck them inside the safest corner of my mind, where I keep precious memories.

"We're going to get him," I tell Sterling. "I'm sure of it."

If I never see another box again, it'll be too soon.

Dumping the two that I'm holding on to the floor, I fish out my keys and lean against my door. I'm so tired.

Going through the donations is taking up all of my spare time, and in order to get my own articles finished, I'm writing on my breaks, in line for coffee, on the toilet.

It's so bad; I spent four hours at work before my alarm went off, and I realized I'd been dreaming the entire time.

I'm scared we won't find what Sterling is after.

I don't want to let him down.

"Hey, let me help you with those," comes a lilting British accent, and as I push off the door and blink my eyes open, a gorgeous man with silky hair and a wide-collared jacket is passing me his coffee and picking up both boxes with ease. Lean muscle, warm eyes, tattoos. Like every singer I had posted on my walls at home.

He's a walking dream.

"Oh, thank you. I've been moving all week, and I really wanted to get these last two boxes done tonight, but my arms are currently on strike."

"Can't have that," he says, smiling down at me. I bet he could lift me as easy as those boxes. "They're lovely. I hope this doesn't mean I'm crossing the picket line."

I unlock my door. "I'll grant you an exception."

"Beautiful and kind." He lowers the boxes onto the coffee table, thighs flexing in his jeans, biceps visible under his jacket.

"What about your coffee?"

"Take it," he says brightly. "I haven't drunk from it or anything."

He looks around, eager and curious. There's not much to see —more boxes and a stack of photos I haven't had the energy to put up yet.

I push it into his hands. "I'm not going to take your coffee."

"Why not? It's great coffee." He punctuates this by taking a sip.

Annoyingly, it smells amazing, but I'm no fool. "Didn't anyone ever teach you about stranger danger?"

This cracks him up for some reason. I watch, transfixed, as the joy plays out over his face, nothing hidden, nothing held back. It's beautiful. I want more of it.

"Love, all my best memories come from talking to strangers."

I want to know everything about him.

"Well, either way, I'm not drinking out of anything I didn't order myself."

"Yeah, that's smart. I guess I'll have to take you out so you can get what you want."

It's smooth as hell. I'm genuinely impressed. "And if I say no?"

The apartment is small enough that it only takes him two strides of his long legs before he's in the kitchen, throwing me a knowing smile when he sees the stack of takeout boxes in the trash.

I've barely moved in, and I'm already getting judged by the neighbors.

"I'd be devastated, of course," he says. "Come over next week. I'll cook you a proper meal."

It's tempting.

"Maybe."

"That's not a no," he says, pleased.

"No," I confirm, the warmth in my chest radiating outward, reacting to his endless enthusiasm, "it's not."

He gets real close, smelling of leather and woodsmoke and reminding me of every dark impulse I've ever had. A silver chain hangs from his neck, thick, like he is. This is a man who takes up space.

"I don't even know your name," I say, a little breathless.

"Lachlan Williams, in 704," he says. "But you can call me Lucky."

"From the note."

He winks. The look in his eyes promises wicked things.

Funny, because I feel like the lucky one right now. "I'm Mia."

"A pleasure," he says, kissing my cheek. "Dinner's at eight, any day you'd like."

My laugh chases him out the door, but we both know I'll be there.

I read through so many pages of transactions; I'm starting to see them in my sleep. Rows and rows of numbers and codes, none of which raise any alarms. It's so boring; anyone else would have given up by now, and that's what keeps me going—because what if that's the point? To bury the dirt under so much monotony that it's barely worth the struggle to look for it.

"When you said it was boring, you weren't kidding."

His lips barely move, but the humor in his eyes feels like a win. I'll take it.

Eventually, we're all that's left in the office, and I dive into my stash of drawer candy to quell my grumbling stomach.

"It's late. You should go home, get some real food."

Sterling loosens his tie, and I try not to stare.

I should.

For weeks, I've been promising myself that I'll order in less, but between the unpredictable hours and constant restaurant reviews, sometimes, the easiest meal is the only option.

"Sorry," I say, closing my drawer. "It's a bad habit."

"I take it, there's no one waiting at home with a hot meal?"

Not unless my neighbor counts.

"Not anymore. He, uh, met someone else and moved back home last month. I'm free to eat as much candy as I'd like."

A yawn I can't stifle escapes me, cracking my jaw. This week has been long, but I wouldn't give it up for anything.

Sterling is currently grinding his teeth, so I know he's had enough.

"By the way, who is it?" I ask.

Sterling grunts what sounds like a question mark—first time I've ever heard anyone articulate punctuation before.

"Your source. You didn't pick Monday arbitrarily. You're on a time crunch to interview someone, and you need this to back it up."

I know I'm right when he spins around to face me.

"Going directly to Cox would never work," he says. "He's too prepared for it. Better to talk to his PA, Rose. She's with him constantly, and she would have intimate knowledge of his calendar and everyone he talks to."

"Wouldn't she be covered by an NDA?"

"Yes, but there are options, if I find the right angle. I know she's in the market for a new apartment, so if I can catch her at a viewing, I might be able to arrange an interview."

I don't like it. If she works as closely to Cox as Sterling says, he'll be paranoid about her spare time.

"That's a big if."

"Which is why it's only a backup. Rose has a single appointment each week that she never misses—lunch with her sister-in-law, Tegan." Sterling pulls up a photo on his phone and passes it to me. "Guess who works at the same bank that manages all of Cox's business and personal finances."

"You want to interview the sister-in-law?"

"I want her to help me convince Rose to go on the record."

A chill licks up my spine. This is serious stuff. "She has to know if he gets spooked, it's her sister taking the fall."

"Perhaps. Unless he's got something over them that's keeping them quiet." His voice is steady, assured, and why wouldn't it be? He's probably dealt with this situation a hundred times before. A thousand. He's probably dealt with worse. I'm the one who has been pushed into the deep end.

Cox isn't who I would have pictured as a real-life villain, but I won't pretend to be surprised. He fits the profile easily enough—generational wealth, a lifelong love affair with fame, with catchy sound bites the press continually eats up. But Sterling is right; if there is any wrongdoing here, Cox has spent a lot of time ensuring it's as buried as it can be.

"You know if you do this, your life is going to get difficult?" I might not stroll the political beat very often, but even I've seen Cox buddied up next to our owner, Hayden Lee.

"It wouldn't be the first time." There's no sign he's bothered by the possibility of a billionaire coming after him. He notices my concern. "Don't worry; *The Observer*'s lawyers are very good at their job."

It's not the lawyers I'm worried about.

"And if he wants to do more than simply sue you?"

A muscle in his jaw jumps. "I'll cross that bridge when I come to it."

It's infuriating. How can he be so blasé about his own safety?

"You really care so little about your own life?"

It's impossible to read anything in his expression. It must be exhausting, staying closed off all the time.

"I know others will pick up where I left off."

The cold spreads, sweeping through my veins and sinking deep into my bones. I can't imagine a world without Sterling Ross in it. I don't want to.

"That isn't the point. You mean something to people." *You mean something to me.*

"A movement can't survive on the back of one person—because what needs to change is bigger than that. These systems are insidious; they're everywhere on purpose. You need to be everywhere at once, you need to get people to listen and hear you, and you need to keep convincing them, over and over again until, as a collective, the system is replaced with something better. That's why we do this. It's difficult and frustrating, and at times, you'll never be more alone."

My heart aches for him, for all of us, deserving of so much more than the world we find ourselves surviving in. A world crafted on purpose by so few, to harm so many.

"You're not alone now." It's as much for me as it is for him. Someone to understand. Someone to see. "I'm here. I can help. Let me. Be here with me."

"I'm not very good at letting people in."

"Oh, I've noticed," I tease, my pulse fluttering at a high speed when Sterling cracks a smile.

I wonder how offended he'd be if he knew how much I wanted to kiss him right now.

"How do you feel about dumplings?" he asks, the app already open on his phone.

"I feel good," I reply, and when he looks up, I know he knows I'm not only talking about the food.

By the time I'm full, I can barely keep my eyes open.

"I can't look at another routing number," I groan. "Please don't make me."

He chuckles, a low, grumbly sound that I'm growing quickly addicted to.

"Go home, Mia. I can handle this."

"No, I'm not going till we find something," I say, but I pick up my phone instead.

Sterling is convinced that the connection between Rose and her sister-in-law is being exploited, but there's no money trail to back it up. There's more to motivate than money though.

If Cox really is an evil mastermind, is Rose even aware? It seems unlikely that someone in close proximity could be fooled, but cults have survived for years on leveraged faith and manipulation.

Her social media matches Cox's public promises of philanthropy. Photo ops fill her feed, with captions extolling the virtues of working with "such a brilliant mind." It takes a few minutes of scrolling to get beyond the fan worship to anything more personal, but she must have scrubbed anything related to family when she took on the higher-profile role.

Hmm ...

Her followers sit at eighty thousand, but she's only following nine hundred, so I start there, checking first for variations of her surname. Tegan comes up on search two, her profile photo one of the two of them from the wedding; it looks to have only been a few months ago, which explains why she's using both her married and maiden names still.

Alice and I have planned our dream wedding many times, the groom changing as often as our crushes were formed, but I always knew I wanted to keep my name. Why wouldn't I? It's mine. I love it. I've worked hard to see it in bylines, although I admit, the idea of something formal, tangible, and legal that stakes a claim on my partner runs a visceral thrill through my veins.

I can see why Tegan would keep both.

Rose might not have any personal posts anymore, but her sister-in-law is full of them, including a lot of the two of them together. It's clear they get along well and were friends before Rose's brother even came into the picture, and the more I scroll through Tegan's posts, the more I see Rose's comments and jokes. It makes me miss Alice even more.

Then my breathing stops.

It's an innocuous photo, smoke rising off a brightly colored cocktail, tagged to a bar two states over. It's not the bar, or the cocktail, or the caption that has me transfixed.

It's Rose's comment.

Peachee is back!!!

Then I see it again on a mirror selfie and again on a photo of the two of them in finery at the races.

That name ... I've seen it. I know I have.

I scramble for the stack of papers I dismissed.

When it first appears, it feels like déjà vu. I've been staring at invoices for long enough now that I can't really be sure if I saw this line already or if I'm simply imagining it.

But, no, there it is again, twenty-six pages later.

Forty-five minutes and two paper cuts later, I have enough evidence that I'm certain. Peachee Holdings, founded last month, with the address of a postbox and no other details.

The same company whose multimillion-dollar donation to

the campaign is exactly what Sterling has had me looking for, and I almost missed it.

Cox was clever—I'll give them that. Tying the money to a name that would implicate both Rose and Tegan means hitting two birds with one stone. Cox is connected by the barest of threads, and outside of an explanation for where the money came from—a question I can immediately guess would be answered by claiming Rose embezzled it without his knowledge—his hands are clean.

"Fuck," I whisper.

If we're not careful about this, Cox won't see a single fine, and we'll destroy these women's lives.

"What's wrong?"

In a blink, Sterling is at my side, the spicy warmth of his cologne making my head swim. My vision fogs over while I picture him tearing off his shirt, no care for the buttons, and commanding me to taste.

"Mia?"

Fuck.

"I've found it. Look at this."

I turn to Sterling to find him watching me. My heart is beating rapidly, fragile as butterfly wings under my skin. Our fingers brush as I pass the papers over, but he makes no move to look away, and I'm all too aware of the heat of him, drawing me in, as if this is where I'm meant to be.

Where he wants me.

"Thank you, Mia."

I hardly dare to breathe, pinned by his gaze and the collective weight of every wish I've cast in his direction.

I'm overcome with the need to know, to see, what it would take to break through his restraint.

What he would do with all of that intensity if I asked.

Not that I'll ever get the chance. I imagine he can read every thought as though it were written clear on my face, and his avoidance of me is as good of a sign as any that what I feel is one-sided. I drop my eyes, turning back to my desk and pushing my foolish hopes away.

This case is kind of intense.

I like it! I'm ready to go to the bank (**turn to page 172**)

21

It takes effort to pull away, to gaze upon the bright rays of Lucky's interest and not bend toward them like a flower in the sun. It would be so easy to shift closer, drifting on borrowed confidence toward the source.

To be with someone who knew where to find this lighter side of myself, who could tend to it, nurture it, simply with their presence. Lucky is wonderfully passionate, exudes it as easy as exhaling, and I can't get enough.

I want to know this funny, freewheeling man who has wrapped his body in armor but leaves his heart on his sleeve. Open. Vulnerable.

Kissing him would take no effort at all.

But I can't. Things are complicated enough; I don't need to confuse them further.

Lucky says nothing as I stand, but I feel his attention on me as I slink off to the bathroom, tail firmly between my legs. It's easier to breathe when the door shuts behind me.

I should be making a plan. That's what capable, independent people who chase their dreams cross-country do, except plans aren't really my strong suit.

Lucky is in the kitchen when I return. He's snooped out my one good pan, moving smoothly with his sleeves pushed to his elbows. He looks like he lives here.

"What are you making?" I ask as the smell hits me.

Lucky steps away from the pan to fill a glass of water from the tap, handing it to me, then goes back to stirring. "Stew. You didn't give me much to work with."

"It smells good," I admit. Better than anything I could have pulled together. "Ma's always been disappointed I didn't inherit her talent in the kitchen."

"What, you think all I'm good for is looking pretty?"

I refill my water instead of answering.

"You should move in with me then," Lucky says, and I laugh until its clear he isn't joking. "Let me feed you."

"I just met you. I can't move in."

"How else do people get roommates?"

Okay, he's got me there.

"You'd really be okay with that? Why do you care so much? You barely know me."

"Since when do you have to know someone to care about them?"

He presents it so simply, and I'm overcome with feeling. I like him. There's no holding back a hug this time, and he accepts it easily, sliding his arms around my shoulders and holding me close.

"I'm serious," he says. "Move in with me."

Make Your Choice:

move in with Lucky (**turn to page 192**)

it's not a good idea (**turn to page 241**)

22

Are you sure?

absolutely certain (**turn to page 136**)

23

Really?

yes. stop asking me (**turn to page 137**)

24

So, that's it then. Time to say goodbye to Chance and everyone in it.

I don't like giving up, but I've made up my mind, and, hey, everything's already packed up.

Chance was originally a dream, an urban fairy tale of steel and glass, but I guess it'll have to remain a fantasy.

THE END

25

In a bit of a rush, huh? Don't worry; I've got your back!

It seems Mia has finally gotten through to Sterling, and he fills her in on the investigation. He suspects Montgomery Cox—tech CEO and public "nice guy"—has hidden millions of secret campaign donations through a series of shell companies.

The problem?

Sterling has evidence that money was used to attempt election fraud. While they continue to comb through the accounts, matching numbers and names, Mia has a light-bulb moment that gives them a strong lead.

She also meets Lucky, her very sexy British neighbor. He asks her out, and while she doesn't say yes, she certainly doesn't say no.

Now you're all caught up!

Are you ready to go now?

yes! take me to the bank (**turn to page 172**)

26

"Keep your guard up."

Sterling comes at me directly, a blur of silver and blue that I meet with equal verve. The sharp clang of steel rings out across the empty courtyard as our swords clash.

"I am."

With the bright glimmer of amusement in his eyes, he pushes against my blade, making me stumble backward. "You're not."

There's no use wiping the dirt from my cheek; I'm already covered in it. Instead, I ready myself for another round.

Satisfied, Sterling starts to circle, slick as a predator.

He strikes from the left, simple and swift. I see the attack coming early and counter, pushing in with my own attack. Perspiration collects at my brow. He's usually faster than this.

I bring the blade down hard, aiming for his shoulder.

Sterling deflects without blinking.

Dust kicks up at our feet. It stains our armor in ochre, painting the tips of my fingers, the curve of his jaw.

There's no doubt Sterling is adept with steel. He is a master of it, as you would expect of my personal guard, but it is not his sole weapon.

Words are.

He swats away my blade as easily as a fly. "Focus, Mia. Do as I told you."

Though Ferntree's harvest has already begun, winter maintains its tight grasp of each morning, and if asked, I will blame my shiver on the chill.

"Again," he commands, a curl tugging at his mouth.

I've long lost hope of my heart fighting off the whims of my attraction for him. It is always dashed the moment his smile appears.

We're alone. We're always alone when we practice. No one likes to watch; the persistent clatter of steel is still too recent of a memory for many to endure. I do not judge them. We all bear our scars differently.

"You're letting me win," I say, dodging his next thrust. "You know how much I want to learn. In a real fight—"

"You'll never be in a real fight," Sterling says, which is entirely unfair. I could if he let me. He's lucky I don't run him through. "As long as I'm still breathing, I will stand between you and the forces against you."

My chest rises with a breathlessness only Sterling manages to achieve. Little wonder that the seed of my affection has rooted itself so deeply in every corner of my soul. Little wonder that he does not feel the same.

He steps to the right, but it's a ploy, and he dodges my next move, countering from above.

"The curse has been lifted," I say. "The sorcerer is gone."

He's holding back, but it's still an effort to keep up with him. I strike harder, faster, angry that he is still treating me like a beginner. Like a child.

"There is no need to fight anymore."

No need except my own selfish reasons to have this time with him. For a year, I've waited for him to call our training off, but he hasn't. Instead, it's only seemed to renew his determination to teach me.

"There is always a need. You should never walk into a room without the certainty that you can walk out."

"That's what I have you for."

We clash, again and again and again. Attack, parry, block. Circling each other. Sweat slicks my hair to my skin, pools under my tights, but I give no ground.

Neither does he.

I dig deep, striking harder, faster, trying to surprise him. To no avail. There's no surprising Sterling. No fight he isn't ready for, no breaking his reserve.

Hauling the sword high above me, I try to strike overhead, but he meets my blade front on. Steel collides with steel between us, and he presses onward, taking me off guard, closing the gap. His armor touches mine.

My lungs startle, breath frozen in my airways. The blazing blue of his eyes lighting my blood on fire.

"Good. Do that again."

I stumble out of the hold, adjusting my grip, my heart thundering in my chest. Frustration builds up within me, heating my blood, tuning my senses to none but him. Each step, each blink, each breath.

I see the opening—the shift in his weight, a step—and I strike.

He blocks the attack in time to keep the blade from his neck, but I'm moving too fast, and I follow him over as he falls back, hitting the ground with a rough thud.

All I hear is the heavy gasps of air pulled into my lungs as awareness filters in. I did it. I actually got him.

He shifts underneath me, and I start. I'm astride him, my knees planted on either side of his hips. His breath gusts against my cheek.

My sword is a beat away from his throat.

I search for a reaction, anything to prove I'm not alone in my feelings, but he's unaffected. Only the pink of his cheeks, unnoticeable under a layer of dirt, would be proof that he's exerted himself.

Years, I've pined, and there has never been proof. Why would he start now?

I get to my feet and offer my hand. He doesn't need it—he's stronger than me by multitudes—but he takes it anyway, and I savor the gruff texture of his palm for the scant seconds it lasts until he pulls away.

"Not many have managed that and lived," he says. "I should be thankful this is our last lesson."

My heart falls, heavy.

It's a sharp reminder of how short-lived that promise will be. I may have him now, but he refuses to leave Ferntree. Refuses to join me in Chance.

"You might be thankful, but I am not." It's petulant, but I don't care.

Once, our world was one. Stretching out from horizon to horizon and beyond. When the sorcerer came into his power, he engulfed the world in water, carving the earth apart, creating twelve lands separated by a dark and riotous sea that he ruled, alongside serpents and horrors.

He is defeated, but the chasms remain.

Hope is a fragile seed, one that I'm determined to help grow and the biggest reason I volunteered to leave. To be wed.

"Equitable," my brother calls it. "A marriage of mutual benefit." Easy for Louis to say; he's not the one leaving his home behind.

"How are you feeling?" He holds out his palm, and I pass him my sword.

My nerves pull tighter with each breath, stretched thin and fraying. I've run out of time. Lachlan will be here—has likely already been received by my brother—and my future will begin. A future that doesn't include Sterling.

Anyone in my position would be nervous because ...

Lachlan is ...

a stranger (**turn to page 153**)
my oldest friend (**turn to page 186**)

27

Actually, why not go with him?

Something tells me it'll be interesting.

He carries my things one-handed as we walk. When his hand brushes mine, I grab on. He's more solid than the ground under my feet, and it's nice to trust that someone else will take care of gravity for a while.

"Is this okay?" I squeeze his fingers. I don't actually remember the last time I held anyone's hand.

His smile is devastating.

Maybe I'm dreaming. Maybe I got clipped by that cyclist, and I'm having a wonderful delusion.

"More than okay," he says.

The walk becomes a pleasant blur, the sky filled with the kind of gray that flattens and dulls everything it touches. Everyone is bundled up against the chill, passing blacks and blues, their eyes peeking out from beanies and scarves and puffer jackets that I want to hug close.

I feel ... light. Lighter than I have in months.

"What are you going to do now?"

It's a great question. I wish I had an answer.

I've always been happier when I was rushing toward something. Being stagnant is ... not enjoyable.

"I honestly don't know."

"Well, the good news is, you don't have to figure it out alone."

It's hard to believe I called him selfish a few hours ago.

"So … boyfriend, job, apartment. Is that it?"

He makes it sound so simple, as though my life hasn't been decimated in the space of a few hours. Like he can make a plan to fix it in no time flat.

"For now."

He doesn't miss a beat. "First one's easy, so no worries there. Second one might be a bit trickier, but I know a guy who owes me a hell of a favor. The third one depends."

"On?"

"On how much you trust me."

We end up in a courtyard overlooking the river. I've never been in this part of the city before, but I can see why he brought me here.

A young girl who can barely be out of high school is performing with her electric guitar, a growing crowd braving the cold to admire her obvious skill.

"The music college is around the corner," he explains. "They come to practice, or battle, or have a bit of fun. Best concerts in the city right here."

I'm captured by the spark in his eyes. I like his energy. He's relaxed and playful, but also deeply passionate. He flirts, yeah, but he also doesn't hide how much he cares, and I like that. It's what draws me to him.

"Did you go here?"

"Couldn't afford to. I learned as much as I could on my own —library books and ten clumsy fingers. The real shit came from favors and kindness, people like this, who play much better than I ever could, people who gave a poor kid a chance. It wasn't serious for me back then. Music was just another way to make a few bucks until it became more. Something stable, something that stopped being a long shot and started being a meal ticket, a home for Mum and my brothers. I owe music everything."

His passion is so tangible that I could reach out and touch it. Hold it between my palms and keep it safe. It reminds me of sitting on Alice's couch with wine and pizza, talking over a movie, or drinking hot cocoa with my parents while wearing matching dressing gowns.

Something about him reminds me of home.

It's so rare to find, and in a city like Chance, it's like discovering lost gold.

We take a seat on a nearby bench. It's close enough to enjoy the show, but far enough to hear ourselves talk. There's a coffee cart nearby and a line of people waiting to order. The air smells like spun sugar.

"I'll be right back," Lucky says, walking over.

Twenty minutes ago, I would have put getting a new job at the top of my list. It should be; walking out of *The Observer*, knowing I won't be back, is a wound I can already tell will take forever to heal. Even now, I'm picking at it.

I should have yelled.

I should have thrown her shitty job back in Monica's face.

I should have found Sterling and done something ridiculous.

But I didn't. I nodded and packed up and walked out with my tail between my legs.

And then I became homeless.

Sighing, I pull out my phone. Best fix this now.

My landlord answers in a rush. "Yep?"

"Bruno, it's Mia in 309. I know I'm meant to be out this weekend, but my new place fell through, and I need to know if there's any chance I could stay a bit longer."

Something crashes in the background, and he swears. "Wait here, would ya?" And then he's setting the phone and walking away, grumbling complaints loud enough to hear.

I wait, watching Lucky charm the guy running the cart. I've

never met anyone so enthusiastically themself before. It's endearing.

"Okay, what was it you needed? Oh, right. Well, you have the luck of a unicorn because the next guy can't move in for another month, so if you can pay me up front, you've won yourself four more weeks."

"I think you mean leprechaun."

"What?"

"Never mind. I'll send the money right now."

"Yep," he grunts and hangs up.

No one hates phone calls more than that man, but, hey, he's efficient. I can appreciate that.

And it's really, really hard to be mad when he just saved my ass.

Lucky sits beside me, a steaming cup in his hand. I'm very aware of how little space there is between us. Everywhere we might touch. How easy it would be to close the gap. How much I want to.

"Please tell me that smile is for me."

"Nope," I say. "I've temporarily postponed my living problem."

He clasps his chest. "Next time, lie to me."

I don't bother to hide my smile.

"I didn't say it before, but thank you for the coffee. Maybe it's the panic talking, but I don't think it's ever tasted this good before." I put the empty cup aside. I fish the doughnut out of my belongings, groaning in pleasure as soon as I take a bite. "I haven't had one of these in a year."

"Why the fuck not?"

"I've been trying to get fit."

Lucky's gaze sweeps over me. "Bullshit. You're gorgeous. What fun is being fit if you can't eat?"

Oh, I want to wrap him up in a box and keep him.

"Wow, I finally found something that annoys you." I don't know what fountain of positivity he dipped himself in, but I need the address.

"It annoys me that your ex would make you feel bad about yourself."

"I never said that."

"You didn't have to."

Lucky stretches out beside me. His legs are so long, denim catching tight across his thighs.

"Does anyone ever tell you that you're a know-it-all?"

He laughs, and it loosens the tightness in my chest. It's so easy with him, easy in a way I've never felt in Chance. Like I belong.

"It's a gift," he says, and I can't tell if he's joking or not. "It's how I know you're smart, although you already know that. You want the world to be better, and you get frustrated when it disappoints you, but overall, it's a good thing. More people should aim to be good. And you're determined—maybe a bit too much because, sometimes, you're so set on a goal that you race ahead before you're ready for it."

What the heck?

I've never had anyone read me so well.

"How did you do that?"

He shrugs, drinks his coffee.

Now that I know I'll have a roof over my head for a little longer, everything feels a little bit more manageable.

"What about you? What is it that you do that makes you such an expert on people? Fortune teller? Politician?"

I can hear the smile in his voice. "I'm a songwriter. Pop mainly, but I mess around with a rock ballad every now and then—you know, get back to my roots."

Ah. That explains this place. "I should have guessed. You have the whole"—I wave a hand over his body, my gaze catching on his arms, thighs, hair; it's ridiculous that anyone can be that attractive —"hot-rocker thing going on."

"Do I?" He leans closer. "Do you like it?"

Very much.

There's nothing I can do to fight the flush that comes to my cheeks, and I know he can see it because his eyes start to sparkle. He really knows exactly the effect he has, and despite wanting to be mad at him for it, it only makes me want to kiss him.

I can imagine it all too well. The scrape of his beard against my skin. His bottom lip, pink and soft against my own. Would he be gentle? Tender? Or would he kiss with the same persistence he's had all morning? Tongue and teeth and passion. I can still feel the force of his hold from earlier, how strong and solid he was against me.

I've been staring at his lips for too long. Tearing my eyes away, I expect to find him looking smug, but he doesn't. Instead, he's fond, as though we've been here before. As if we're reliving a cherished memory.

It sets my insides going more than his flirting does.

"Do you like it?" I ask because I need a second to think, and maybe if I get to know him better, I can remind myself of why falling for him is a terrible idea. "Writing music?"

"I love it. It's been my dream since I was a kid."

My childhood dreams once seemed so possible. Now they feel like a fantasy, wild hopes wished on distant stars, never to be realized.

And yet ...

Lucky makes me want to believe.

"What brought you here to Chance anyway?"

"Love," he says.

And has there ever been a single word more capable of encapsulating a life? It's thick with meaning, pure, drawn from the very source of him.

"Running to it or away from it?"

His eyes shine amber in the sunlight, flecks of gold glimmering with kindness. "Bit of both."

"I'm surprised you stayed." Would I?

I suppose I already am, and there is much more in Chance to love than another person. It's easy to discover. The laugh of the kid running the coffee cart, every note pouring smooth and easy from the guitarist, a dad getting on one knee to fix the zipper on his daughter's jacket.

"Some risks are worth taking," he says.

He's right.

Risks require unparalleled trust, as does love, and both require a strong heart. Why else would I have moved to Chance? This city is full of risk-takers. I admire that. It's every reason I was drawn here and drawn to him.

"Or you're just stubborn," I say, and I mean it as a compliment. I'm stubborn too.

"See," he says, sliding his arm around me. "You do know me."

We're joined, knee to hip to shoulder. We fit well together.

It gives me an idea.

"What are you doing on Thursday?"

"Anything you want, love."

Hmm. Maybe there is a way I can salvage this. I can't find a job in two days, not in this economy, but that doesn't mean I can't delay the apartment a little longer. Nothing major ... just a nudge to give myself a little more time.

Can we skip ahead? I want to see Lucky again.

it's a date (**turn to page 163**)

28

NOTHING HAPPENS.

Like missing a step on the way down, I'm gripped by a jolt of panic that snaps me back to reality.

The surface of the stone is smooth to the touch—too smooth—and I laugh to myself when I find it's not a real gem but plastic, the light emanating from a small bulb. I find a switch on the back and turn it off.

"I guess that's as good of a sign as any that I should call it a night," I say.

"Or that I've been overworking you."

"I agreed to it."

His brows climb. "So, I am overworking you?"

"No!" I rush, and the shock of seeing him actually smile makes me go a little wild, until I'm batting him across the shoulder like we do that—tease and touch each other. It lands like a house cat swatting a lion—barely felt—until I look up and see a dimple appear.

I did that.

"I really should go," I say, though it's the last thing I want to do. But my apartment won't move itself, and there's so much more work to do. "I'll see you tomorrow?"

Looking up at him, the stark overhead light bearing down into my eyes, I could swear there is longing in his eyes. Something syrupy sweet, rich and oversaturated in the same way the air smelled minutes ago. It makes me sway closer, a call and response from one heart to another.

I really shouldn't have skipped lunch.

But if I'm dreaming or hallucinating, I'm not sure I want to stop because the warm cradle of his palm cups my cheek, and no reality could ever be this good.

"Thank you. I know I'm ... difficult," he says, and I really am too tender about him because everything softens within me. "I'll be better."

Gripped by an urge I can't explain, I stretch up, pressing the ghost of a kiss to his cheek. "Good night, Sterling."

His eyes are still closed as I turn to walk away.

Make Your Choice:

come back to the office tomorrow (**turn to page 119**)
I'm in a rush. gimme the short version (**turn to page 138**)

29

STERLING IS precise as he removes the armor from my shoulders and chest—never careless, never touching more than is necessary, lingering only in presence.

Since the day of my twenty-first birthday, he has been by my side, hair as dark as shale after the rain, eyes bright as a summer sky. He towers over most, even Louis, yet rarely uses it against me, only coming to full height when he's standing between me and a threat.

Not that there are any of those since the sorcerer was destroyed.

"I'll be married tomorrow," I say, not as a reminder—neither of us needs one—but because I can't avoid it any longer. "And gone a day after that."

The lines by his eyes tighten, but he swallows whatever is causing it. His words are gruff. "I'm aware."

I expected Sterling to leave as swiftly and mysteriously as he'd arrived, but he hasn't. Though he never wishes to explain why, he stays.

I hoped it was for me—a silly ember of hope that was extinguished when I found that I'd be traveling to Chance alone.

Once the weapons are stored, there is nothing left to do but prepare for today's introductions. I may be bound by duty and circumstance, but that does not mean I need to go easily.

"I'll miss you." My admission lands feather soft in the

silence. Delicate. Fragile. "Everything I've read tells me I should be happy there, but I can't imagine it. Who will train with me and tell me when I'm dragging my feet? Who will find me when I sneak into the orchards at night and sit with me as I count stars?" What kind of marriage can I have if half of my heart remains here?

"You're easy to love, Mia; you will not find yourself alone for long. Despite his"—he pauses—"relaxed manner, the prince is a good man. You have nothing to fear from him."

"I'd feel less lost if you were with me."

Sterling shakes his head. "You know I can't."

I sigh.

Anytime I think there's something between us, something personal, something deeper than heir and guard, mentor and friend, he retreats. Perhaps leaving is the right thing. I'm not sure how much more of this I can withstand.

Better to face the unknown than the pain I'm slowly conflating with love.

"*You can't, you can't*—that's all you will tell me. I don't understand it. Make me understand it, please."

Disapproval creases his brows, drags his frown lower. "Your brother is waiting."

I stay Sterling with a hand on his arm. "So, he won't mind waiting a little longer."

"Mia," he says, his tone as sharp as the dagger hidden at his side, "he isn't the only one waiting."

I huff. I hardly need him to remind me.

"Sterling," I plead, and the rare use of his given name melts his reserve—a trick I learned quickly. "There's something ... if I'm going to go through with this, let us part honestly. Ever since we met, I've grown to care for you, as a friend, but also as more—"

He cuts me off with a command. "Mia, don't." His fists are clenched at his sides. The muscles beneath his beard shift like water in a stream. The crack in his calm facade is hardly a consolation.

I wait, but he says nothing more.

He always does this. Silence. Vagaries. He's impossible. Getting to know him has been a fight, and don't get me started on his past. The reasons for his move are vague, as are the details on his life before Ferntree.

How am I ever meant to know of anything of the world when he and Louis conspire to keep it hidden from me? Anything of him?

"It seems I am alone after all. I knew I would be once I left on the prince's arm, my name signed over to his, but I thought I had at least one ally left. Hoped it so."

"You don't know how hard this is for me—"

"No, you do not know." I push a finger into his chest, my traitorous heart spinning at the feel of hard muscle beneath cloth.

"You say you care, but you always stop me before I say … before I can tell you …" I shake my head. I thought if we were anything, we were friends. But now, I'm not so sure. "You promise protection but refuse to stay by my side when I need you the most." My voice breaks as tears flood my eyes, and I hate how young I feel, as lost and naive as I'm accused of.

"Mia, please …"

"No." I can't be here anymore; it's too painful. "Excuse me, I need to meet my future husband."

I storm off before he can stop me.

Louis opens the study door with his mouth in a hard, flat line. "You're late."

I meet his stare with my own. Who cares? There's no getting

out of this arrangement, whether it happens now or later. No changing the fate that I agreed to—agreed because I had the childish expectation that my friend, the one who had sworn to protect me, would be by my side.

Well, if the Chance's crown prince isn't a patient man, we will have worse issues than my timekeeping.

Louis drops his gaze to the floor and sighs. I'm still wearing my boots from practice, their bright tips poking out from under my skirts.

"My apologies," I say, stepping into the room. "But it won't be the last time, so it's better you know now, and we won't have to waste time with sorries in the future."

There's an unfamiliar chuckle, and I turn to face the man I'm here to meet.

"I rather like waiting when the reward is so lovely, and I thank you for your honesty. It's how every good marriage should start."

Prince Lachlan is as handsome as the rumors say, which is a pleasant surprise. Tall and well defined. Older than Louis, but not by much. His hair falls past his brow, soft and clean, a shade darker than his honey-brown eyes. It brushes along sharp cheekbones, begs to be touched. Tousled. Ruined.

Yes, he is very pleasing to look at.

Strange that he's unwed. As the only son, he should have been married off years ago.

Is there secretly something wrong with him that my brother hasn't told me?

If there is, I must make my peace with it now.

Sterling is adamant that the prince is a good man, and I trust him, but this isn't a love match. It's a responsibility to unite our provinces and heal the scars the sorcerer cleaved out between our communities. I pushed for this, and I will honor my choice, no matter who this stranger is.

Louis looks eagerly between us, twitching with excitement.

It's no wonder; he was raised to take over our father's role on the council, and trade between Ferntree and Chance is about to increase twofold.

"How was your journey?" I ask.

"Enjoyable," Lachlan answers. "The waters were calm. Have you ever sailed?"

"No." I offer nothing else.

"You'll love it, I promise. I'm an excellent captain."

"And modest, clearly."

Louis gapes. "I apologize for my sister—"

"Please don't," Lachlan says, smiling wider. "Is there anything else you need, Louis? Only I'd like to get to know my fiancée."

"I shouldn't leave you alone," Louis says, cautious. "Why isn't your guard here?"

"That's a question we'd both like the answer to," I say, not hiding the bite in my voice.

Louis looks like a drowned puppy when he pouts. "I'll call one of mine to stand watch." He touches my arm. "At the first sign of trouble—"

With a flick of my wrist, I free the dagger Sterling gave me. "I know what to do."

Louis's eyes almost fall out of his head, and I prepare for his wrath, but Lachlan tips his head back and laughs.

"Oh, I believe this will be an even better arrangement than you promised, Louis."

Flushed to the tips of his ears, my brother apologizes anyway and excuses himself. I take the opportunity to put a little distance between myself and this wayward prince.

I sheathe my dagger. "Mia Finnegan. Nice to finally meet you," I say, dipping my head.

"Lachlan Williams, or Lucky if you prefer, and the pleasure is all mine, I assure you."

His eyes are alight with more joy than I would expect for a

man who has been strong-armed into an arranged marriage—or perhaps it's only me who has been dreading this.

He's not the one losing his entire world. My chest aches with the need to have Sterling here.

"Your brother mentioned you were well read, but not that you were also skilled with a blade."

I look down at my hands; the tips are still stained with dirt. "He doesn't approve."

"That's a shame. I find it admirable."

He has a lovely smile. Warm, where I expected him to be cold. Interested, where I expected indifference.

He walks behind my desk, beckons me over. I'm curious.

"I brought you something."

He passes me a scroll. It's large, half the length of me at least, and I lay it over the desk to roll it out. Lucky holds the opposite end, and what I find steals my breath.

"It's a map."

There's a similar one on the wall behind us, drawn before the world was split. I've studied it long and hard over the years, tried to imagine where the breaks were, swallowed down the pain of a wound we'd never be able to repair.

Before me is the new world, and it's ... beautiful. I didn't think it would be. I've never seen the sea before, only ever heard of the horrors the sorcerer enacted with it, but this is ...

Gosh, it's so very blue.

A familiar, striking blue.

Lucky sets a candleholder down, holding the map flat. "We'll leave from here," he says, pointing to our only port, far in the north. He has nice hands. Large, sun-kissed, with strong veins. "My crew is still there, looking after the ship and no doubt getting into trouble." He turns his head toward me. "You'll fit right in."

I duck my head, hiding my blush. Chance sits to the east, the city spilling out from the summit of a cliff, where the land has been carved away. But they didn't give up; they embraced their scars and celebrate them. It's beautiful.

"The port must be filled with yellow blossoms by now."

"You've done your research," he says, pleased.

I have, but that's not how I learned of it. "My guard, Sterling, has said many good things about Chance. I must admit, I'm curious to see it for myself."

He's close enough that I hear his breath catch. Curious.

"Do you know him?"

It's not a thought I've had before, but perhaps I should have. Where else would Sterling have trained?

The prince considers the map, his features held still. Too still. "The name is familiar, but I cannot recall more than that."

He's lying. I want to poke and prod, tease out the details that Sterling has so long denied me, but the look on Lucky's face stops me. I've seen it before.

It's heartbreak.

Rocked, I turn and walk to the window, with the pretense of admiring the view. It makes sense. Sterling has never dated since he arrived, and he's always careful to keep my advances at a distance. I thought he was protecting me by letting me down gently. Now I know there's so much more to it.

"It's beautiful," he says. "What will you miss most?"

Not, *Will you miss it?* No, there's no question I will. I'm glad he understands that; it will make things easier. The real, honest answer is not a what, but a who—not that I'll reveal it.

Instead, I point into the distance, deep into the neighboring forest.

Ferntree is largely flat, far as the eye can see, with rich soil and good seasons. We've been fortunate to live off what we grow, and we are careful never to ask for more than that.

Beyond the orchard to the east, the horizon is flush with greenery. Oaks, taller than any home I've seen, flourish there, and all of my childhood summers were spent hiding from Louis in the undergrowth.

"Not many know of it, but there's a cottage one day's walk from here, where the woodsmen camp. Otherwise, it's left empty. All my life, it's served as a secret refuge whenever I was scared. I'd wait until the moon was high and the house was still and sneak out. No one else could find me there, not even my brother. I'll miss having it nearby."

"Then we'll have to visit often," Lucky says, surprising me with a smile. "And while I hope you will never be scared while you're with me, I know a few great hiding places of my own that I'd be willing to share with you."

I want to like him. I think I already do, but nothing new can survive in the shadow of my feelings for Sterling, and I have one night left to rid myself of them.

I owe it to myself to try.

"I'm ..." *Speechless*. "Thank you," I say, caught off guard by how little I dislike him.

Sterling was right; he's lovely, so why don't I feel any better?

I skip dinner.

Louis will be intolerably angry, but I don't care. I'm only here for two more nights, and then it won't matter. He won't have to worry about me anymore. No one will.

I've decided I won't wait. The prince isn't a bad man; in fact, he is warm and rather sweet. I could even see myself falling for him one day. The worst thing I could say about him, if I had to choose anything at all, is that he's perhaps too friendly.

That's not why I'm leaving.

Something twists in my stomach—part hunger, part frustration. I throw another dress into my satchel. It won't be enough; nothing will be. I could fit everything in this room into this bag, and I still wouldn't be leaving with the one thing I want.

I don't mean to disappear for long, but I need to think. One night in the cottage will be enough to purge these painful feelings.

I step into the hallway ...

Straight into Sterling's arms.

"What's that?" He's looking down at my bag.

"You know what it is."

"No."

I gape. "You can't stop me."

"You're not running."

"Why not? You did."

I've never had a reason to believe he ran from Chance, but he flinches, and I know I'm right.

"This isn't about me."

Of course he'd think that.

"It has *everything* to do with you." He opens his mouth to speak, but I won't let him; I can't. "No. You sing the prince's praises, and yet you won't tell me why or how you know this about him. I know you have a past, Sterling, one you keep hidden from me, but unless you can convince me to choose a loveless life, I can't stay here. I thought you'd understand. I thought—hoped really—that you might choose me as I choose you."

"Of course I—" He pauses. "Can't you trust me?"

"I've done nothing but trust you since the day you arrived, asking my brother to join the guard. I requested you specifically."

His expression changes. "And I am grateful for every minute we've had together."

"Then why won't you let me tell you?" I step closer than I ever have before, past the boundaries I've held myself to for so long. Close enough to touch, as I've longed to. "You're not a fool, Sterling—we both know that. You must know—you have to," I whisper, hearing my own desperation, but this is my last chance. For years, I've held my feelings at bay, never sure of their return, fearful of heartbreak.

Footsteps echo down the cold hallway, too many to be an accident. No doubt Louis has sent more people to find me.

"I love you. I don't remember when I started, only that it has grown deeper with every day. I know you don't feel the same way, but I can't pretend any longer. I have to leave here, and I can't carry this with me anymore."

Sterling's face tightens and crumples. He glances toward the approaching footsteps, his movements quick. Panicked. "Mia, please. We can't do this now."

My heart sinks to the stone beneath our feet. "Then leave and don't look for me."

A deep sigh emanates from his chest, one I hear every time I test his patience, but it's the strain in his expression that knocks the air from my lungs.

Voices reach us, closer now, and it won't be long until we're found. If I want to leave, it has to be now.

What do I do?

Make Your Choice:

run (**turn to page 204**)
hide (**turn to page 266**)

30

THURSDAY ROLLS AROUND IN A FLASH.

It's all too easy to lose time when I have nowhere to be and even easier when all my time is spent crushed under the pain of job hunting. Meeting Lucky for coffee in the morning—or more accurately, *late* morning because he doesn't believe in alarms—has become the highlight of my unemployment.

"So," Lucky says, eager, "where are you taking me on this date?"

"It's not a date. It's an apartment viewing."

His brow furrows. "That was fast. I thought you had another month to look for a place."

"I already had my eye on it."

Lucky curls his hand around my wrist, bringing us to a stop. "I don't think that's a good idea, love."

"I just want one last look," I lie.

I can already tell he doesn't believe me. Damn his uncanny people skills.

"No, you want to torment yourself. I get it; it's hard to let go of something you had your heart set on, but it'll only make it worse."

Sounds like he's speaking from experience.

"Come on," he says, slipping his hand in mine. "Forget the apartment. Let's go in there."

He gestures to a shop across the street, and immediately, I can see why it got his attention. With its black wooden door, dusty windows, and the creeping sense that it's of another place and time, Chance's Curious Creations is unmissable.

It does look interesting ...

Make Your Choice:

go to the viewing (**turn to page 201**)
go into the shop (**turn to page 167**)

31

"I'm not so sure that's a good idea." Especially now, while I can still feel the heat of his lips.

"Agree to disagree," he counters. "You need somewhere to live; I need a roommate. It's win-win."

"It's a recipe for disaster." But I can't deny that I want to take him up on the offer.

"Scared you won't be able to keep your hands off me?"

Yes, but like hell am I telling him that. "You're ridiculous."

He holds his hands up. "All right, all right, I won't push."

The silence grows limbs, stumbling awkwardly, like a newborn calf. Kissing him seemed like a good idea at the time, but maybe I read the signs wrong. I need to clear my head, and I can't do that with him here.

I've already made one bad decision; best not make it two.

"I'll think about it." It's a lie. I've already made my mind up.

Lucky slips on his jacket and reties his hair. "I hope you do."

He looks around for a few seconds, delaying the inevitable. I wonder if this will be the last time I see him. Kind eyes, tight jeans, generous heart. I hope it isn't; it's nice to have a friend in this city, and Lucky is a rare one.

"Hand me your phone," he says, stepping close enough to trip my heart up.

I do it without thinking, watching as he enters his phone

number. The power to see him again will be within my control, if I want it.

But what do I want?

I know what I need. It's a rather long list at the moment, and I don't have much time to solve it. Lucky is offering me a piece of that puzzle, but my feelings for him will make it complicated.

If I can't find a solution, I'm going to have to consider the one thing I've never wanted to do—give up.

I stare at the door long after he leaves. It's not too late.

I can still change my mind.

Make Your Choice:

I changed my mind; I want to move in (**turn to page 181**)

it's time to leave (**turn to page 117**)

32

It's a strange little place, candles and incense so strong that my lungs seize as we enter, but something is calling to me, leading me deeper inside.

The shopkeeper is a short older woman with faded pink hair. It's put up in pigtails, and it sways as she moves. Her dark eyes are framed with equally dark glasses, but she wears no other jewelry, except for a bright orange pin with the name Moira.

She says nothing as we enter.

Inside, the store is tiny, as if someone took a shoebox and stood it on its short end. The ceilings reach high above us while the walls seem to close in, stuffed from floor to high beams with crystals and artifacts of every size.

Shelves spill over with tiny bottles, carrying ingredients like *yeti fur (freely shed)* and *crushed phoenix egg (hatched)*. Hanging from every conceivable point are wind chimes that gently whistle and sing despite the stillness.

How odd.

"Wow, this is great." Lucky is already bouncing around like a kid in a candy store, which is an interesting look for a guy who's six-two and covered in tattoos.

It's hard not to absorb his enthusiasm—something I suspect I'm going to have to get used to if we're going to be friends.

Funny how, a few days ago, I didn't think I had any of those here, and now … well, it's nice. Like Fate is reassuring me that I was right. I'm meant to be here. Things will work out.

"Look at this," he says, pointing at a bronze dagger, its sheath covered in runes.

There's an inscription in the blade—*Beyond earth, moon, and mortal rule.*

I'm suddenly desperate to press my fingers into the words, but as I reach out, Lucky stops me.

"I didn't take you as superstitious," I say, amused.

I'm expecting a joke or a wink, something playful because that's how he's been about everything so far, but there's only sincerity in his eyes. "Some things are beyond human understanding. I choose to respect that."

Well, well, well. He really is full of surprises.

"You aren't even a little curious about what could happen?" I know I am.

"I don't need all the answers to life," he says, trailing his hand reverently in the air, careful not to touch the shelf itself. "Mystery is what makes it beautiful, you know? And we're all free to give it our own meaning. That's beautiful too. For as long as we've been around, we've created ways to share that with each other. That's what interests me."

The aisle is narrow, leaving no room to pass each other without touching. It draws me closer to him, and he must feel it, too, stepping closer, filling my vision.

"But that doesn't mean I won't go after what I want."

My eyes flutter closed, each breath deep with heat and him.

"Curiosity is a rare gift," I say. "Respect even more so."

"What are you curious about?"

You. I don't say it, but I swear he hears it anyway when I look up and watch as his smile curls deeper into his cheek.

Knowing. Sure.

"People," I admit.

There's a box on the shelf beside him, beside vials of swirling ectoplasm and dried flowers. It's ajar. The need to open it, to look inside and discover, is overwhelming.

I don't need all the answers, but, wow, do I love looking for them. Always have.

"We've proven time and time again that we're capable of anything."

Great feats of strength, exploration, science, art, empathy ... you name it, and humans have tried to excel in it, but we've also discovered new depths of cruelty, apathy, and greed.

For good or for bad, we always find a way to do more, and if we can do better and we don't, that's not an accident.

That's a decision.

I think I'm becoming addicted to Lucky's smiles. The fluttering in my stomach increases, and like a glass overflowing, I feel more words tumbling out, filling up the silence.

I let them. It's either that or kiss him.

"Our choices matter. They change us and the people around us, and I never want to forget that. And maybe that makes me rush sometimes; maybe I'm young and inexperienced and need to slow down, but I don't want to."

"You want to soak up as much life as you can, while you can. I know the feeling."

I expect he does.

We move deeper into the shop, which goes farther than I thought it would. New corners appear at every turn, like mirrors facing each other, a series of infinite reflections.

Moira is nowhere to be seen.

Ingredients, bundled in fabric pouches, promise insight into the future, new love, and protection.

Lucky pauses, and I follow his gaze to a deep blue bottle. The label reads *forget your regret*. He lingers.

I desperately want to ask.

"There should be a *hex your ex* potion around here somewhere," I offer.

He turns to me, and the memories play so vividly over his expression that they almost project outward, like his body is here, but his mind is in another place, another time. "He'll be doing that to himself; he won't need any help from me."

The memory ends, and his attention refocuses on me. Not sharp, no. Lucky's attention is always gentle. But unwavering. Like nothing else exists.

"But I'll gladly cause some problems for yours."

"How sweet of you."

The air pressure changes, heats. My breathing deepens, and each rise and fall shifts my clothes like a caress against my skin. I imagine it feels like his hands would.

"Any regrets?" he asks.

"No." It's a whisper. Huey has no place here, not in my future. "I need someone who wants what I want."

Lucky steps closer, his voice soft. "And what's that?"

The lights seem to dim.

"Everything."

The touch of his palm on my waist is electric.

"I thought we weren't meant to touch anything in here," I whisper, letting him press me against the shelf.

"I'm making an exception."

He teases the tip of his nose along my cheek, sending tingles through me. It wouldn't take much to kiss him. He's right there; all I'd need to do is move, tilt up, and make our lips meet, but I don't.

The wait is a delicious kind of agony. Each second, each breath turns the heat of my blood up a little bit more, until wanting him is a song I can't stop replaying in my head, over and over and over.

The kiss, when it comes, is lightning to my skin, more than

the firm press of his mouth, more than the eager, searching curl of his tongue around mine. It's overwhelming. A bass thumping deep into my bones. Moving. Vital. Life-giving.

It feels like falling, and I reach blindly for the case behind me, my palm catching on a strange stone. I pull back from the kiss and pick it up.

It's glowing.

Faint pink light coats my fingertips, illuminating the deep, swirling patterns within the crystal itself. They have no beginning or end, stretching endlessly into the stone itself, although it's no bigger than my hand.

I can't look away.

"Touch it," I tell Lucky. I don't know why.

Slowly, he reaches out ...

Make Your Choice:

something magical happens (**turn to page 227**)
nothing happens (**turn to page 246**)

33

I DODGE a guy in a baseball cap as he stomps down the sidewalk. We're only a block away from the bank now.

"I'm assuming we aren't going to just ask her straight up about it."

Sterling presses a hand to my back, guiding me around a group of suits.

"Correct," he answers, a hint of pride in his voice.

We both agreed he's too recognizable, so I'm meeting Tegan in his place, but he put his foot down when I suggested coming alone. Honestly, I'm grateful for it. We make a good team.

"You'll need to ease her into the conversation first. She thinks you're here as a potential customer, so she'll be eager to please, but if you mention Cox or her sister-in-law too soon, she'll likely clam up, and then we'll have lost our lead."

"So, this is like recon."

There's a short huff of air that could be a laugh, but it's hard to tell with him. "You watch too many movies."

The sidewalk clears ahead of us, but his hand remains. I don't mention it, selfishly pleased he hasn't noticed.

"I need to know you'll be okay in there," he says. "There's a chance she'll get defensive if she feels cornered, and you can't let yourself get intimidated. You need teeth to survive in this job. If you want to find the truth, you need to be able to do what it takes to pursue that truth to its conclusion. Understand that it will get messy. You'll upset people because you're disrupting their comfort, and some will hate you for it, whether they benefit or not. Are you prepared for that?"

"Yes." I am.

I will be.

It's clear today but cold, the sky a shocking blue, the air damp from last night's storm. Everyone's covered up, thick scarves and long coats, heads down and shoulders up as they walk. My stomach grumbles as we pass a spot selling the most delicious-smelling waffles, and I'm tempted to stop.

I'm nervous. This is all I've wanted, and if I screw this up, I'll lose Sterling's trust.

We round the next corner, and the bank appears.

Sterling's hand closes around mine, pulling me to a stop.

"Okay, deep breath. That's it."

I do as he said.

"It's only a conversation. You'll ask some questions and only push when necessary. You can do this."

He sounds certain. It helps.

"Got it?"

I nod again.

"Say it back to me, Mia."

Gosh, he's beautiful.

I roll my shoulders back, stand a little taller. "I can do this. Now, let's go before I'm late."

I swear there's a hint of a smile on his face.

Chance's Reserve Bank is a fortress. With five floors of stone above ground and two below, it's hard to imagine anyone brave enough to try to penetrate its defenses.

The public entrance is contained, manned outside by a single guard and inside by two more. The windows are small and barred with wrought iron.

It's intimidating in every way.

Trust us, it promises, *your money is safe here.*

We enter.

Gleaming white tiles and arched, vaulted ceilings continue the impressive display.

Sterling points out a thick door on the west side of the hall. "Tegan will be down that corridor, with bank management."

He explains how the offices upstairs are only accessible via a separate entrance, in case of emergency. It allows this part of the bank to be locked down without affecting regular operation.

"God forbid anyone take a few minutes off while there's a robbery."

The curl of his smile feels like a victory.

There's a fresco on the floor, surrounded by Latin, and I'm sad to say I don't remember a word of it.

The foyer is vast, tellers lined up behind an ornate brass counter that runs the length of the longest wall. Every employee is dressed to impress. Every surface shines.

This is who you want to trust with your valuables.

This is who Cox trusts.

It's also, hopefully, where we'll discover his secrets.

For midday on a Monday, it's busier than I expected. There's at least fifty people here. Sterling lets me lead, keeping distance between us, but the feel of him at my back is assuring.

I'm asked to wait, and at twelve on the dot, I watch Tegan cross the floor to greet me.

"Hi, Mia, is it? Lovely to meet you."

Her fine blonde hair falls perfectly straight along her collarbone, and there isn't a wrinkle to be seen in her uniform. She meets my gaze easily and smiles freely. She looks more like someone who would offer cookies at a bake sale, not a mastermind.

"Thank you so much for making time for me."

Tegan smiles. "Of course."

She gestures in the direction of the offices, and I can't risk a look at Sterling, but I can see him hovering in my peripheral vision.

Then gunshots pierce through the quiet.

"Everyone on the ground—now!"

A second round of gunfire makes his point. We all drop.

Eight armed men, dressed head to toe in black, burst through the front entrance.

A hulking guy in a tight sweater drags in the guard from outside and throws him to the ground before barricading the door. The guard is pale as his hands and feet are tied.

His radio is ripped from him.

It shatters loudly on the floor. Someone screams.

On the floor beside him are the other two guards, already knocked out.

Another round of shots goes off.

"Empty your pockets! Bags on the ground!"

We all rush to obey.

Someone behind me is crying, and there are muttering pleas nearby. I press my rabid heart to the floor, twisting my head to find Sterling a few feet away, already watching me.

His steadiness is my lifeline. I grab hold with both hands and borrow from its strength.

I start memorizing as much as I can.

The assailants all wear matching ski masks, covering their faces.

They're all adults, roughly the same height, all a similar build.

Each of them has the same black backpack strapped on their front.

All but one.

He stands out, wearing a motorcycle helmet in place of the mask, and moves deliberately while the rest are a flurry of activity, shouting and laughing as they terrorize us.

This is the leader.

"Hands on your head."

We obey.

The leader stands over the fresco, keeping watch. His hands are covered with gloves, and his sleeves are strapped tight around his wrists. There's no visible skin, bar a sliver between his coveralls and helmet. No visible marks. No tattoos. He won't be identifiable after the fact.

The rest either didn't get the memo or they want to be remembered. Rings, tattoos, scars. They're trussed up like holiday poultry, ready for a sketch artist to make them famous. Strange. It's the kind of obvious that makes you wonder if it's a red herring. No one can be that obtuse, right?

Right?

"Start tying them up," the leader commands.

No one argues with him.

He takes two of his friends and stalks toward the corridor on the west wall, the same door Tegan and I were meant to go through.

Screams follow.

Then silence.

Five of his team remain in the hall, making their way through the crowd, pulling an endless amount of zip ties from their backpacks, binding people's hands as they go.

One of them is wearing a loose silver wristwatch. It jingles as he bounces around the room. His glee sends ice down my spine.

When fear makes people happy, the worst things you can imagine won't touch the depths of their depravity.

The leader returns with his hand twisted in a woman's hair.

Her feet drag along the tiles as they walk, one heel already gone. She's crying.

He throws her to the feet of one of his crew. "That's the manager. She'll have the vault codes."

His friend nods and holds her at gunpoint while the leader starts giving orders.

It's simple; we're all going to be restrained and moved. If we're calm, no one gets hurt. They get what they want, and we get to walk away.

The manager's hands are shaking.

They'd better be right about no one getting hurt. I hate the thought of leaving her with these men.

The leader stops in front of the one who dragged in the guard. "Get everyone in the back. Use the offices to the left." His friend nods, but the leader slaps his chest before he can walk away. "Be quick about it."

The Hulk grabs the hostage nearest to him by the back of his shirt, which stretches around his throat. He scrambles to his feet.

"All right! Move the fuck along."

Everyone except the leader yells. It's jarring, and if it's a tactic to keep us on edge, it's working.

Instead, he stands guard while they poke and prod and sneer, quietly watching over his twisted kingdom. Like he has all the time in the world.

They start to move us in groups. The closest first, working their way across the floor. It's impossible to see where they're taking them; once they reach the corridor, they turn left and disappear.

Then they return and repeat.

Tegan and I are still close to the eastern wall, where she greeted me before they came in.

It'll take a few minutes for them to reach us, so I've got time to think.

Beside me, Tegan is shivering. Tear tracks cut through her blush.

I reach out and squeeze her hand.

Then I lift my head and seek out Sterling.

He's staring. *Okay?* he mouths.

I check that no one is watching, then nod. He doesn't look relieved; in fact, that's his planning face. Christ. I hope he isn't thinking of doing anything heroic.

A few feet away, I watch as the leader bends to zip tie an older man in scuffed jeans and heavy brown boots. They look like the kind my uncle wears on the farm—thick and sturdy. Working boots. Not the sort you need to wear into a bank, but then this was probably just an errand for him. In and out.

Quick and painless.

That's when the shouting starts.

It's the man in heavy boots. He's terrified.

The leader grabs him by the throat and lifts him onto his feet. The sounds of his struggling are loud in the shocked silence.

Sterling gets to his feet. "The fuck are you doing? Let him go."

I push up to my knees, but I can't stop him.

I'm too far away.

The older man is still choking. He aims a punch at the leader's stomach, but it mustn't connect because there's no reaction. The leader does drop him though, punching the poor guy once in the nose before Sterling is across the floor and in front of him.

The leader brings his gun up.

Aiming straight between Sterling's eyes.

Sterling, finally seeing sense, takes a step back. "I'm not asking for trouble, okay? I'm trying to help you." He holds his hands up in front of him.

"Oh, really?" comes the leader's response. There's no hint of an accent, no way to really tell what he sounds like through the helmet. It's smart.

He gestures with his gun, and Sterling takes another step back.

"I don't think you want to add a murder charge today, do you?" Sterling's voice is low and controlled.

I don't believe it. He's still fucking calm.

We'd better make it through this alive because I'm going to kill him.

The leader cocks his head. Like he's playing a game. "You sure about that?"

The older man tries again, pushing up to his knees, only to be backhanded with the gun. Blood splatters on the tiles.

I hope, this time, he stays down. For his sake.

Meanwhile, a different mask, this one leaner and jumpier than the Hulk, grabs Sterling before he can move, kicking the back of his legs.

I watch Sterling fall to his knees, his jaw tense.

His gaze is furious.

The jumpy one fits a zip tie around Sterling's wrists, pulling tight enough that I can see the skin go white.

Fuck.

The leader hovers over the older man, waiting.

He stays down.

"J," the leader says over his shoulder, and the guy beside Sterling looks up. "Keep an eye out. I'm gonna make sure this asshole is situated." Then he leans down and grabs the older man by the collar.

"Sure thing, T."

Using initials instead of names—that's smart. They prepared for this.

I don't know if that makes me more comfortable.

T drags his prize toward the offices along the west wall, but he turns right. He must be throwing him into a room by himself. Cut off from the rest of us.

A door slams shut. The seconds pass, and no sign of T.

I'm praying there won't be a corpse in there later.

Tegan is pulled off the ground, still shaking. I stand, stepping between her and the guy who moves to touch her. He stinks of cologne.

I look over his shoulder, and my heart lurches.

Sterling is herded to his feet, and I know with a certainty that they're going to separate us.

I won't even consider what might happen if he's put in the same room as the other guy.

There are only seconds left to decide.

Stay with Tegan or try to get to Sterling?

What the hell do I do?

Make Your Choice:

stay with Tegan (**turn to page 214**)

find a way to Sterling (**turn to page 280**)

34

FATE MUST BE LAUGHING at me.

Lucky's apartment—a beautiful two-bedroom that hugs the long side of the building and boasts the most incredible morning light—happens to be in the same building that I was supposed to move into.

Ha-freaking-ha, Fate. I tip my hat to you.

In any case, his apartment is lovely. Three times the size of the corner studio I wanted and filled to the brim with all things Lucky.

Floor-to-ceiling curtains soften the exposed brick, guitars collected in one corner, a vertical vinyl player attached to the wall. Everything he loves is on display, in the kitchen especially. If I didn't know better, I'd assume he was a chef. Cast iron pots hang over a white tiled backsplash and a magnetic strip holds an impressive selection of knives.

You're not beating those serial killer allegations here, Lucky.

Plates are stacked in the cupboard above the stove, bowls as well, glasses above the sink. Just like my parents' house.

It's like stepping inside his heart, warm and lively, and now I get to call it home.

"Are you sure you want my stuff mingling with yours?"

Lucky watches as I flip mugs over before storing them—because you only need to discover a bug inside your coffee once before you're scarred for life.

"Mum does that too," he says, a smile softening his features.

"You must miss it," I say, closing the cupboard and mirroring his stance. We face each other, two brackets surrounding the memory of our kiss. "Being far from home is difficult, especially somewhere like this. I never knew it was possible to feel lonely in a city of four million people. Or in bed with my own boyfriend," I add with a sting.

Smoke and leather fill my nose as Lucky sidles closer, the heat of him sending a shiver down my spine.

"Ex-boyfriend," he corrects. "As he deserves, if he let you feel lonely for even a second."

My gaze drops to his lips, and I remember how soft they were against my own, but I promised myself I wouldn't do that again.

"I do miss it," he says, and I swear he's getting closer. "It wasn't all great, in fact; most of it was pretty shit actually. Having a roof over my head and food to spare—it's a relief, but it's hard not to miss my family."

It hints at a roughness belied by his open friendliness, easy grin, and cocksure attitude. Explains the steely resolve in his gaze, the hell-or-high-water persistence that seeps from his pores. It's no wonder he made a success of himself.

"Would you ever go back?"

"No. The past is where it belongs," he says, "for the most part."

"But?"

Breath ghosts my cheek as he chuckles softly, making me aware of how close we are.

"No buts. I'm exactly where I want to be."

It's clear he means it, but there's something underneath, a double meaning I don't have the context to unravel yet.

"Me too," I admit, believing it for the first time since I moved here.

His smile grows, and I can't help but look at his lips again, wanting more than anything to cross the gap. When Lucky steps away to mess with something on his phone, I have to stamp down the urge to follow with my hands and lips.

If I can't get a grip on this crush, I'll be homeless again in no time.

Music fills the room, a gentle guitar strum I don't recognize, and between one blink and another, Lucky is back, pulling me into his arms and leading me into a waltz.

"Of course you can dance."

"I'd be happy to show you all my moves, love; you only need to ask."

"Just don't be mad if I step on your toes. I haven't danced since my middle-school formal."

"A few bruises don't bother me," he teases. "Feel free to mark me up however you'd like."

I guess that answers my question about whether that kiss would make things awkward between us.

He spins me out and back again, catching me in his arms with ease.

"Is this what I have to look forward to as your roommate? Home-cooked meals and impromptu dances? My ex didn't even like cuddling."

"No offense, but there's something wrong with him. How long were you together?"

"Ten years. He was my first love—or I thought he was, but now I'm not sure I know what love is. It was nice to come home to someone who knew me though. To be chosen."

One song leads into another, slow and sultry. We're chest to chest now, and I hide my smile in Lucky's shoulder when he starts mimicking chords along my spine. Every brush of his fingers sends lightning through me.

"First loves are funny like that," he says, his voice soft. It reminds me of sleepovers and shared secrets. "Most erode over time, like rock giving way to water. Others are immutable, no matter how long it's been."

The pain is clear in his voice.

"Do you forgive him?" I ask, pressing closer.

He takes a long breath, my cheek moving with the sigh he releases. "It took a while, but going triple platinum a few times helped." He breaks into a smile when I playfully push at his chest.

Trust him to find a silver lining, even in the deepest of pain, the innate light within him piercing through any storm. It's intoxicating.

"I've always thought Sterling was the smartest man I've met, but if he walked away from you and wasn't destroyed with guilt, he's the Devil himself."

The warm umber of Lucky's eyes is intense as we sway, and this time, it's his gaze that drops, sending my heart skittering between my ribs.

"Has there been anyone since?" I ask.

His gaze holds on my lips as he licks his own, and he pulls me closer. "Yes," is all he says, and we must move in tandem because we're kissing, and it's all I remember and more. Better actually because there's nothing to dull the slide of his tongue against mine. No way of missing the grip of his hand as he slides it into my hair, guiding my head back as he devours my mouth.

My lips tingle when we pull apart. "I thought you didn't want to do this," I whisper.

"I wanted to do it right," he says, kissing me again. "You're not a drunken one-night stand, love. We can take it as slow as you want—"

"No." I slip my hands under his shirt, groaning internally as my fingertips slide over and between the groove of his ribs. He's gorgeous. "I don't want slow." Clutching his shirt in my fist, I haul him back to me.

There are few opportunities in life where you can be certain of something, but in this, I am sure; Lucky came into my life for a reason, and I might not know where we're heading, but I'm going to enjoy every second of the ride there.

Make Your Choice:

don't stop there! gimme the good stuff* (**turn to page 210**)
no spice? no problem! (**turn to page 220**)

35

It's been many years since I've seen my dear friend.

We've been betrothed since we were born, before the sorcerer ripped the earth apart and separated us from each other. For over a decade, my only contact with Lucky has been through letters.

Our marriage will be one step toward peace, one I have been thinking of for a long time.

"Mia, I want you to be careful. You may think you know him, but a lot has changed since you last met. He will not be the boy of your memories."

"If you'd read what he wrote me—"

"Words can be faked, truths hidden beneath pretty promises that never need testing."

"Why are you so against him? I know he's changed. I'm not the same as before, so why should he be? But I trust that he's a good man, Sterling. The rest we will discover together."

Sterling frowns.

I know he dislikes my leaving, but surely, he must see that there is little to fear.

"Aha! Here you are."

My face splits into a smile at the sound of Lucky's voice, and between one blink and the next, he's crossed the courtyard and spinning me around.

"Hello, love," he says, his eyes sparkling. A sudden lightness has eclipsed all other senses, tilting the world, even after I've regained my footing on solid ground. "You're more beautiful than I remember."

So is he. Lucky's smile is wide and free. It's a direct strike, weakening my defenses immediately.

I bow my head in greeting, noting how he has not retreated to the safe distance typically respected among unwedded couples, much to my brother's chagrin. He strides across the stone in long steps, giving the dirt covering my *everything* the raised brow of disappointment.

Behind me, I feel Sterling looming. He's always been protective of those entering my space.

It doesn't matter. All that I care about is here before me, in glorious flesh and blood. Propriety be damned, it's so good to finally, finally see him.

He grew fast as a child, taller than me from an early age, but, my, he's grown. Not just in height, but in build. *Oh.* His tailors should be praised; they have crafted clothes that complement every inch of him. His hair is tied back, his skin glowing in the morning sun, almost as brightly as his smile.

Oh, how I've missed him.

Lucky darts his gaze over my shoulder. He leans in, smelling of woodsmoke and earth after rain. "Say, there's a rather fetching man behind you, attempting to end my life with his thoughts. Is he a friend of yours?"

"I can use my sword if you'd prefer," Sterling growls.

Something wicked dances in Lucky's brown eyes. "Is that a promise?"

I'm hot all over.

Louis claps Lucky on the shoulder. "Sterling is Mia's personal guard, and though you've been trained by the best, perhaps we should hold off on any duels until after the wedding."

There's a collective pause, and I hear Sterling sigh before the heat of him steps back. It isn't often that he acquiesces, and I can imagine the valley between his brows growing deeper in frustration.

"I do find it's much more enjoyable to get to know my opponent before we cross swords," Lucky teases.

He's warm to the touch, and he doesn't seem to mind my inability to stop putting my hand on him. I can't help it. He's here. Real. My senses are alive.

"How are you, friend? It's been far too long."

"Surely, that's an improper greeting for your betrothed," Lucky teases, and the relief of having my dearest friend back in my life becomes complete.

I should never have doubted. Sterling's warnings dug under my skin, but Lucky stands before me, as familiar as my own voice.

"How are you, husband?"

"You're not married yet," Sterling clarifies, but Lucky ignores him.

"I'm infinitely better now that I'm here. Shall we walk? I've been promised a tour of your lovely home, and I can think of no better guide."

I nod, eager to relearn who he is. Ignoring the rules that say Lucky and I should not be alone until the night of our wedding, I cautiously slip my hand into his, marveling at the feel of it. His skin is surprisingly rough around the edges, reminding me of Sterling's hands instead of those of a noble.

As we leave the room, I hear my brother say, "I trust you'll look after her," and it isn't until I hear footsteps following us that I realize he was speaking to Sterling and not Lucky.

I stop in the hall and turn to him. "We don't need a chaperone."

Sterling's frown is etched in. "I disagree."

Ridiculous. I'm a grown woman; how dare he treat me like a child in my own home? In front of my future husband as well.

I spin on my heel. "What are you expecting will occur? Do

you truly believe me so far gone in my feelings that I cannot uphold my propriety for a single stroll? I should think I've given you, of all people, enough evidence that is not true."

It's more than I should have said. To admit the existence of feelings where they are both concerned is highly improper, but I'm oddly thrilled at having laid it bare finally.

However, despite the working of his jaw, Sterling is not dissuaded from joining us.

"And you should know by now that I will always put you first."

Lucky curls his fingers in mine, covering the join with his other hand. "Come. If your man is determined to join us, let him command the rear." He raises a brow in challenge. "Am I right in guessing that's the position you favor?"

Sterling growls in response.

I tug Lucky along. I have no time for petty games, especially between two of the most important people in my life. "Please, I'd like us to be friendly."

To my surprise, Sterling drops eye contact first, bowing his head and taking a step back, but keeping close as we start down the hall.

When dinnertime arrives, I fear my body is more nerves than bone. Nothing fits right, but I've gone through every dress I own, and it's clear that the issue is me.

Two quick raps sound at my door—Sterling.

"Come in."

I smooth my hands down the front of my dress. Fix the collar. Pull at the sleeves. I'm suspiciously damp under my arms. Maybe I should change back to the black.

"You look lovely," Sterling says, appearing behind me in the mirror.

Sweet of him to reassure me, but he always says that.

I need Lucky to think it too.

He brings his hands up to my shoulders, turning me to face him. Usually, his unshakable reserve steadies me. I'm the one prone to whimsy and dramatics, quick to act once I'm decided on something. Not Sterling. I've never once seen him lose control.

"You have nothing to worry about."

Gosh, this dress is so tight. Has it always been this tight? Maybe I should change.

"We don't know that."

Lucky is a good man, the kind who would follow through on a proposal because it was the right thing to do. It doesn't mean he feels the way I do.

"Mia."

I look up into Sterling's unwavering gaze.

"You didn't see how he looked at you."

Warmth sparks in my belly. "How did he look at me?"

"Like the stars hang in your eyes."

Does he really think so?

"Perhaps it was a trick of the light."

"No," he says, resolute, a storm brewing within the blue of his eyes. "I recognize the signs of a man in love. Trust me on that."

My eyes flutter shut as a flush washes over me. No matter what I do, I can't shake how much he affects me. With Lucky here, I thought ... but it hasn't changed a thing. My heart still beats faster when Sterling is close. When he says my name. When he touches me.

All of it will be gone once I leave.

He can forget his no-hugging rule; I won't get a chance after tomorrow. I throw my arms around his neck, crushing us together. After a deep inhale, he brings his own around my back, pressing me tighter to him.

"Sterling," I whisper, my heart beating wild in my chest. Surely, he can feel it. Surely, he knows what he means to me. "There's something I should tell you."

Will you...

confess your feelings? (**turn to page 245**)
say nothing? (**turn to page 279**)

36

LUCKY'S APARTMENT is exactly what I expected when compared to the little I knew of him—a little thrown together, a lot cozy, and an overabundance of everything. This is no "starving artist." This is a very successful musician.

A pile of laundry sits, folded, on the couch. A large television dominates one wall, next to a stack of vinyl records, the player hung vertically beside three platinum records. An acoustic guitar is propped up against the coffee table next to a navy sweatshirt, and two electrics sit on stands in the corner. Music sheets litter every surface.

The kitchen is open and bright, separated from the living room by a thick pillar. It's well stocked and gleaming. It's hopeful and hearty, exactly like the man who lives here. Exactly like Alice's oversaturated studio or my parents' nautical themed living room.

I don't really know where to put my stuff, not that there's much of it. Maybe that's better; everything has a place here, and right now, I'm not even sure where I'm supposed to be, let alone where my extra chargers and hair ties should go.

I shift the phone to my other ear. "I don't know, Ma. I guess I'm torn. I'm grateful to Lucky for letting me stay, but maybe it's time to be more realistic about my future. Just because I've been dreaming about Chance for years doesn't mean I belong here."

"Of course you belong there," Ma assures me. "You've always known that."

Sure, but that was before I lived here.

"Don't let a setback put you off course," Pa calls out before Ma shushes him.

"I won't," I groan into my tea. I certainly don't *want* to.

The mug is faded, the camp logo half gone now, and there's a crack in the handle that always reminds me of counting lightning strikes when storms hit my uncle's farm.

"I'm thinking of visiting soon."

"You don't need to do that," Ma says.

She's right, but I want to anyway.

"I miss you." It's easy to admit. I always miss them; I don't ever want to be too old to stop. I am glad that Lucky is out, playing a set at a club right now. "Why don't I come spend a few days there for your birthday?"

It's a few months away. I'll either have my life together again or I'll be buying a one-way ticket.

"Come whenever you want; we'll always be here for you."

I know, and it's high time I started being here for myself.

Lucky stumbles in at two a.m., shirtless, his jeans slung low enough on his hips that I'm impressed with their stamina.

"Wasn't expecting you to be up," he says.

"That makes two of us. But I decided what I'm going to do next, and once I started writing it down, I couldn't stop. Next thing I know, you're here."

He kicks off his shoes and scrubs a hand through his hair. "That's great," he says.

There's something off about him, and now that I'm looking, I catch the strain of his smile.

"Did something happen?"

He flops on the couch next to me, throwing his head back to stare at the ceiling. "I guess ten years was long enough for Sterling to apologize."

"He was there?"

"Yeah." He continues to stare in the abyss, and I imagine all the words he isn't saying filling the spaces between us.

"Do you forgive him?"

"I shouldn't."

"But you do."

"I've missed him. I know how ridiculous that sounds. I'd been angry for so long, and I really gave it to him tonight, everything I'd been wanting to say to him for ten years finally out in the open."

"That must have felt good."

"You have no idea, and you know what he did?"

I shake my head.

"Stood there and took it. Accepted how shitty he'd been and then told me he wanted to make it right."

"What do you want?"

A long breath explodes out of him, and he rolls his head over to me. "Is this an interview?"

"Just a conversation between friends."

His smile is soft. When his gaze dips down to my lips, I don't dare to breathe, too caught up in the memory of the last time we were this close. I didn't kiss him then, but I wanted to, and I want to now. Except the timing is terrible.

Lucky lifts a hand to my cheek, and my eyes flutter closed as the rough edges of his fingertips drag lightly over my skin. I feel them everywhere at once and want his hands on me with a ferocity I've rarely known.

When I open my eyes, he's watching me, and I'm once again torn with what to do.

"What do you want?" I ask again, a whisper between us.

“I want a lot of things,” he confesses, a weight behind his words that I can’t help but feel settle against my skin.

He’s torn, and no matter how I feel about him—these burgeoning feelings that I sense are reflected in him—there’s someone else in his heart.

I pull away.

“It’s late,” I say, standing. “I know he hurt you, and maybe that wound is too great to ever heal, but you’ve had a decade of questioning if it could work between you. Don’t you think you owe it to yourself to find out?”

I leave before he can answer, burying myself under my blankets.

The answer, it turns out, is that I now have a very inconvenient crush on my roommate *and* his boyfriend.

Lucky took my advice, visiting Sterling the very next night so they could clear over a decade’s worth of air. Once the fog of old hurt passed, it took no time at all for them to rekindle what they’d started all those years ago.

All while I watch from the sidelines.

It aches. Not all the time, but every so often, the light will catch in Lucky’s hair, falling over his closed eyes as he hears notes compose themselves in his head. I love watching him work, love seeing him create beauty out of silence, and, my God, it makes him so happy, fit to burst and so freaking gorgeous in his joy that I can’t get enough.

Then there’s Sterling.

Seeing him like this—stern, like I’ve always known him to be, but softened, domesticated—it’s ... difficult. Impossible actually to see him like this—his bedhead and cotton shirt rumpled first thing in the morning, the glare he sets on the coffee machine like it personally wronged him by not starting itself, the perfectly sweetened caramel latte he makes for me when he returns from his run.

How am I supposed to know these things and not want more?

It catches me off guard, presses into the healing bruise just to check that it still hurts. It does, but it's getting better. Easier. They're too perfect for each other, and I'm not getting in the way of that.

"They want you to tone it down?" Sterling frowns at my laptop. "It's a class action suit. They lied about the sets being flame resistant and put thousands of kids at risk. If anything, I think your copy is a little too lenient."

It is. I've been through three drafts already, and I can't type the phrase *eight-year-old suffers severe burns* without crying.

"I don't know what to do." I take my computer back, fighting the urge to fling it into the wall. "It's like this with everything. The station only wants the facts, and I get that, but these are people's lives, and it makes me fucking angry. I don't want to calmly report that a little boy went up in flames because another influencer wanted their own merch. It's disgusting."

My eyes sting as I force myself to take a deep breath, avoiding Sterling's all-too-seeing eyes. A heavy quiet settles between us, and I wait for him to tell me to quit.

Maybe I should.

"It's good that you care."

I wait for more. It doesn't come. "But?"

"No *but*," he says, and I don't believe him, but all that's there when I look over is sincerity. "People are owed the truth, and caring about that is what will keep you going when everyone else tries to stop you from finding it. You've already been through this."

Have I ever. My time under Monica is still a sore point for me.

"If this isn't working, you need to go after what you want. Wishing for it won't make it happen."

I should start my own radio show, call it *News No One Paid For*. Maybe then I'd finally be able to call people out instead of gently wagging my finger.

"I know the editor of *The Herald*. Let me give her a call."

"You don't have to—" The last thing I want to do is take advantage of him.

"I know," he says firmly.

Well, okay. Tamping down the flare of warmth in my chest, I nod. "Thank you."

It's still strange to have conversations with Sterling, even more so when he's dressed in running tights and a compression shirt. His already-dark hair is pitch-black with sweat, and I grip my mug tighter as I ignore the overwhelming urge to know what it might feel like to run my fingers through it, the way I've seen Lucky do.

Lucky wanders in from the bedroom, and for a man so meticulous about laundry, you'd think he could find a shirt. He pauses on his way to the kitchen, scrolling his social media in one hand, even as he leans down and kisses Sterling. It's all tongue, deep and filthy, and I can't look away. He follows it up by kissing me on the cheek. His hair is damp from the shower, and he smells divine, soft and warm and a little like lavender. He must have used my shampoo again.

I feel the imprint of both their lips on my skin.

Lucky starts dinner, peeling vegetables over the sink while half watching his phone. His jeans are snug, and his ass looks amazing. Sterling catches me, of course—he catches everything. I simmer in mild panic, feeling the weight of his eyes on me, and I wish I could tell what he was thinking. He's so damn inscrutable all the time.

Sterling pushes off the couch and follows. He'll do that sometimes, orbit Lucky, keeping him close. Penance for the years they lost.

He fits himself to Lucky's back. "Less spice this time."

"It's good for you. Your taste buds just aren't used to flavor. You'll live."

Sterling hums.

"Oh, I got the tickets we wanted. Front row." Lucky slips out of Sterling's arms and checks the oven, waving off the steam that escapes. I'll never understand what he's looking for, but that's why I'm not allowed in the kitchen. Satisfied, he closes the door and turns to me. "Clear your calendar for the twenty-eighth."

Finally. Ever since they started dating, I've expected them to ask me to clear out or at least give them a night to themselves.

"Perfect. That new hotel opened up on Riverside. I'll book a night there." I know I sound a little too chipper, but I want them to know I'm supportive. It's got nothing to do with how lonely it will be in the apartment without them.

Plus, I've always wanted to have a staycation in town.

Lucky is uncharacteristically quiet. Maybe I should have offered sooner.

"Don't go on our account," Sterling says. "We'll go instead."

"Don't do that." Although I am curious.

Sterling still has an apartment, but they never spend any time there. I've asked why, but all Lucky will say is, "Because you're here," which I'm assuming is code for our shower having better pressure or something.

I'm not complaining.

I like living with them. For the first time in two years, Chance actually feels like home and not somewhere I've been squatting in, clinging to its foundations while it tries to pry me off.

After dinner, we collapse onto the sofa to watch a movie. Lucky pulls my feet into his lap, which is how I know it's Sterling's night to choose.

Sterling's taste in entertainment is … surprising. The show is great. I just never pictured him watching anime—rude, I know—or really anything this gory and outrageous.

"I read more than the news," Sterling defends.

Lucky presses his thumb into the arch of my foot, and I bite back a moan.

"Mac here wanted to be a comic artist as a kid."

"Really?" I've seen the doodles he makes in the margins of his notes, an irresistible urge to draw in quiet moments. I imagine his textbooks must have been filled with them.

"After the accident, I took a break, and I never really picked it back up."

Oh.

Sterling talks about losing his parents like that, never shying away, just a direct statement. *Lost them at sixteen, drunk driver, instant fatality.* It never fails to be a punch in the gut, and though he rips the Band-Aid off, it's clear in the raw edge of his voice that the wound won't ever heal.

It's a stark contrast to the free-flowing emotion Lucky shares with the world, but it runs just as deep.

I pull my legs back.

"What's wrong?" Lucky asks.

Sterling speaks before I can answer. "It's about your mother's birthday, isn't it?"

"How did you—" I cut myself off.

Of course Sterling worked it out; it's what he does.

"It'll be the first time I'm seeing everyone since I left."

It'll be my first time seeing Huey since *he* left.

"Nothing to worry about, love," Lucky says.

But there is.

"Mia"—Sterling's voice is low—"you won't be facing him alone."

What?

"You didn't think we would sit back and let you go by yourself, did you?"

I did actually.

Make Your Choice:

home sweet home (**turn to page 290**)
pine away (**turn to page 244**)

37

I GIVE Lucky the sad puppy eyes that always work on my brother.

It's sweet to see how little he fights it, be it because he wants to please me or he's simply too curious to see what will happen. I like that about him.

"That's an unfair advantage, love."

"All's fair," I say, grabbing his hand and continuing down the street.

He slips his palm away, choosing to throw his arm around my shoulders instead, and he's right; this is much nicer.

The only other person in my life who's ever indulged me in this way is Alice.

No one cheered me on to move here more than she did. I miss her every second of every day. No amount of video calls can replace my best friend, but I made us both a promise when I moved here, and that was to do everything I could to try. Some days are easier than others.

He laughs when I tell him the address. "Starting to think this is fate."

"Only because you're an incurable romantic."

His face lights up with pure and unadulterated joy. The force of it is too strong to look at. "Ah, that explains all the Grammys then."

I've never seen Lucky with an instrument, but it's not difficult to imagine, with his nimble fingers and tactile nature. I like that about him too.

I pull his arm tighter around me.

There's a steady flow of people entering the apartment, and every one of them has the potential to rip this place out of my hands.

Lucky is two steps ahead of me, his long legs projecting him out of the elevator toward the apartment. From this angle, I become acutely aware of how well his jeans fit around the curve of his ass.

Bryan recognizes me. "As you can see, there's a lot of interest."

Even as we stand there, more people are filtering in. Jealousy is swimming in my gut. There has to be something I can do.

"Are you sure you can't convince the owner to hold off a little longer? It's not going to take me that long to find a new job. I've already had a few offers." It's a lie, but I feel desperate. I need this apartment. I need something to go right.

My heart plummets as Bryan shakes his head.

"Sorry. The owner is determined. I've been told to have someone signed on by the end of today."

Damn.

"Can I at least take one last look around?"

Bryan nods. "Sure."

Lucky pulls me back before I walk in, speaking low. "I don't like this."

Anyone would think I'm walking into battle. "Don't worry; I'll be quick."

Worry carves itself deeper around his eyes, pinching his mouth.

With no curtains to hold it back, light floods the room, casting a spotlight on the cramped space.

It's all too easy to picture myself here.

The couch pushed into the corner, facing the windows so that I can start every day watching the sun rise over the city. A bookshelf on the opposite wall, with a jar of spare hair ties to replace the ones I'm always losing, and a dish for my keys because I'll forget them if they are anywhere else. An oven I'll never use and a sink I'll pretend I'm not eating over when I'm in a rush.

Candles in the bedroom, perfect for nights when I get sleepy before eight p.m.

Losing this place is awful.

But I'm going to. I can see it in the eyes of everyone else. They see what I see. They are imagining themselves here.

And I can't let them.

An idea strikes me. This is an older building—beautiful, yes, but showing signs of wear. Cracks in the paint, grout that will never be white again ...

It probably hasn't had the plumbing updated since 1992.

Did I mention my dad is a plumber and used to take me on jobs after school because we couldn't afford babysitting? And that I learned everything I could ever want to know about how to fix—and subsequently break—the pipes in a bathroom?

It wouldn't even be a break. Just a small, inconvenient obstruction. Carefully placed to buy me some time.

Make Your Choice:

embrace your inner rebel (**turn to page 240**)
maybe you shouldn't (**turn to page 387**)

38

I TURN TO GO, and Sterling's hand wraps around my wrist.

"All I've ever wanted is for you to be safe."

Everything I've ever known tilts and falls away when Sterling gathers my face in his palms and kisses me. I gasp. The brush of his beard on my cheek is real. The softness of lips against mine isn't imagined.

"What—"

He grabs my hand. Candlelight shimmers in his gaze. "There's no time to explain, but you have to know I'll follow you anywhere."

We run.

It's easier than I thought it might be. I hide in shadows and behind coves, and no one questions Sterling commanding orders. We get to the stables. There, this stallion, Rogue, greets us, butting his head against mine.

"Just one. It'll be safer."

Sterling doesn't waste time fitting a saddle, using his long legs to project him onto Rogue's back and reaching down to pull me up behind him. We take flight, galloping out of the stables, through the orchards and into the forest as fast as we're able.

We make it to the cottage before sunrise. It's empty, but there is wood by the fire and freshly picked food in the pantry. We can't stay long.

Sterling starts a fire, the long line of his back giving away nothing.

"Why didn't you say anything?" I press my fingers to my lips. "All this time, we could have ..."

"We couldn't," he says, turning. His face is marred with sadness. "There were bigger concerns, and after, I wanted to talk to you. I wanted to tell you everything, but I waited too long, and you accepted the proposal. I couldn't jeopardize your chance at happiness."

I grab his hands and pull him to me. "How could I ever be happy without you? If this is how you felt, why wouldn't you come with me?"

"And torture myself every day, watching as you gave your heart to someone else?"

"Never." I pull him down into a kiss. "I cannot give away what is already yours."

He wraps me in his arms, lifting me easily. He fits perfectly between my thighs, hard and hot, and I've never needed anyone like this before. These clothes need to be gone. I have half a mind to shred them myself, claw my way under and finally get my hands on him. My lips.

"Please," I plead. "I need you."

Something cold and solid touches my back, and—oh, it's the wall. Good. Sterling presses me against it, and the friction is delicious. I rock against him, tasting his answering groan.

"I wish I could put into words what I feel for you," he says, kissing the hinge of my jaw. "You've reignited a fire inside me that I thought long extinguished. I've been consumed with want, aching every time you step into sight. My heart wails every time you leave, then fills my dreams with you as punishment. Now that I have you, I'm going to make up for every lost moment. I'm going to strip away every thread that stands between us and relish every inch of you until you are screaming my name, and then I'm going to do it again."

Oh God, yes.

There is a knock at the door.

We freeze. My heart stills in my chest. It's far too polite to be my brother, but who else knows we're here? Could it be a passing farmer, checking in? Or a guard from the castle? Perhaps our tracks aren't as lost as Sterling thought.

The knock comes again.

"I'd much rather not wait here all night, but I can."

Lucky.

He sounds more playful than mad, but Sterling looks like he's seen a ghost. He lets me down and steps back.

"How did you find us?" he asks, his voice strangled.

There's a long pause, and with much less humor, Lucky says, "Miss Finnegan made mention of this earlier today. I thought it best to check my hunch before I said anything to Louis."

I'm gutted. In the rush, I completely forgot that I'd told Lucky about the cottage.

"I'm sorry," I whisper, but Sterling shakes his head and opens the door.

"Lucky."

"Hello, Sterling."

They stand feet apart. All at once, I know why Sterling refused to meet him. Refused to join me. The breadth of a shared history hangs in the air between them, thick and vicious and raw.

Outside, the sun peeks over the horizon, splitting and shimmering through the trees, painting the forest floor in a bright glow.

"Come inside at least," I say, pulling a blanket tighter over my shoulders. "And then one of you is going to tell me everything. No more secrets."

The sky is light by the time the story is complete. They met as boys, grew together into men, then friends, then more. They ate, trained, slept, and dreamed in unison, but it didn't last.

Sterling sighs and seats himself on the bed. "When the world split, many of us were asked to leave, to help protect and train the other realms, and I accepted. We fought, and I left. We haven't seen each other since."

"Did you know he was here when you asked for my hand?"

Lucky reaches for me, his tone earnest. "No. When you said his name yesterday, I was blindsided. My intentions to you were—and still are—honorable."

I squeeze his hand. Running from my problems isn't going to work and helps no one. I have a responsibility to meet, no matter where my heart lies, but surely, this makes things easier?

My fear was always leaving Sterling behind or being locked in an uncaring and unkind marriage. It's clear neither needs to be the case.

Oh, how foolish we've all been, tormenting ourselves against the sharp edges of our heartbreak when the solution is staring us all in the face.

Intertwining my fingers in Lucky's, I turn to the man who continues to brood beside us, his frown directed at the exact point where our hands meet. "We need to go back."

Sterling's expression falls, but I'm not letting him go so easily. Not now. Not ever again. I know what is in his heart, can see it clearer without the haze of my own fears. I will never leave him, nor will I let him walk away from Lucky a second time.

"Come with us," I say, surer than I have ever been that he must. There is no other option. "We'll have the wedding, as promised, and return together to Chance. As my guard, you would be permitted to live in the house. You could see us both."

"Mia, what are you saying?"

I drop Lucky's hand and kneel before Sterling, holding his face in my hands, the same way he did with me last night. "I'm saying, stay with us."

Sterling looks over my shoulder with such naked hope on his face that it almost hurts. Waiting for Lucky's response.

"Please," Lucky says, his voice hoarse. "I don't think I could lose you twice. My heart wouldn't survive it."

Blue eyes drop back down to mine, brimming with a storm of emotion. "This doesn't change how I feel about you."

"I know."

He makes his decision, telegraphing it as easily as his strikes, and when he leans forward, I'm already there. Ready to meet him. Ready for anything and everything that comes next.

When we part, he rises, reaching for Lucky and crushing him in a kiss. I wait for jealousy to hit, but all I see is love, and it is beautiful. There is more than one way to find happiness, and bearing witness to their passion fills my heart.

Lucky pulls away, still gripping at Sterling's tunic with clenched fists. In inches, as though it pains him to look away, he faces me. Steps closer, breathing fast, his expression broken open. Joy spills out and over the top, and it's difficult not to bask in it.

I'm smiling as he cups my cheek.

"There's no possible way to thank you, Mia. Except perhaps this."

His kiss is gentle, almost chaste, but my body reacts all the same. Tingles spread through me from top to toe, cascading until I'm trembling with the need for more. I don't ask, pressing up for another and another, which Lucky grants, deepening each kiss until the heat in my belly is licking at my skin.

When we part, he sounds as breathless as I feel.

"If we don't mean to miss your wedding, we should leave."

I reach for Sterling, finding his gaze dark and hungry. "As long as it's together."

"Always."

THE END

39

He presses me against the counter, his hands eagerly ridding me of my shirt. Then his. I can't get enough of him—all that bare skin, scorching hot, lean and limber—and, my God, I can't wait to see what he can do with it, but right now, I just want his mouth on me.

I need to be naked *now*.

Some men kiss like it's a test, like there's only one right answer, and if they follow the formula, boom, they'll get what they want. Two plus two equals sex. It's uninspired, sloppy, and overly wet.

Lucky kisses with creative abandon. He dives in, adjusts, reacts, until our lips meet perfectly, uniquely, harmoniously, over and over, no wrong answers, only the pulsing joy of it reaching every inch of me.

"Wanted you ever since I saw you, ever since you bit my head off."

"You were so arrogant." Shit, his abs are amazing. Not an inch of body fat. "I didn't know if I wanted to smack you or kiss you."

He kisses along my jaw. "Could do both. I wouldn't mind."

Another time maybe.

I've been itching to get my hands on him all day, and he has clearly had the same problem. His hands are everywhere—my back, my waist, my breasts, my ass. I moan into his mouth as he teases his fingers along my crack to my aching pussy.

I'm already addicted to his lips, his taste. The bristles of his beard are a delicious scratch along my neck as he sucks and licks, pulling away only to divest himself of his shirt. Finally, I get a look at his body, and—holy shit. Ink spreads over his broad shoulders, and I spot a jack of clubs on his collarbone and a jaguar crawling down his ribs before he's pulling me back in and attacking my lips once more.

Fuck. "Don't stop."

"Not in the cards, love."

His skin feels amazing against mine. I know we're moving fast, but I can't make myself stop or slow down. I want everything with him, and I don't care what order it comes in. Something tells me he'll be ready for more than one round as well.

When he's finally free of his pants, I almost drop to my knees. His cock looks amazing. The flushed head peeks out of his foreskin, seeping pre-cum. He's thick, not too long, and I can already tell sucking him off will be my new favorite thing.

"Lucky," I plead.

"Please," he says, kneeling on the floor. "Let me do this."

"Okay, y-yeah. On your knees. That's good."

He presses a kiss to my knee, peeking up through his lashes at me as he sucks a mark on my inner thigh. His breath gusts over me, warm and only making me wetter. I buck into the air, needing his mouth on me, whining as he takes his time.

"Fuck, this is all I've thought about." With a gentle hand, he hooks my knee over his shoulder, smiling an inch away from my bare pussy, teasing me.

"Do it," I whisper. "Please, please touch me."

"Since you asked so nicely."

He looks hungry, and when he puts his tongue on my clit, he takes his time to eat me out.

I'm sweaty and panting and one orgasm down by the time I choke out the words, "Fuck me."

Fuck, his hair is just as soft as I imagined it would be, gliding through my fingers while his tongue circles wickedly.

He moans, alternating between stroking my clit and trailing his tongue down, licking deeper, fucking me with it until I cry out. I scratch and pull at his hair, gripping and holding his face between my legs.

His palms come up underneath, and he slips his fingers between us, opening me wider, dipping into the wet slick of his spit and pushing it into me with two fingers as I cry out. Fucking me like that as he sucks my clit just the way I need it.

Fuck, I'm so close already.

Heat is pouring off my skin, and yet I'm trembling, shaking with pleasure and chasing his mouth for more. I need more. I need all of him.

"Lucky, wait, please."

He pulls back, wipes his mouth on my thigh. "What is it? What do you need?"

He's fucking art like this. On his knees, eyes blazing, hair a mess. He's organized and thoughtful and a menace with that mouth. I don't know how I'm supposed to ignore it now, knowing exactly how talented it is, how gorgeous he looks, soaked in me.

"I need you to fuck me."

He hums, dives in for one more taste.

Ah fuck. Damn it, he needs to stop that, or I'm going to come, and I need him inside of me.

He stands, pulling a condom from somewhere—I don't care—and I'm so glad he's a planner, that he thought ahead to this and knew we'd need something close, that I wouldn't be able to wait because he's lifting me up effortlessly and pushing his thick cock inside of me, and it's glorious.

"Fuck, love."

Yes, please.

I can taste myself on his tongue, love how I can feel his cock pulse when I suck at it, gripping at him in hopes of getting closer. I'm already too worked up, too close to do anything more than eke out pleased little groans as he fucks me.

"Ah!" My orgasm crashes over me so fast that I race to catch up, catch the air that's squeezed out of me as Lucky grunts, his hips stuttering as he follows me over with a curse, his final thrusts making me tremble with aftershocks.

"Oh fuck."

"Thank you," I pant, and Lucky's eyebrow rises in surprise.

"This isn't a transaction, love."

He slowly pulls out, his grip tight on my arms as he lowers me down, keeps me steady.

"No, no, I didn't mean it like that." I bite my lip, searching for the right words through the haze. "I just—"

He kisses the corner of my mouth. "Just teasing. I know what you meant, and you're welcome."

He pulls me closer, arms wrapping around my waist, his breath warm on my neck. "It's been a long time since I've felt this way about someone." He tightens his hold. "Thank you."

That was satisfying.

let's see what happens next (**turn to page 220**)

40

I CAN'T LEAVE HER.

Sterling said it himself; the story is what's important. We didn't work our asses off last week to miss an opportunity like this, even if it's not exactly the one I pictured.

Tegan's hands shake as her wrists are bound. She's whispering to herself, words I can't make out.

I try to reassure her, "It's going to be okay."

"Shut the fuck up," comes the reply of the man in front of me.

I might not be able to see his face, but from the brutal way he tightens the zip tie, I can tell he's enjoying himself.

I stare at the cross around his neck, gold and garish against his white skin.

I stare until I can picture it behind my eyes.

I will not forget.

Sterling shifts, about to step closer, but I shake my head. He's already made himself a target. I won't be responsible for him getting hurt.

I'm going to prove I can handle this.

I'm going to get him his story.

The jerk in front of me slaps my face. "I said, move it, bitch."

This gets Sterling moving again. "Touch her again, and I'll rip your throat out."

I blink back tears.

There's more shouting.

Sterling is shoved violently to the floor, and the guys around him are raising their guns, and I can't breathe.

A spurt of gunfire cuts into the noise.

Dust falls from the ceiling, where T's bullets decimated the molding.

Everyone is silent.

"Stop wasting time," he says, his voice cold. "We've got work to do."

"But, boss—" The jerk who hit me sounds put out.

"What did I say? Put 'em in the back and keep a lookout. The alarm's been triggered, which means we have minutes before the cops start setting up outside. I need you up here."

"Fine." The jerk spits the word out but then stays quiet.

Tegan and I are being shoved down the corridor and to the left, into a room that is already full of hostages.

The door is closed behind us.

More footsteps sound in the hallway, but Sterling never appears.

They must have taken him to the same room as the other guy.

Fuck.

Most of us sit on the floor, although one or two people are standing, propped up against the wall. One man is curled up into a ball in the corner, his head in the lap of a woman—partner, friend?—who is trying to soothe him.

There's a window high on the left, closed and barred. Likely glued shut.

Even with the heat on, the chill seeps through.

If the movies tell the truth, they might turn that off soon, and I worry what that will mean for the older gentleman who is already breathing in rasps.

"Do you have your inhaler?" I ask him. Alice always keeps hers nearby.

He nods with jerky movements. "My—my pocket."

I push up onto my knees and shuffle closer. "Can I help?"

"Please," he says. "I can use it, but I can't—can't reach."

"It's okay. I'll get it for you." I slip my fingers into his jacket pocket, feeling for the inhaler and almost falling over with relief when I pull it out.

As soon as it hits his hands, he uses it, and I stay with him, matching his deep breaths until I'm sure he's okay.

"Thank you."

I don't know how to tell him that he shouldn't need to thank me. That anyone could and would do the same, but I've lived here long enough to know it's not always true.

Still, I want to believe.

"The cops will be here soon," I assure him. "I heard them before they dragged us in here. We'll be home before you know it." I hope.

As if I timed it, we hear a chorus of sirens outside. Relief ripples through the room, and soft murmurs of conversation start to pick up.

I return to Tegan. She's silent now, but her eyes are glassy. Far away.

"Do you know the first thing I'm going to do after we get out of here?" I ask her. "Have the greasiest, cheesiest burger with extra pickles. I've been craving one all weekend."

Tegan sniffles. Blinks. Someone nearby coughs.

She doesn't answer.

It's fine. I cross my legs, pick at a loose thread on my pants, and try not to think about Sterling, lifeless in another room.

I can't stop hearing his scream when I was slapped.

The sound of him hitting the floor. Seeing the guns pointed at his face.

Fuck. It's probably ridiculous to worry about him. He's the

most capable person here. No doubt he's already talking his way into an exclusive, and what am I doing?

The minutes pass slowly.

My stomach rumbles, loud enough to hear. I could really go for that burger now.

Tegan's voice is small. A whisper. "All I want is a pint of cookies and cream."

I lean closer, resting our shoulders together. She presses into it.

"When I was little," I say softly, "I used to sneak into the kitchen when I thought my parents were asleep and eat the top layer straight out of the carton so they wouldn't know it was gone. Then my brother would dig a ditch in it and ruin the secret."

Her smile fights through the fear. "Rose used to do that too."

The plan was for me to ease into the conversation. Tegan doesn't know who I am or why I'm here, and if we weren't in the middle of a robbery, I would have taken my time, but the longer we're here, the more panicked and scared she'll be.

No. It's a risk I have to take.

"Your sister-in-law works for a bad man, Tegan."

Her eyes widen.

I continue, as gently as I can, "We know he's been funneling money into hidden accounts at this bank. We know an LLC was registered under the name Peachee at the same time that a sizable amount of money went missing from last year's profit statement. We know that money was used to attempt voter fraud. We also know it's not Cox's name tied to that company. I think he used you and your sister to hide that money."

Tegan's gone white.

I put my hand on her knee. "If this goes public, he isn't the one who'll pay the price, Tegan. It'll be Rose, and it'll be you because he designed it that way."

Her face crumples in an instant. “He told us if we said no, he’d bury us in court. I can’t … I’m still paying off my student loans. I couldn’t do that to my parents.”

“I know.”

“I’m scared,” she whispers, rubbing at one eye with her knuckle. “Rose keeps telling me not to worry, but she’s too close to him. She says he’s a genius and he’ll look after us because we’ve proven our loyalty, but ever since she started working for him, it’s like she’s a different person. I barely see her anymore. He’s got her wrapped around his finger.”

I want to be sick. First, it’s late nights, weekends; then it’s separating her from her family and friends. Until there’s no one else she trusts but him.

I want to ruin Cox so badly that even the sound of his name will make people gag.

“Can you protect us?” she asks, fresh tears in her eyes.

Can we? I want to.

“I’ll do everything in my power to help you.”

Sterling trusts *The Observer*’s lawyers to protect him, but it might not be enough. Cox is massively wealthy. Guys like that built the very system that protects them.

“What will I need to do?”

“We need proof that Cox knew about this, that he knows what the money was used for and signed off on it. Ideally, you and your sister would make a statement.”

She shakes her head. “He’ll just deny everything. No one will believe us.”

“We have to try.”

“Okay.”

I look around. The sounds from outside are getting louder, orders being shouted and repeated.

I drop my voice low. “There’s a waffle place down the street; do you know it?”

Tegan nods.

"I'll be there with a friend of mine tomorrow morning before work, and we can talk."

Pins and needles start to prickle at my ankles. There's no room to stretch out, so I roll and stretch them as best I can and try not to think about the worst-case scenario.

"Older or younger brother?" Tegan asks, her voice small.

"Older, by four years. I love him now, but he was a little shit when we were kids. Last year—"

Footsteps in the hallway stop me cold. I stare at the door.

There are sounds of a struggle, followed by a loud thump that doesn't sound like anything good.

"It's them," Tegan whispers.

She's gripping my hand, her nails almost piercing skin. She's shaking. I look around; there's nothing to protect us. I've got nothing. Can do nothing except wait for whatever fresh horror is about to come.

The handle rattles.

I shuffle forward, shielding Tegan with my body. Whoever comes through that door will have to go through me first.

The lock clicks open.

"Sterling?"

They're saved!

you can't just leave it there. what happens next? (**turn to page 313**)

41

Two weeks later, I'm exhausted.

The job market is awful. I'm done being an advertising shill, but it's all anyone wants to hire me for.

"I just need to find a real story," I tell Lucky as he strides out of his bedroom, and everything stops.

He's helping launch a new bar, but with the way he looks, he'll also be sending a thousand hearts into orbit from that stage.

My eyes almost drop out of my head.

Loose black denim hangs low on his hips, paired with an equally low-cut vest. His tattoos are worn like a shirt. Like bait. Like he's a siren, ready to lure you into the deep blue sea.

His hair is let down tonight, soft and tucked behind his ears, dusting his chin, and the black eyeliner he's wearing stands out like a beacon.

Holy shit, he's so gorgeous; I can't breathe.

"Start with yours," he says, and I completely forget what we were talking about.

"Huh?"

He has to know the effect he has. Has to. And, yes, that glimmer in his eyes before he pulls me into a deep, longing kiss tells me he knows exactly what I'm distracted by.

He tugs on my bottom lip, then straightens. I manage to catch my laptop before it drops to the floor.

"All those articles you wrote, how many people do you think

took them at face value? Wouldn't you want a friend to help you understand if you were being led on? So, be that friend."

Huh. He's right. I don't have his stage presence, but I have brains, a camera, and an internet connection.

Better people have done more with less.

"Help me set up my phone before you go?"

He kisses me again. "Happy to, love."

I didn't wake when he came home, but it must have been late. His boots were kicked off by the door. A half-finished glass of water sits beside his keys on the counter and a note.

The scribble is almost indecipherable, swirling across the page at an angle. It says, *Wake me when you read this. Bring coffee.* I pocket the note, unable to hold back a smile as I change the coffee filter and wait.

Lucky is sprawled across his bed the same way his words were, freely haphazard, and I place the coffee gently on his bedside table before jumping on the bed, straddling him.

Lucky is already gripping my hips before he blinks awake, a smile slowly curling up one side of his mouth. "Need you like this every morning."

"Guess what."

Lucky's grip grounds me, the only thing keeping me from flying apart in the face of last night's experiment and this morning's rewards.

"I'm incredible, and you couldn't wait another second to kiss me."

"Obviously," I tease, leaning down with the intention to keep things chaste, but Lucky slips one hand up into my hair and holds me there, sucking on my lower lip. I pull back, a thrill running through me at how dark his eyes are. "Check this out." I pull my phone out of my back pocket, bringing up the video from last night.

After Lucky left, I followed through on his advice, filming an introduction and promising to share an insider's look at what journalism has become. I've already planned it out. Using my own articles as examples, I'll do an entire series, pointing out all the tricks used to hide advertising and consumer persuasion techniques. People deserve to know when they're being manipulated, and from the analytics on last night's video, they agree.

"Look at that view count, and it's still climbing. Comments too."

Lucky opens the comments section and starts to scroll. "Well done. You've given them enough to chew on, but left them wanting more, and, boy, do they. They're scrambling to hear the rest." The admiration in his eyes sends a shiver down my spine. "Have you planned out what you'll do after this?"

It's a good question and one that kept me up last night. "Mostly. I was hoping I could run it by you though. I watched a lot of your videos last night, and you really know what you're doing. It's the perfect mix of vulnerable and fun."

"As much as I like hearing you compliment me, I won't pretend that I don't get by mostly on looks."

He's not wrong; at least half his videos feature a half-buttoned shirt, filled with comments asking him to finish the job.

"I'm sure that's what you want everyone to think, but you're smart about what you share and how often you share it. I already know what I want to present, but you know what people respond well to. If I were writing this all down, it would be different—the medium changes things. But I want to reach more than a single article could, especially since I don't have a platform to publish it right now. But this proves that there are people who want to hear what I have to say, and I really think this is going to be my best shot at doing what I want to do."

Lucky takes my phone, discarding it on the side table and grabbing my ass with both hands. "Then put me to work, boss."

The erection pressing into my thigh is a pleasant distraction, and I sink my fingers into his hair as I pull him up for a kiss.

"You got in late," I say. "How did it go?"

Lucky pauses in his mission to cover my throat in kisses and groans. "Gig was great until Sterling showed up."

"What?"

Lucky raises himself enough to make eye contact, but we're still plastered together. "Bad timing all round, I'd say. Now, where were we?"

"Uh-uh-uh." I hold him back, my hand on his chest. "What happened?"

His head falls back to the pillow with a sigh. "I played, rocked some worlds; he came to talk to me after. We had it out; I left. My biggest issue is the gorgeous reporter in my lap who isn't kissing me right now."

"That's it?"

"For now," he says, threading his fingers through my hair. I sigh at the touch. "I know what I want, and she's right here in front of me."

My heart thumps loudly in my chest, pestering me to let Sterling go. This is where I want to be.

"Let's start fixing your other issue then," I say, grinding into him.

"Best idea you've ever had."

Groaning, I silence my third alarm and sit up, choosing to linger in bed instead of getting coffee started.

I know; I barely recognize me either.

It's now been six weeks since I left *The Observer*.

I have a shiny new job at the second-biggest newspaper in Chance, and I didn't even have to work the lifestyle beat to get it. My front-page dreams are within reach now, closer than they've ever been before, and I'm having a hard time believing I'm not hallucinating.

Mentally, I flip a coin—heads, doomscrolling; tails, emails—and I open my mail.

"Oh my God."

There's no way.

"Hnrg?" Lucky groans beside me. He rolls over and drapes an arm across my waist.

If this is an elaborate fantasy, I've got to hand it to myself—it's damn good. Lucky's a pretty great cheerleader, gorgeous and distracting, but always behind me, encouraging every win. He's more than his songs, more than the success or the box the public has put him in—the troubled past with a bleeding heart. He's loyal and sweet and a phenomenal cook.

I shuffle against the headboard, staring down at my phone, eyes barely open, still trying to believe what I'm looking at.

An email. Not unusual on its own.

No, it's who it's from that has caught my breath in my throat.

"Sterling emailed me."

Sterling knows my personal email address?

More importantly, why is he using it? I have to know.

Lucky cuddles closer, eyes closed, head almost in my lap now. It always takes him a while to wake up.

Technically, I still live in the guest room.

In reality, we pass out in whoever's bed is closest at the time, and I've had more sex in the last six weeks than the last two years combined.

"What's he want?"

I have no idea.

Opening the email is more confusing.

"He's apologizing for what happened with Monica." Which makes no sense because it was hardly his fault, and why the hell does he even care? Then there's the last part. *I look forward to being dethroned as Chance's number one reporter. If there's ever anything you need, you only have to ask.* "Strange, right?"

"Not really. He's relentless when he sets his sights on someone."

I scoff, "Sterling Ross doesn't have his sights set on me."

"I wouldn't be so sure about that," Lucky says, awake now and slipping his hand under my shirt. His touch is electric. "Mac's clever enough to know brilliance when he sees it."

I'm still pinching myself that *The Herald* has hired me as an investigative reporter. I finally feel like I'm doing the job I was born to do.

I know you will achieve great things, the email says, but does he mean it?

"Whatever," I whisper as I lean down to kiss Lucky.

"Come on. You can be smug about it. I know you admire him." Lucky's voice is rough with more than sleep. He drags his fingers along the waistband of my underwear, pulling them lower to kiss my hip.

"He's the reason I picked journalism as my major. The reason I came to Chance."

He smiles up at me, the coincidence not escaping either of us. I'm glad for it. This connection between us is a lovely thing.

"And?" he coaxes, tossing my phone to the side and pulling me down the bed. "Is that all?"

"What are you implying?"

Lucky drags his lips along my neck. "You want him." My first instinct is to deny it, but I don't. "I'll let you in on a secret, love. I want him too."

"Oh," I whisper.

This morning just became infinitely more exciting.

Make Your Choice:

keep that door wide open, please* (**turn to page 235**)
I prefer it closed (**turn to page 243**)

42

THE SHOP IS GONE.

Gone are the towering shelves and burning incense and warmth.

Instead, there are bricks and car horns and the thick stench of nicotine. A violent shiver runs through me.

We're outside. How did we get outside?

The crystal has gone cold in my grip. My body feels strange—tingly and unstable. My vision ripples, like the moment before a migraine, flaring bright, but it's gone as quickly as it came.

Like nothing happened.

"What the hell was that?"

I stare at Lucky. I wish I knew.

I open my mouth to reply, then freeze.

Lucky's gone.

My heart pounds. He was just here. I'm sure of it. I—

He reappears, slotting right back into reality like he never left.

"What ... what is happening?"

Lucky's eyes are wide. "I don't know. One minute, I was here, and then I started thinking about home and"—he snaps his fingers—"there I was. Next blink, and I'm back."

It can't be ...

Will it work anywhere? Or only places he knows?

"Think of somewhere you've always wanted to go."

"Why?"

"I have a hunch," I say.

Lucky smiles, and it's so playful; it makes me briefly forget the spiky tendrils of heat that are steadily growing at my fingertips. I clench my fists.

"All right. Let's try the top of the Empire State Building." He closes his eyes.

A second passes, then two. When five have gone by and nothing has happened, he opens them again and shrugs. "Guess I can't go anywhere I haven't been before."

I share the disappointment that's tugging at his lips.

"Bit of a bummer, if I'm honest," he adds.

I agree, although it's probably for the best; there are some horrific ramifications once I start to think about it. Who knows how teleportation works? What if you phased into a wall? Would you die instantly? And what about the space you take up? Does that disappear forever or swap places with you? What about moving through time?

"Whoa, that's a nifty trick you've got there, love."

Lucky's voice drifts through the thick cloud of questions consuming me, and I must have closed my eyes at some point because I open them and find the world around us has shifted a few feet higher than before.

No, wait. Not the world, just every static object in a six-foot radius. What the fuck?

I jolt, and everything comes crashing back down with a resounding boom that shakes my bones. "How did you do that?"

"Not me, I'm afraid."

My heart is pounding so fast; it feels like a blur in my chest. I need air, but we're already outside.

"Deep breaths, love," Lucky says.

The garbage beside me starts to rattle violently, an echo of my own strangled nerves.

"Let's try this," he says, close enough that I can feel the heat of his body through the thin material of his shirt.

Jeez, he's burning up.

Taking the crystal from my hand, he meets my gaze. Earlier, his smiles seemed manipulative, but there's nothing false about the soft curl of his lips. They're red and tempting, and, oh God, I'm staring. I tear my eyes away. Sound quickly rushes back in.

The alley is quiet again, the objects around us settled and silent.

He slips the crystal into his pocket.

"Can you control it?" he asks.

I don't know. My fingers are tingling now, pins and needles and lightning under my skin, but I take a deep breath and close my eyes, swaying on my feet. Lucky's hands come up to my elbows, his palms warm. They are a little dry, a few calluses grounding me to his touch, and I hold on to that as I try to picture the trash can beside me.

Up, I think and wait for the sound of it moving.

Nothing.

Hmm.

UP. The word echoes louder in my mind, my teeth aching as I clench my jaw, but all I can hear is Lucky's breathing and the distant sound of a bus stopping down the street.

I feel his whisper hit my cheek. "Deep breath. Relax. That's it." He smells like leather and shaving cream. "Now, picture it in your mind."

Rather than imagining the can lifting on its own, I change directions and instead picture myself picking it up, raising it in the air. It's not light, spilling over with leftovers the restaurant couldn't keep. The tingles move up my arms, sparking lightly where Lucky's fingers rest on my elbows, before concentrating in my biceps.

Metal scrapes against the pavement in a screech.

Did I just …

"You're a natural," comes Lucky's voice, setting off fireworks under my ribs, and I open my eyes to see the trash can hovering a foot off the ground.

Holy shit!

For a second, my grip slips, and an empty Styrofoam box falls to the ground as the can tips on its side, but I quickly right it.

Then, all at once, it's easy. The box hovers, frozen in the air between us.

Giddiness bursts between my ribs. What else can I do?

Keeping my gaze on the can, I shift focus to the box that fell out, imagining the feel of the foam, the lightness of its shape in my hands, until, in my peripheral vision, I see it float up beside the trash and settle to the top.

"Show-off," Lucky jokes, his voice light. "What else have you got?"

Remembering the way the alley shifted before, I extend my mind out, reaching and touching everything I can see in front of me. With a deep breath, I lift.

It doesn't happen straightaway, but after a few pounding beats of my heart, half of the disposals start to rise up off the ground.

"What the hell?" someone shouts in the distance, shattering my concentration and slamming everything back down to earth.

Lucky's grip tightens. Between blinks, the world condenses and swells, and all of a sudden, the street is gone, replaced by a black leather couch and a bright red electric guitar mounted onto the brick wall. Light streams in from floor-to-ceiling windows, pooling at our feet in a puddle of heat, like a cat purring in greeting.

I swallow hard, trying to shift my stomach down from where it lodged itself in my throat.

"Next time," I choke out, "warn me first." I think I might have left my kidney back there.

"Sorry, love. Just wanted to bring us somewhere safe."

I throw myself on his couch, desperately trying to wrangle my wild heart under control. "Got a beer?"

I'd prefer vodka, but there's a better chance Lucky has a case on hand.

I'm right, of course, but when I go for the bottle, he puts it out of my reach, knocking my hand away when I sit forward to grab it.

"Nuh-uh. You need the practice."

With a groan, I know he's right. I just hope he's ready to lose a lot of beer.

Two spilled bottles and a broken lamp later, I can successfully move an object from the coffee table to my waiting hand. It's not perfect, but I'm getting better.

Between blinks, Lucky appears in the kitchen and then the living room. He'll forget how to walk at this rate. "Picking pockets would have been a breeze with this."

I can't tell if he's joking or not. "Chores certainly would have been easier if I could have done them all while sitting down." I stifle a laugh, thinking about how my uncle's old hen Mabel would have taken to watching her eggs float out of the coop.

"Nah," Lucky corrects, escalating the test by replacing the pen with his half-finished tea. "You don't strike me as the type to like sitting too long."

It should surprise me that he knows me this well already.

Shaking, the mug rises. Tea sloshes against the rim, but doesn't spill.

"Did you ever get caught?"

"A guy almost broke my wrist while I was trying to take his wallet, but he let me go with a warning when he realized he was hurting a kid."

The mug hovers in the air between us, still now. Holding it is becoming easier.

Lucky smiles when it arrives at his waiting hand. "Ready for something trickier?"

My wide smile mirrors his. "Hell yeah, I am."

"Where are we now?"

The beach stretches out as far as I can see, a fine layer of snow dusting the ground. Dead grass climbs the dunes behind us. The ocean knocks against the land like it's asking for entry.

It's like standing in someone else's dream.

Lucky has been silent for a long time.

"It's, uh"—he blows out a breath—"somewhere my ex used to talk about. His parents grew up 'round here, and they visited a couple times when he was a kid. It was one of the few good memories he was hanging on to. Always said he'd come back someday. So, about a year after I moved to Chance, I packed a bag and drove out; I had this absurd idea he'd be standing here, waiting for me. He wasn't, of course, but ..."

"You wanted to see him again."

He stares out at the ocean, chewing over his memories. "Yeah."

Closing the gap, I slip my arms around his waist, holding tight. Lucky hugs back.

I hope, one day, he'll get to meet his friend here. The view is beautiful.

“I used to think the hard part was over,” I say. “I’d found someone who wanted to be with me, so I was set. I didn’t know the hard part was choosing to stay.”

“Everything good in my life took effort to get. Love’s the biggest win of all if you can find it, so I figure it deserves all of me. All in, through good times and bad.”

I ride the rise and fall of his chest as he takes a deep breath.

“Mac used to say I could form an opinion on anything, but I just liked seeing him riled up. I’d find him in the library, hunched over like a gremlin, hissing at people if they got too close. It took a month of sitting there, talking at him, until he finally cracked. Then he wouldn’t shut up. Fuck, I had known he was smart, but hearing him talk was something else. He just lit up. Most beautiful thing I’d ever seen—before you.”

“You still love him.” I don’t ask because it was obvious from the moment we arrived. This guy is special. A once-in-a-lifetime love.

Lucky turns away from the view, staring deep into my eyes as he raises my hands to his lips. “That’s the great thing about love though; it isn’t limited. I’ll always love him, but it doesn’t mean I can’t feel it for anyone else.”

“I feel the same way.”

A shiver I can’t account to the wind runs through me. When I next blink, we’re back in his apartment, and the burn of his lips against my knuckles lasts the rest of the day.

We hear the sirens before we see the news. A robbery in action at Chance’s Reserve Bank. At least three assailants are confirmed, but likely more. Hostages are estimated at fifty or more.

“We should help them,” I say.

"I'm loving the gung-ho attitude, but what's the plan here? Free the hostages, stop the bad guys"—he blinks to life behind me, nosing the sensitive skin under my ear—"get the girl?"

I step away. "I'm serious. We need to help."

"What? We're only civilians. We can't just rush in there when we barely have any control over these powers."

That's exactly why we should be helping. Right now, people with power and money use it for self-interest. If they have any inclination to change the world, it's for the worse. There's no *all for one* in a world of *what about me?*

It's time to evolve.

"Why not? We don't know how long these will last, and I don't know about you, but I don't like my chances of sleeping tonight if I could have helped and didn't."

There's no choice. I've been given this gift, and I might not understand how or why, but I do know what I'm going to do with it.

I'm going to make a difference.

Make Your Choice:

go be a hero (**turn to page 329**)
stay here (**turn to page 323**)

43

"I …" My face flushes, and the sparkle in Lucky's eyes tells me he knows it's from more than his wandering touch.

Reaching into my underwear, he strokes, featherlight, licking his lips. "Is it just the thought of him that makes you this wet? Or something else?"

"Lucky," I gasp, rocking into his fingers. He parts my pussy and teases me, circling my clit before going lower.

He kisses my neck. "You've done this before—touched yourself and imagined him. Haven't you?"

"Yes." Of course I have.

It's not just that he looks amazing in a suit, but how controlled he is. I can't decide what I want more—to break his control or be under it.

Both. Definitely both.

"Tell me what you think about," Lucky says, slowly dragging the tip of his finger around my entrance before dipping inside. "His hands? His mouth? How do you want him?"

"His hands." I've spent hours thinking about them. On me. In me.

Like a command, Lucky slips his fingers into me, slowly fucking me. "Yeah, that's right; he's got good hands. Long fingers. You feel them inside you?"

"Yes." *Fuck.* "Did he use them on you? God, did he taste you?"

He grunts and rocks his hard cock against my hip. "Is that what you want to see?"

"I want to see him kiss you."

It sounds so simple compared to what he's doing to me, too sweet, but it's the truth. I love the way Lucky kisses, and now that I know to listen for it, it's obvious that love still lives within him.

His lips meet mine instead, and I slip my hand into his briefs to stroke his cock, which is already wet with pre-cum. Spreading it around the leaking head and coating my palm, I match the push of his fingers.

"Fuck, that's it," Lucky pants. "Tighter—that's how he'd want it."

Oh fuck. My imagination explodes, a lightning burst of fantasies coming to life under Lucky's touch. Sterling in Lucky's place, hot and hard and leaking in my grip. Then standing over us, watching, directing. Lastly, all three of us tangled together, sweat-slick and writhing until the pleasure is more akin to pain.

I want it all.

"Lucky ..." I whine, needing more. More fingers, more friction, *more.*

He must understand, must hear it in my voice, because he doubles his pace.

"I wish he could see you like this," he says, licking along my neck. "So wet for us. Can you feel him, love? Fuck, yes, I know you want it. I can feel you clenching tighter at the thought. You want him inside of you? Want both of us?"

"Yes. Oh God, yes."

The Sterling in my mind smiles—a private, heated thing—and runs his palm over his cock, thick and straining his pants. He won't get himself out; he enjoys the wait, testing to see how long he can hold out.

He's patient. A predator watching his prey.

Watching us.

"Focus," he says. No, demands. *"Feel the way he fills you up. Imagine it's my cock inside of you, fucking you like you deserve. Can you feel it? I'm never going to let you feel empty again."*

I whimper into Lucky's mouth.

Fucking hell. The picture is all too clear as Lucky pumps his fingers inside of me, stroking the pleasure higher and higher. I imagine Sterling enjoying this, giving Lucky commands to go faster, slower, bite here, suck there.

My heart pounds against my ribs. I'm close.

"Come on, love," Lucky says, his breath hot against my neck. "Let go for us."

"Yes, Mia. Come."

My whispered, "Yes, yes, yes," fills my ears, and it's the thought of Sterling commanding me to come in that low, stern tone he has that catapults me over the edge.

I'm still trembling as I pounce on Lucky, rolling onto his chest. "How did he do it? Was he rough with you?" I graze his nipple with my teeth. "I know you like that."

"Fuck, love. More."

I tighten my grip on the up stroke, focusing the pressure on the weeping head of his cock.

Lucky grunts and fucks into my fist. "That's good, just like that."

It's so hot; I could come again.

Pre-cum pools at the head, slicking the way as he fucks into my fist. Lucky likes it rough, so I tighten my fist and let my nails skim the sensitive underside of his cock.

He bares his throat on a drawn-out, "Fuck."

He's never looked hotter.

"You going to come?" I ask between kisses.

His hips stutter out of rhythm. Yeah, he's going to come.

"Come on. Do it. He wants you to."

This does it, pushing Lucky into orgasm just as quickly as it did me, his cum spilling over my fist, pooling across his stomach. His cock pulses, and I drag out my last few strokes to the point of overstimulation, loving Lucky's punched-out moans.

Panting, I finally pull away, letting Lucky clean the cum off me with his boxers before he throws them in the hamper he keeps by the door.

He collapses back on the bed and pulls me into his arms. "I'm glad I asked," he says, breathless.

His skin is damp with a fine sheen of sweat, his heartbeat loud under my cheek.

"Lucky?"

"Yeah, love?"

It turns out, a great orgasm makes me brave. "If you still have feelings for Sterling, why haven't you gotten back with him?"

Lucky's chest rises and falls with a long breath. "Because I'm in love with you."

Oh.

"Look, I've loved that man most of my life, and a part of me always will."

"What if you could have both of us?"

"Well, that's the dream, isn't it?"

Yes, it is. I curl tighter around him.

"Feel good?" he asks.

Sparks trickle along my skin where he's gently stroking my back.

All I can manage is a contented hum. It's as close to a dream as it's possible to get, consciousness a soft and syrupy thing that will come later. For now, I have the warm embers of pleasure running through my veins, a great job, and Lucky, who has reignited wonder within me, freely offered anything and everything I could ever need, and proven what I knew to be true—that there are people with endless kindness in their hearts, who brighten the world and illuminate its beauty.

Getting to sun myself in Lucky's glow is a joy I am grateful for every day.

I'M GOING TO NEED AN ICE BATH AFTER THAT!

But what about Sterling? (**turn to page 254**)

44

The coast is clear.

Lucky is busy talking with Bryan by the front door, and the other viewers are distracted. I enter the bathroom and lock the door, turning on the overhead fan. It should drown out the noise I'm about to make.

As soon as I open the cabinet under the sink, my hopes lift. The P-trap is backtracking into a ninety-degree elbow, but the joint is loose—a temporary installation that they likely planned to glue later, but never came back for. Shoddy work, honestly.

Perfect.

Are you sure you want to damage someone else's property?

yes (**turn to page 301)**

I'll be good (**turn to page 387**)

45

"No, I don't think that's a good idea."

"If you're sure."

Am I?

The silence grows limbs, knocking us both off course.

"Maybe I should go," Lucky says, and I have the sinking feeling I won't see him again if he walks out the door. "I think we could really help each other, but I respect your decision."

Everything is moving too fast. When I woke up this morning, I had a job, an apartment, a life.

When he reaches the door, I find my legs, rushing over and catching his arm. "Wait, um, I just wanted to say thank you, for this afternoon. It meant a lot."

He leans in and kisses my cheek. "My pleasure."

I'm stunned when he reaches into my pocket and pulls out my phone, adding his number to my Contacts after I've unlocked it. "If you change your mind about the room."

I stare at the door long after he leaves. It's not too late.

I can still change my mind.

Make Your Choice:

move in (**turn to page 192**)
it's time to go home (**turn to page 135**)

46

Decided to skip past the sex? Don't worry; I'll catch you up.

So, what did you miss? Well, Mia confesses that she has a crush on Sterling, and although their recent reunion didn't go especially well, Lucky is into it.

A lot into it.

In fact, he admits that he, too, has lingering feelings for Sterling, and he's very interested to see just how interested Mia is. Clothes come off, hands explore ... all while they talk about what they'd want him to do to them if he was there.

It'll certainly be interesting the next time they see him—that's for sure. But then, hey, maybe Sterling would like the idea. You'll have to keep reading to find out.

ALL CAUGHT UP?

let's get back to the story! (**turn to page 254**)

47

"You don't want to come home with me."

They can't possibly. How would we explain it?

Lucky pulls me closer, determined. "And miss out on seeing where you came from? You're joking."

"It's up to you, Mia, but this isn't pity. We care about you." Sterling is serious—he's always so serious—but I can't find the crack in his argument, can't see anything but honesty and blue, blue, blue, and my heart spins on its heels.

Great, now I'm crying again.

Lucky pulls out his phone. "Right, tickets. First class, yeah?"

There's no place like ...

home sweet home (**turn to page 290**)

48

"WHAT IS IT?"

He waits, ever patient.

"I ..."

The fire's already been lit, and the flames coat his cheeks in a fine glow, caressing the curves of his mouth in a way I've always longed to. Leaving without him is already a wound I've been tending to. Must I push the knife deeper? What would telling him achieve?

"Mia?"

I turn away. "If we don't leave now, we'll be late."

"Mia, stop."

I wait, one hand on the door, but he says nothing else. Slowly, he comes close, until I can smell the soap he used to wash with.

"Forget I said anything," I say and leave.

YOU WERE SO CLOSE!

go to dinner (**turn to page 315**)

49

We both laugh quietly.

"I don't know what I expected to happen."

"Magic," he says, his voice kind.

I should put the crystal back, but something tells me to hold on to it. A good-luck charm or maybe a reminder to temper my expectations—who knows?

"Silly, right?"

He covers my hand with his. "Hope is never silly."

Moira bags up my purchase with a twinkle in her eye. Oh gosh, she probably saw us kissing back there.

My blush holds firm as we make it back into the frigid afternoon air.

Lucky grabs my hand. "I've got an idea."

"Um," I say, looking up at *The Observer*, "what are we doing here?"

"We're going to get your job back."

I stop in my tracks, and the man walking behind me grunts his frustration but passes by when Lucky glares at him.

"Monica will never go for it."

"So, there's nothing to lose." He pulls me into the elevator.

If there's one constant in the world, it's that musicians are always trouble. Always. In the best and worst ways.

Or perhaps it's because I've never been able to resist a man with a guitar.

Trust me, I know it's an issue. I'm working on it.

At least, I'm trying to.

Which is how I know Lucky is *bad*, bad news.

Because every fiber of my being is currently screaming, *Touch him*. I know how good it'll be too—those strong hands gripping my hips, palms big enough to really get a handful of my tits, biceps that look like they could haul me anywhere I want to go.

See?

Trouble.

Sterling is at his desk when we arrive. I'm praying he doesn't see us, except, no, Lucky's walking us straight toward him. My heart slips and bangs against my ribs, struggling for purchase.

"Lachlan?" Then he sees me. "What—"

Lucky grabs Sterling's arm and keeps walking, now with the two of us in hand. "Conference room's back here, yeah?"

"Yes, but—"

Lucky isn't listening. He's on a mission, and apparently, it's to steer Sterling and me into the conference room, ignoring the obvious stares along the way. He closes the door behind us, and I drop into the nearest chair. It doesn't help much. I still feel like the rug has been pulled out from under me.

Sterling doesn't look much better.

"Are you done? If you wanted to talk—and I know we need to—there—"

He's stopped by Lucky's brow rising. I've never seen Sterling stop for anything. Anyone.

"Nope, this isn't about us; it's about Mia."

I'm not sure what to focus on first. The us? Somehow, I've

managed to wedge myself in the valley between their past and present, and I shouldn't find that as enticing as I do.

Even if the glimmer in his gaze makes it clear Lucky would be on board for that. Emphatically, hungrily, eagerly on board.

There goes my heart again.

Flushing, I blink up at Sterling. That should be safer; he's never looked at me with anything other than ...

Oh.

Lucky was right. I shouldn't have touched that crystal.

"I don't understand what's happening."

"What's happening is, we're going to make things right. You wouldn't have been late this morning if it wasn't for me, and—"

"That's not true." I would've been late regardless.

"If anyone has the pull to change that, he does."

"I want to help—you have no idea how much—but it's complicated."

"Always is with you."

I freeze. Sterling is staring at me. The seconds pass, a slow trickle, until he looks away, blowing out an explosive breath.

"There's more going on here than you realize, Lucky. I'm already too involved, and—"

"Fuckin' hell, Mac." Lucky squares off against him, tall enough to be eye to eye. "Again? I mean, not that I'm surprised. She's—tell me you at least handled it better this time."

Sterling looks away, causing Lucky to curse again.

I'm lost, and it's completely different from losing myself in my work or chasing what I want off the beaten path. That's the good kind of lost, where I still know where I'm going and how I got there.

No, this is the type of lost that is too close to cluelessness, to standing beside a group of people who all turn their backs on you.

I've never handled that well.

"Make it right, would you?"

Sterling nods. "I'll talk to Monica."

I give in to the urgent buzz under my skin and get up to pace. "No."

Their attention follows me. Whatever. I can't ... let them see the anxiety. I need to breathe. I really wish this room had windows.

"She's made it perfectly clear she doesn't respect me, and I won't work like that. I don't need your pity, and if the only reason I have a job is because the great Sterling Ross commanded it, I'll spend the rest of my career wondering if every opportunity is simply someone trying to get into your good graces."

They share a look, and I know how it sounds. The naive little girl, trying to be a grown adult in a big, bad world. I've heard it all before.

I fall back into a chair. "Look, it's nice that you want to do the honorable thing here, but—"

Lucky lets out a laugh that quickly morphs into a cough when Sterling elbows him. It's the most ... *human* I've ever seen Sterling, like I'm looking at a different version of him.

This can't be the real him. He's too expressive, too responsive.

He's *kneeling at my feet.*

"Uh ..."

"Mia." That's it. One word. Laid between us as if it answers anything. Said like it answers everything.

"What is going on?" I ask.

His glasses do nothing to limit the impact of all that blue—nothing—and it's not fair. How dare he look at me this way, after all this time! It's all I've wanted.

"You're usually more observant than this," he says.

And he's right; I'm never blindsided like this because I'm a damn good reporter, but how does he even know that? He doesn't know me.

When was he going to tell me how well he knew me?

"I thought you hated me. Now you're looking at me with stars in your eyes. It doesn't make any sense. Why have you been pushing me away?"

"I'm trying to protect you."

Protect me ... right. By staying as far away as possible. By making me think he hated me. It worked.

The chair drags against the carpet as I stand. "No, you're trying to control the situation by hiding. You've made a career out of exposing everyone else's secrets, but you can't handle your own. Is that it?"

He pushes up to stand. It puts him above me again. A tall tower, far from anyone's reach.

"All right, you'd like honesty?" he says. "I think you're scared."

Of course I am. I'm terrified. Is that all he's got?

He ducks down, trying to catch my eyes. "Two years of writing articles you hate. Why?"

"Monica would have—"

"There are other papers. You could have gone anywhere you wanted—"

Anywhere? There *is* nowhere else.

"No, I couldn't."

Lucky has retreated, keeping a watchful eye. Close enough to step in if this gets out of hand.

Sterling's gotten closer, keeps getting closer, and I'm not prepared for it. I've gotten used to him keeping his distance, damn it. I figured out how to handle it, how to crush my silly feelings into a tiny pebble and get used to the blisters.

"Why?"

I step back. He follows.

"Because." It's a weak argument, and we both know it.

"You're scared."

"Because ..."

He's close enough now that I have to tilt my head up to look at him. This is unfair. He's right—of course he's right—but he doesn't understand.

"Because you're not there."

It's the answer he's been waiting for, apparently, and hooray for him, knowing so much and being head of the class. Have a gold star.

He touches me, sliding his fingers along my jaw. It's instinct to press my cheek to his palm, the heat of his skin sparking lightning in my veins.

"Stop looking at me like that."

"No," he says. "I don't think I will."

He's smiling—holy hell, he should never stop. I never want him to stop. Is this why Lucky brought me—oh God, Lucky.

My stomach drops to my shoes. How could I forget? An hour ago, it was Lucky I was kissing, and now he's ...

Watching. Waiting.

"Fuck, Mac, just kiss her already, or I'll do it for you."

In the breath before Sterling kisses me, my heart migrates three inches to the right.

Everything stops, stills, restarts.

I don't know how to prepare for this; it's never been a possibility, never in the realm of anything close to reality, and yet my eyes fall closed, and he's there, skimming his thumb along my jaw, keeping his touch tender, but there's no denying the strength beneath it.

Sterling Ross. The man who can't be moved ... wants me.

My lips part on my next breath, and there's no warning before his mouth meets mine. It's electric. Tingles flare to life across every inch of my skin, waking up parts of me I forgot existed and some that have never been touched before.

Everything narrows down to him. The press of his glasses

against my cheek, the soft gust of each breath he takes, the all-too-tender way he's handling me.

"Let me talk to Monica," he says, his lips skimming mine. "I pressed her to hire you because I could see your potential, and she took my interest out on you. It's why I've kept my distance. Let me right the wrong I should have two years ago. You deserve this chance, Mia. You're going to be better than I am. Let me help you."

"Okay, yeah, yes." I want that. I want him.

When Sterling pulls back, I can't help that I search out the last unknown—Lucky, who's leaning against the wall, legs crossed, radiating an air of casual contentment. He's smiling, soft and small, but it doesn't reach his eyes, which is weighed down at the corners with something he's intentionally holding back.

It's unlike him.

One last kiss, and Sterling leaves us alone, acting on his promise to make things right. Monica isn't going to like it, and she might actually make life harder for me after this, but all of that can be dealt with later.

I step up to Lucky, place my hand on his arm. "Thank you." There's so much more I want to say, but this is the most important.

"Anything for you, love."

There's the smile I'm used to. Deep. Honest. Beautiful.

"I owe you one. Now you have to tell me what you want, so I can repay the favor."

I wait for his answer, but I don't need it. I know what he wants. It's obvious. It's been clear since I met him, since he grabbed Sterling's hand and led us both into this room. All he has to do is admit it.

He reaches up, brushes my hair out of my face. "Some other time," he says. "You're about to have your hands full, and I feel a song coming on."

Disappointment sinks heavy in my gut. “Oh, okay. Of course.” Still, I hate leaving things like this, so I lift up and kiss his cheek, breathe in his heady scent. “Promise me it’ll be a love song.”

More of that innate joy shakes loose in him. “It’s never going to be anything else, is it?”

Yes, I think before he leaves. *It’ll always be love.*

Oh, Lucky …

please tell me there’s an epilogue (**turn to page 417**)

50

"Sure you're ready for this?" Lucky asks, getting frustrated with his bow tie.

He's on his third attempt to tie it. I'm no help, and honestly, he'd look better without it—or any clothes, but it's not that kind of party.

"I hate these blasted things." He groans and rips it off, stuffing it into his pocket.

"More than ready," I say, meaning it.

Tonight is a big night, a celebration of the city and my biggest opportunity yet to make the connections I'll need to support my career.

I earned this invite.

I don't even care that Monica will be there.

She's always gloated about being the only attendee from *The Observer*, and I am especially looking forward to wiping the smile off her face by walking in with my head held high.

Lucky sneaks up behind me, sliding his hands down my full hips. His tattoos peek out from his tuxedo and make him look more dangerous, not less.

"You look incredible, love."

"I was just thinking the same thing about you."

Adrenaline builds in my belly as we step into the ballroom. The mayor is here, along with half of the city's elite. If ever I wanted a pull quote, now's the time. It might be fun to hound a slippery CEO while they sip champagne and have to play calm.

Maybe next year ...

Lucky slips his hand from my back to my waist, protective. "Christ, look at them all."

The room is a blur of starched collars and polite smiles. "Almost makes me want to ruffle some feathers."

"Attagirl."

The evening is, in short, a black-tie networking event. Sure, there'll be a speech and some toasts to a better tomorrow, but it's largely a self-congratulatory pat on the back. Safe. Gentle.

"The point is not to do anything, but to be seen," my new boss, Zia, told me as she handed me the embossed invitation.

Slowly, we begin to circle the room.

"Seen the demon yet?" Lucky asks.

"Not yet. She must have ..." Any thought I have dies because six feet away is Sterling Ross.

He never comes to these things. He hates parties and pretending, and he absolutely abhors schmoozing.

He barely likes people.

Why is he here?

"I'm going to get us a drink, love. There's a bar over ... holy fuck."

Oh good, I'm not hallucinating. Lucky sees him too.

"He looks incredible," I say, my mouth dry. "Black's always been his color."

Lucky fits himself to my back, his arms coming possessively around me as we both stare. "He'd look better without it. What do you say? First one to get in his pants wins."

Brazenly, Lucky traces his thumb along the underside of my breast, sending my pulse skyrocketing.

I know he's teasing, know he's not really suggesting we try to do something as ridiculous as flirt with Sterling, but, fuck, just thinking about it ...

My God.

Then the impossible happens.

Sterling locks eyes with me, and my heart crashes to a standstill. He's not wearing his glasses tonight. I didn't know it was possible for his gaze to get more intense, but it is.

"Do you think he knows how much you want him?" Lucky asks, his voice rough.

"He wants you too," I add, like a defense. I'm not used to anyone knowing about my crush. It's hard to remember Lucky is okay with it.

More than okay, from the way Lucky presses his hips closer, his arousal obvious. Fuck.

Sterling looks between us in long, silent breaths. I don't know what I'm expecting. Surprise? Disappointment? Anger?

But it never comes.

Of course he already knows about our relationship. Sterling is always three steps ahead.

Holding our gaze, he lifts his glass and nods. A toast to ...

"Still think he's not interested?"

My nipples tingle from Lucky's heat and Sterling's attention. I'm not sure I remember my name right now, let alone anything else.

I step out of Lucky's arms, tearing my gaze from Sterling, in search of a drink.

To my relief, I find Zia, smiling and waving me over. Good. I need a distraction.

"I'm going to go say hi," I tell Lucky.

"That's a great idea. I think I'll do the same."

And I don't need to ask who he's going to talk to because he hasn't taken his eyes off of Sterling since we spotted him.

I catch Lucky's hand. "Find me later?"

He raises it to his lips, his eyes blazing with mischief. "Always."

I'm not ready to talk to Sterling yet. If at all. I'm not convinced he cares, no matter what Lucky says.

Zia looks fantastic in a patterned gown, embroidered with gold, her black pixie styled in finger waves, her lips a rich purple. She looks like a movie star.

"Take this," she says, passing me a thick tumbler, garnished with orange and mint, that matches the one she's already holding and clinking our glasses together. "Cheers. I hope you enjoy yourself tonight. It's going to be an interesting week ahead."

I know. First thing tomorrow, my article—exposing a popular sleepwear company of lying about the fire resistance of the fabric used in their kids' line—hits the front page.

The fallout will be messy.

"What if they sue?"

She smiles. "That's what I pay the lawyers for. Besides, the evidence you collected stands up. I wouldn't have green-lit the article if I didn't think we could protect you."

Have I mentioned how amazing Zia is? Easily the best boss I've ever had—the complete opposite of Monica in every way. Warm, interesting, and incredibly smart.

I'm going to be a better reporter for working with her.

"Relax," she adds. "Getting on people's shit list is a good thing. It'll stop them from underestimating you."

She's right, and I feel my earlier confidence returning, solidifying like concrete under my feet as I turn back around, instantly finding Lucky and Sterling across the crowd.

It's not difficult. They're taller than everyone else.

Hotter too.

"Have you seen Monica?"

Zia looks surprised. "You didn't hear?"

I whip my head back to her. "Hear what?"

She leans in conspiratorially. "Sterling Ross had her fired. He threatened to quit if she wasn't let go, and there's rumblings that he wants to sue her for workplace harassment on behalf of another reporter, but no one will tell me who." Zia shrugs.

The industry is small. If it is true, it won't be long until she finds what she's after.

She doesn't seem to notice that I'm shocked silent. This isn't a coincidence. I know that. When something walks like a duck, talks like a duck ... well ...

Quack, quack.

What I don't understand is *why*.

Zia continues, "The next thing I know, I'm getting a call, telling me her noncompete excludes us from offering her a position, and we weren't the only ones."

Holy shit.

She touches my arm. "Oh, got to go. I see the mayor trying to slip into the restroom, and I'm not leaving tonight until I get us that interview."

"Good luck."

I last five seconds before turning back to the source of my attention.

I can't take my eyes off them.

Sterling stands out, his dark curls brushed back, his cheekbones sharp under the glow of the chandeliers, casting shadows over his strong jaw. The three-piece he's wearing might as well be painted on. It highlights the broad stretch of his shoulders and his trim waist, and my mouth goes dry every time I look for too long.

Beside him, Lucky is no less delicious, the top few buttons of his shirt open at the collar, and while his jacket can't do his arms and ass justice, I know Sterling is aware of them. Even from across the room, I can tell when Sterling's gaze drops and looks away from Lucky's body. I don't blame him; it deserves its own wing in a museum.

Watching them like this, I can picture them together. Lucky is doing most of the talking, his trademark smirk in place, while Sterling sips on champagne.

All of a sudden, his gaze shifts, meeting mine in an instant, holding as Lucky leans in to say something in his ear. Sterling licks his lips, and I flush from head to toe.

I have to know.

I stride over, my pulse racing, letting the tart taste of the cocktail fuel me.

"Ask, and she will appear," Lucky says, pulling me in for a kiss that makes my knees weak.

"Let her breathe, Lachlan."

Lucky complies, looking a little smug. "Couldn't help myself."

Sterling unbuttons his jacket with one hand. It's effortlessly charming. "I think you could, if you were properly motivated."

I have no idea what is happening right now, but if it gets any hotter in here, I'll catch on fire.

Maybe I should go, and I would, except Sterling turns those endless blue eyes on me, dark enough to be the night sky itself, and my legs won't move.

"I wasn't expecting to see you here tonight. You usually hate these things."

"Still do," he replies, proving nothing has changed. "I came because I knew you'd be here."

"I ..." When the rest of my words dry up, I swallow the ash with my drink. *Come on, confidence.* "Here I thought, you were only here because you were working."

His eyes cut across the floor, tracking someone or something intensely.

"Wait, are you working right now?"

Sterling says nothing, but as he slides one hand into his pocket, I catch it—the slightest flicker of a smile.

He is. He's working. I knew it.

"Claire Westlin has been particularly difficult to get an interview with. In my experience, that's an indication of fear."

I find the airline COO a few feet away, alone with an empty glass. She's tall and statuesque, with an air of detachment, but Sterling's wrong.

"She doesn't want to talk to you because you're intimidating, not because she's hiding something. Lucky, go talk to her; show him he's being ridiculous."

Lucky smiles at Sterling while kissing my cheek. "Happy to."

We both watch him walk over.

"Does he always do what you tell him?" Sterling asks, his voice low.

"Yes, he's good like that."

"I remember."

A shiver rolls down my spine.

"What about you, Mia? Are you good? Would you do what I told you?"

It's getting difficult to breathe. My pulse is fluttering in my throat.

Yes, my heart whispers.

My body agrees.

Across the room, I hear Lucky laugh, but I don't look. I can't. I'm afraid if I do, Sterling and this moment will disappear.

"Sterling! There you are. Hiding, as always." Out of the crowd appears a beautiful woman. Her thick blonde hair is cut into a very flattering bob, and the silky silver dress she's wearing is making me question my sexuality.

I smile. This industry is too small to not start off on the right foot. "Hi. We haven't met. You must be ..."

She finally notices that there's someone standing beside Sterling and holds her hand out. "Alexis."

Over the next fifteen minutes, I learn a lot of things. Alexis York is the new me at *The Observer*. She's sick of servers recommending tiramisu at every Italian restaurant—which … what? She's single, she's clearly interested in Sterling, she doesn't ask either of us a thing—I'm pretty sure I'm invisible to her—and she will not stop talking about herself.

One glance tells me Sterling is in hell.

"Oh my God," I say, touching Alexis's elbow mid-sentence and turning her away from Sterling. "I can't believe he did that."

"I know! Unbelievable, right?"

Her attention successfully diverted, Sterling makes his escape, taking off in the direction of the balcony.

"I know! And then I said—"

"Would you excuse me?" I cut in. "I just remembered I left my cat by himself, and I need to go check on him."

It's not a *complete* lie. Sterling's about as friendly as a leopard. Silent. Solitary. Mysterious.

Thick curtains block the bulk of the chill from outside, and I slip through, eager to escape the cloying fog of aftershave for a breath of fresh air. The balcony is empty, save for one man. His broad back to me, one hand shoved in a pocket, Sterling looks out over the city like a dark protector.

"Don't worry," I say, coming to stand beside him. We don't touch, but we're close enough that we could. "She'll learn how antisocial you are."

He huffs a laugh. "I'm not so sure."

"I did."

"Alexis is not you."

I don't think I've ever heard him so gruff before. I'll take that as a compliment?

The city glitters before us, reflecting off glass and steel like fireflies in spring. From here, the party is muffled, leaving us encased in quiet. Sterling's natural state.

"In a weird way, this reminds me of home," I say softly.

He shifts, and I feel his gaze on me like a caress. "You've come a long way since the front page of the *Ferntree Gazette*."

God, how does he even know that?

"You should be proud of yourself."

What's that supposed to mean?

"I am." It comes out defiant, but I'm not about to apologize for it. Not to him or anyone.

When I finally look at him, I see the hint of a smile.

Jeez, he's confusing.

"Do you ever regret the choices you've made?" I ask him, turning back to the view.

Four million lives occur simultaneously around us, unique from each other. How many are happy right now?

"Some," he says. "It's hard for me to trust people. To let them see me."

It's more honest than I expected from him.

"You're different tonight."

The hint of a smile cements into something real. "Lachlan has reliably informed me that the surgery was a success."

"Surgery?"

"To remove my head from my ass."

Oh.

"Congratulations." I raise my drink, a mirror of how he greeted me earlier.

"I'm sorry for what happened with Monica."

In a night full of surprises, it catches me off guard. "You have nothing to apologize for."

"Don't I? I wasn't exactly welcoming to you."

That's putting it mildly. "I was new and very enamored with

the star reporter," I admit. "I can see why you'd want to distance yourself."

"That wasn't why, Mia."

A flush rushes to my cheeks. God, his voice is so low, like the rumble of thunder during a storm.

He steps closer, his jacket brushing my arm. Goose bumps spread like wildfire. I finish my drink. The air is thick, humid. It clings to my skin.

He's still looking at me. Why won't he stop looking at me?

"The office misses you."

I laugh. Sterling Ross has a funny sense of humor.

"No one misses me."

"I do."

I finally turn to him. "Sterling, you never talked to me. I wasn't sure you ever knew I existed."

"For as long as I've known you, I've been aware of little else."

Whatever I was about to say, it's stolen by his admission.

I shake my head. "I don't understand you."

"Yes, you do. It's not complicated. Why do you think I'd say these things?"

I know why. Of course I do. I've known since Lucky teased me about him. Since Zia mentioned Monica being fired.

I just don't know how to accept it. It sounds ... like I'm dreaming. Like I'm going to wake up right before the good part and have my heart crushed.

"You're interested."

Pleasure is written all over his face. He's proud I figured it out.

"All this time?"

"Avoiding you isn't something I'm proud of, but at the time, it seemed like the best defense."

"God, you're an asshole."

"I've been told."

I'm sure he has, by Lucky if no one else.

"But you hate me."

"I would sooner hate my own heart for beating."

I brace my hand on the balustrade while my understanding of him shifts and changes like sand in a storm, rearranging itself to fit the man in front of me, the one gazing down with open interest.

"What does that even mean?"

Sterling cups my cheek. "Let me show you."

Lucky appears, sliding in behind me, and I look up, expecting Sterling's mask to return, but it's not there. No, there's only heat in his eyes. For me. For Lucky. It's lightning in my veins.

I know Lucky feels it, too, because his voice has the same gritty edge it gets when we fuck. "You know there's a party going on," he says. "But I can see it's much more interesting out here."

"It is," Sterling agrees. "But I think it's time we took Mia home."

"Great idea." Lucky slips his arm around my waist, pulling me tight against him. His breath is hot against my skin. "How about it, love? Is that what you want?"

"You know what I want."

He hums. "Yes, but I think Mac here should hear it."

Sterling's eyes are blown black. "Tell me, Mia." His shoe knocks against my heel as he presses himself closer. "Be good for me."

I crush my eyes closed. It's all too much, and I don't want to wake up yet.

Someone's thumb—must be Sterling's—slides along my jaw, tilting my head up. I let the words escape, ready to see where tonight will lead. Ready to follow anywhere they want to go.

It should split my heart in two, wanting them both, each calling to a separate side of me, but it's the opposite. A fusion of every part of me, light and dark and everything in between. Like opening a door and discovering a room I never knew existed. Like magic.

"Take me home," I say.

THEY'RE PERFECT TOGETHER.

yes! now show me the epilogue (**turn to page 446**)

51

STERLING'S HAND curls around mine. "There's no time. If you really want to know about him, we must hide."

I go to reenter my room, but Sterling stops me.

"They'll look there first. Come."

We run down the hall and take the closest room, which is usually an unattended guest room, but it's, unfortunately, not unattended. It's empty, but there are trunks and fine clothes about, making it clear whose room it is.

"It must be Prince Lachlan's room."

"I ..." Sterling stands frozen in place. "We shouldn't be here."

It's my turn to stop him. "You promised. Now tell me what is going on."

"The prince and I know each other."

"Yes, that much is obvious. I mentioned your name earlier, and he—"

"What?" It's the most eager I've seen him.

"He pretended he didn't know you, but I could tell he was lying."

Everything that was open in his expression shutters closed. There's no sadness in the fall of his shoulders, only resignation.

"I knew him in Chance. We were ... close. I had a choice, and I chose duty over him."

So, that's why ...

Oh, Sterling. Oh, Lucky.

"That is why I cannot accompany you. It's simply too painful."

Everything makes sense now. "I'm sorry."

Sterling shakes his head. "Thank you, but it is I who should apologize."

"Perhaps there is another way. You could tell him how you feel, and we could speak with Louis—"

"No, it's too late for that. Even if the wedding were called off, he wouldn't want anything to do with me."

A familiar voice stops my heart. "Are you talking about me, or is there another man whose heart you broke beyond repair?"

I didn't even hear the door open, but it must have because there Lucky is, openly staring at Sterling with pain clear on his face.

"I was a coward," Sterling says, not yet facing him. "You deserved better."

I dare not interrupt, but there is noise in the hallway, and my gut is telling me that if we are found, any hope these two have of talking will evaporate. Fortunately, Lucky blinks out of his stunned stupor, quietly closing the door.

"Yes, you were, and I did. So did you." He looks uneasy in the space, his gaze darting around at his trunk, the bed, the floor. Me. Landing on Sterling in between each item, as though he must check he's still here. "You knew I was here, in Ferntree."

Sterling nods.

A breath rushes out of Lucky. "Right."

He walks over to the fireplace, leaning a hand on the mantel, looking like a man ready to crumple under the slightest weight. It's awful and so far from the man I met earlier that I hate to see it.

"I wanted to talk to you. I wrote you a hundred times, but no words ever seemed like enough. Sorry never seemed enough."

"Better to make me think you were ignoring me or dead. Did it mean anything to you?" Bitterness laces Lucky's tone.

"It meant everything to me."

There has to be a way to fix this. To save them from themselves.

Because if anything is obvious to me now, it's that they are too stubborn for their own good. I could call off the wedding. Louis would be disappointed, but he'd get over it. It would be the right thing to do, to get out of the way.

Except look at them. Steps apart, clearly drawn to each other, but they can't even look at each other. If I call this wedding off, all that will happen is that Lucky will sail back home, and the two of them will continue this miserable dance until one or both of them are dead.

I refuse to let them.

I walk to the door, my steps trampling over my own feelings in the process, but they're not important right now. I'll have plenty of time to rest my wounded heart in Chance—*after* I've righted this wrong.

"I'm going to find my brother, let him know I'm not well. The wedding will continue tomorrow, but there will be three of us traveling back to Chance, not two."

My gut is telling me Lucky is a good man, one who deserves the choice Sterling took from him. "Unless you have any objections?"

The tight line of his shoulders softens as he steps close, raising my hand to his lips for a gentle kiss. *Thank you,* it says as loudly as if he'd spoken the words.

His palms are rough from sailing, but warm. Tender goose bumps rise along my arms as he trails his thumb across my skin.

"Not a single one," he says. "I gave you my word to be a good husband, and I'll give it again, now and tomorrow. I only wish for your happiness, and I will do everything I can to ensure your life is as comfortable as possible."

I nod. There's only one way I can see that occurring, and I'm going to do everything in *my* power to make it happen.

The wedding is a simple affair. We hold it in the courtyard, now clear of dust and debris, a local officiant presiding and my family in attendance. We swap vows of commitment, sign the paperwork, and it's done.

No feast, no kiss, no issues. It's all very polite, as long as you ignore the hulking mass of dismay in the corner.

Sterling has said very little since last night. He and Lucky appear to have reached a mutual agreement to accept each other's presence, but do no more than that. I barely restrain myself from rolling my eyes during the ceremony.

We travel three days by road and seven by sea. It takes two sunrises to gain my sea legs—a fact that amuses the rest of the ship's small crew. By the third morning, I'm glad I no longer need to greet the water with the contents of the previous night's dinner, and I can finally start pulling my weight, shadowing whichever crew will let me and following their lead.

The horizon stretches unfathomably far.

The ocean greets us like an old friend and holds us calmly as we sail, which I'm reminded—many, many times—is a good sign. Salt stings my eyes and nose, but it's worth it to witness Lucky in his element. He leads well, and the crew trusts him.

But it's the view that steals my breath. All that's before us is sea, on and on. More water than I could have imagined. It must be endless. I've never seen anything like it, even in my dreams.

"Terrifyingly beautiful, isn't it?" Lucky asks on one of the occasions he catches me staring.

It is.

At night, the stars track our progress and serve as a reminder of forces beyond our reach.

I've long known my purpose would be to leave Ferntree, to stand as consult to the assembly with the knowledge and honor of our province. I believed myself prepared to leave behind the flat farmland and familiar faces of my home, but as our destination approaches, awareness rushes in. Nothing will be familiar anymore. I must conduct myself in respect of that which I do not know and learn all I can.

The task alone does not daunt me, although I must admit to a growing loneliness that's taken root beside my heart. The crew is friendly, if brash, and Lucky is exceedingly welcoming, answering every question I have and even teaching me to steer and navigate. I took him to be improper, uncaring of courtesy, but I see now he's a man of rules when it suits him. Gone is the stifling propriety that he adopted in front of my family, shed as soon as his boots touched the worn tread of the deck.

Where he once came across cavalier, he's now relaxed and generous.

"You've taken to this well," he says, smiling.

The sun is finally relenting after a day of bearing its full weight upon us. Not a person among the crew, including myself, is without a thick sheen of sweat. I long for a bath. Lucky wears exertion well, his shirt plastered to his firm chest and slender waist.

"Dare I say, you have begun to enjoy it?"

"It has its merits," I admit and delight when he laughs.

"Indeed, it does."

Tomorrow, we'll reach the cove, and as such, morale is high among the crew. Someone hands Lucky an instrument I've never seen, and he leads the rest in a bawdry shanty that makes the tips of Sterling's ears pink. I can't wait to tell Louis about it in a letter.

Sterling is starboard, brooding. Since we left Ferntree, he has draped himself in a blanket of solitude, even though he never lets me out of his sight. Admittedly, I don't want him out of mine either. He is already watching me when our eyes meet. I offer him a smile he doesn't return, but he does not turn away, exuding the same intensity he always has. There's something there I can't decipher, hidden in the darkness, writ large in his expression.

I miss him dearly.

Oh, how I long to know what he is thinking.

Lucky tears himself from the group and finds me at the bow. He leans his weight on the railing beside me. Once, my future appeared as vast and endless as the horizon. Now, the shape of it has coalesced into that of two men, both of whom are as bound to each other as they are to me.

I only wish the prospect brought all of us more joy.

"I see he is the same as I remember. Not one for revelry."

"Challenge him to a duel. That usually puts him in a good mood."

Lucky chuckles, the sound lost to the breeze. "Let me guess. He let you win as well."

"Yes! Did he also compare your footwork to a newborn foal?"

"I believe mine was akin to a freshly hatched duckling."

I return his grin with my own. It's nice to talk to someone who knows Sterling, who understands what it's like to be in his orbit, under his thrall. "I'd like to see that sometime."

"If you think you can take me," he says, and the delicious curl of his mouth sends my pulse into the heavens. "But I promise you, I do not yield lightly."

The moon paints his lips with a gentle brush, coating them in silver. I can't seem to look away.

"We shall see," I reply.

"We will."

Perhaps another man would let the shadows cover my darkened cheeks, but Lucky isn't like anyone I've ever met. My eyes fall closed as he reaches up to touch me, skimming his thumb over the heated skin.

"Does it scare you to leave home?"

It should perhaps, but not anymore. It's easier with Sterling here.

"I've never been out of Ferntree before, but I dreamed of it. I've always known I was meant for somewhere else, but I've never been able to picture where. It will be good to finally fulfill the role I've been given."

"There's more to life than serving a role. There's art and music, good food and great friends."

"Love?" I risk.

"The richest of spoils. Is it not something you seek?"

Difficult to seek that which you've already found.

"At present, I'm pursuing more attainable things."

In my peripheral vision, I see his head turn, but I keep my eyes on the quickly evaporating horizon, the full force of his attention too much for me to face.

"I hope you won't mind my company in the meantime."

"I'm glad for it," I admit, realizing how true the words are as they leave me.

Days ago, I knew nothing but rumor of this man, and I wrongly expected him to be a mystery to me. Yet there's no veil between him and the world. What he feels is open for all to see.

It's surprising, and already, I find myself hungry for more.

"Have you always felt an affinity for sailing?" I ask.

"Yes. My father wanted me to learn the value of contribution. No one person above any other. Everyone works in unison toward shared goals. I've learned from blacksmiths and cooks, painters and helmsmen."

"I imagine you've seen wondrous things."

"Nothing so beautiful as home," he says, facing the shadow of the city, which looms large in the distance. If not for the many lights painting the dark, I'd have no idea it was there. "But the biggest lesson I've learned is that home is not a place, but people. I have many companions in Chance, but I have been lacking in anyone to call my own."

Briefly, he shifts his gaze over my shoulder, where Sterling's voice carries on the breeze.

Lucky returns his eyes to mine, bringing my hand to his lips. "Which is why I'm so grateful you're here."

We dock by midmorn.

Chance is as beautiful as Lucky promised, white rock rising triumphant from the blazing blue sea. The city climbs the land surrounding the cove. It's vibrant, an explosion of color and culture and life.

He calls out greetings to the workers who meet us, and they laugh and call back. The sun bathes Lucky in its glow, doing its best to make him even handsomer. It barely needs to try.

At its peak stands the castle. On the way here, Lucky explained that though he retains his royal title, it's an honorary one, as the city governs itself. The castle itself has been turned into communal housing, but he was gifted the highest floor of the east wing for himself, including three bedrooms, two sitting rooms, and a study.

"Although the study is off-limits for now," he says as he waves us past the closed door. "A little light remodeling I'm doing, but it will be ready soon."

We end the tour at my bedroom, a bright, airy room that faces his own. A vase of yellow blossoms sits by my bedside, and I don't know how he did it, but it had to have been Lucky.

Sterling's room is one door down—awfully convenient for my plans.

Sterling says nothing as he leaves. It's clear his intent is to hurt Lucky, and Sterling might not see the attack land, but I do.

I lay my hand on Lucky's arm. "I wanted to thank you. I know the situation isn't ... ideal, but I want us to be friends." All of us. "You know, I've never been married before, but so far, I like it. You make it something to look forward to."

We are both still caked in layers of salt and dirt and days at sea, but none of it dulls the fire in his touch as he takes my hand in his and presses a tender kiss to my knuckles. "It is I who needs to thank you. I'd accepted that love was a thing of my past, and I left it there, content to give my all to my work. But then I met you, and I see that love is not so far out of reach. It is surprising and unpredictable, and I mean to cherish it."

I know now how Sterling fell for him. It's easy. Lucky makes it easy.

My motivations for being here have not changed, but there are new motivations now, layered overtop or perhaps weaved underneath. A history I have stumbled upon and now play part in crushing beneath my feet.

It is too late to salvage my own heartbreak, but that does not mean there is no hope to restore the love Lucky and Sterling once had and will have again.

The next morning, Lucky greets me with flowers. "These are only one of the blooms local to this area. They are a family emblem."

"Sweet Williams," I answer, recognizing them from my

research. "They're beautiful. Thank you. I have nothing to gift you in return."

"Your company is gift enough."

There's a disgruntled sound from the door, revealed to be Sterling when Lucky turns. He stares at the flowers in Lucky's hands, averting his eyes when I take them from him and set them by the window.

"I was hoping you'd like to walk with me."

"Very much so."

No one asks Sterling if he'd like to come, but we don't need to; he follows anyway, keeping close enough that he must overhear every word we share, although he never offers anything of his own.

I'm set to finally confront his childishness when a much older man calls out to him from a large drawing room.

"Emile Jackson," Lucky whispers in my ear.

Ah. Emile is dressed impeccably, his beard a shock of white against his navy tunic.

"Sterling! I thought that was you. Come, come. I need to borrow your brain."

Nothing happens for a moment. I know Sterling heard him, but he isn't moving. Well, unless you count the glare he's directing toward Lucky and me. I say nothing, but I hook my hand into the crook of Lucky's arm and smile sweetly.

Sterling's eyes flare in frustration. Then I blink, and he's gone, following the voice into the drawing room, leaving silence in his wake.

"Finally, we're alone," Lucky whispers conspiratorially. "Shall we get up to mischief now that we are unsupervised?"

It sends a giddy warmth through me, and I find it's easy to agree. Lucky's idea of mischief is little more than entering the kitchen in search of cake, but it's rich with cinnamon and absolutely heavenly.

With our bellies full, we venture outdoors to the southeast courtyard, where I finally beg Lucky for a rest.

He lights up. "Perfect. I have a surprise for you."

It's impossible to not want to follow him when he smiles at me like that.

He leads me back to the study. "Close your eyes," he says, and with a thrill, I do.

There's the creak of a door, and ...

"Open."

Oh my.

From the wooden desk to the soft drapes to the candles, he's thought of everything. He even hung the map he'd gifted me on the wall. I could very well be transported back home, standing here. And the books ... oh, the books. More than I have ever owned. More than I can count.

How did he ...

"Do you like it?" he asks.

Yes, I think, looking at him. *I really do.*

It's a wonder.

I'm curious about the effort he is going to. Flowers, flirtation. We're already wed. I'm flattered, truly, but confused.

"If I didn't know any better, I'd think you were courting me. Yet we both know your heart lies elsewhere."

He gathers my hand in his—always touching so gently—admiring it while he speaks. "I often thought myself ill-formed in pursuits of love, as there always seemed room within me for more than one."

My heart excites.

"Would it be so difficult to feel affection for me?" he asks.

Not in the least. I wonder, too, about my ability to love more than one.

"It is not difficult at all," I admit.

He smells of salt and sun, and I step closer. Close enough for him not to mistake my intention.

It has been all too simple to fall now that I think of it. Easy as breathing.

His lips welcome mine eagerly, the sound of my gasp lost between breaths. I'm weightless, a bundle of nerves alight by his presence, his touch. It's different from what I feel for Sterling, but not lesser. Lighter. The ember of something I already know will grow into more.

The door slams shut, and we tear apart. Sterling is standing there, a mixture of heat and anger in his eyes.

"What cruel plan was this? To demand my presence here, only to watch you take what is left of my heart and crush it?"

I hardly know which of us he's talking to or about.

Lucky steps between us. "Then you admit you love her?"

"Of course I do," he roars. "How dare you act as if you have not been aware of that since you walked back into my life? To what end was this destined for? If you meant to kill me without a blade, then congratulations; you've managed it."

He stumbles back as I crash into him, pushing against his chest with both hands. He steps back, never stopping me, letting me take it out on him. How could he? And he knew how I felt. He knew, and he said nothing.

I should carve out his stubborn heart.

He hits the door with a thud. My breath rushes from me, and I follow, clinging to his tunic, crushing our chests together.

"I hope you are not dead because you have brought me back to life."

Where the kiss with Lucky was tender, soft, this is brutal. Devastating. This—*this*—is all I've wanted. All I've desired and never thought possible. I tried in vain to not imagine it, but no dream could ever match the reality.

Sterling holds me tightly to him, his grip strong and sure, his lips devouring my own.

We're separated by a throat clearing.

"I must apologize for my meddling," Lucky says. "But I couldn't let another day pass without you finding out how we both feel about you."

It's unbearably sweet.

"You fulfilled your promise," I tell him and beckon him closer.

It's Sterling who takes his hand. "I am sorry for hurting you. Again."

Lucky brings his palm to his lips. "Make it the last time and promise to love us as we deserve, and I'll forgive you." He winks at me. "We both will."

My knees weaken as Sterling smiles. Fortunately, he's holding me up.

"I promise."

THE END

52

"What is it?"

Sterling waits, ever patient.

"It's nothing," I say. "Nerves." I can tell he doesn't believe me, but I move past him to the door. "Come. We'll be late for dinner."

Maybe it's for the best.

go to dinner (**turn to page 315**)

53

I CAN'T LEAVE HIM.

While the masked man next to me is occupied with getting Tegan's wrists tied, I rush over to Sterling, where I'm stopped abruptly. The muscles in my neck pull tight as the guy next to Sterling grabs me by the hair, and I fight off a scream. My heart is pounding.

There's a scuffle to my right, shoes in my peripheral vision, and then a loud crack!

The grip in my hair is gone. The man responsible stumbles back a step, holding his bloody nose in his hands.

Sterling stands between us, his hands tied, his knuckles bloody.

"I'm gonna fucking kill you for that," the man says and slams his fist into Sterling's jaw.

"The fuck are you doing?" T appears, his voice unnervingly quiet as he pulls the other man back and gets in his face. "We're not here for that. We're here for the gold, and you're wasting time."

"He fucking hit me."

"He's nobody. Now, put them in the back and get where you need to be. We don't have time for your ego."

Flashing lights flood the room from outside.

The room freezes.

Then ... chaos.

"Fuck."

"They're not supposed to be here yet. What the fuck?"

"Boss?"

The masked men all look toward T, who is unnervingly still.

There's shouting outside.

"How the fuck did the cops get here so fast?"

The only one who doesn't seem worried is T.

He speaks low. "The silent alarm must have been triggered. It doesn't matter. We planned for this. B, you stay up here. Make sure they don't get in."

The Hulk grabs Sterling and grits out, "Yes, sir."

"Stick to the plan," T says to the others, who are standing by.

The rest of the floor is empty.

Tegan is gone.

T grabs the manager and keeps walking. "Let's go."

The rest of the men fall in line, leaving Sterling and me with the Hulk and his jittery friend to watch as they all step into the elevator with the manager. Off to the vault they go.

"Take care of it," T says before the doors close.

Jitterbug grumbles. "Fuck it. Put them with the older guy T cleared out. We need to get downstairs."

The guy Sterling punched spits blood onto the floor, forgetting that'll be evidence or just not caring. "Fuck! Fine."

We're dragged to the corridor. There are scuff marks in the carpet and spots of blood that turn my stomach. The walls are lined with financial ads and praise, and the banality only makes this whole situation worse.

I'm readying my feet, turning to the left, where they took everyone else.

We're pulled to the right.

Oh God.

The door opens, and it's a relief to see the man from earlier alive. He straightens, surprised as we're shoved inside. Sterling hits the ground first and catches me. The door slams behind us, and we're left alone.

I slide down the wall to sit, my shoulder bumping Sterling's. The other man sits opposite, curious.

"I'm Mia."

"Hal," he grunts, his gaze shifting between us. Anxious.

"They hurt you," I say, keeping my voice gentle.

"It's fine," Hal says. His hair is gray at the temples, shaved close to the scalp. Late forties, if I had to guess. "It'll be over soon," he murmurs, eyes on the door. "The cops are already outside."

He's right, of course; we've all heard the shouting from the street. It should be a comfort, but I can't help feeling like prey caught between predators.

Nothing happens for a while. Is it strange that they left us here alone? Probably not. We're zip-tied, and they're armed. We hardly pose a threat.

The office we've been stuffed in has no windows, and no doubt any attempt we make to open the door will be noticed.

Two desks flank the room, topped with chunky computers and a matching set of stationery. The monitor on the left is blinking, a thumb drive nestled among a swarm of cables, abandoned when the alarm sounded. The name plate on the desk says this is Tracy's desk. I hope she's okay out there.

"Brutes," Sterling calls them, and I see Hal's lip curl before he's covering it under a shaky hand.

"Maybe they're a little rough about it, but can you really blame them for wanting a piece back of what's been taken from them?"

"And what's that?" Sterling asks, ever the investigator.

He's started pulling at the laces on one shoe, but I'm not sure why. Maybe they came undone while we were being dragged in here.

"Dignity. Pride." Hal pauses, and it isn't until his shoulders sag that I realize how tall he looked before. Curled over his knees again, he looks small and timid. It seems so much more like an act now.

I need to start paying more attention.

"What sort of work do you do, Hal?"

His eyes flash, and I watch as his index finger taps a rhythm on his thigh. I guess the shock hasn't worn off yet.

"Construction."

Tap, tap, tap.

I perk up. "Oh? Houses or commercial? My pa did his apprenticeship with New Build before he came home and started his own business."

The gift of personal information works as I wanted it to, smoothing a little of the tension in his jaw.

"Oh, yeah? I got a bunch of guys who started there, too, before they all got pushed out because of budget cuts." His words are laced with bitterness.

I gentle my voice. "It's a good thing they have you looking out for them now."

The tension is back.

Tap, tap, tap.

"Yeah, they do, and I'm gonna make sure they can take care of their families because I'm not a heartless corporate fuck."

Beside me, Sterling stills. He drops his shoelace and looks over at Hal, his body tight, like a violin string. Poised for action.

"Being a boss takes a lot of responsibility," Hal says. His knuckles are dark with dried blood.

The tapping stops.

"You got a family?"

The weight of Sterling's, "No," hits me in the chest, the delivery thick with meaning.

"Well, my crew is family, and that means making sacrifices."

Said with the conviction of a man who isn't planning something, but executing it.

I need to move. Sterling is stuck in place, eyes locked on Hal while Hal stares back. I leave them to their odd little standoff, twisting my wrists inside the zip tie. It doesn't budge.

I sigh. What would I even do if I got my hands free? I can't fight. But I can't sit here and do nothing.

At least if I could reach the computer, I could—

That's it!

Both men jump as I shuffle forward on my knees. I can't believe I didn't think of it before.

"What are you doing?" Hal asks, his voice tight.

"Mia?" Even Sterling sounds concerned.

They should both be thanking me.

It takes longer than I'd like to get to the desk, but I pull open the second drawer, happiness exploding in my chest as I look down at a pair of scissors, exactly where I expected them.

I take care of Hal's ties first, nodding when he offers a quiet, "Thank you."

Sterling is silent as I snip his bindings off, the plastic falling to the floor between us. He pockets it before taking the scissors from me and cutting mine off.

"Smart move," he says, his voice warm against my skin. He places the scissors on the floor beside him.

"Thanks."

Have I ever noticed how long his lashes were before?

There's no first aid kit in the room, so I make do with tissues and water.

"I don't mind a few extra scars."

Extra? How often is he throwing himself in the way of danger? And why isn't anyone protecting him?

"Well, I do," I huff. I start with his hand, eager to avoid the endless blue that I can feel staring at me.

"Phone's dead," Hal says, dejected.

I didn't even notice him move over to the desk.

"And the computer's locked. There's no way to call for help."

Great.

"Shouldn't the cops be inside by now?" I ask Sterling.

His jaw tics like he's been chewing on the same thought. "Maybe, but with this many hostages, they'd be reluctant to trigger any retaliation."

There's something in his tone, like he only half believes what he's saying. Whatever he's thinking, he's keeping it to himself.

Hal settles back on the floor across from us, elbows on his knees.

"You're incredible," Sterling says, his voice soft.

I feel Sterling's eyes on me like a caress. Heat radiates outward through my skin like a burn.

"What?" *He can't be serious.* "You're delirious, clearly." I hold up my hand. "How many fingers can you see?"

I think my heart straight-up falls over when he smiles. It's so unlike him.

It's gorgeous.

"I'm serious. How did you know where to look?"

I shrug. "I guessed."

"No, you didn't. You picked that desk and that drawer. How did you know?"

My pulse flutters in my throat. I'm still recovering from hearing him say I'm incredible. Maybe I'm the delirious one. What if this is all a really bad dream?

"Everything on the desk is organized into its own position. Neat and sensible. It makes sense that someone who keeps a desk like that would be prepared for anything."

"Exactly," he says. He's still smiling. "Incredible."

"I'm sure you thought of it," I deflect. The tissue is starting to dissolve in my hand, but I can't look at his face yet, so I keep dabbing the clean skin around his knuckles to hold off the inevitable.

"I didn't actually, but I was working on my own way out."

Of course he was.

"When we get out of here …" he says.

When … not if. A weight lifts off my lungs. If Sterling says it, it must be true.

"I'm going to tell Monica to take you off Lifestyle and give you some real assignments."

Don't make promises you can't keep, I want to say.

He reaches to scratch his cheek, and I gently slap his hand away. His gaze finally catches mine, and it's just as intense as I expected.

Soaking more tissues, I start on his face. "You can't just let someone help you, can you?"

He's quiet. "It's been a long time since someone wanted to. The last time didn't end so well."

"For you or for them?"

"Both of us, but it was my fault. I …" He swallows. "I chased my dreams instead of him."

"Well, you've got one up on me," I say. "I chased my dreams, and it was my ex who ran away from me."

"What an idiot."

I smile. "You studied in the UK, didn't you?"

He nods. "Manchester, where my great-uncle lives. After the accident, I wanted to disappear. Get as far away from reality as I could, and it seemed like a good idea at sixteen." His hand lies in a fist on his knee, fingers digging into his palm.

I can't even imagine. If I lost my parents …

My heart aches for him. "Was it?"

"Best decision I ever made. Followed by one of the worst."

"Is that why you moved home?"

"Partly. Grief is a funny thing, honestly. Once the anger

passed, I hated the thought of being so far from them, and I saw how much good I could do here." Every word slips heavy from his lips, two decades of pain stitched into the syllables.

"You must have had every paper in the city chasing you."

"I did," he says. "I almost went to work at *The Herald*. I'm extremely glad I didn't now. That was the second-best decision I ever made."

"*The Herald* is a great paper."

"The editor is a friend of mine, but there's one thing *The Observer* has that they don't."

The trail of his fingers along my wrist shoots electricity through my veins, down my spine.

"What's that?"

He says nothing for a breath, leaving me to deal with the aftershocks of his touch. I want him to do it again. I want him to never stop.

"Terrible coffee," he whispers, and the secret curl of his smile doubles down on the wave I'm experiencing.

Sterling reaches up slowly enough that I know it's coming, but I don't move. He curls his fingers around mine, and all I'm aware of is how close we are, each breath he takes, how much I want to kiss him.

Water trickles down my wrist from where I'm squeezing the tissue too tight.

I pull away. It's just the situation playing with my head.

"It must be lonely," I say, dropping my hand into my lap. Two of my nails have gotten chipped since we arrived. "Only relying on yourself."

"I'm not good at letting people in," he confesses in the space between us. Dropped quiet, like snow. "But I want to get better at it."

He covers my clasped hands with his. "Maybe you could help me."

I stare down at where our hands are combined. His strong palms encompass my own.

When Sterling crosses to the door, my heart jumps into my throat.

"Where are you going?"

"All those guys are downstairs; I'm going to get to the other hostages and get us out before they come back."

Of course he wants to do that. I've already witnessed him risk his life twice today. If this is the way he runs his investigations, I'm starting to understand why he kept telling me I wasn't suited for it.

It's honorable in a way I already know him to be, but I'm selfish; I don't want anything to happen to him. Sterling doesn't seem as bothered by that idea.

"Maybe you should both go," Hal says, and I whip my head over to him. "I would join you, but that guy has it out for me. I think it's best if I stay here, wait it out."

Something doesn't feel right.

I turn back to Sterling. "What if they aren't all gone?"

He places his hands on my shoulders. The heat of him is a relief. "I'll be okay. I need you to stay here. It's safer."

"Makes sense for you to leave then." I'm being snarky, but I don't care. I'm not the one choosing to put myself in danger.

What if the cops rush in and think he's one of the bad guys? They don't have a reputation for calm conflict resolution.

Or forethought.

"Promise me, Mia, you'll stay here."

"Promise *me* you won't get yourself killed. I ..." I swallow. "I can't finish the story without you."

The sound of my pulse is loud in my ears. Sterling's lips part, but his gaze darts to Hal, and whatever he's about to say is cast aside.

I can't shake the feeling I shouldn't let him go. He said it himself; it's safer here. Why can't he just stay and wait?

Make Your Choice:

let sterling leave (**turn to page 325**)
convince him to stay (**turn to page 330**)

54

I LOVE BEING HOME.

I love my parents. I love that I know Larry's daughter wants to be a teacher and that Mrs. Davies is going stir-crazy, recovering from hip surgery. I love sitting in Alice's kitchen, hands cupped around a hot cup of coffee, while she rolls out dough and makes me laugh until I cry.

I love the wide spaces and thin roads and being able to see the stars at night.

But right now? I'm nervous as hell.

Not because of Huey—oh, no, that became clear as soon as we stopped for gas. There he was, two pumps over, back turned, smiling to himself, unaware that I was only a few feet away. I stared at him, waiting for anger, tears, betrayal to bloom within me, but there was only relief.

He's happy here, and I'm happy in Chance. It's better this way.

That aside, I did point him out to Lucky and Sterling and got a wicked thrill at how much they instantly hated him, smiling as Lucky came up with ways to pay him back somehow.

"Brilliant decision, this," Lucky says as he pops a piece of pork in his mouth.

We made it to my parents' house in time for dinner, and he was given strict instructions to stay out of the kitchen. Ma quickly slaps his hand away from getting a second, but she's smiling back at him when he tells her how good it is.

"Go make yourself useful."

Lucky's laugh follows him out the kitchen, and even Sterling's smiling until Ma rounds on him too.

"You too. Come on. Out."

He nods with all the weight of a man given a royal decree, and I'm so immensely thankful to have them both in my life that I forget I'm not alone until Ma's hustled so close to me that it's like she's trying to mind-meld with me.

No, the reason I'm nervous has nothing to do with Huey and everything to do with the two men I'm certain I'm falling in love with.

Ma took one look up at them when she opened the door, her thick auburn hair piled high, and said, "I see trouble has arrived."

She knows. In that Ma way of knowing, I know she knows. And from the way she's looking at me now, she knows I know she knows.

This is why I'm nervous.

"Honey, are you sure you're eating enough?"

"Yes, Ma."

Jean Finnegan is a smile, wrapped in a hug, stuffed into a person. She talks loud and sings louder and doesn't care that she's never been in tune. She also has as much tact as a donkey.

"Because I know you don't like cooking—"

"Don't worry; Lucky always makes sure I have at least one home-cooked meal a day."

Ma squeezes my shoulder. "He's a sweet boy."

Here we go.

"Yes, he is very sweet."

"And handsome."

Oh my God.

"He's here with his boyfriend."

Pa steps into the room and doesn't miss a beat. "I seem to remember you being obsessed with a Sterling before you left."

I can hear murmurs of conversation coming from the dining room, which hopefully means they aren't hearing this.

"I wasn't obsessed."

"Those aren't his articles you have pinned above your desk?" he teases.

Oh God, he's right; they are still there. New rule: Sterling and Lucky cannot see my bedroom.

"I should go help them set the table."

Ma shoves a butter knife in my hand and sets me in front of the rolls. "They'll figure it out."

Pa is less subtle. "They care about you."

"We're friends."

"It would be okay if it was more. Relationships don't always look one way. If three of you want something different, then you should have it. Don't hold yourself back from something good because of what anyone else might think."

It sucks all the air from my lungs, and I lower the knife to force a full breath back in. "It's not ..." I start, but one look at him, and I know he knows too. "It's just me, okay? It's not—they're not—" I take another breath. "They're happy, and I'm happy for them, and I'm dealing with the rest of it. It's fine. It'll be fine."

He shares a look with Ma over my shoulder, but I'm saved from any further discussion of a throuple situation when Alice's car pulls up outside.

She rushes me as soon as she's in the front door, almost dropping the stack of Tupperware she's carrying before Sterling steps in and rescues it. I squeeze her tighter and bury my face into her shoulder. Every bad thought melts in the face of sugar and flour and cinnamon.

"I've missed you so much."

She lowers her voice to a whisper. "There's extra cinnamon rolls in the car."

"I love you."

Alice is the best person in the world. Hands down, no competition.

Hilariously, the first time I ever heard the term *polyamory* was after Alice and I marched up to our parents to tell them we were getting married someday, only to then have to explain to them that we meant as friends, obviously, and that we'd also have husbands, duh.

A few awkward explanations—and my ma excusing herself to cackle in the kitchen—later, a whole new world of possibilities opened up to me.

Alice is sharp, of eyes and mind, a riot of black ringlets cascading around her at all times, with a laugh that will restore joy to your heart.

She's my moon, my stars, my faith when all is lost. I can't imagine life without her.

"Oh my gosh." She pulls back. "Remember the state fair I was telling you about? They got back to me! I'm in. This time next year, you'll be looking at a gold-medal baker."

"Heck yeah, I will be. That's amazing." That's Alice for you. "Hey, I'll come cover it, get some photos you can use for the website. Make it a girls' weekend too. Drink a little, flirt a little ..."

"You might not want to tell your boyfriends that in case they do something drastic."

"We're just *friends*." Why is that so hard for everyone to understand?

"Who you're in love with."

"Shh." I cover her mouth with my hand. "That's between you, me, and the cinnamon rolls I'll be comfort-eating later."

After dinner, Ma puts music on, and Lucky pulls me out of my chair to dance. Mostly, he picks me up and spins us until I'm worried dinner will make a reappearance, but it's the lightest I've felt in months.

When the song ends, Sterling holds out his hand. "May I cut in?"

I step back so he can join Lucky, but it's Lucky who moves away.

"Look after our girl for me."

Sterling's hand is warm in mine. His other settles on my back, and I'm trying desperately not to notice every little detail—the buttons at his collar that he loosened during dessert, the heat radiating from him like a sunburn, his grip, his lips, his *smell* ...

"Missing the city yet?" I ask to distract myself.

The music has slowed, and Sterling moves us in a gentle sway.

"Not at all." He pauses, corrects himself, "A little."

I thought so. "Thank you for getting us from the airport in one piece."

"You're welcome. I couldn't let Lucky behind a wheel." His eyes are always so bright. "Thank you for letting us be here."

For a second, I could swear he wants to kiss me, but that can't be right.

I drop my eyes, try to corral my heart back into place. Lucky has started washing the dishes, and I can hear him swapping recipes with Alice while Ma referees.

"What was he like in college?"

"Worse," he says, and he's not smiling, but there's glee in his eyes.

"What were you like?"

"Worse," he repeats.

I can barely imagine it. "I'm picturing you holed up in a dark corner, planning a horrific fate for anyone who dared disturb you."

The laughter fades from his eyes.

Oh no. "Sorry, that was a terrible joke."

"Is that really what you think of me?"

"No, no, of course not." At least not now.

"But you used to."

I sigh. Trying to lie to him is impossible.

"I didn't know you then. You were this super-scary-slash-impressive big-time journalist. In my defense, the whole office was afraid of you."

"I don't care about them; I care about you."

"Well, obviously, I'm not afraid of you now." *Just the super-scary-slash-impressively-big feelings I have about you.* "I'm so sorry. It was a really bad joke; I just wanted to make you smile. Can we just forget I said anything?"

I take his silence as a yes, but I know I hurt his feelings, and it cuts deep. I need to fix this, but I'm not sure how. I didn't know I could hurt him, and now I've messed up. I'll need to ask Lucky what to do.

When the song ends, Pa calls it a night, and I do, too, walking Alice out to her car to say goodbye and get my hands on her treats.

It's been years since the farm was operational and about six months since Louis convinced my parents to turn the barn into a vacation home. They agreed mostly to keep Louis busy between jobs, but he did good, lots of warm colors and soft touches. The light from the main house gives it a gentle glow, and by the time I step inside, the hum of crickets and smell of new grass soothe over the fraying parts of my soul.

I'll always have a home here, always leave a part of myself behind when I go. No matter how far away I am, it's waiting for me when I return. I could do that—come back, save myself more months, years, of wanting what I can't have. My folks would welcome me. Alice too.

But I'd miss the city like a limb, and I'd be leaving two-thirds of my heart behind.

Lucky and Sterling are sitting together on the couch when I step out of the bathroom. I'm pinned by their joint gazes, a delicate trap I can't help but feel I've laid a hand in setting.

It's not their fault I love them. I should have moved out when they got back together. I knew I'd end up here, somehow, someway.

Where Lucky is a warm and inviting beach, Sterling is the cool and unknowable sea. As powerful as a riptide, as beautiful as the endless horizon. And I've let myself go adrift.

"Come," Sterling says, the low command rearranging my body temperature.

I want to, but there's a line between us I know will be crossed if I move.

Do I go?

Make Your Choice:

confess your feelings (**turn to page 298**)
go to bed (**turn to page 297**)

55

"I THINK I should go to sleep."

"Mia," Sterling says. It's not a request.

I slip into the armchair facing them, my heart trying to escape my chest. Maybe if it hides before this conversation starts, we can go home and pretend everything is fine.

I don't want to move out. I don't want them to spend all their time at Sterling's, where I can't see them or touch them.

I don't want to lose them.

But when Sterling speaks again, I know I might not have a choice in it. "There's something we need to talk about."

I DON'T THINK YOU CAN AVOID THIS.

hear them out (**turn to page 298**)

56

It's fine. I've been expecting this for a while; I've known that, one day, I'd have to face my feelings. They're too observant. Why wouldn't they work out that I've been hiding my feelings for them?

"I'm sorry about before." Maybe if I get ahead of this, I can salvage their friendship.

"Sorry for what?" Lucky asks.

"Um ..." The words stack up in the back of my throat, making it hard to breathe. I know what I need to say, so it should be a breeze, right? Except they don't want to move—they're stuck—and the longer the silence plays out, the less I want to say anything at all.

Sterling takes pity on me. "We heard what Alice called us."

Oh God.

"We're not mad about it," Lucky adds.

"The opposite actually."

I'm not sure my heart rate has ever been this quick before ...

"Mia"—Sterling pulls my hands into his—"it's okay. We've wanted to talk to you about this for a while."

They have?

"You have?"

"We want to be with you."

The wind picks up outside, sweeping up the leaves and shaking them out again. A chorus of frog calls follows. The sound often invades my dreams, as familiar to me as the terra-cotta tiles in the main house.

Maybe I'm dreaming right now. It's the only explanation that makes sense.

"Wait. All of us?"

"Of course," Lucky says.

Oh, of course.

Sterling slides his fingers in mine, gently pulling my hand into his lap. I've always loved his hands, as talented as Lucky's and always steady. Always strong.

"Yes, all of us. We both care about you and each other, and we know you care about us."

I do.

"Who's to tell us that we can't be together?"

No one, I want to say because I want this too much.

"How? How would this even work?"

"However we want. There isn't a rule book we need to follow. We only need to talk to each other."

Lucky snorts. "Your specialty." He is unrepentant in the face of Sterling's unamused brow.

"I'm working on it." Then his attention is back, joined by Lucky's, and my heart picks up once more, whipping and spinning like the wind against the windows. "We've already talked about this, but we need to know how you feel. Is this something you want?"

I can't believe he even has to ask.

"More than anything."

I want to fall into Lucky's arms when I'm sad and have Sterling understand when work frustrates me. I want to be with them because when I'm with them I'm seen, and I'm inspired, and I'm brimming with so much love that I don't have room for it all, and every second I've spent trying to stuff it down, it only gets bigger.

My jaw creaks on a yawn. I want to sleep.

"Come on. We can talk about it more tomorrow. You're coming with us."

Without waiting, he scoops me into his arms. I scramble to catch myself, but there's no need. Sterling has me and isn't letting me go. Lucky walks ahead, turning off the lights and turning down the bed. Their bed.

Sterling lowers me onto the mattress, and I'm treated to the sight of the two of them stripping down to their boxers. I want to ask them to stop, to let me stare and memorize them—the hair on Sterling's chest, Lucky's tattoos, the peaks and valleys of their hips and chests and shoulders—but sleep is taking me fast, and they slide under the covers before I can say anything.

Lying on either side of me, they leave no distance. One arm across my waist, a thigh slid between mine. Holding me close. Keeping me.

"Sweet dreams, Mia." Sterling's voice follows me into sleep.

But I don't need dreams because nothing could be sweeter than this.

THE END

Or you can stay for more* (**turn to page 307**)

57

You rebel! Just remember …

actions have consequences (**turn to page 302**)

58

THE PIPES GROAN as the joint comes undone, and—oh no. One thing Pa taught me? Pipes groan for a reason. And that reason is pressure.

Water spits out, free of the pipe, covering me in seconds. I cough and splutter against it, tightening the fitting as fast as I can, my fingers slipping in the water.

Damn it!

A deep voice calls through the door. Finally, after it feels like I've been covered in a metric ton of water, I screw the joint back in place. There's still a trickle of water leaking from the pipe, but it'll hold. For now.

I crumple against the floor.

The door bursts open. I almost don't want to look, but I can't help myself.

Lucky leans in the doorframe, curious. "How is the tour going?"

I smile up at him. "Could be better. I think there's a small leak in the bathroom."

Bryan appears, incensed. "If you leave now, I'll keep this from the owners, but don't let me see you here again."

"Come on. We'd better get out of here." Lucky offers me his hand.

I take it, the warmth of his hand a sharp contrast to my cold everything.

"This will be a fun walk home," I say, taking in the soaked condition of my clothes. Guess I should have thought of that before I got handsy with the sink.

We stand in the tiny bathroom, damp and dripping, and I'm caught between wanting him to make the first move and running from it. It would be easy to take a leap, if I hadn't already left my bravado sitting with my dignity on a bathroom floor.

"My place is closer," he says. "If you want."

Oh, I want. I want a lot of things, and maybe that's the problem.

It's a sweet gesture, but I've already embarrassed myself enough today. "You don't want to say *I told you so*?"

Lucky reaches out and tucks a damp piece of hair behind my ear. "How would that help?"

I close my eyes. He's a good man.

"I should go, but thank you for today. For ... all of it."

"Make it up to me. Take me to dinner tonight."

It pulls a laugh from me. Why not? "I hope you like takeout then because that's all I can offer."

"Love, as long as you're there, I'm happy." He kisses my cheek.

"It's a date then." The first of many.

I GUESS IT WORKED OUT AFTER ALL.

that's it? I want more (**turn to page 304**)

59

I LEAVE Lucky's apartment with a promise to return in a few hours with food and shuffle to the elevator, wrapped in his coat. It's thick and luxurious, and it smells like him. A small mercy after my actions today.

There's already someone waiting, likely from the viewing, and I stop beside them, my nose buried in my collar, eyes on the floor. It's only when I hear my name that I look up.

"Sterling? What are you doing here?"

Clearly, it's for an article—he's in his work suit, with a thick black coat over the top—but he looks so good that he might as well have stepped out of a photo shoot. Even the curl that's dangling over his eyebrow looks perfectly placed.

He takes his time getting a look at me. The oversize coat, the soaked pants, the shame. I shiver under the scrutiny.

"Checking in on a source I'm interviewing—or attempted to before a pipe burst."

Ah. "Sorry the interview didn't pan out."

"It was a long shot."

The elevator arrives, and Sterling holds the doors open for me. "I'm sorry about what happened with Monica. Had I been there—"

I cut him off with a gesture. In the past week, I've been yelled at by my boss, hit on by a rock star, and waterlogged by my own envy. Now Sterling is eager to have a conversation?

It's too much.

"That's nice and everything, but—"

"Let me make it up to you."

If I wasn't standing here, water seeping from my scuffed sneakers onto the speckled tiles, I'd swear I was dreaming. Heck, maybe I am. Maybe I slipped in that water upstairs and hit my head and I'm actually hooked up to seriously good meds right now because what is happening?

"Dinner," he says, and he isn't joking. He's serious.

"I ..." I don't know what to say. *Yes* is the obvious answer, the one every atom in my body is screaming at me right now, but ... I made plans with Lucky, and I want to honor them. "I already have a date tonight."

"Tomorrow then," Sterling says. "I've waited a long time to ask you out, Mia. One more night is nothing."

Two years ago, I packed up my bags and told the most important people in my life that Chance was where I wanted—no, where I *needed* to be. If the future burned with possibilities, then surely, the spark had to be lit here.

I've waited two long years for that to be true.

Something tells me I'm about to find out.

"It's a date," I say, overwhelmed with déjà vu. I know I shouldn't complain here, but how is it fair that two great guys asked me out on the same day? Am I supposed to hope one of them is secretly awful so it's easier to pick between them? "If only I could have two boyfriends," I joke.

Sterling's gaze lingers on my lips. "Who says you can't?"

There must still be water in my ears because there's no way Sterling just suggested that. "I don't know if you're joking or not."

"There's a lot you don't know about me—yet. But you will. I'm done hiding from you, Mia."

My clothes are sticking to my skin, and there's a blister on my pinkie toe from walking in wet socks, but Sterling catches my hand in his, and I've never felt more beautiful.

First Lucky and now Sterling. Is Fate trying to tell me something? I don't want to be forced to choose between them.

The elevator reaches the ground floor.

"Can I walk you home?" Sterling asks.

I nod.

Maybe Sterling is right; maybe I don't have to choose.

THE END

60

GRUMBLING, Lucky pads into the living room—no shirt, boxers low on his hips. He looks like a god, if gods had bedhead and got cranky when they didn't have a sleep-in.

"Nope," is all he says as he throws me over his shoulder.

"Lachlan—"

He cuts Sterling off. "You too."

It's not often Lucky will make demands, and why would he when he begs so sweetly? But as the floor changes from wood to carpet, I see Sterling following behind.

Lucky is sweet as he lowers me back onto the bed, stripping me of my pajamas and enveloping me in his body heat before the morning chill can hit my skin.

The bed dips again, and Sterling is brushing hair from my eyes, kissing me softly as he settles back in.

Lucky charts a tender course along my back with his fingers and buries his face in my shoulder, breathing deep and slow. Over his shoulder, the red glow of the clock makes his point. It's Sunday. What's a few more hours in bed when it's this good?

I could live happily in this very spot, in this very moment, and never need anything else. Lock myself away in a cocoon of comfort and skin, being held by them, shielded from the outside world.

It's still hard to remember this isn't a dream.

I must fall back asleep because when I blink awake, I'm sandwiched between them again, our legs threaded together, except this time, there's no barrier between us. Nothing except skin on delicious skin.

I start to move, desperate to finally touch them.

Lucky's arm slips around my waist, pulling me back. "Not yet," he says.

I want to laugh. Like hell I'm leaving this bed. Maybe later. Maybe never again.

I hold back a groan as his erection presses into my hip.

Sterling kisses me, his own cock hard and hot against my thigh, and I know I'm not going anywhere.

Lucky fits himself against my back. The slick tip of his cock leaves wet kisses along my ass as I roll against him, slow with sleep. "Mmm." His low hum in my ear goes straight through me. "Morning, gorgeous."

Sterling slides his hand down my hip to my thigh, gripping tight as he pulls my leg up and over his, leaving me open. His cock finds a place between my thighs, but he doesn't push in yet. He teases his fingers along the sensitive part of my thigh while he nips at my neck.

Lucky stretches as he watches, his smile growing lascivious. "I knew you'd look good like this, love. Don't you think so, baby?"

"I do," Sterling answers.

Lucky leans down and takes my nipple in his mouth. "Better than we imagined."

All I can do is whine with pleasure.

"She likes that," Sterling says, sliding his hand closer to where I want it, but still not touching where I really need.

With my nipple caught between his teeth, his tongue swirling around the peak, Lucky looks up, all smiles, and, fuck, they've barely done anything, and I'm already close to begging.

He looks good like this, hair out of control, eyes a little hazy with lingering sleep. I grab the back of his head, gripping his hair, and haul him up to kiss me. It's loose and filthy, his lips softer than melted butter.

Fuck, his mouth is so good.

I want it everywhere.

Sterling chooses this moment to finally circle my clit, and I gasp into Lucky's mouth.

Lucky pulls back with a groan, grabbing the base of his hard cock as he watches Sterling's fingers. "Fuck."

Reaching behind me, I twist and catch Sterling's mouth with mine, bucking as Lucky's hand joins his between my thighs, dragging through the wetness and circling my pussy in a tease.

Fuck is right.

"Please," I whine.

Sterling sucks on my lower lip. He shifts, gripping my hips with enough force that I moan, and it's followed by his when Lucky's hand disappears, his knuckles dragging along my skin in a way that tells me he's stroking Sterling right now.

Then he's lining Sterling's cock up, and Sterling pushes inside, and—holy mother of God, yes.

Lucky kisses his way down my body, until he's between my open thighs, licking his reddened lips as he watches as Sterling slowly fucks into me.

Sliding his hands up my thighs, Lucky parts my pussy with his thumbs, letting out a hot breath across my clit. I buck into it.

"Don't be cruel, Lucky," Sterling says. "Help her."

Lucky smiles up at us both. "Hold her, baby. Help me out."

Sterling grips my thighs. "Gladly."

Lucky sinks down into the mattress and dives in, sucking my clit into his mouth.

I shout.

Caught between the pleasure on both sides, I can't do anything but hold on and enjoy the ride. Sterling keeps his pace slow and steady, and Lucky seems content to stay down there forever, so why not? I never want it to end.

"That's it," Sterling says. "Show that pussy the worship it deserves."

He ghosts his fingertips along the curve of my breast, making my back arch, trying to get more of his hands on me.

"I could get used to waking up like this."

Lucky teases my clit with his tongue. "Fuck, you're beautiful."

Lucky's tongue disappears lower, and then Sterling is growling in my ear.

He thrusts forward hard. "Shit, Lucky, your fucking tongue."

Ah, so that's where he went.

He's eager, curling his tongue around where Sterling is inside of me, teasing his way inside, making me scream.

Lucky rises up on one hand, licking his lips. "You taste so fucking good, both of you." He dives back down, alternating between us, his talented fingers rubbing my clit as he tongues my pussy where Sterling is pumping in and out.

"I'm close," I whine.

Like a call to action, Sterling takes this personally, reaching down with one hand to sink his hand into Lucky's hair and holding him firmly against my clit.

"Fuck his mouth, beautiful. Take what you need," Sterling whispers in my ear, a wall of heat behind me, his arm a vise over my chest.

Lucky's moan vibrates through my pussy, ripping a wrecked moan from my throat.

"She likes that. Do it again," Sterling says. "Slower. Make it last."

Lucky moans. Obeys.

I'm at his mercy, both of them. My only option—the only

option I want—is to fuck myself between Lucky's mouth and Sterling's cock. There's no better place to be.

Slowly, I rock up to Lucky's searching tongue, then back, until Sterling's dick is so deep inside of me that I might burst. The stretch of him is gratifying, full enough for there to be a dull ache, but it fades the deeper he goes, the longer he's inside of me.

Each push of my hips makes me hotter. Sweat beads along my nose, over my lip, under my breasts. It pools along my spine, between our bodies. It does nothing to cool my skin or ice the fire in my veins.

All I can do is hold on to Sterling, one hand gripping his forearm, where I'm locked against his chest, and the other tangled with his in Lucky's hair. It's a lifeline, a feedback loop through me to them and back again. All of us connected.

Just as we should be.

My thighs start to tremble, the muscles pulsing. Lucky sucks my clit into his mouth, not letting up, and my hips move on their own, fucking faster now, chasing my climax.

I pant with each breath, little *ah, ah, ah*s escaping me.

Yes. Fuck yes.

Sterling digs one heel into the mattress and starts to fuck into me. He slides his hand up to my throat, then my jaw, gripping, turning me into a fierce kiss that knocks our teeth together.

That's all I need.

Fireworks burst across my body, leaving me a twitching mess between them. I hear nothing but my own cries, loud in the silence. Fuck, I hope no one in the main house is listening.

The shocks go on and on, reignited when I feel Sterling's cock pulse within me as he comes.

Sterling pulls out, and Lucky is there, lapping up his cum from my sensitive skin while I shake. The slick sounds of him jacking himself off only make it hotter, and when he comes, it sets off a second round of electricity through me.

Panting, he drops his forehead to my thigh. Sweat covers every inch of me, and my chest rises and falls hard as I try to wrangle my breathing under control. It's no use; I'm completely spent, a pool of melted wax between them, liquefied by pleasure.

I sigh into Sterling's tender kisses along my jaw, whine a little when he rolls us onto our sides, never taking his hands off me. Lucky crawls up the bed and collapses. I use the last of my strength to pull him closer, tasting the combination of us on his tongue.

If I could come again, I would from that alone.

I want to explain everything they mean to me. How knowing them has changed me, how much I value Sterling's inner strength and Lucky's warmth and humor. That, sometimes, I can't breathe because my heart overflows and I might drown in how much I love them.

"Fuck," is all I get out.

Lucky makes a sound in agreement.

"We know, Mia," Sterling says, his voice thick. "We feel it, too, and we're not going anywhere."

THE END

61

Sterling bursts through the door like a tornado. Blood on his cheek, jacket rumpled, and ... his shoe untied?

He isn't alone. Everything gets louder as the cops start to clear us out.

Sterling rushes over, his hands moving rapidly as he checks my face, arms, hands. "You're okay." It's an answer more than a question.

He doesn't let go, even as the EMT forces him to sit down so they can look over his cheek.

Sterling keeps his gaze on me the entire time.

Gone is the crisp, restrained man I've always known. His shoulders are hunched forward, his breathing is labored, his temples are damp with sweat. He never lets anyone see him like this.

He's letting me see though. He's keeping me here.

Doesn't he know I'm not going anywhere? Not now, not ever.

"I got the story," I say, squeezing his hand.

Today has been an adrenaline rush I'll be happy to put behind me, but at least it wasn't for nothing.

The EMT finishes up and moves to another patient.

Sterling stands. "I don't care about the story."

He reaches up, cupping my cheeks with his palms; they're

warm and steady, and I've watched them write treatises that tear down powerful people, but right now, he's gently holding me.

"I've spent my life putting the story first, but watching them take you ... Mia, I've been cruel to us both. I'm sorry. I know you'll be angry—you deserve to be—but if—"

Ridiculous man.

Grabbing the lapels of his jacket, I pull him down into a kiss.

Make Your Choice:

awww how cute! (epilogue now, please) (**turn to page 441**)

no, I want more! (**turn to page 378**)

62

"I SEE you still enjoy tormenting your brother," Lucky says, hiding his chuckle into his wineglass.

Meanwhile, Louis sits at the head of the table, pink at the tips of his ears. The conversation around us has returned to full volume, but I keep my voice low to save him more embarrassment.

"It's character building," I say. "He's head of this family now that our parents have retired. He needs to be able to keep calm in the face of frustration."

It's a lie; I simply like teasing my older brother until his face matches the drapery in his room. Lucky smiles knowingly.

"Do you still disappear into the forest when he bothers you?"

The mention tickles me. "I can't believe you remembered that."

"I forget nothing you've shared," he says, and his gravity pulls my heart ever closer. "You spend summers in the fields and your winters in the study. Which brings me to this." He passes me a scroll. There's no room to open it, so Lucky explains, "It's a map of the new world. Now that the seas are safe, I've been helping to document the new routes. Wait until you see the ship, Mia. It's fantastic. And the water ..." He clasps a hand to his chest. "When the light hits it in the morning, you'll swear you're still dreaming."

Sterling is wrong; this is the boy I remember. Spirited, teasing. A smile that rivals the sun.

"Sailing suits you."

"It'll suit you too, I think."

You suit me, I want to say.

Sterling, who has spent the evening acting as a silent sentry on my other side, leans forward to address Lucky. "I've heard there are rapids by the south islands. How did you navigate the area without taking damage?"

I could hug him again for putting in the effort. I know it's only because I asked, but it still means everything to me that he would.

"Who says we didn't?" Lucky replies, a teasing glint in his eyes. He tucks a lock of hair behind his ear. "I won't lie; it was difficult, but I have an excellent crew, and they deserve all the credit for delivering me in one piece."

"What was it like?"

I smile down at my plate. This is exactly what I hoped for. Sterling is as curious as they come, even more so than Lucky or me, but he rarely lets anyone see.

"Incredible," Lucky says. He leans closer, placing his elbow on the table, until the two of them form a barricade around me. It's intimate. "I've never experienced anything like it. The rush ... it's indescribable. There were times I was sure we would flip, turn so far over that the sea would block out the sun."

"Any man who thinks he can best the ocean is a fool," Sterling says, a wry smile twisting the corner of his mouth.

"A swordsman and a poet," Lucky says, his voice low. "What other skills should we know about? I bet you're excellent with your hands." He reaches forward, brushing his finger along Sterling's knuckles.

Sterling's fingers twitch before he pulls his hand away.

He says nothing.

"Sterling has many talents," I say, reaching for my water glass. My pulse is racing. "And few equals."

When there's no reply, I look up to find his eyes on me while Lucky looks between us.

"Curious why you're not joining us on the journey back tomorrow, Sterling." Lucky picks up his glass and takes a sip. "I must admit, I'm disappointed. Why would you stay while Mia leaves? Do you value your vow to her so little?"

Hurt cuts across Sterling's expression as surely as a blade, but before he can answer, a scream rings out from beyond the house.

Both men stand in a rush.

Even Louis is at attention, already storming toward the door. "Get Mia out—now."

More screams call out, indecipherable, except for one phrase —*in the sorcerer's name*—and my blood runs cold.

"Come," Sterling says, his dagger drawn.

Damn. I left mine in my room.

"I'll keep you safe."

"We both will," Lucky says, taking my hand.

Sterling looks like he'd rather swallow glass, but he agrees.

We move quickly to my rooms, Sterling leading and Lucky behind, keeping one hand on my back the whole way. I expect them both to leave me when we arrive, but they don't, and the tension follows us inside as Sterling closes the door.

Wonderful. A possible madman outside and two stubborn ones locked in with me.

The fire has shrunk since I left, and tending to it calms my mind as I add fresh wood and stoke the flames.

"Do you think he's returned?"

It shouldn't be possible. My parents promised me. They saw him turn to ash with their own eyes.

"No," Sterling says from the other side of the room. He has been guarding the door since we entered.

Lucky is closer and cups my shaking hands between his. It

helps. "I'm sure it's nothing, but even if it isn't, we won't let anything happen to you."

It can't be a coincidence. There has been no sign of unrest in over a year, but the night before our wedding, a stranger appears, calling out the name of the man who attempted to destroy us all?

"Promise me you won't go out there," I plead, slipping my hands free to grip at Lucky's clothes. "I just got you back. I can't lose you. I ..." What if this is a sign of worse to come? There may be more men tomorrow, and I'll never get to tell him ... never get the time back. "Lucky, I love you."

"Oh, love." He cradles my face in his palms, lifting my face so I can see the truth ring out in his gaze. "My heart is—and has always been—yours."

The kiss is a relief. Years of longing released in the breath between us, in the eager press of his lips on mine. I don't let go—I can't—using my hold on him to bring us closer together. I never want to be parted again.

Let evil return. I will not let it separate us.

A knock comes at the door, pulling us apart. Sterling gives us enough time to separate before inching it open. It's a relief to see Louis on the other side.

"Some of the farmers' sons broke into the distillery, and this was their idea of a joke. They've been taken home now. Nothing more to worry about."

Oh, thank God.

"Best we all get some sleep before tomorrow," he says and excuses himself.

"Well," I start, unsure of what to do now.

Neither Lucky nor Sterling makes a move to leave.

"After you," Sterling says, waving Lucky toward the closed door.

"Be my guest." Lucky steps between us. "Unless you're worried about leaving us alone?"

Silence.

"Or perhaps *jealous* is a better word," Lucky adds.

Nothing.

I'm frozen in place as Lucky steps closer to Sterling. Even from a distance, it's clear how hard he is breathing.

"I wonder," Lucky says, "what do you imagine we would do if you left us? Would we stop at a kiss? A touch? Can you picture it?" He comes to a stop, less than an arm's length left between them.

All at once, I notice they are the same height. Eyes, nose, mouth ... all aligned. I know how soft Lucky's lips are, and now I want nothing more than to see them fit between Sterling's own.

Separately, they're handsome, but together ...

I'm entranced.

"Which of us would you be more envious of?" Lucky asks.

The tension snaps. Sterling surges forward, gripping two large fists of Lucky's tunic, their faces a breath apart. "Why are you so insistent on this? It's none of your business."

Despite the snarl aimed at him, Lucky is undeterred. "Because I recognize the fight in your eyes. I've been there too. Don't pass up on the chance of happiness that is being offered to you."

Carefully, as though the floor is littered with broken glass, I make my way to them. "Is it true? Are you truly jealous?" I can hardly believe it.

He lets Lucky go, dropping his head. "It does not matter. You are in love with another, betrothed, and I have accepted that." Sterling's words are rough, torn from him.

"I wish you'd said something. I didn't know ... I thought ..." My hands tremble. "I've loved you in some shape or form ever since we met. I buried it because I was certain you'd never feel the same, but it's only grown, and my only consolation was that I wouldn't have to decide between you two."

"You're wrong, Mia." Sterling comes over, cupping my cheek. "No one could love you more deeply than me."

"Why would you have to decide?" Lucky says, surprising us both. A smile plays on his lips. He toys with Sterling's collar, and I clearly hear the hitch in Sterling's breath. "Have us both."

Then Lucky kisses him.

Ahhh! They did it, they kissed!

I hear wedding bells (**turn to page 321**)

63

THE WEDDING IS INTIMATE. Lucky shines in a golden embroidered tunic, silk draped over one shoulder and cascading to the floor.

When we brought the news to Louis, he threw his head back and released an exasperated cheer. There was no surprise, and as he binds our hands together—forever connecting Sterling, Lachlan, and me—his eyes are fond. Welcoming.

"Repeat after me ..."

My dress is beautiful. The stitching is fine work, the jewels catching and holding the lamplight, radiating a soft glow. The rich red embroidered gown weighs me down in ten layers, no doubt Louis's amusing game to deter me from fleeing.

Ridiculous. There's nowhere else I want to be.

Sterling stands on my left, severe in all black, his sword hanging at his side. He's handsomer than I've ever seen him, but it's not the work of cloth and soap. It's the naked adoration in his gaze—a sight I've seen before, but never known how to interpret.

We complement each other. Sterling's strength, my passion, Lucky's fearlessness.

With our hands intertwined, we recite our vows in unison. The truth in every word binds us together, for now and eternity.

"What I feel will last beyond flesh, beyond breath, beyond life. When every light in the sky fades out of view, I will continue to be guided by my unending love for you."

THE END

64

"No," Lucky says, "we don't have to be saviors."

"Standing here and doing nothing is one step down from being the bad guys."

"That's not fair. Of course I want to help, but I don't think unnecessarily dying helps anyone."

Love. Protection. Community. It used to be understood as a basic human trait. Now I'm not sure what is base about humans beyond our ability to surprise ourselves.

"Then stay. I'll go by myself."

He blinks himself into my path, stopping me. "Oh, no, no, no, no. Christ, what is it about you journos? I'm cursed to want you, and you're cursed to break my heart."

He pushes both hands into his hair. I don't have time for his internal struggle; there are lives at stake, and if I'm on my own, I need to leave now.

Lucky huffs. "I'm just a musician. I write down my feelings, and sometimes, it sounds good. I'm not a bloody hero."

"You don't need to be," I counter. "I'm asking you to be a good man."

"Fuck it. But if I die, don't let Bentley fucking Michaels anywhere near these guitars. That prat's had his eye on 'em for years, and I'd rather get up close and personal with his moldy balls than let him touch my babies."

Later, when all this is done, I'm going back to the shop and asking Moira for something to remove that image from my head.

"I promise. Can we go now?"

What are you waiting for?

let's do this (**turn to page 329**)

65

STERLING LEAVES.

Hal is twitchy, the way Louis used to be when he was hiding something. Alarm bells are ringing in my head. He darts his eyes over to the computer again. Something is definitely wrong.

While he's distracted, I pull my knees into my chest, hugging with one arm. Nothing to see here, just a girl getting comfortable in the middle of a hostage situation.

The recorder is still in my pocket, and if Sterling were here, I can imagine the little look of self-congratulations he'd wear. I argued that having my phone out would look less suspicious while talking to Tegan, but I can see now that he was right. Finding the recording button is as easy as reaching into my pocket and pressing. No unlocking a screen, no finding an app, no concern I'll accidentally press stop through the material of my shirt.

Just one simple click that I hide by clearing my throat.

"You don't think they'll bring me some water if I ask, do you?" I joke softly.

If I'm right about this—and I'm hoping I'm not—I can't spook him.

"I'd be more worried about them discovering your boyfriend out there," he says.

Against my will, my face heats. "Not my boyfriend," I correct.

Maybe I was imagining it earlier. Is there any chance it isn't a response to the—oh, I don't know—traumatic experience of being held hostage in the middle of a Monday?

I'm certainly not going to jeopardize my career to ask a boy if he likes me.

My spine pops when I stretch. "I definitely didn't wake up this morning and expect this." It's the truth, but not the reason I'm bringing it up.

There's something that's been nagging away at me about Hal. It's grown the longer we've been in here. It's like what Sterling said about gut instinct.

There's a story here; I simply need to uncover it.

Hal hasn't responded. I'm not sure he even heard me.

I keep my tone light, conversational. "How old are your kids?" I ask, finally getting his attention. "You asked about family before," I explain.

"Three and five."

"Exciting ages. My ma said those were the best and worst years for her and pa. Apparently, my brother and I liked hide-and-seek so much that she considered getting us to wear bells."

"Yeah, I've been there." He chuckles. "Lola, my youngest, started coughing one night and wouldn't stop. Scariest thing that's ever happened to me. By the time we got to the hospital, she'd gone from red to purple to white. We thought we were going to lose her."

My heart breaks, only saved by the phrasing. *Were.* "How is she now?"

As he blinks, his eyes shine with unshed tears. "Better. Hasn't happened again since, but after, I spent six whole months sleeping on the floor of her room, listening to her breathe. And I still wake up in the middle of the night, terrified."

"I'm glad she's okay."

Hal says nothing, staring into a distance I'm suddenly sure is dark and tormented.

"She has a good dad."

He opens his mouth, but a quiet beep cuts through the silence, and he stills.

It came from the computer.

The same one he said wasn't working.

I'm on my feet in seconds, but Hal is too. I barely have my fingers around the thumb drive before my head is slammed into the desk. It's quick and dirty, and I slump to the floor in a heap. My head is pounding.

He ejects the thumb drive and pockets it, standing over me.

"What is that?" I ask.

"It's my winning lottery ticket."

The computer screen shows a customer profile.

"You're taking ... people's information?"

"You'd be surprised what some people are willing to pay for a few letters and numbers."

Actually, I wouldn't.

"Why do this?"

"So my daughters can afford to live. So my mom can stay on her medication. So we don't have to starve. Why the fuck else would I risk it?"

"Whatever's in the vault isn't enough for you?"

He laughs, and—*oh*.

"You're not after that, are you?" I ask. "This was the real plan."

"Had to get back here somehow, didn't I?" His smile is no longer reassuring. "What they take can be tracked. This right here? Ain't no one even gonna know it's missing."

"You'd really sell out thousands of people just to save yourself?"

"Yes!"

"You're no better than the people you hate."

"Lady, I don't give a shit what you think about me. You know why? Because I'm about to solve every problem I've ever had, and I'm going to sleep well at night, knowing I took care of mine and my own when no one else did. You think the fucks on the board of directors will give a shit about today? About you?"

"What would your daughters think?"

"Fuck you. Don't you talk about my kids."

"Hal, you think you're sticking it to the same unethical corporations that put you in this position, but I promise you, you're only going to hurt people who are in the same situation as you. The people at the top? They have protections in place, and insurance, and lawyers. I understand why you want to do this, and if your only target was the assholes running the show, I would close my eyes and pretend we didn't have this conversation, but—"

"But what?"

My blood runs cold.

"But I can't let you condemn thousands of people just to save yourself."

"Then I'm sorry," he says. "Because you're never going to get the chance to tell anybody about it."

Crashing into me like a boulder, he wraps his hands around my throat and squeezes. There's no hesitation, only desperation in his eyes. He's bigger and meaner, and I'm not strong enough to pull him off me.

Make Your Choice:

you get the upper hand (**turn to page 346**)
Hal overpowers you (**turn to page 348**)

66

"ALL RIGHT, love, let's do it."

I could kiss him.

"Do you think you can get us into the bank?"

Lucky places his glass on the coffee table with a thud. "Course I can."

ALL RIGHT, HEROES!

to the bank! (**turn to page 339**)

67

Sterling turns the handle, and I change my mind.

"No, wait. Please don't leave."

I'm aware that I'm gripping his arm too tightly, but I can't let go. Can't let him go. I don't know how I know, but he needs to stay, needs to be here right now.

Maybe it's panic finally catching up with me. It would make sense. It's not every day you find yourself nose to nose with an automatic weapon.

"Breathe, Mia."

Am I not?

His fingers are cold against my cheek, a relief from the thundering beat of my pulse. I close my eyes and lean in. Sterling's arms come around me.

"How are you always so calm?"

Heat bleeds through his clothes, and for long-drawn-out seconds, I do nothing but listen to his breathing, steady enough that I could set a clock to it. His heart thumps out of time for a beat, then returns to normal.

Sometimes, it's good to know he's still human. I stifle a giggle at the thought.

"Did I miss something?" he asks.

No, but I did. "You have a heart," I say, looking up at him. Only when his expression turns cold do I hear the words and scramble to explain. "Bianca called you a vampire once; I don't even know why I'm remembering that right now, but I shouldn't have said anything. Gosh, that was so rude. I'm sorry."

I pull away. I don't want to leave the comfort of his arms, but I'm sure I'm making him uncomfortable.

"She really called me a vampire?" He looks amused.

"You work all hours of the day, you only wear black, you're a little mean ..."

"Only a little?"

Okay, that's funny. I didn't know he was so funny.

"I'm paraphrasing."

"Ah." He settles back against the wall, abandoning his plan to leave. I'm more grateful than I can say, especially when he puts his arm around me and pulls me to his side. "Are you sure I'm not?"

"What? A vampire? Or mean?"

There's a pause. I can sense Hal watching us with interest, but I'm not ready to leave the little bubble of Sterling and me that exists right now, so I look down at my knees and pretend we're the only ones here.

"I know you're human, Sterling."

Sterling mustn't want to shatter the bubble either because he's whispering low into my ear. "So, you're not afraid that I'll mysteriously appear in your bedroom tonight, hungry for a taste?"

I think my heart stops.

I'm not sure because, right now, it's doing a sort of triple axel jump in my chest, and I can't remember how to breathe.

"Is that why you don't date?"

"It's complicated," he says, the words jagged with his typical gruffness. "Hell, I'm complicated. You don't need that."

Jeez, he's so ridiculous, and I'm so helplessly in love with him.

I twist to look him in the eyes. "It's okay to be complicated. Believe it or not, I like you this way."

I'm not sure I'll ever get used to the spotlight that is Sterling's undivided attention, but I'm also sure I never want it to stop. God, I wish I could cross this divide, reach out and touch the vulnerability I know is underneath the prickliness.

Hal coughs, and reality rushes back in.

The minutes pass slowly. Sterling is staring at the door. I wonder if he's still planning on leaving.

"What is it?" I ask.

His brow is knitted tight. "You're right; we've been in here too long. Something's wrong. Anyone with access to the silent alarm is trained to hit it when suspects are leaving, so why press it early?"

"Fear?" I guess. "Everyone's terrified."

Sterling hums, but his frown stays. "That's the other thing; not everyone has access to the alarm, and it went off when half the floor was already tied up and moved. It's strange."

"You an investigator or something?" Hal is staring intently at Sterling. It plants itself like a splinter in my mind.

Something doesn't feel right. It irks me, but I can't get to it, can't work out what it is.

"Reporter."

Hal's shoulders relax. He dabs at his mouth with his sleeve. The bleeding has stopped, but it'll be swollen for a while. Maybe he's jumpy. I know I am.

"Are you one of the ones protecting the corrupt fucks who run this country or one of the good ones?"

"He's one of the best ones," I answer, offended by the mere suggestion Sterling would ever go against his morals.

Hal nods, but doesn't look convinced.

"You're right to be angry at them," Sterling adds, his tone steady. It's his interview voice. "There's a lot to be angry about, but there are ways to go about change that don't involve putting other people's lives in danger."

Hal scoffs. "Oh, really? What have you done? I don't remember seeing your name on my daughter's medical bills."

I don't like this. I don't like his tone or the way he's looking at Sterling like a threat.

"Why did you come to the bank today, Hal?"

Hal's eyes harden, and my blood runs cold. Sterling's grip tightens around me.

I think back on how we got here. Hal fighting back as T tried to tie his wrists, the way he kept getting in his face, how he wouldn't stay down until T really hurt him.

If he's really working with them, why go to all that trouble? Why get hurt?

The rest of them are all downstairs in the vault.

Sterling must be thinking the same thing. "Are they doing your dirty work for you?"

Shockingly, Hal laughs at this. "I don't let anyone do my dirty work for me. You're fishing in the dark, son."

No, that's not true. Sterling knows as well as I do that something isn't right here. I've been feeling it since we came into this room.

But why?

Why be at the bank at all?

I'm so close to the answer that it's frustrating. I need to think.

"You're here for a reason though," I say. I'm certain of it.

Slowly, as though he's afraid Hal will be spooked if he moves too quickly, Sterling removes his arm from my shoulders. It feels like he's gearing up for a fight.

Oh fuck! The recorder.

Luckily, all of Hal's attention is on Sterling, so I'm able to slip my hand into my pocket and start the recording. I'm not sure why it feels so crucial, but I'm going to trust my gut.

"There's one thing that I've been wondering," Sterling starts. "The guy calling the shots out there? He's all about control, and yet he lost it with you. Made sure to separate you too. Put you in here, away from everyone else. That's interesting to me."

Hal's smile turns sharp and dangerous. The room reshapes itself with this new light, no longer a safe haven, keeping evil out, but a trap slash cage, where the hunter is here with us.

And Sterling is baiting him.

Carefully, cautiously, I shift my hand to my side, inching toward the scissors.

"Why is that? As far as I can see, you're not a threat. So, that makes me think you needed to be here for another reason. That maybe something in this room is valuable to you."

I curl my pinkie finger around the handle.

"You're pretty slick—you know that?" Hal says.

He's too happy. I don't like it.

"No, no, don't stop now. Keep going. Tell me about this master plan I'm supposed to have. Since you're *the best*."

I freeze when his eyes cut to me.

Sterling's hand forms a fist on his thigh.

Careful, I plead silently. *Don't spook him*.

"I imagine a sick child is quite stressful," Sterling says.

It tears Hal's attention back to him.

"It's the most terrifying thing you could imagine."

The tension goes ice cold.

Quickly, I pull the scissors in, hiding them under my thigh, my fingers curled tightly around them.

"I can imagine," Sterling replies. "You said yourself; family is important. A scare like that could drive a good man to desperation."

"Oh, yeah? What the fuck would you know about desperation, huh? Nothing, I bet. Bet you've never known loss in your life. Got everything handed to you. Yeah, I see you, with your fancy watch and your expensive suits. Does this make you feel important? You trying to impress your girlfriend here, get her all wet by—"

"Don't you dare talk about her," Sterling growls.

It's exactly what Hal wants. He crosses his arms, pleased. "You're just like the rest of them. High on your fucking soapbox because you've never had to get your hands dirty when shit gets real. Well, news flash: some of us don't have the luxury of the moral high ground because we're too busy making sure we can fucking eat."

Gone is the quiet man from before, replaced with a burning fury that is shaping around my suspicions. Sterling is right. Hal wasn't pulled away from everyone else; he was put here on purpose.

But there's nothing in here. No money, no way out. Only two desks and a couple of computers, and Hal hasn't made a single move toward them.

Hal stands, and Sterling rushes to his feet.

I feel very small.

Hal points at him. "You think wagging your finger at some politicians is gonna change anything? Oh, you talk a big game, but when it comes down to it, you're not prepared to do what it takes."

Sterling steps forward. They're only a foot apart now.

"And you are?"

"You bet your ass I am. I'm about to change lives, and there's not a goddamn thing you can do about it."

Something about the computers is bugging me. It's that flashing. It's still going.

I remember how jumpy Hal got when I went for the desk earlier. And all those times I caught him staring over there.

Oh my God.

Sterling and Hal are still talking, but I can't hear it, can't think of anything, except, *I need to get to that thumb drive.*

It's got to be that; it's the only thing that makes sense, and I'm only going to have one shot to try and get it.

My heart pounding, I shift onto my knees, thrusting the scissors into Sterling's hand. I can't stop to make sure he grabbed them. I have to keep moving, lunging for the light that's been flicking on and off all afternoon.

Behind me, there's movement and noise, but I can't look back. I have to trust Sterling will be okay. I reach the computer with my arm outstretched like a relay racer, and with one swift pull, I free the USB from the port.

The light dies, and I hear Hal roar.

A body slams into me, throwing me to the ground. I curl up, sliding my hand under my belly, protecting the drive. Hal pushes and pulls and scratches at me, until the weight pinning me down is gone, and I look up to see Sterling standing between us.

Protecting me.

Hal stands, a sneer taking over his face. He's wrestled the scissors from Sterling, and he wields them now, slashing at the air, trying to push Sterling back.

"I'm not leaving here without that drive."

I shove it in my pocket, next to the recorder, and scramble toward the door.

Hal lunges for Sterling, who twists his shoulders before pushing forward, catching Hal in the face with his fist.

Hal drops immediately, out cold.

I blink up at him, and all I see is blood.

"Shit," he says, curling his fingers over the cut on his palm, trying to stem the blood flow. Hopefully, the fact that he's still able to move them is a good sign. No nerve damage. Maybe the cut isn't that deep.

"Are you okay?"

Me? That's who he's worried about right now?

"Good," I lie. "You stayed with me."

"Of course."

Of course. Like it's nothing. Simple. Because I asked, so *of course*.

"Why?"

I might as well have asked him if he hunts for sport.

"What do you mean, why?"

"You stayed."

"Mia, of course I stayed."

He keeps saying that.

This is a man who has dedicated his life to his work, who has faced lawsuits and threats because he dared to put the truth before his own safety. The same man who I could barely utter a sentence to for two years, and today, I asked him to abandon his plan to help a room full of hostages because I had a hunch.

And he just ... did it.

I fill my lungs, finally able to take a full breath. "I should have let you leave."

He drops to a crouch beside me. "I'm fucking glad you didn't."

Hearing him swear is stirring up all kinds of feelings, and I wish he'd waited until he wasn't bleeding and I wasn't sitting on the floor during a bank robbery because I can't do anything about how much I want to tear his clothes off right now.

"I can't imagine what would have happened if I'd left."

He cups my cheek with his good hand. I lift my eyes to his, and it's electric.

"This is going to be incredibly unprofessional, but I've already wasted two fucking years, so here it is. I'm so desperately in love with you that I'm sick with it. I've thought about you constantly, but I never wanted to be the reason your success was questioned, didn't want anyone to think you hadn't earned it, because you're brilliant, and not enough people recognize that. But I'm sorry. I—"

I put my hand over his mouth, grateful for the quiet. My head is pounding, and my heart still hasn't crawled out of my throat. I love what he's saying, but I'm going to need him to repeat it when I'm not feeling so lightheaded.

Preferably while he's naked.

"Can you please just kiss me already?" I whisper.

His lips curl into a smile under my palm, and he places a sweet kiss there before carefully lowering my hand and leaning in.

"Sterling, I ..." I stall out, lost.

There aren't any words to finish that sentence because what I want to say is too big to fit into something as finicky and limited as English. It needs an orchestra, and sweeping hills, and torrential rain. Something elemental and raw.

All I have are my hands and my mouth, and they're going to have to be good enough because he's looking at me as if he'd suffer a thousand more cuts. Like there was no other choice for him. No choice at all. Because when it came down to his plan or me, I came first.

Of course I did.

Our teeth click together when I dive in to kiss him, and Sterling briefly sways back with the force of it, but recovers quickly, cupping my cheek and kissing back.

Oh, how I've dreamed of these lips.

Make Your Choice:

not ready to leave yet?* (**turn to page 436**)
take me to the epilogue (**turn to page 441**)

68

ONE BLINK, and I'm staring at a series of dancing waffles, next to a crude haiku and what I really hope isn't someone's actual phone number.

I'm almost afraid to ask.

"Lucky, where are we?"

"Sorry, love, this is the closest place I could think of." He's already opening the bathroom door, surprising the young girl about to enter.

Lucky pulls me out the door and through the restaurant, which appears to exclusively sell waffles, and—oh my God, that chocolate stack with ice cream and fudge sauce looks amazing. I'm definitely coming back here.

Then we're out the door and on the street.

"The bank is on the next corner," he says, but he needn't have the dance of red and blue lights and cacophony of shouts do the job for him.

Police cars block the entrance, and a crowd has formed around the barricade, people trying to sneak a look at the drama happening in front of their eyes.

"Can you see anything?" I'm too short to get a good look.

"Yep," is all he says, gripping my hand and pulling me past the crowd.

There's a break between the buildings across the street, an

alley that stings my eyes with the smell of urine and trash, but I follow Lucky until we're hidden from view.

"The foyer mostly looks empty. I could only see one brute inside, but he looks bored as fuck. I can take him."

"You're not going without me."

He brings my hand up to kiss. "Wouldn't dream of it, love. You ready for this?"

Instead of answering, I raise a pointed brow and slam the lid of the dumpster closed behind me. Lucky laughs.

Okay, I'll admit it; this might be a little bit fun.

It doesn't stop my heart from racing when he wraps his arms around me and closes his eyes. There's a violent tug in my gut and …

We're standing inside the bank.

"What the—who the fuck are you?" The man we've surprised raises his gun, but Lucky is quicker, moving us behind him in the blink of an eye. "What the ever-loving hell is going on?"

The man now stands in front of us, frantically searching the space we were a second ago. He's dressed in black from head to toe, a mask covering everything but his eyes and a backpack slung over his shoulders. There's something jittery in the way he moves. Nervous maybe.

Lucky lets me go to tap on the man's shoulder. "On your left."

He blinks out of view when the guy whips around and appears behind him again.

He taps again, smiling wide. "Oops. Your other left."

The man lets out a guttural sound. "I'm going to kill you."

He finally realizes I'm there and trains his firearm on me. My pulse rockets up in my throat. We might have a handle on our new skills, but are either of us faster than a bullet?

I'd rather not find out.

With a flick of my eyes, the gun flies out of his hands and skitters across the floor in a clatter.

"Yo, B, what's all the noise about?" A second man, clad in all black, appears across the room. "Who the fuck are you?"

Lucky and I share a look. Two-on-two. Okay. We can do this.

I nod, and we move.

Forcing the guy in front of me on his ass is simple; one swift push with my imagination, and he's down, his eyes wide as he stares up at me.

Yeah, that's right, asshole. Try threatening me now.

Out of view, Lucky continues to goad the other guy. "Almost got me that time, mate. Oops. No, missed again."

"Fucking shitbag, quit moving!"

I bite back a smile and knock the guy he's teasing against the wall. He slumps to the floor at Lucky's feet.

"Aww," he says, appearing beside me. "I was about to ask him which Henchmen 'R' Us he got his outfit from."

A laugh escapes me. Is that bad form in the middle of a crime scene?

"You two are crazy," B spits.

Rich, coming from a man who put a mask on and terrorizes innocent people.

"Oi, don't talk to her like that." Lucky knocks him out in one punch.

He squats down and rips open the backpack, but there's no money there, just more ammunition and zip ties. They must be using them to tie up the hostages.

"What do we do with them?"

There's a glint in Lucky's eyes. "Wrap them up and post 'em. Let the cops deal with it."

I follow his gaze outside and read between the lines. He's right. Better outside than in, especially if they wake up anytime soon.

We tie up their legs and hands, and I slide B across the floor until he bumps into the other guy. I'm tempted to take their masks off, find out who we're dealing with, but we've already spent enough time on these two guys, and we have no idea where the hostages are or where the rest of the crew is.

"Be quick. Don't be seen."

Lucky pulls his ball cap lower and ducks down to press a quick kiss to my cheek before disappearing with the two guys.

Barely two heartbeats pass before he's back.

"What a rush."

"Come on. I think everyone's back here," I say, already walking down the corridor.

A door opens to our right, and nothing could have prepared me for who walks out.

Sterling Ross.

Lucky huffs, the first break of his good mood I've seen. "Of course you're here. Is there a story you won't put yourself in the middle of?"

Sterling looks between us, surprised.

"Go back," Lucky orders, pointing back in the direction he came from.

"Excuse me?"

"Wherever you came from just now, find your way back to it and get out of here before anyone sees you."

Sterling steps closer, meeting Lucky's glare with his own. "I can't leave."

"Yes, you can. I don't care what story you're chasing. Be a hero another day."

They're the same height, almost nose to nose now. Any closer, and they would be kissing.

"Lach—"

"No. I know you know how to disappear," Lucky spits, his pain ripping at the tender underside of my heart. "So, do it."

There is no room for argument, and the math completes itself in my head. Sterling is Lucky's once in a lifetime.

Oh.

Sterling stills. "I don't care how angry you are. I'm not leaving either of you."

"Better late than never," Lucky grumbles.

The crease between Sterling's brows deepens as he sighs. "How did you even get in here?"

"Oh, that? That part's easy," Lucky says, his signature smile starting to peek through. His ability to bounce back is impressive. "Are you watching?"

The space he's standing in clears, and I can pinpoint the exact moment when Sterling stops breathing. Yep. I remember how shocking it was the first time.

The next second, Lucky is back. Gone long enough to make his point and now staring at me.

"Go on, love. Show off for him."

Any other time, and I might. But this situation has only gotten more complicated since we arrived, and the personal history we're tripping over right now can wait.

"Can we keep focus, please?" I ask. "The news said there were half a dozen guys inside. Is that true?"

Sterling recovers. "That's right. The leader is wearing a motorcycle helmet, answers to T. He took three down to one of the vaults with the manager and left two up here to keep the police out."

"Okay, so that leaves us four to take care of."

"You're not going down there," Sterling says, and it turns out Lucky can get angry.

"Look who has an opinion about my life after ten years."

"This is hardly the time to—"

"You just can't handle not calling the shots—"

Oh my God, this cannot be happening right now.

Their hands slap over their mouths with a clap, and the silence is a blessing.

Sterling's eyes are wide in terror, and Lucky looks knowingly at me.

"Sorry, sorry, but you do both remember that there are hostages here? I don't know what happened between you, and I'm not taking sides, but I think we have bigger issues at hand."

I drop my control, and Sterling rips his hands away.

"Mia?"

"Sorry," I say again. "I should have warned you I could do that."

"No, I ..." The rest of the sentence is lost.

There's a slight flush to his cheeks, and I feel my own heat as I trace the color down his neck. Usually, he's in a full suit, but he doesn't have a jacket on right now, so I get to be quietly tormented by the stretch of his black shirt over his strong chest.

Shit.

Sterling shakes off the shock, and the man I've seen at work every day for two years reappears. "We need to get the hostages out of here safely."

"No one's stopping you," Lucky responds, and if they don't kiss and make up soon, I might have to make them.

"Lucky's right," I say. "You should stay here and help them. We can go find the rest of these guys."

Of course, it's too much to hope that Sterling will listen to reason.

"No," he says. "It's too dangerous. Whatever ... powers you have, the men down there have guns, and unless you're invincible or invulnerable, you'll be safer away from them. I'd rather you hold back and let me take care of this." He turns to Lucky. "There are still six of them down—"

"Excuse me," I say—because what the fuck? He cannot be serious right now. "Don't you dare dismiss me like that again." I push him backward without touching him, using more force than I would if I wasn't filled with rage. He backs into the corridor and hits the wall with a thud. "I can look after myself, and I think it might be better if you stayed here."

I don't even need to see Lucky to know he's smiling.

"Mia, please," Sterling pleads, finally dropping the polite indifference I'm used to. There's pain underneath—so much pain—and a longing I know matches Lachlan's own.

It's enough to make me crumple, to change my mind.

Oh, Sterling …

take him along (**turn to page 351**)
keep him safe (**turn to page 362**)

69

I'M NEVER GOING to win a hand-to-hand fight on my own—I know that. Hal is bigger and stronger. But that can't mean it's over; I won't let it be.

I just have to think of something … use something …

Searching frantically, I knock a pen to the floor. Hal reaches for it, but I'm faster.

It sinks into his thigh.

"Ah fuck!"

I scramble away, but he doesn't stop, pulling the pen from his flesh, soaking his jeans in more blood.

He throws the pen to the side, lunging again.

I'm ready this time.

My foot catches him in the stomach. I don't stop; I can't pause long enough to think beyond my next move. I need to get out of here, need to find Sterling.

There!

I see them. The scissors are in front of me, where Sterling was sitting, and I crawl faster.

I'm almost there.

Hal grabs my hair, pulling me back. Pain shoots through me, but I keep moving.

He pins me to the ground, straddling my back, the force punching the air out of my lungs.

I feel his hands tight on my throat.

I just need to stretch a little more.

My fingers graze the handle of the scissors.

So close.

Just one more inch ...

Spots appear in my vision.

Hal's grip tightens, and tears flood my eyes.

I'm running out of time.

I make one final reach and ...

Yes! Got it!

I grip the scissors with as much strength as I can muster and stab blindly.

I can't breathe.

My chest is convulsing, begging, pleading for air.

The scissors catch his hand, his arm, or maybe his shoulder. I can't see enough to tell, but he releases my throat.

Every breath is fire burning through me.

There's a thump, and the weight disappears off my back. I want to turn, make sure he's not going to try to kill me, but I can't move. Can barely breathe.

Darkness fades in.

You did it! You're a hero.

you can't end it there! (**turn to page 360**)

70

In the hours after, arrests were made, statements were taken, and Sterling was left to make the last call he'd ever wanted to make.

Mia was dead.

Emergency services was only able to tell him so much—multiple stab wounds, a crushed windpipe, head trauma. Blood under her nails and tongue. She'd put up a hell of a fight.

One she lost.

The sound her mother made over the phone tore through him, and he knew he'd be hearing it in his nightmares for years.

He shouldn't have left her. He should have protected her.

He never should have asked for her help.

Years of keeping his distance, only to betray himself, but when they'd stood in that elevator, Mia flustered and bright—beautiful as ever—he couldn't stop himself from storming into Monica's office and demanding she end whatever petty scheme had been holding Mia back. He should have discovered it sooner. He'd been the one to convince Monica to hire Mia; it shouldn't have taken two years to help her.

Disgraceful. He'd known about her crush, flattered himself with it, and now she was gone.

All because of him.

Hal was nowhere to be found in the aftermath, and in the coming days, Sterling would be haunted by discovering that Hal wasn't a Hal at all, and he'd known exactly how to keep his face away from the cameras.

He had known something was wrong, but he pushed aside his instincts to play hero—a ridiculous, overwhelming instinct he'd followed his whole life. He trusted it would carry him safely, as it always had.

He'd been wrong.

Mia hadn't been though. She'd gotten the entire confession on tape, and Hal must have cared more about making his getaway than checking her pockets because the EMT found it, still recording, and passed it to Sterling. It wasn't protocol, but he still had friends and favors, and he'd pull every single one of them to make sure she hadn't died in vain.

When the press requests flooded in, asking for his firsthand account of the day, he rejected them all, not wanting to relive it beyond the dreams he frequently woke up from in a sweat. But he couldn't let her pass quietly, and so he began to talk, about her tenacity and spirit, her quick thinking in the moment, and ultimately, her kindness.

He'd long suspected love to be at the core of his boxed-up feelings about her, despite how little they'd known each other. There wasn't any way to explain it, and now there was no way to know if she could have loved him back.

One thing he was certain of: Mia had thought he was a good man, and he would spend the rest of his life living up to that.

Congratulations on reaching one of the few "bad" endings in this book. You can thank my friend, who talked me into writing this, as they love consequences. If you, like me, hate bad endings, please accept my deepest apologies and make yourself feel better by going back and making a different choice.

THE END

71

"Fine, but you stay behind us," I say, annoyed.

"Fuck. You're gorgeous like this."

I freeze. "Say that again."

Sterling's brow creases. "I didn't say anything."

Lucky appears at my side. I know I'm not hearing things. Despite saying it to myself and hearing it from Lachlan a hundred times a day, I've never once imagined Sterling calling me gorgeous before.

Unless he was talking to Lucky.

"You called me gorgeous, or you called him gorgeous—not that either is really appropriate right now." As soon as I say the word, Sterling's entire body stills. He'd better not deny it. "I know what I heard."

"Guys, what's going on?"

Sterling shifts against the wall, and I wait. Wait for this man to explain why he's thinking about me as though he hasn't kept his distance for two years. Wait for him to take it back so I can use the shattered remains of my broken heart to cut out the crush I've held on to for all this time.

His thoughts come through, slow and steady, his eyes never leaving mine.

"There's an earring on your desk—a gold stud with a ruby in the center. You lost the other half, but you won't throw it away

because they were a gift from a dear friend. Best friend, if I had to guess."

I nod. They were a gift from Alice.

"You call your parents every week, but only during Monica's lunch breaks."

"You look amazing in every color, but green always makes your eyes shine brighter."

"Uh, guys?" Lucky is really starting to look worried now.

Sterling hushes him.

"You love crosswords, and you beat yourself up when you can't finish them, even though you shouldn't. I know the guy who writes them, and he's an asshole."

I want to laugh. Cry. Scream at him for keeping this from me. But above all, I want to fall into his arms.

"Seriously, what's going on?"

Sterling turns to Lucky. "Mia just discovered she's telepathic."

It's alarming how fast Lucky's head turns. *"You can hear this?"*

I nod.

"That's amazing. Tell Sterling he's a prick."

"No."

"Spoilsport."

Sterling, meanwhile, is making it difficult to not regret letting him stay. He disappears into the foyer before I can stop him, checking over the guards before striding over to the front door and putting himself in full view of the police.

Fuck, now he's waving someone over.

Lucky looks as appalled as I feel—because you don't just make yourself an easy target in the middle of an active robbery. I can't believe this is the smartest man I've ever met.

Grabbing my hand, Lucky blinks us out of view, too close to the entrance for them to see. I try to melt into the wall while Sterling gives them an update on the situation. I don't listen; I can't hear anything over the sound of my heart panicking.

Lucky waits until the coast is clear to grab Sterling by the back of his shirt and yank him into the shadows. "I'm not fucking working with them," he hisses.

Sterling is annoyingly calm. "You don't have to, but I'm making sure these people are safe."

"Did you even think about us? If even one of them sees what we can do, we're in trouble. I'm not going to let them make us a science experiment or a fucking weapon."

The thought is terrifying. I press closer to the wall, until the chill permeates my clothes, cools my overheated skin. I can hear them mobilizing outside, boots and guns and vests and body cams that may or may not work when questioned.

There are so many of them. We wouldn't stand a chance.

Sterling must have considered this.

Must have decided it was a risk worth taking.

His blue eyes fill my view, complicated and intense. There's so much going on behind them—things I have always wanted to know, things I could know now, if I only looked.

It's like holding the golden ticket.

Like breaking into someone's house.

It's too much.

"I won't let anything happen to you," he says, and I believe him.

This is Sterling Ross. The man who can't be moved. If he says we'll be safe, then I trust him.

His thumbs rub reassuringly over my arms, and I sink into the warmth. My heart calms.

He turns to Lucky, leaving his hands on me. "Look, I promised to get the hostages to safety, but that doesn't mean we have to let anyone in." And, goddamn it, even I can hear the smile in his voice. Of course he had a plan all along. "How many people do you think you can move at a time?"

"Four or five maybe, as long as I've got ahold on them. Where are you thinking?"

"There's a bar a block over—The Little Llama. It doesn't open for a few hours, so you'll be able to come and go without being seen, and the hostages will have water and access to a bathroom while they wait."

Lucky nods. "Yeah, I know it. Then what? I get identified by a couple dozen people who say I magicked them out of the building?"

"Not if you're wearing a mask," Sterling says, walking over and pulling the balaclava off the thief closest to us. He's younger than I expected, with a shaved head and bruising under his eye.

Lucky puts the mask on and takes our hands. Even covered up, his smile is impossible to miss. "Buckle up."

The corridor reappears.

Sterling takes a step, stumbles, grabs on to the wall to steady himself. "Fuck, that's weird."

Lucky slaps his shoulder. "You'll get used to it."

Moving the hostages is quick. They're eager to get out, and I don't blame them. We work well as a team; I open the locks, Sterling explains the plan, Lucky moves them.

The minutes drag on, even though Lucky works as fast as he can, and I spend the entire time worried the robbers will come check on their friends.

They don't.

When we've finally cleared the room, I hear Sterling arguing, and my pulse spikes. I race down and find him in a standoff with an older man. He's in scuffed jeans and heavy boots, and he looks angry that we're saving him.

"How do I know you aren't trying to trick me?"

Even his thoughts are shouting. *"And where the hell is Tony?"*

Jeez, the poor guy must be terrified. He's separated from his friend, worried about him, and Sterling is arguing.

I step into the room. "Hey, I know today has been a lot, but I'm sure Tony is just fine. We're getting you all out, so you'll see him soon, okay?"

He recoils like I slapped him in the face, backing up to the desk behind him. "How do you know that name?"

Shit, I really need to start being more careful. Sterling lifts his hands, approaching slow. Easy.

It doesn't work.

The closer he gets, the more agitated the man looks. He starts pulling drawers open, yelling at Sterling to get back.

The next thing I know, he's slashing the air, a pair of scissors in his hand.

I see red.

It's easy to take hold of them with my mind, flinging them to the other side of the room. Sterling grunts, and then Lucky is rushing in.

I point him at the other guy. "Get him out of here!"

The guy roars, but it's gone before a second goes by, Lucky disappearing with him.

I rush over to Sterling. He's bleeding, cut across his biceps, where I must have clipped him.

"Oh my God, I hurt you."

It's hard to tell how much blood because of his obsession with black, but the area around the cut is mostly dry so I'm going to use everything I learned from fourteen seasons of hospital soap operas to say that it's fine.

"I'm okay. It's a graze. I've had worse."

Oh, worse, he says. That's reassuring.

"That's not good enough. This is why we wanted you to leave."

He cups my cheek. "I'm not going anywhere. If you're both here, so am I."

"If anything happened, I'd never forgive myself."

"Maybe we should all leave then," I say as Lucky blinks back into existence.

"Fuck that," Lucky says, shaking his head. "What's the point of being able to help if we just stand by and watch?"

He's using my own words against me.

"Getting yourself killed isn't helping," Sterling says. "You've already saved innocent lives—"

"And let these assholes get away to try again later?"

"The professionals know how to do their jobs," Sterling argues.

"Sure," Lucky thinks. *"That's why so many innocent people are incarcerated."*

"Only the great Sterling Ross is allowed to rush into danger and save the day with his mighty pen—is that it? We're supposed to go home and what, sit and wait?"

Sterling starts pacing, pulling at his hair. This is the most animated I've ever seen him before. His mouth opens and shuts, starting and rejecting sentences as he goes.

The force of Sterling's feelings for us steals my breath. I never knew ... could never have guessed this was fueling his distance, but I can't deny what is passing through his mind right now.

The longing, the regret, all of it circling back on himself until he returns to the same conclusion—we're better off without him. But he's wrong. So wrong. And I don't need to read Lucky's thoughts to know he feels the same.

Touching his arm, I stop Sterling in his tracks. There's only one way to convince him he's wrong. One way to tip the scales past his resolve.

I lean up and kiss him.

He takes control, cupping my face and tilting my head back. His kisses are as controlled as he is, deliberate, deep. Hungry for more.

Sterling kisses with intention.

I melt into him, not caring. He'll hold me up; he'll keep me safe. All I need right now is this—the safety of his arms, the trust that everything will be okay.

Stroking my jaw, he pulls back. *"You don't know how long I've wanted to do that."*

I smile. "I do now."

He grips Lucky's shirt in his fist and reels him in, their mouths meeting hard and fast. It's over as quick as it started, but the look in Sterling's eyes says he's not nearly done with us. "We have a lot to talk about, but first, I think we need to finish this."

Lucky steals another kiss from Sterling, then picks me up and attacks my mouth so filthily that I almost forget what we're doing here.

I'm panting when he puts me back down.

Even Sterling is biting back a smile. "Let's go."

The cops aren't too pleased that we aren't letting them in, but too bad; they'll need to break the door down themselves. Besides, they should have their hands full with the hostages, especially that last guy.

At least he's with his friend now.

"Must have shut the elevator down," Lucky says, pressing the button again.

Sterling isn't deterred, running behind the teller's desk. "Then we take the stairs. There are only two levels below this; it won't take long to find them."

The stairwell is hidden but unlocked, and we don't waste any time.

"This must be their escape plan," I say.

"I don't see how. There's no exit except the foyer," Sterling explains. "None of this makes any sense. The silent alarm was triggered almost as soon as they walked in; they're taking gold, which is difficult to move and even easier to track; and they've been here long enough for there to be a full contingent of officers outside. It's almost as if they want to be caught."

"Mate, you know I love how your brain works, but some people are just shortsighted. These aren't criminal masterminds we're dealing with here."

Our whispers echo back to us, effectively shutting us up. We can't risk them hearing us.

"Your ass looks amazing in these pants, by the way."

I look over my shoulder at Lucky, shooting him my best, *Now? Really?*

He grins widely.

"Keep up," Sterling thinks, his expression as clear as it usually is.

A thrill runs through me. I have a fast pass to his inner thoughts now. No more guessing games. Nothing else for him to hide behind.

This skill is really going to come in handy.

When we reach the first basement level, Lucky opens the door a crack.

It's silent. No voices, no thoughts. They're not here.

Down. I point, hearing their silent confirmations.

We continue down the stairs. My heart rate rises.

When we reach the last floor, I know we're in the right place.

Tension pulls my senses tight, and I don't even need Lucky to open the door to hear them in my head.

By the time we've stepped out of the stairwell, it's too late.

There they are. Five guys in masks, one in a helmet. Just like Sterling said.

They stand outside the vault door, packed duffels in hand, stilling at the sight of us.

“The fuck?”

The bags hit the floor with a bang. They raise their guns.

“Mia,” comes the command in Sterling’s mind, and maybe he yells it as well, but they’ve started shooting, and it’s all I can do to rush back into the stairwell, taking the stairs two at a time.

I’m already at the next floor when Lucky calls out. Shit, I forgot.

Lucky grips Sterling’s hand and holds the other out for me. “We have to go.”

I can’t reach him; they’re too far away.

The stairwell bursts open.

Bullets pierce the walls, cut through the gap between us.

Sterling’s eyes are pleading, but it’s too late. They need to go. Now.

“Go!” I scream at Lucky. “Get him out of here.”

Make Your Choice:

they go (**turn to page 381**)
they stay (**turn to page 374**)

72

THE WORLD IS MOVING. I can't see it, but I feel it, swaying gently.

I'm surrounded by warmth.

Slowly, the rest of my senses filter back in.

Noise and light and a screaming pain in my lungs. My head is pounding.

"I shouldn't have fucking left you."

I know that voice, but it's coming from a strange place. Above me. Close. Almost as if he's ...

I blink my eyes open to find Sterling holding me. No, not holding—carrying me. The cut on his cheek is bleeding again, and there are tears falling from his eyes.

"Don't you dare die on me," he says.

"Who's dying?" I croak out.

"Fuck. You scared the shit out of me."

"You should see the other guy," I joke, but I'm pretty sure it's ruined by the coughing fit that follows.

Sterling walks faster. Then more hands appear, and I'm lowered. Someone starts taking my vitals. Oh. Right.

The EMT works around Sterling since he won't move from my side. Hasn't stopped staring at me since I woke up, like he can't quite believe I'm still here.

"You shouldn't have taken him on alone."

"Why wouldn't I?"

It's a fact of life that bad things are going to happen. Of course they are.

How do you protect the people you care about? When the attack can come from any side, intended or not?

You stand up. You fight for change. You give voice to the voiceless. Because the powerful will always try to make you believe they are louder, hoping for your silence.

I will never be quiet about what's right.

"What happened to Hal?"

Sterling's expression hardens. "He's been charged. They have the flash drive, thanks to you. You saved a lot of people from trouble today."

"I learned from the best."

The EMT smiles as they give me the all clear and move on to treat someone else. I don't even think I thanked them.

Oh God, Ma's going to kill me. I mean, after she plasters me in bubble wrap and makes me promise never to wage a one-woman war in a hostile situation.

"Come on," Sterling says, holding my hand. "I'll take you home."

Make Your Choice:

take me home* (**turn to page 424**)
go home alone (**turn to page 398**)

73

"Where are the hostages?" I ask.

Sterling points at a door down the hallway, then stumbles as I push him toward it.

"Mia, come on. Be smart about this." Then, inside my head, he says, *"Don't do this. I can't protect you from here, and I can't lose you."*

I freeze, my knuckles white on the door handle. My voice is a whisper. "What did you just say?"

"I said, be smart about this. I can help you."

That's not what I heard though.

I have to try something. "What's your favorite color?"

His confusion is understandable, but I need to know if I just did what I think I just did. I keep my eyes on his lips and do not blink. In fact, I'm not sure I'm breathing right now.

"What?" *The red of your hair.*

Oh my God.

"Uh, Lucky?"

Lachlan comes to my shoulder. "What's taking so long?"

"We need to talk." As quick as I can, I open the door and shove Sterling through. "You'll be safer here." I pull it closed and focus on turning the pins in the lock. They click and settle into place as the handle rattles from the other side.

It's Lucky's voice I hear next.

"So, you'll fight for her, but not for us."

Okay, so not a fluke then. "I think I might be telepathic."

To Lucky's credit, he takes it in stride, merely looking behind me and asking, "What happened to saving the hostages?"

I feel heat pouring from my cheeks. "It's like you said, no one is stopping him." I probably shouldn't have locked the door behind him, but he's already escaped once, and maybe now he'll think twice before he underestimates me. "Now we can go downstairs and finish this."

He kisses me before I can prepare for it, a quick press of lips that lights me up from tip to toe. "Is it too early to say I love you?"

No. "That can't be a serious question."

"You wound me, love. Here we are, two examples of the wondrous mysteries of the universe, and you're going to doubt the breadth of my feelings for you?"

"You're going to write a song about this, aren't you?"

"I feel another Grammy coming on."

He's so ridiculous. I'm definitely falling a little.

We run to the elevators, but pressing the call button does nothing. They must be shut down, by either the robbers or the cops, and what has my life become?

The doors slide open easily, and I get a thrill from the pride Lucky turns on me when I manage it without moving. Little does he know, that's the easy part.

The bad part is that I'm afraid of heights, and it's bad enough that I can't even stick my head in to see where the elevator is. What if I lean in and it rushes by and cuts it off?

I catch myself on his arm, lightheaded. Shit.

"Are you all right there?"

Nope. Not even a little. My lungs feel like they're being crushed slowly, and the room is tilting. No, that's me, sliding to the ground.

"Fuck, what's wrong? Was that too much?"

He's right in front of me now, warm palms checking me for a fever, grounding me. I press my palm to his chest, drinking in the heavy beat of his heart and feeling my own start to slow to match its beat.

"Heights," I choke out once I can breathe again.

He sags and places his hands on my shoulders; his relief is palpable. "Say the word, and I'll zap us out of here."

"No." Using him as leverage, I push up to standing, keeping my eyes off the open elevator doors. "I just needed a second. I'll be okay."

"Mia, please." The raw pain in his voice is what convinces me. He's really worried. "Don't power through if something's wrong, all right? Promise me you'll tell me, and we can get out of here. I'll take you anywhere ... anywhere you want to go, but you have to tell me."

"Yes, of course, I promise."

"Okay." He exhales a long breath, shakes out his hands.

I hate seeing him rattled like this. Pulling him into a hug, I close my eyes and concentrate. Every time I've used my power, I've had the object in sight, but there's also been this ... feeling, a sense of it in the air around me. Maybe if I can reach out with my mind, I can find the—

Yes!

There's a groan of metal on metal beside us. It's not moving yet, but I can make out the shape of it, I think. I just need a little more ...

The day I left, I cried in Pa's arms. He held me and explained how he'd gone out that morning to buy a photo frame so he'd have something to put my first *Observer* byline up in. I hadn't even been hired yet. He was that certain I'd get the job. Said it was only a matter of time and tenacity—ever since he had gotten Word of the Day toilet paper, it was like living with a thesaurus.

And he was right, even if my first byline didn't look how I'd thought it would.

Some things are only possible when you put your mind to 'em. Those are the important things.

It's just a fancy set of pulleys and a box. How hard can it be?

The groaning gets louder.

Closer.

It's moving.

Oh my God.

It's moving.

I can actually feel it rising, like a magnet drawing itself nearer. When it reaches our floor, I finally open my eyes, and it's a good thing Lucky's got a good hold on me because I feel a little wobbly now.

"Okay?"

"Good, but I probably shouldn't try that too many times."

He helps me onto the elevator, and I'm grateful when he doesn't let go. Based on how far I had to pull the cab up, they're in basement two. Gravity takes the pressure off of getting us down there, and now that I'm not fighting against it, the fog behind my eyes clears.

"What if there's someone waiting?" I whisper.

"I only need to see where I'm going, yeah? We'll keep to the front, out of sight, and you open the door enough that I can move us without them seeing."

It's a good plan, as long as there's somewhere safe for us to move to.

The doors groan and screech as I pull them open the few inches Lucky needs to see beyond. My heart jumps into my throat when I hear the thump of something hitting the floor, accompanied by overlapping voices, but it's distant, echoing from another room.

Okay. Distant is good. I like distant.

Nodding to Lucky, I watch as he flickers in place, gone one second, back the next. "It's clear."

I slide my hands in his, and we're out.

The room is barren, a sterilized corridor, bookended by the vault and the exit. We stand between them, with no shield and no plan.

The vault door is huge, thick as a tractor tire and swung wide open. Inside is another room of white walls and tiles. Five men stand with their backs to us, their movements accompanied by a heavy thump as they load six large black duffel bags with gold bricks, one by one.

Anxiety has sharpened their personalities to a deadly point. I'd bet they're seconds away from turning on each other.

There's a woman's body on the floor near the open door, and I tap softly on Lucky's hand to get his attention, pointing to where she's lying.

"Hostage?" he thinks.

I nod.

"Fuck. Okay."

Lucky disappears, and I hear the rustle of clothing before it's gone again. But he doesn't reappear, and my veins turn to ice at how quiet it is.

No movement. No thumps. Not a single word.

Shit, shit, shit.

Then ...

The click of a safety getting pulled back.

Then another.

And another.

Lucky ... where the hell are you?

I need to get out of here. Put some space between me and six guns.

Or else slow them down a little.

The vault door slams closed with a force that rumbles beneath my feet. It won't keep them away for long, but I just need it to be long enough to get to the elevator.

Lucky blinks back in as the shooting starts.

"What the hell happened?"

"They heard you, and I had to improvise."

I start running for the elevator, Lucky at my side, when he skids to a stop.

"Wait." Lucky slows, incredulous. "Why are we running? Take my hand."

Oh, right. I forgot.

It actually hurts to stop, my heart pounding and my entire body telling me to move. The vault door starts to swing open, screams filling the room.

I catch sight of the man Sterling described, imposing in his helmet as he stalks confidently toward us. Then Lucky transports us back upstairs. No scary men here. Just the terrifying afterimage of one seared onto my trembling heart.

The foyer is empty, but everything is louder now, the shadows outside creeping in closer. Footsteps crashing up the stairs.

We're about to be in the middle of a gunfight.

I start pacing. "What about the hostages?" What about Sterling?

Lucky watches the entrance. "All out. That's what took me so long. I was arguing with one guy who wouldn't leave."

Wait. "What?" There's someone still back there?

"Beats me, but I had to get back to you. I've got to hope Sterling sorted him out. Nothing stopping the professionals coming in now."

"Maybe we should get out of here ..." Stopping the bad guys seemed like such a good idea a few minutes ago, but the very real and imminent threat of having my face blown off makes a girl reconsider some things.

The door to the stairwell crashes open. It's hidden in the far back corner of the room, behind the tellers. Well, that would have saved me some trouble with the elevator, but it's not like I can do anything about it.

Who would I even complain to? The fire department? City council? The mayor?

Hi, I recently thwarted a robbery at the Reserve Bank but was disappointed with the internal design. One out of ten for inconvenient stair placement during a rescue.

I run toward Lucky but drop to the floor as bullets cut through the air. He blinks away just in time, and I manage to get behind a pillar just as dust surrounds me.

The men storm out of the stairwell, laden with their loot, and at the sight of them, there's a roar of shouting outside. A voice starts yelling commands via a megaphone.

They don't let the sentence end before they're shooting again. I'm terrified Lucky is going to get caught in the cross fire if he tries to get to me.

I use the bags they were holding, throwing them at them to distract them, while Lucky blinks in and gets a few punches in. One catches him in the face with a punch, and I see red.

With a scream, I send a shock wave across the room. The guy flies four feet away until the wall stops him, and he crumples to the ground. I look around. Everything is a mess, dragged outward in a wave from the force of my push. But I can't see Lucky.

Shit.

"Lucky?" What if he's gone? What if I … did something? I wasn't really thinking, just trying to stop the guy from hurting him again.

"That's some trick you've got there," comes from behind me, and I rush over to crush him in a hug.

"Don't leave me again."

"Not even to piss?"

"I'm serious. I thought I'd hurt you. I thought …"

"Shh, it's okay. You can't get rid of me that easy." He kisses the top of my head. "Hell, a lifetime stuck with you? Sounds like heaven to me."

I hug him closer, breathing in deep. A week ago, we were strangers, but we're linked now, by fate and magic. Bonded.

A voice I don't recognize appears in my head.

"What the fuck happened here? Where the hell is Tony?"

He's behind me.

Turning, I see him. A man in a suit, blood on his lip, creeping cautiously around the corner, shock clear on his face. First Sterling and now this? These were some sloppy robbers.

"It's okay," I call out, walking toward him. "It's safe. They're all knocked out. Help is on the way."

The man stands, but says nothing. He's not coming closer, and he's eyeing Lucky and me like we're the bad guys. Jeez. What's a girl got to do for some fanfare? It's not every day you save people, you know.

Without taking his eyes off me, he sidles sideways until his leg hits the body of one of the bad guys, his arm outstretched, knife still in his grip even though he's out cold.

"Careful there, pal," Lucky says. "Maybe you want to think about sitting down." Then adds, *"Maybe we should get out of here before they storm the place."*

He's right. There's not much more we can do here, and I'd rather not have to answer any questions about how Lucky and I managed to subdue a group of armed guys on our own.

Especially because I'm still not quite sure how we did it.

Oh, Officer, it was nothing, just these neat new powers we got after I touched a glowing rock. What's that? You want to take us to a secure location and never let us leave while you study us for eternity? Sounds great. Let's go.

No, thanks.

Even if these guys wake up soon—and they won't—they

aren't getting away. I can already hear the shouts from outside getting closer and glass smashing as the cops break through the front doors.

"You ready?" Lucky asks.

I reach for his hand, only to be pulled backward with enough force that I stumble straight into a hard body, the knife now at my throat.

What the heck?

The man from before is huffing and puffing behind me, mumbling something that I can't hear over the loud cursing in his head. He's swearing so much that my mom's probably blushing all the way back home.

"Get away from her!" Lucky yells.

I hold up my hands to calm him. The poor guy is just confused. I'm not exactly thrilled to be on the receiving end of it, but the key is to play it calmly. Talk him down.

"Hey, we're not the bad guys."

"Shut up," he spits.

I feel the sting of steel before I remember. I learned a new trick recently.

He screams when I fling into the pillar beside us and finally backs away.

The last thing I register is the grip of Lucky's hand on my arm before we're back in his living room. As soon as I recognize where we are, I collapse onto his sofa.

I'm panting like I've run a marathon.

"What about Sterling?"

Lucky disappears into the kitchen, and my whole body aches as I twist around to see him. I'm not ready to let him leave my sight again.

He runs the tap and ducks down to take a gulp, wiping his mouth on his sleeve. "He'll be fine. Pissed—that's for sure."

"Maybe I shouldn't have locked him in."

"Hey, he's safe because of you. You saw the equipment those guys were carrying; we only stood a chance because of what we can do."

He's right. Lucky passes me a glass of water, and I stare down at it.

"The red of your hair."

His favorite color. From anyone else, I'd think it was creepy, but from Sterling, I'm just confused. He's barely talked to me.

I always thought he hated me.

"What's wrong, love?"

Lachlan's moved, now kneeling in front of me, hands gently placed on my knees.

"He said something before. Thought it, I mean. He doesn't know I heard him, and I can't stop thinking about it."

"I can't lose you."

My pulse is racing, and I'd blame it on the adrenaline rush of the robbery, but I know the real reason.

"It's going to be okay; you can tell me."

Can I? I'm not so naive that I can't tell there's some history between them.

"I don't want to get between you two."

Lucky sighs. "That's all in the past."

Bullshit. "It didn't sound like it."

He cups my cheek. "You're too clever for your own good," he says, then sighs. "Wait here." And in a blink, he's gone ...

I'm all alone.

Fear, panic, frustration—it all finally breaks, crashing over me, and my eyes run white hot as tears spill over onto my cheeks.

"Sorry, love, had to evade the fucking cops—"

Sterling drops to his knees, cupping my face in his hands. "Mia," he says, breathless, and then he's staring daggers at Lachlan. "What the hell happened to her?"

And just like that, I snap. I'm sick of him talking to anyone but me.

"You happened," I spit, pushing his hands off me with a thought. He sways backward with the force. "How could you?"

"What are you talking about? I've been locked up in that room, thanks to you—"

"Red. That's the color you thought of when I asked you. I heard it."

His lips part. I wait for a denial, an explanation, anything ... anything to make sense of this. I know what I heard, know what I want it to mean, but how can it be true?

Always so unflappable, Sterling recovers. Surprise melts into tenderness, softening the lines around his eyes, mouth. Oh. He's always handsome, but this ... this is new. This is life-changing.

The veil vanishes before my eyes. What was hidden is now on full display in his expression, in his *thoughts*. It's too much.

I gasp for air, trembling without any warning at all, and Sterling doesn't miss a beat. Collecting me in his arms, he pulls me in, and I go, falling down into the safety of him, the surety of it.

He rocks me gently. "I didn't know how to tell you. You already had someone, and I never want to complicate your life. You mean too much to me. All I want is your happiness, with or without me."

"No," I say, lifting my head to lock eyes with him. "There is no without you. Not now."

He takes a long, deep breath, and even if I couldn't hear it, it's impossible to miss the fight playing out in his head.

"You have no idea how much I want ... but if it doesn't work, if I mess it up, I can't ... either of you. It's too important. You're too important."

Lucky joins us on the floor, taking one of Sterling's hands in his. He places a gentle kiss in the center of Sterling's palm, whose eyes fall closed.

"I'm not good at this," he says.

My heart overflows with the rush of longing Sterling feels.

"But I've tried to stop loving you, and I can't."

"Then stop trying, you beautiful bastard." Lucky wastes no more time, curling his other hand around Sterling's neck and pulling him in for a kiss. "We deserve better than that."

"I know you do." He turns his endless blue on me.

I don't need him to say anything. He's already shouting it from every angle, every atom reaching out for us, practically glowing. It floods the air, fills my lungs with every breath, leaving me no choice except to reach up and touch the source of it, kiss the love from his lips and meet it with my own.

Someone pass me a tissue.

I don't want to leave yet. is there more? (**turn to page 421**)

74

"Go!" I scream.

Lucky's face falls. It hurts him, but I know he'll do it to save Sterling.

Sterling must know this, too, because he rips his hand out of Lucky's grip just as another bullet catches the wall by my head.

"Not without you," he screams back, and time slows to a crawl as he reaches for me.

Our fingers brush as the bullet catches him in the shoulder, throwing him to the ground.

"No!"

I throw all of my power out at once. I have to do something, anything, to get rid of the threat closing in on us.

The pressure in my head expands, growing infinitely; it's too much, and I can't contain it. White noise makes my ears pop, and I fall to my knees, closing my eyes against the piercing light.

There's a sickening crunch, and the pressure breaks, leaving me gasping on my hands and knees. I heave in breath after breath. Every bone in my body aches. They crack and grind as I push myself up.

I stumble into the wall.

Everyone's on the ground, pushed as far as possible away from me.

The leader's helmet is cracked, the visor shattered and broken.

Their thoughts are silent. I'm too afraid to know if they're not breathing.

I'm not sure I could stomach killing someone.

Even Lucky is a little dazed, looking up at me in awe. It looks like he got hit with the least of it, and relief threatens to bring me to my knees. Despite the power raging through me, all that matters is keeping him and Sterling safe.

Noise from upstairs gets my attention. The calvary is here. We need to go.

I find Sterling.

Oh my God.

My heart is hammering in my throat. He's propped himself up against the wall, shirt stained with blood. He keeps pressure on the wound with one hand, the other outstretched.

I clasp it in mine. "You need to see a doctor. There are EMTs outside—"

He shakes his head. "Don't leave me."

Lucky looks at me.

The shouts are louder now.

"We can't stay," I say.

Sterling pushes himself to standing with a grunt. "Take me with you."

Lucky's grip is tight in mine, his eyes blazing.

"We can't seriously be debating this; you've been shot—you do realize that, right? A bullet went into your body."

"I've patched myself up before."

Lucky and I drop our jaws.

"This is ridiculous. You're going to a hospital; I'm not taking no for an answer."

"You heard the lady," Lucky said. "Let's go."

Sterling is in the hospital for four days. The first twenty-four hours is the worst because he disappears into surgery, and no amount of us calling him our partner gets us into his room. We sleep in fits and starts in the waiting area.

By the end of day one, I've plucked enough secrets from hospital management for us to leverage. It gets us into Sterling's room, and we keep a vigil for every second of visiting hours over the next three days.

The nurses always joke that we appear out of thin air in the mornings.

Sterling wakes as grumpy as ever, but there's color returning to his cheeks, and he never complains when I'm gripping his hand tight enough to leave nail marks.

If the bullet had hit two inches lower ...

It's too horrible to think about.

He's no less obstinate once he's discharged. "You shouldn't have paid my bill," he complains.

I'm still skeptical that he's been released so soon, but luckily, the bullet missed the bone, so as long as he rests, he should recover well.

"Sorry that I saved you from thousands of dollars of medical debt," Lucky responds without an ounce of apology in his voice.

I set a glass of water at his bedside. "Is there anything else we can do?"

"Yes," Sterling grunts, catching my wrist and pulling me close with his good arm. "You can come here."

He's propped up against the headboard of his king-size bed, taking up space, and there's no mistaking what he wants. Not anymore.

He's here, and he's ours. No returns, no refunds, no more running away.

Beginnings always feel powerful, and this is so much more

than a beginning. It's the whole damn story. The lead, and the answer, and my future, wrapped up in one.

We're linked together now, all three of us.

Make Your Choice:

more please* (**turn to page 406**)

oh, wonderful. there's an epilogue (**turn to page 421**)

75

FUCK. The elevator is taking too long.

"Come on. This will be faster."

I grab Sterling's hand and don't wait for a reply, amazed that he's letting me drag him to the stairwell. I'm half convinced this is a dream. That I didn't really kiss him and he didn't really kiss me back, and I'm about to wake up, back in that room with Tegan.

Sterling stops me at the second step, crowding me against the wall and teasing his lips over mine. "Slow down." I can taste the humor in his voice, feel it as he pulls me into a deep, dragged-out kiss.

His grip, my God. He lifts me with ease, pressing his weight into me. I can't get enough.

I need more. Need him closer, harder, faster.

He groans when I scratch my nails across his scalp, and finally —*finally*—he gives me what I want.

"Eager," he says, pulling back from the kiss as he rocks into me.

Through denim and cotton, I can feel the hard line of his cock, impressive already, and I need it inside of me now.

"I saw you go into the other room, and I wasn't sure I'd see you come out," I pant, gripping him tighter with my thighs.

"I needed to know you were safe." The drag of his thumb along my jaw makes me ache, slow and gentle, in direct opposition to how frenzied I feel.

There's too much clothing in the way.

"Please."

"Tell me what you want, Mia."

"You. It's always been you."

I yelp as he picks me up and carries me the rest of the way.

Is it bad form to be grateful for a hostage situation?

Sterling gets us to the seventh floor, not even letting me down as we exit the stairwell and start down the corridor. I've loosened the top buttons of his collar, burying my nose in the deep scent of him as he walks me to my door.

The door where Lucky stands, bearing dinner, looking delicious in a tight sweater and jeans. They hang low enough that the V of his abs is showing.

Oh.

Apprehension grips the cage of my ribs as he turns and recognizes what he's looking at. Who.

Then ... something unexpected happens.

His gaze lifts from me to Sterling, and ... a sly grin curls into place. "What do we have here then? Playing hero again, Mac?"

Mac?

Sterling's chest rumbles with a soft laugh. "I see you haven't changed. I don't suppose you made enough for three?"

"Only one way to find out." He turns his charm on me. "It's up to the lady."

I ... a zip of electricity travels up my spine. There's a tension here I'm enjoying, even if I don't fully understand where it came from. But, boy, am I interested in finding out.

Sterling's hand shifts on my back, his thumb brushing the soft, tender spot between my shoulder blades, and my hunger grows into something feral, something with teeth.

Yes.

Slowly, I meet each of their gazes. "If you think you can satisfy me."

THE END

76

STERLING OPENS HIS MOUTH, angry, and Lucky promises, *"I'm coming back for you."*

They disappear.

I barely make it to the first floor.

The door crashes shut behind me as more shots go off, and I hold it closed with my mind.

Bang!

I jump as someone thumps against it.

The room stretches out in front of me, doors mirroring each other on each side, branching off into smaller rooms of lockboxes.

Bang!

A second body throws itself against the door.

I won't be able to hold it much longer.

I run to the end of the room, throwing myself behind the last door on the left as my grip breaks.

Bang!

I hear the door splinter.

Pasting myself to the wall, I slow my breathing as much as I'm able.

"G, find her. If she's a cop, you know what to do. If not, tie her up and put her with the others. We gotta get this stuff out of here."

Their footsteps continue to charge up the stairwell, until it grows quiet. G—whoever he is—knows how to tread silently. If I were anyone else, I'd have no way of knowing where he is.

But I've got something no one else has.

"Come out, come out, wherever you are."

His tone sends a sick shiver down my spine. This does not sound like a man willing to take me alive.

He's still in the hallway, close to the first set of rooms now.

"Too bad I'm in a hurry, princess. We could have had some fun together."

He's closer now.

I need to think quicker. I have no way of telling Lucky where I am. Even if he does risk heading back to the stairwell, he can't get into this room if he's never seen it before.

I need to get this guy to walk into a side room. I should be able to close the door behind him. I won't be able to hold it for long, but if I can get back to the stairwell ...

Maybe I'll have a shot.

The distance between us closes with every passing second. I can't stop it. Can't escape it. He's going to reach me, and when he does ...

My fingers tremble. I squeeze my hand into a tight fist.

What if I'm not fast enough? What if I freeze? All it takes is a split second. Or maybe he won't shoot to kill. Maybe he'll take my legs out or catch my spine. Put me to sleep.

Where the hell is Lucky?

There's nothing in here. I can't rip open any of the lockboxes quietly. As soon as they open, he'll know where I am. Where he can find me.

And I can't think about what happens after that.

"Oh, I'm getting close, aren't I? I can smell you."

He takes a rasping breath, and my skin crawls.

"Taste good."

I can feel him on the other side of the wall.

He's right outside.

There's nowhere to hide. Nothing between us except some drywall and the stench of his intentions.

I need to think. What would Lucky do? What would Sterling do?

Squeezing my eyes closed, I reach out in my mind for the room opposite me, imagining it as a mirror of this one. Concentrating.

Fear fogs over my thoughts, and I fight to clear it. Adrenaline is wearing off, leaving behind ice-cold panic. I reach out with my mind, feel the mirror of the floor, walls, and safes. There are too many doors. Too many pins to move. But I don't need all of them.

Come on. Just one. That's all I need.

The squeal of his shoe against the tiles claws up the back of my throat. I can almost feel the putrid heat of his breath on my skin.

He's enjoying this.

He's toying with me on purpose.

"I'm going to love taking you apart."

My hands shake. A tear begins a slow descent over my cheek, down my neck.

Why are they taking so long? I shouldn't have told him to leave. Should have jumped, reached, anything. Then I wouldn't be here.

What if I can't do this?

Pops sound as multiple boxes open, and immediately, he's firing inside the room. I risk a glance.

His back is to me, and he's inching inside. I need him to take one more step ...

He takes it.

Got you, you little shit.

I slam the door closed behind him.

Then I run.

Lucky is waiting for me when I break out into the stairwell again, and that's when I hear gunfire upstairs.

"What—"

"No time," he says, swallowing me in a hug, and I feel a familiar tug in my gut.

Sterling is mid-yell when we blink into Lucky's apartment. "… meant to be protecting her. Anything could have—Mia, fuck, are you okay?"

Am I? I don't think my knees are working. They're liquid beneath me, folding as I slide down to the floor. My heart is racing.

"You're late," I whisper.

The floor is shaking. No, that can't be right. It must be me. It's hard to tell. There's nothing to focus on, nothing but a blank void of space in my mind, a white expanse with nothing to cling to.

Pressure closes in on me, enveloping me in heat and the familiar scent of Lucky's shampoo, Sterling's aftershave. Oh, that's nice. I let them gather me up off of the floor and sink into the solid feel of someone's chest as my eyes close.

"We shouldn't have left her."

Sterling.

We sink down. The couch? I don't care. It's nice here, in the heat of his arms. Safe. Still. I hear his heartbeat. It's strong, like him.

There's a distant echo of movement, a cupboard, the tap.

"I know. I thought I was fast enough, thought I could get you out of there and get back to her, but she wasn't there, and I—"

"I know. Fuck, her heart is beating really fast. I think she's having an adrenaline crash."

Am I? All I can feel is warm and safe. Then the cool press of a glass in my hand. Oh, water. I blink open my eyes as I take it from Lucky and feel his fear like a physical thing in the air between us.

"It's okay," I say—because it is now.

I'm here, and he's here, and Sterling is here, and we're all okay.

"It's over now."

"Yes, it's over," Sterling assures me.

Oh good. I'm glad.

"Come on," Lucky says, slipping the glass out of my grip and —oh, it's because I drank all of it. "Let's lay you down."

Awareness seeps back in slowly as I rise from Sterling's lap and let them both lead me to Lucky's bedroom. Sterling becomes a hazy blur at my feet while he helps slip my shoes and socks off. The lighting shifts, disappears, enveloping the room in darkness. Ah. Lucky closed the curtains.

My senses return as I lie down.

The woodsy smell of his cologne, the comforting softness of his stark white sheets. Even the way he and Sterling bicker in whispers to each other as they tuck me in makes me smile.

I find my voice just as they turn to leave. "You'd better not be leaving me."

It's a little cruel perhaps to use this against them. Too soon definitely, from the way they both whip their gazes to me, apologies writ large on their faces, but maybe I've earned a little selfishness. We might all be safe, but they're standing too damn far away from me, and right now, I'll use anything and everything I can to correct that.

I hold my hand out. "We don't have to do anything; I just want to be close to you."

I close the door softly behind them.

Lucky recovers first, smiling softly as he teleports beside me. I'm impressed; appearing under the covers is a nice touch, and I don't need to read his mind to know the kiss is coming.

It's soft, gentle in a way that betrays his concern, and I don't push, instead replying to every slow press of his lips with my own, letting the easy rhythm of it soothe my still-racing heart.

There's a dip in the mattress on my other side, then tingles roll down my spine as Sterling kisses the curve of my neck.

I turn my head and catch his mouth.

Make Your Choice:

don't leave me hanging; it was just getting good* (**turn to page 412**)

I'd rather read the epilogue (**turn to page 421**)

77

What am I doing?

Pa would be horrified to know this is what I'm using his advice for. Have I really lost enough hope that I'd sabotage someone else's property and risk a fine—or worse?

Closing the cabinet, I stand up, almost too afraid to meet my own gaze in the mirror. This is what it's come to, huh?

Lucky is leaning on the wall in the hallway when I exit. "Pretty sure you're not meant to use the facilities at these things," he jokes, but his eyes are scanning me worriedly.

It's sweet that he's concerned about me. It makes me feel about ten percent worse than I do.

"Water pressure is important to me," I say.

With his forearm perched on the doorframe, he leans past me to take a look inside, reigniting my shame. "That's something we have in common."

He's not even going to say he was right, is he?

Eager to leave, I'm almost at the door when I see a familiar face, his dark hair standing out easily above the crowd—literally a head above—and if I didn't think Fate was laughing before, well, bumping into my most decorated coworker after being unceremoniously fired would do it.

Sterling stops and stares.

What's really interesting though is that he isn't looking at me. No, he's staring straight at Lachlan as he walks over.

"Mac?" Lachlan asks, and they must really go back if he feels comfortable calling Sterling that.

"Can we talk?"

Lucky's expression is strained. It pinches under my skin, the sight of it, ill-fitting and unfair. He's hurt, and I need to do something about it. Find who did it. Make them apologize.

Reach out and make the pain go away.

"Now's not a good time."

"Okay. Look, uh ..." And Sterling does something I've never seen him do—he pauses.

This is not a man who is without words. They're his livelihood. But right here, right now, Lachlan—and whatever history they have—has taken them.

"I wanted to—" He cuts himself off, no longer looking at Lucky, but at me. There's a flicker of surprise and ... something else I don't catch before it's gone.

Lachlan shoves a hand in his pocket, drops eye contact. "Mia and I were just on our way."

"Lucky ..." Sterling takes a step forward, reaching for him but pulling back before they touch.

Oh. Oh. Well, that would explain why none of the girls at work have ever been able to score a date with him. Except Lachlan has done nothing but flirt with me all morning, so maybe this isn't as cut and dry as I think.

"Don't worry about me," I say because it's clear there's something here they need to talk about and it won't happen if I'm around. "I promise not to start any fires."

For all his earlier joking, Lachlan can be intense when he wants to be. As we stand together in the cramped hallway, his eyes locked on mine, I have the urge to cover up somehow, like he's seeing everything I'm feeling lit up in neon.

"No, I think I will worry. So sorry, love, but you're going to have to come with me." He looks at Sterling. "You too, it seems."

This will be interesting.

Lucky is sprawled in the center of his sofa, arms and knees wide, looking like lord of the manor. "Aww, Mac's gone shy."

Sterling, who is brooding by the window, huffs out a breath like this isn't a new accusation and he's going to humor Lucky, which is not something I thought he was capable of.

But he's a man who calculates his exits, and right now, he's standing as far from the door as possible. He wants to be here. He just doesn't really like it.

"Maybe I don't always have to fill every silence."

"No?" Lucky asks, a smile pulling at his mouth. "Is there anything you do want to fill?"

"Stop," Sterling commands, but it's marbled with fondness.

Lucky's apartment is an extension of the man himself—aesthetically pleasing, surprisingly warm, and brimming with curiosity. There are more records than I can count, separated by genre tabs with labels like *Eardrum Destroyers* and *Warning: Will induce imposter syndrome.* The kitchen looks professional, full of cast iron and stainless steel that Ma would drool over.

It resembles a showroom, but there are small touches—a dish towel by the sink, a couple of spice jars left by the stove—that prove it's a hub of contentment.

Not that there's much of it in the air right now. Lucky is putting on a good show—I'll give him that—but he can't go five seconds without glancing at the line of Sterling's back.

I take a seat in the armchair across from him. "What happened between you two?" I direct the question at Lucky—because of the two of them, he's more likely to spill the goods.

"Oh, just your classic tale of a daft kid getting a crush on the strong and silent guy from across the pond, becoming best mates with him, and accepting that's all they'd ever be, only for this guy to crush his heart and run off forever."

"Jesus, Lachlan, could you be more dramatic?"

Lucky leans back, crossing his arms over his chest with a pained smile. "How would you tell it then? You kissed me, if you've forgotten."

"I remember every second."

The smile drops off Lucky's face. The only sound is the ticking of the clock on the wall.

"Everything but my number then," he finally says.

"What do you want me to say? I fucked up—I know that. It won't change anything."

"Sorry is a good start, if you give a shit."

Sterling finally decides to join us, and I can see how much it means to Lucky for him to be the one to bridge the divide. "Of course I'm sorry. I haven't stopped being sorry since I left. I know what I gave up. Why do you think it's taken so long for me to come here?"

Lucky scoffs. "What happened to you? I know you've always been a surly bastard, but now you're downright sour."

"Why shouldn't I be angry? It used to be that reporting on criminal actions put a stop to them. Now, it's an advertisement for them. The world is in the equivalent of a ten-car pileup, and I might as well be standing on the sidelines, selling tickets."

He pushes forcefully off his knees. "If I point out someone's misdeeds, I'm labeled a hater. Call out injustice, I'm performing outrage ... I don't remember the devil having so many defenders. Live and let live used to stand for peace and acceptance; now it's the slogan of people who never want to be criticized." His chest heaves. "Of course I'm sour."

Sterling leans forward, elbows resting on his knees. It stretches his button-up across his shoulders and biceps, the material taut. "I've missed you."

Lucky scoffs. "Couldn't have missed me that much."

"You're the one who told me to go fuck myself, remember? I've tried to forget you, but I couldn't. I've dialed your number, but never called. I thought you'd moved on, that I would be dragging you back to something you didn't want, and then it was one work assignment after another. I was always away, and I never knew when I'd be back. I didn't want to do that to you."

"You gave up so easily. You didn't even fight."

The pain they're holding pills over and clouds up the space between them, fills the room like smoke, thick and acrid.

"You were better off without me."

Lucky curses. "You've always been such a shitty liar."

"Only to you." Sterling lets out a breath, smoothing his hands over his pants.

"Was it worth it?"

Sterling opens his mouth, hesitating. He never hesitates. "That case made my career."

"That's not what I'm talking about."

"I'm proud of what I've done, and it's been hard. I've almost lost my job multiple times. I've brought down bad people, helped class action suits, found secrets people thought were buried or burned. I've done good in a world where that feels increasingly impossible."

"I know. I'm proud of you." Lucky's voice is soft. "Was it worth it?"

Sterling's gaze whips up to meet mine, causing a tremor to run through me. "Don't ask me that. I—I can't ..."

I should leave. I'm only an interloper, and I'm clearly getting in the way of them being honest with each other.

Lucky follows the trail, finds me, nods to himself.

I don't know what it means.

He slaps his knees, walking to the kitchen. "Drink? I'm assuming you still drink that fancy shit?"

"Whatever you have works."

He brings back a bottle of beer for each of us, but my stomach is in knots so I wave it off. Lucky shrugs and puts the extra bottle on the coffee table, handing the other to Sterling, who takes it and looks at the bottle for a long time before drinking. His eyes fall closed on the first sip.

"You've done well for yourself," he says, waving a hand around the room. There are records on the wall, a Grammy on a shelf, alongside a few smaller awards. "Not that it was in any doubt."

Lucky chuckles, something tight releasing in his chest. This will be okay—maybe. "Pretty sure Chuck would have a few words against that."

"How is he?"

Lucky shrugs. "Good, last I heard. He's somewhere in Ohio now—wife, kids, cats, the whole thing. It took a long time for him to come round after I left the band, but even though we're cool now, we don't talk much. Best I get out of him is a Christmas card."

Sterling smiles around his next sip. "Things were easier then."

"Things were harder too."

"You can't still be pissed about the party."

"Fuck off. I can. The one time I convince you to come to a party, and he ruins it. Expected you to scuttle off back to your shadows, but when I came inside, there you were, talking up Maisey by the kitchen."

Sterling loosens the top two buttons on his shirt. "We were partnered on an assignment. I was asking her if she needed help, not flirting."

"I know." Lucky smirks. "Everyone knew she had a crush on

you, except you. She was pissed that she gave you all her best moves, and all you wanted to talk about was research methods."

Sterling lowers his beer. "She put our work at risk over a flight of fancy. I wasn't going to encourage her when the feelings were one-sided."

Lucky gapes before laughing. "I forgot how much of an arrogant prick you were back then."

"I don't think caring about my education is a bad thing."

"Here we go. Like I didn't hear enough of this when we were in school. I bet nothing's changed, has it? Still working till you burn out, then working some more. No parties, no dating, no fun."

"I have fun."

"Oh, yeah?"

"I know how to."

This time, Lucky's whole body loosens up with laughter. He stands, taking Sterling's empty bottle, and comes back with two more, throwing himself back on the couch with a sigh. There's a little ghost of a smile on Sterling's lips, smug for making a joke, pride in Lucky appreciating it.

"Gotta be honest, it's weird, seeing you sitting here," Lucky admits. "Ever since I moved here, I've been bumping up against your ghost wherever I go. Sitting at bus stops, walking down the street, staring at me from across the bar. Started to worry I wouldn't recognize the real you anymore."

"I could lose every memory I've ever made and still know you."

My heart is pounding at the obvious pain they still feel, and it's time I got out of here. I'm almost at the door when I hear Lucky call my name.

"Stay. Let me cook for you. As a thank-you."

I shouldn't. They've just made up, and I'm ... more invested in either of them than I should be. They need a friend, and I could be that ... one day, after I figure out how to handle my feelings for them.

But before I can say no, Sterling is there, holding my hand, and all thoughts of leaving burn to ash from the intensity in his gaze. "I'd like you to stay. We both would."

Breathless, all I can do is nod.

Make Your Choice:

it's getting hot in here* (**turn to page 400**)
I'd like to skip to the end (**turn to page 446**)

78

"Actually, I'm going to go." I don't wait for them, quickly turning on my heel and catapulting myself out of the club, where the cold midnight air can cool my nerves.

It's for the best if they work things out alone. I'll just be in the way.

Am I disappointed? Sure. My lips tingle with the echo of Lucky's kiss, and I really wanted to follow that mouth and see where it led, but I also know how much Sterling means to him, and they deserve a shot at getting their shit together.

My crush on both of them will pass in time. Maybe.

By the time I get home, dinner is on its way, and I have just enough time to scrub the club out of my pores before it arrives. I hate washing off Lucky's touch, and before I can overthink it, I trail my fingers over every place I remember his hands being—and some he never got to—until I'm wet in more ways than one.

What would have happened if I'd stayed?

Knocking interrupts me. Shit. Must be the delivery guy.

It's a race to get the water off and a towel around me. Last time I made them wait, my food magically disappeared, and no amount of complaining made it or my money reappear.

Not this time.

I swing the door open, halfway through humming the chorus of one of Lucky's songs.

It's not the delivery guy.

"Fuck me," Lucky says, staring openly.

A similar, albeit whispered, curse escapes Sterling, and I grip the towel tighter, lust roaring in my ears. I didn't think this through.

On the plus side, they have my burger.

"Get inside," I hiss, retreating to my bedroom and throwing on the first thing I can find, which is an oversize sweatshirt and bike shorts.

"Cute outfit," Lucky says. "Think I prefer the last one though."

"Gimme that. I'm starving." He hands me the bag, and I tear into my burger. "Why are you here anyway?"

"You ran off," Lucky says, stealing a fry.

I glare at him until he backs off. "I was giving you time to talk."

"We talked on the way here."

I take another bite and nearly moan. If I'm going to end the night having to hear the two guys I like politely reject me, I'm going to do it with salt and extra cheese. "And?"

"And," Sterling says, leaning his elbows on his knees, "we agreed we needed to speak with you."

"Okay. So, talk."

They share a look, maybe debating who goes first—I'm not sure. It doesn't matter who delivers the apology. I just need them to get on with it so I can finish my food and lie down.

"I'd rather show you." Lucky pulls the box away from me.

"Hey."

"I'll buy you another one."

He'd better.

There's a light tug on my hand, pulling me up.

"Now, before we were rudely interrupted," he says, slipping his hands to my waist, "I think we were right about ... here."

His hips meet mine in a vivid re-creation of earlier, and even though I can't hear any music, it's all too easy to fall into the rhythm, bringing my arms around his neck and swaying into him.

There's a rustle of clothing behind me, steps coming closer until there's heat and pressure along my back—Sterling—and, oh God, I'm never recovering from this.

We move slow, still unsure of how we fit together, but working it out quickly, the press and grind of bodies enough for now. Their hands are everywhere—on me, on each other—and it feels so good that I lay my head back on Sterling's shoulder and close my eyes.

They don't kiss me, not yet, teasing me instead by dragging their mouths over my neck, my shoulders, then ghosting by my ear. They're relaxed. Whatever they needed to get out of their system is gone, the tension boiled down to something filthier.

"You look like you need to be kissed," Sterling says, slipping his thumb under my jaw.

"I do," I breathe. "But I can't decide."

Sparks follow Lucky's fingertips as he trails them across my lips. "Then don't. Have us both."

Okay.

So, I do.

You made the right choice.

go on. have a little more. (**turn to page 446**)

79

I shake my head. "It's fine. I can get home okay. Nothing's going to happen to me."

Let's hope. This has been enough adventure for one day.

But today isn't over yet.

Sterling helps me stand, hovering like he wants to take over or —dear God—carry me. I'd probably faint a second time if he tried, but I definitely wouldn't stop him.

"It won't because you're going to get in this car and let me drive you home."

Blood rushes to my cheeks so fast that I can't hide it, and it doesn't help that he's standing so close. The deep edge of his voice stirs up a burning heat between my thighs, and I hope to hell he's doing it on purpose because I'm about two seconds away from throwing myself at him.

Warm breath gusts over my ear. "That wasn't a request."

Oh fuck.

I slip into his passenger seat and let him fuss over the temperature. Let's hope he drives fast.

Make Your Choice:

take me home* (**turn to page 424**)

go straight to the epilogue (**turn to page 441**)

80

"I THINK you should kiss and make up," I say.

Lucky's smile etches itself under my skin. He looks over at Sterling, whose expression I can't see. Lucky sits beside him, not letting me step away, keeping me there. They're touching each other but looking at me.

"How do you want me to kiss him?"

I look to Sterling for ... permission? Approval? And he licks his lips. Flames lick up my spine.

Oh.

"Get in his lap. You should ... use your tongue."

The sight of Lucky following, listening to me, and moving into position makes my pulse race. I could get used to this. Even hotter is the way Sterling's hands immediately come up to meet him, sliding from knee to hips to waist, gripping the tight muscle underneath Lucky's shirt. My knees go weak beneath me.

I fill the empty space Lucky has left, glad for the new perspective and the stability. I've liquefied to nothing but a single point of focus, and they soak it up, putting on a show for me. Lucky doesn't waste time diving into Sterling's mouth, each exhale released like a moan. Sterling is no better, becoming a man possessed as soon as Lucky's lips meet his.

"Rougher."

They claw at each other, breathing loud in the silence, and my heart is racing.

I startle when I feel Sterling's hand on my thigh.

They pull out of the kiss and pin me with their gaze.

Lucky reaches for me, and I fall into him.

His kisses are warm and comforting. He ducks to meet me, easing the strain on my neck, and I slide my hands under his shirt, stripping it off of him.

Goddamn. How dare he hide this body from the world! It's a crime. One I plan on reporting just as soon as I investigate it—thoroughly and with both hands. Mouth too.

When Lucky drags his lips down my neck, I search for Sterling. He has all the power of a king observing his court, watching us with dark eyes and an intent so pointed that I feel myself getting wetter.

"Lucky, on your knees. I want to show Mia just how talented that mouth is."

Lucky drops to the ground and licks his lips. "Gladly."

I shudder as pleasure ripples through me. He looks incredible.

"Come here," Sterling commands me, smoothing one hand down his thigh.

The apartment has become a pocket dimension. Safe from the outside world. Nothing matters except us three.

Sterling turns me around, pulling my back against his chest. Strong fingers slide through my hair, and I gasp as he grips and draws my head back, sucking a bruise on to my throat. *Fuck*. I would happily die like this. Sterling brings his other hand between my thighs to grind his palm against my aching pussy, dragging a moan from me.

Lucky slides his hands under my skirt. My thighs clench in anticipation.

"Feels so fucking good, Mia." He nips at my ear as I whine. "Shh, we're going to make you feel good."

His cock is hard, and I roll my hips. My skin is on fire, and he's barely touching me.

Sterling drags his nose along my jaw, moving his hand out of the way when Lucky reaches under my dress and pulls my underwear off. It's a slow, torturous drag along my skin, his eyes shining like he can tell what it's doing to me.

"Have you thought about it?" Sterling asks. "Looked at that sinful mouth and thought about it sucking on your clit?" His words stoke the fire within me. "Hmm? Did you touch yourself and imagine it was his tongue tasting you?"

"Hold her up," Lachlan says, and Sterling hooks his hands under my knees and pulls, until I'm curled into myself, opened wide to Lucky's hungry gaze.

He grabs my ass with both hands, thumbs dipping into my pussy, spreading the wetness. I moan and try to push closer to his mouth, but Sterling's grip keeps me in place.

"Fucking hell," Lucky says, kissing my thighs. "Look at you. I could feast on you for weeks."

"Then do it," I gasp. I need his mouth on me. Anything.

Lucky leans in, licking a long stripe along my pussy. He slides his hands down my legs, under, fitting in between Sterling and me, massaging his cock as he sucks my clit between his lips.

Oh my God, *yes.*

Sterling grunts, his grip tightening. It stretches me wider. "Fuck. I didn't tell you to do that."

The points of Lucky's teeth shine as he smiles. "Should I stop?"

"No. Take it out."

Lachlan does one better, dragging Sterling's pants off. The searing heat of his cock is sliding between my cheeks. We both groan.

Lucky drags his fingers down my pussy until he reaches Sterling's bare skin, following the trail with his mouth. Sterling groans, low and deep, as soon as Lucky's tongue reaches his cock.

"Fuck, Lachlan, your mouth," he moans in my ear, and an answering moan comes from below us.

Lucky sits back on his feet, pleased as anything. He continues to pump Sterling, his fingers brushing my skin.

I twist in Sterling's lap to kiss him. He bucks under me, groans into my mouth. I need him inside of me—*now.* We break apart, and I surge forward, falling into Lucky's lap and sending him onto the floor. He catches me, and I kiss my way down his chest, scrambling to get his jeans open.

"Easy, love."

"No," I say, pulling at his waistband until his cock—thick, red, glistening—is freed. "I will not go easy. Now, be good and let me suck your cock."

Without waiting for an answer, I drop my head and take him as deep as I can.

"Fuck." Lucky drags the word out, deep and low. His head drops back with a thud.

If I could, I'd smile. Instead, I lift up and swirl my tongue around the head, letting saliva drip from my lips, coating his cock all the way to his balls.

"Yeah," he grunts. "That's it. Fuck, you're good. Keep going."

Someone threads their fingers in my hair, pulling it away from my face, gripping it tight. "Don't you dare stop, Mia."

And, oh fuck, it's Sterling. I moan loudly, mouth full, taking Lucky so deep in my throat that the muscles start to convulse around him.

"Ah fuck, Mia, I'm going to come."

Good. I want to take it all.

Except Sterling's fist pulls me up, lifting me off Lucky's cock, which twitches and bobs in front of my face. He's soaked.

"Goddamn, Mac, you're cruel."

Sterling's low chuckle only makes me wetter. "Don't worry;

I'll let her get back to it soon. But I need to fuck this pretty pussy before it starts to feel neglected."

He's already pressing two long fingers into me. I arch my back, my neck pulled back by his grip in my hair.

Bare skin hits mine—he's ditched his shirt—and he catches my earlobe between his teeth, adding a third finger and thrusting them faster. "You looked incredible, Mia, these beautiful lips stretched all the way around his cock. So hungry for it, aren't you?"

I moan, pushing back on his fingers.

"You are. Fuck. You couldn't wait to get him in your mouth. Are you going to swallow all of his cum while I fuck you?"

"Yes."

I whine when he pulls out his fingers and rubs his cock across my pussy. I need him to stop teasing me and fuck me already.

"On your knees, Lucky. We're going to give our girl what she needs."

Fuck.

Lucky sits up and moves to his knees in front of me so I'm on all fours between them. Sterling releases my hair to wrap his big fucking hands around my hips, and I love the feeling of his fingers digging into the soft parts of my waist, holding me in place as he enters me in one hard thrust.

This is it. I've found nirvana. Call off the search.

Lucky holds the base of his cock tightly, stemming the blood flow. I stick my tongue out and look up, my chest heaving, and he squeezes himself tighter. Oh, he's not going to last long at all.

He curses and feeds me his cock. Each time Sterling fucks into me, it pushes Lucky deeper down my throat. All I can do is breathe and take it, my moans lost around Lucky's dick.

It's so good. I'm full, everywhere, sweat pooling along my spine.

"I'm close," Lucky says, and I start to swallow around him, making him groan. "Ah fuck, Mac, kiss me."

They shift above me. I want to look up, see the pitch-black of Lucky's eyes as they darken, but it's impossible at this angle. Instead, I feel how his cock pulses, filling my mouth as he comes. I swallow it all.

My own orgasm hits me out of fucking nowhere, rocketing through me, my pussy clenching hard around Sterling, who growls so deep that I can feel the vibrations in my bones.

His hips stutter, and then he slams in hard once, twice more as he comes.

I collapse to the floor the second they both pull out. They drop down beside me, sweat-slick and panting.

"Once my brain stops leaking out of my ears, we're going for another round," Lucky rasps.

I have just enough strength to throw my leg over his, kiss the closest part of him to me—his biceps. "I like the sound of that."

Sterling trails his fingers along my back, kisses my spine. "Good, because we're not nearly done with you yet."

I've always wanted to visit Paris.

no! it's over? okay, I'll go to the epilogue (**turn to page 446**)

81

The nurses were very strict. *No vigorous activities.* I can already tell holding him to that will be difficult. It's a good thing that I've gotten very good at controlling things recently.

I take my time crawling onto the bed, enjoying the slow, satisfied smile that spreads onto Sterling's face. He reaches for me with both hands, but it pulls on his stitches, stretching the skin and muscle across his gorgeous chest as he lifts his hands.

I stop, rising onto my knees. "Uh-uh, you're meant to be resting your shoulder."

His hand hovers midair before continuing its journey. So goddamn stubborn. He traces a gentle line over my thigh, sending sparks along my skin. Sexy and stubborn. Fine. If he can't play by the rules, I'll have to help him out.

I've had time to practice, during our vigil in the hospital, focusing my concentration, seeing how often I could loosen the laces of Lucky's sneakers before he noticed. Undo the clasp of his chain. Keep his elbow from slipping off the arm of his chair when he inevitably fell asleep.

I don't even have to look away from Sterling's gaze as I do it, pressing his hands to the mattress at his sides with my mind, getting a front-row seat as hunger darkens the deep blue.

"That's better," I whisper, leaning up to kiss him.

It's one thing to see him in this bed, petulant and bored after days of rest, and another to feel him alive under me, mouth eager and seeking, the reassuring gusts of breath that prove he's here, he's real. He made it.

The moment in the stairwell is burned behind my eyes, stained on my memory like an afterimage. Sterling, slumped on the floor, blood—so much blood—his body as limp as a rag doll while I was frozen in horror at what I'd done.

I was so close to losing him forever.

He must know this. Even without the use of his hands, he's reassuring, pressing up into me, seeking with lips and teeth and tongue. The heat of his mouth is addictive, and I lose myself to it, to him, painting over the memory in broad, hard strokes.

Lucky comes up behind me, skirting his hands up my sides and back. I moan into Sterling's mouth, reminded of my goal. Sterling tries to chase me as I pull back, but my hold is firm, and I slide off his lap as Lachlan takes my place. He's gloriously naked, crawling up the bed while pushing Sterling's shirt up to his armpits, kissing and biting his way along the exposed skin.

"Fuck." The soft curse is paired with Sterling clenching the sheet in his fingers, the only movement I'm allowing.

"I like you like this," Lucky says, playfully biting Sterling's hip.

I trace Sterling's lips, slipping two fingers into the waiting heat of his mouth.

Lucky groans and, in a swift move, pulls Sterling's pants off, leaving his bottom half naked, his cock hardening against his thigh.

Sterling twists his head toward me, swirling his tongue over and around my fingers.

"He wants your mouth," I tell Lucky, reading Sterling's thoughts.

"He does, does he?"

Sterling groans around my fingers, a slew of obscene images flowing from his mind to mine. Fuck, that's hot.

Lucky kisses the base of Sterling's cock, which twitches in interest, no doubt trying to get closer to where it wants to be, but Lucky pulls back in favor of rolling a condom down Sterling's hard length.

"I've got a much better idea."

I pull my fingers free of Sterling's mouth while he tries to buck up into Lucky's hand. Stripping what's left of my clothes, I use my soaked fingers to circle my clit. Sterling's head turns, and he can't seem to decide where to hold his attention. That's okay; we can solve that for him.

"Don't worry; we're going to take care of you."

I circle my clit while Lucky reaches behind himself, sinking what has to be more than a single finger in by the way he moans and throws his head back. The tendons in his neck stretch, and the sound of him pumping his fingers in and out of his ass is only making me wetter.

"Fuck," Sterling says again, and I sense the strain against my hold of his chest and arms. It's not enough to break free, not even close, and it's obvious how much he likes that.

Christ, I can't wait to find new ways to use this power in the future. Putting a plug in Lucky before a show and manipulating it while he's onstage, edging Sterling under the table hands-free ... so many possibilities.

Sooner than expected, Lucky decides he's ready, pulling his fingers back to coat everything in more lube before slowly lowering himself onto Sterling's cock.

"Fuck, you feel good."

"You too."

I can't wait any longer; the sight of Sterling filling Lucky up leaves me empty, and I buck against my palm as I finger myself.

"Fuck, Mia, you smell incredible."

"Let me taste you," Sterling growls as Lucky starts to ride him.

"Please."

His wish is my command. Carefully, I straddle his face, intending to take this slow, but Sterling has no such plan and uses what little leverage he has to immediately lick from my pussy to my clit.

"Ahh." I fold forward, catching myself on his waist. "Yes, that's it. Right there."

Lucky starts fucking himself harder, grabbing me by the neck and pulling me into a deep, filthy kiss, tasting each sound Sterling pulls out of me while he swirls and spears his tongue into my pussy.

"I want to devour you."

I can see Sterling's hips start to flex and rise, and without planning it, I expand my reach, pushing back against them until his body is prone against the covers. All he has left are his mouth, fingers, and toes, and they spasm as he moans loudly and sucks on my clit.

"Do you know how many times I've thought about you like this? Every time I caught you staring at me, I wanted to fall to my knees and worship this perfect pussy. You'd get up to leave, and I wanted to walk you out, but I couldn't because I was too fucking hard under my desk. I'd get home and fuck my fist, imagining what you'd taste like."

Oh my God.

My nails dig into his skin as I come, bucking and writhing against his mouth.

He keeps going, talking and licking and sucking, and doesn't stop.

"Sterling—ah, yes, fuck. More."

Lucky grunts. "Fuck, Mac, she's loving it."

"That's it, baby. Ride my face. Give me everything. I'm going to

make you come again. Come as many times as you need because you're mine now. You both are, and I'm always going to make sure this pussy gets everything it deserves."

Sterling is usually quiet, but his head is a riot of noise right now, and it hits me that I've been given an all-access pass to a man who prides himself on his own control. Control he's giving over to us now. Fuck. Adrenaline rushes through me as my thighs flex and tremble. Sterling moans and licks deeper.

Oh fuck. Yes, yes, yes.

"He's close," I pant.

Lucky fucks himself harder on Sterling's cock.

We work in unison, the lines blurred between the three of us, the thread pulling tighter. There is no separating the ties that bind us. We are all, or we are none. What matters to them, what brings them joy or pain or pleasure, comes to me as well.

In this, we seal our commitment.

My second orgasm hits me lightning fast, before I'm ready for it, throwing me off the cliff so hard that my whole body trembles. Sterling doesn't stop, keeps licking and sucking and tasting every part of it, until I'm sensitive and whimpering.

It sets off a chain—Sterling grunting low and deep, his knuckles turning white as they grip the sheets as he comes, and then Lucky is gone, pulsing and throbbing as his release shoots onto Sterling's stomach.

The last vestiges of my energy drain out of me as I slide off Sterling to melt into the bed. I'm no longer holding him down, but he doesn't seem inclined to move as Lucky makes his way to the bathroom and returns to clean up. He curls into Sterling's other side when he's done, and the room is silent, save for our heavy breaths.

Even Sterling's mind, so usually full of thoughts and ideas and plans, is quiet.

"There's only one more thing I want," he pants.

I lift my head. "Oh?"

"An exclusive."

Well. I … might need to cool off. You go on. I'll catch up.

Okay, take me to the epilogue now (**turn to page 421**)

82

THEY'RE TRYING to keep it slow, just kissing, petting, breathing, but my senses are back with a vengeance now, and I don't want slow. Don't want gentle.

I missed them as soon as they left the room, felt twin pieces of me rip out from under my ribs after they disappeared. Felt that void every second that I was alone, waiting for them to return, waiting for it to be over, for good or for bad. I don't want to feel the emptiness now; I want to be surrounded by them.

I don't use my gift, using my hands instead, touching every way I can. I can't bear to stop, can't stand the thought that they won't be here if I let go.

They indulge me, pulling off their clothes and mine, closing the space between us, even when it slows us down. I don't stop though. I won't. I can't.

I catch my breath as Lucky and Sterling kiss, sighing in the proximity of their desire. Its roots are thick and strong with age, but they light up like a fresh bloom. It soothes something in me, and I'm grateful they found each other again. That they get to have this. I'd be happy for them even if I wasn't here.

It hits me, now that the residue of today is slipping away, that I'm fully dressed, and I shimmy out of my shirt and pants, glad to be free of them. A shower would probably be better, but that would mean leaving this bed, and there's no way that's happening.

The tangle of sheets and clothes and limbs is rapidly getting in the way, so Sterling rips the sheets back and tosses my stuff to the floor, following it quickly with Lachlan's shirt. He meets Lucky's mouth again, and I take advantage of the newly bared skin to kiss down his chest, swirling my tongue around his nipple and taking a bite of the firm muscle underneath.

Lucky slips his hand into my hair and hauls me up into a kiss. His other hand drops to my waist and pulls, shifting me to straddle him, rocking me against his hardening cock.

A second set of hands skates from my shoulders, down my arms, undoing and removing my bra. The bare heat of Sterling's chest hits my back as I arch into him and grind against Lucky, trapped in a delicious feedback loop. Sterling kneels behind me and pulls me upright, attacking my neck with his mouth while Lucky cups and massages my breasts.

"Do you want him to fuck you?" Sterling asks. He must have taken care of his pants, too, because I can feel the wet kiss of precum on my lower back.

"Yes, please fuck me."

"You heard her."

It's an inelegant scramble to shuck the last scraps of material that separate us, and Sterling, ever prepared, takes the opportunity to torture Lucky by rolling the condom on and jacking him, tight and slow, until Lachlan's entire chest is flushed red under his tattoos.

Lucky's hands skim up my thighs and grip. "Fuck, get on with it already, unless you want me to bust early."

"You'd never do that," Sterling says.

"Won't have a choice soon," Lucky grunts.

Sterling smiles as he kisses me, but he does let go, sliding his hand up my thigh. "You don't come until I say."

My head falls back against Sterling's shoulder as he slides his fingers along my pussy, circling my clit with his thumb while he teases the tip of a finger inside me. I've always loved his hands, broad and thick and strong, and they feel just as good as I imagined. I think I could come just from rubbing up against his palm like an animal in heat.

"Have you taken two at once before?"

I shake my head.

"You'll like it," he says, kissing my jaw. "Now, you're going to fuck yourself on Lucky's cock while I get you ready, okay? Show me that you can take what you need." Then he sucks his finger into his mouth and groans. "Fuck. You taste good, but I want to see how good you can be."

He lets go to get lube and another condom, and I flush white hot at the thought of what they want to do.

"Yes," I answer, pulling away from Sterling to sink down onto Lucky's waiting cock.

We moan in unison.

Lucky wraps his arms around me, distracting me with long, deep kisses while he rocks into me. It's not enough to get off, and he knows it, letting me writhe against him, my body begging for more. I don't have to wait long.

Sterling circles a wet finger between my cheeks, teasing my hole. "Next time, I'm going to open you up with my tongue," he says, and, yes, I want that, need this time and next time and all the times, if they're anything close to as good as this.

I clench around Lucky when Sterling pushes in, and, fuck, it's good, it's perfect, it's not enough. I need more. I need him filling me.

He's efficient, but he doesn't rush, fucking my ass with his fingers and pulling sounds out of Lucky and me every time he curls his fingers inside of me until Lachlan can feel it.

He pulls his fingers free and lines himself up, entering me in a slow, delicious push.

Oh fuck, oh fuck, oh fuck.

There's sweat pooling between my breasts, on my brow, down my spine, and Lucky's hair is damp with it. His fingers are gripped tight in mine as Sterling fills me completely. It's ... like nothing I've ever felt. The two of them, hot and hard and throbbing inside of me. My blood is on fire, lightning in my veins as every nerve ending jolts and sparkles to life.

"Please," I choke out.

I don't know what I'm asking for. I don't care. They'll figure it out—Sterling probably, and I know he'll take care of me.

He does, brushing my damp hair over my shoulder and blowing a cool breeze over my skin. Lucky's gone still underneath me, panting hard. He's as close to coming as I am.

"Feels so fucking good," he grunts. "I can feel you—shit. Fuck, you gotta move."

I lose track of everything when Sterling starts to move, pleasure whiting out reality. I feel him—at my back, in my mind, inside of me—and I feel Lucky, but everything else is an electric storm of sensation. A bite mark on my shoulder, sweat under my breasts, hands ... everywhere.

I scream when I come, and it must set Lucky off because his thrusts stutter and start while he moans deep into our kiss. He has one hand wrapped around my neck, and he doesn't stop kissing me as Sterling continues to thrust.

He groans into my shoulder as he comes, bracing himself on the mattress with one arm, and he falls against my back. My thighs ache with the stretch now, and I know I'll be feeling it for days. Good. If I could, I'd find a way to etch this moment into my skin—the togetherness, where bodies blur and I feel their heartbeats as surely as my own.

Sterling manages the cleanup, and I have every intention of showering, just as soon as I can move my legs again. Or I could nap. A nap sounds good. Just a small one, and then I'll get up. I need to eat too.

Maybe I can convince Lucky to cook something for us.

"Mia?"

The mattress dips, and Sterling climbs under the covers, his body a hot line at my side. He guides me onto his chest. "You did so well."

I sigh as he kisses my forehead.

"How do you feel?"

"Good." I'm a puddle of good. An ocean. Endlessly buoyant.

"I'm glad. You scared me before"—there's a soft grunt behind me—"both of us. Never again. I'm not going to lose you, all right? Either of you." He pulls Lucky closer, each of them a parenthesis around me. "You matter too much to me. I'm not letting you go."

"We love you too," Lucky says.

I swim through the fog of exhaustion to blink up at Sterling, sliding a free hand into his hair, making sure he's looking at me when I say, "He's right, and we're not letting you go either."

I fall asleep to the vision of him smiling down at me.

Ready for the end yet?

not even a little (**turn to page 421**)

83

SIX MONTHS LATER

"YES, I read the audit reports you sent, and you're sure they're accurate?" I crush the phone between my ear and shoulder as I type.

"Absolutely sure. There's no story here, Miss Finnegan."

Yeah, we'll see about that.

"Okay, thank you for your time. If I think of any other questions, I'll be in touch."

There is a heavy sigh on the other end that I mirror after I hang up.

"No luck with the bank?" Sterling pushes backward from his desk, rolling over to take a look at the reports on my screen.

"They're adamant that there hasn't been an external breach of their system. No customer data has been compromised." I repeat the stock response I've been getting since I started looking into the story. "And the reports back it up."

"Who ran the audits?" he asks, not taking his eyes off the screen.

I've grown used to his uncanny ability to maintain a conversation while researching. It's what makes him so good at his job.

"The bank ran their own internal investigation when the initial complaints came in, then hired two objective third parties to complete independent audits after the first lawsuits were filed. All got the same result—their system is secure."

"How many lawsuits are there now?"

I return to my notes. "Twenty and counting, with over four hundred complaints. They're looking at a class action now."

The whole thing is nagging at me. I can't put my finger on it. The data isn't lying, but it doesn't explain how hundreds of customers of the same bank have suffered identity theft in the last two months.

It's too much of a coincidence, and Sterling doesn't believe in coincidences.

When I look up, his eyes are on me, a telltale smile tucked into the corner of his mouth. Tingles shoot up my arm as he traces his fingers lightly over the back of my hand.

"What is that brilliant mind thinking?"

Right now, all I can think about is tasting that smile with my tongue, digging my fingers deep into those dark curls and likely getting us both fired.

Instead, I flip my hand over and curl my fingers around his. "I've traced the complaints back to the earliest case, and it all started right after the bank was robbed. Something happened that day—I'm sure of it."

"Want my help?"

Always. But there's satisfaction in getting the result on my own.

I shake my head. "I'm going to keep looking, put together a timeline of events from that day so I can see if there's even the slightest chance it fits."

"You'll piece the puzzle together. You usually do."

"What can I say?" I lean in. "I learned from the best."

"Don't you two ever stop? This is an office, for fuck's sake. I'd like to work without losing my lunch."

"And I'd rather the Sports column had none of your insipid,

bullshit takes," Sterling says, directing a cold stare at Andy, "but we can't all get what we want, can we?"

Andy rolls his eyes and walks away.

Sterling rolls back to his desk, but not before I catch the spark of celebration in his eyes. Sterling's quiet is soothing. His focus helps me focus.

A wolf whistle silences the entire floor. There's only one man it can belong to, and I'm grinning before Lucky steps out of the elevator.

He places a cake box in front of me.

"What's the occasion?"

"It's my birthday."

Ah, so that's what the note in Sterling's calendar is for.

"And you brought your own cake? I feel awful."

" 'S all right, love," he says, flattening the box on top of a coroner's report. It's a much better view. "You can both make it up to me later."

"Jesus ..." Sterling whispers under his breath.

"I meant presents, but if you've got something else in mind, please, share."

If left to themselves, I swear Lucky and Sterling would do nothing but stare at each other. I, however, want cake, so I steal the knife and start cutting a generous piece for myself. If they want any, they'll have to stop flirting long enough to get it.

"Oh, was I supposed to get you something?" Sterling teases, settling back in his chair with his arms crossed.

"It's tradition."

"Hmm. Thought maybe you'd want to take something instead. You do it so well."

Fuck. It might be a while.

Sterling isn't wrong though; Lucky *does* take it well. I have firsthand experience of that, and on a good day, I can go, oh, about three hours without thinking about it. Remembering it. Wanting it.

The three of us have fallen into a rhythm, smooth and easy, a lot of talking. It works.

I could never choose between them. My feelings have grown roots, deep and nourishing, seeking out both of them. There's no favorite, no second place, just us—fitting together so perfectly that I think I missed them my whole life.

Maybe I did. Maybe that's what this great, aching need inside of me always was.

Some have questions, but the people who are most important are supportive. It doesn't need to make sense to anyone else. It makes sense to us. I'm happy. *We're* happy.

THE END

84

SIX MONTHS LATER

I RINSE out the last of my conditioner. "Lucky," I call out. "Can you get me a towel?"

You know what no one ever tells you about having powers? That, sometimes, you'll forget they're there. It's only after Lucky pops into existence in the bathroom that I remember I could have moved it myself.

He's a blur through the frosted glass, a yellow square in his hand. "This one?"

"Thank you."

Lucky opens the door, and instead of passing it to me, he hooks it around my shoulders and pulls me into him, kissing and licking into my mouth as he backs me against the shower wall.

"You're getting wet," I whisper.

He starts kissing my neck, adding to the marks that he and Sterling left yesterday. "Damn right. Look at you." He presses closer, the hard line of his cock evident through his sweats.

"Lucky ..." I melt against the tiles, arching into him.

"He's right, Mia. You look good enough to eat."

Sterling leans against the doorframe, watching us, unfazed at the water spreading out on the floor.

Oh hell. I don't want to resist them.

"Get in here already. I'm cold."

The only move he makes is to raise a brow. "Make me."

Gladly.

An hour later, my hair is still drying. The other interesting part about having powers is all the parts of life they don't help you with.

Sterling stalks after Lucky as he crosses the apartment in a blink. "Obviously, I can't stop you from going," he says, "but can you please pack an extra mask this time? That kid almost caught you on camera last week."

There's also the small issue of one rather tall, rather broody mother hen.

"Hey, I don't ask these assholes to rip it off me," Lucky says, unperturbed by the handsome shadow he's gained. "If the glue held better, it wouldn't be an issue. And you hated the body paint—"

"The bathroom was stained pink for a week."

Lucky finally comes to a stop, addressing the room with a cocky grin. "I looked hot though."

He really, really did.

"That's beside the point," Sterling says.

I step between them, stuffing an extra mask in Lucky's pocket. "The new glue is arriving tomorrow; I just got a shipping update. It's what they use for movie effects; it'll hold up."

Sterling thanks me with a kiss that weakens my knees, which is how I prefer to be thanked by him. "This meeting shouldn't take too long."

"No need to rush it. We're not going anywhere."

"I know," he says, kissing me again.

I swear Lucky is rubbing off on him.

After the bank and Sterling's exclusive, living together made sense. It started as an excuse to keep each other—and our secret—safe, and then one month turned into three, which turned into six.

Sterling still has his place, which he escapes to when he gets a little too lost in a story, but he's getting better at texting back, no matter how deep in his research he is.

Lucky's busy with his phone, typing rapidly enough that I know he's in someone's comment section again.

I pluck the device from his hands, leaving it hovering in the air above his head, out of reach. "Stop power-splaining to right-wing comic fans. You know it pisses them off."

Last week, it was a whole argument about teleporting and the earth's rotation, and ... well, it's better not to know.

"But it's so easy to annoy them." Lucky grins, having too much fun.

"I'm sure." I laugh. "But I need to finish your profile for *The Herald*, so sit down and answer some questions."

He falls into the armchair, sprawled hedonistically, oh-so-long legs splayed wide in invitation. I'm ignoring him on purpose. I've already tried to interview him twice this week, and both times, he distracted me.

Not today.

Okay, not *twice* today.

"You've got me at your mercy, Miss Finnegan. What do you want to know?"

I cross my legs tightly. "Let's just start from the beginning, shall we?"

THE END

85

"I CAN GET UPSTAIRS BY MYSELF," I tell Sterling as I close the passenger door. "I promise I'll call you if I need anything."

He doesn't look appeased. I keep expecting him to throw me over his shoulder and camp out in my living room, where he can keep an eye on me, but eventually, he relents.

The weight of his attention follows me as I walk into the building. Honestly, it's nice. It's been a long time since someone doted on me, and I never expected it to be Sterling.

"Hey, neigh—fuck, love, are you all right?"

Standing at the elevator is Lucky, looking gorgeous in black jeans and a leather jacket.

The adrenaline must be wearing off because I stumble before I reach him. Luckily—*ha, because of the name*—he catches me.

"Whoa, okay. Don't worry; I've got you. Come on."

He does too. Like Sterling, he's built of muscle, and he smells amazing, and maybe it's better to stop acting tough and let someone look after me for a little bit.

One second, I'm closing my eyes and leaning into him, and the next, we're at my door.

"Are you going to be okay? Do you want me to call someone to stay with you?"

"You're sweet," I say before I can stop myself. "Hot and sweet."

He looks concerned. "I'm not sure I want to leave you like this."

I push my key into the lock, and if it wasn't for Sterling, I'd be inviting Lucky in right now. Shame really. If only there was a way to have both.

I really should get inside before I say that out loud.

"It's fine, I promise." I'm already a little more awake now that my bed is within reach. "But thank you for walking me home."

"I'm right down the hall if you need anything, anything at all."

He really is quite sweet.

I've just closed the door behind me when there's a knock. Honestly, I know today was a lot, and I probably look as banged up as my uncle's old sedan, but I'm not so hurt that I can't walk the eight feet to my bedroom.

But it isn't Lucky at my door.

"Sterling, what are you doing here?"

He doesn't look good. He might actually look worse than me as he steps inside, brow furrowed and unblinking.

I worry about what he sees.

It's not that I'm messy. I've just ... had other priorities lately. It's been easier to forget the socks I left in the bathroom because I almost wore them into the shower or the pair of headphones under my pillow because I fell asleep watching a two-hour deep dive on the drama surrounding a niche hobby I'd never heard of. It's the mug that never makes it back into the cupboard because keeping it next to the coffee maker saves me five seconds and the collection of charging cables plugged in at all times for easy access.

But Sterling never stops looking at me long enough to notice.

"I never left. I've been stuck in my car, debating whether or not this is a terrible idea, but I don't give a shit anymore. I need you." He stalks forward, catches my face in his hands, and kisses me, hard and desperate.

Oh, finally.

I fall into him, clawing at his clothes, clinging to him, the last threads of my energy turning my need for him up to eleven.

He kisses down my neck, but I'm too aware of where we've been.

I push back. "Wait. I've been sitting on the floor for half the day. Let me clean up first."

"Let me," he says, picking me up and walking to the bathroom.

"You don't need to worry about me. I can manage."

He's gentle as he sets me down, as though I'll break if he moves too quickly, presses too hard. "Please, Mia. Let me take care of you."

"Okay."

He strips me carefully, gently, keeping me out of the shower until he's satisfied the temperature won't scald me. The water's a little colder than I like it, but he's pulling his shirt off and his zipper down, and I don't care about the water anymore.

Long, lean legs and broad shoulders aren't the only impressive things he's hiding under his suits. His dick is gorgeous, thick and hard between his thighs, and I'm glad I didn't die before I got to see it. Touch it. Taste it.

He walks in after me, kissing me again, and I let go, standing still and safe while he pours some gel in his hands and starts to wash me. He's methodical, never stopping to tease, but, oh, does he look.

When he's done, he rinses it off, and then he redirects the showerhead to hit the wall, crowding me against it. The tiles are warm from the water, and it's so like him to think of a detail like that. Hotter than that is his body, which presses against me as he kisses me again.

When he drops to his knees, I have to grip his shoulder to keep upright.

"Say the word, and I'll stop."

But I don't have any words, and I don't need them because he licks between the seam of my pussy, sucking my clit into his mouth, and I'm consumed by white-hot pleasure.

His fingers bite into my hips, but it's a delicious reminder that I don't need to hold myself up because he's here, he's got me, and so I dig my fingers into his damp hair and lose myself to every swipe of his tongue.

"Don't you dare stop," I gasp.

The air is thick with steam, sticking to my skin, making me hotter.

He eats me out like a man starved for it, and all it takes is finally looking down, seeing the great Sterling Ross, hot and hard and hungry between my thighs, and I'm gone, overwhelmed by him, my stomach tensing under his palm as I rock into his mouth.

When it gets to be too much, he relents, placing gentle kisses on the inside of my thigh, along my hips, holding me through the aftershocks.

I can't keep myself up when he moves, but I shouldn't have doubted him. He wraps me in a towel and scoops me back up, walking me to the bed.

"Stay," I say, and he hugs me tighter.

"I'm not going anywhere."

And they lived happily ever ...

not so fast. I want an epilogue. (**turn to page 441**)

86

Lucky grabs his gear, and we walk out of the club together. Sterling has his hand on my lower back, and Lucky has his arm around my shoulders.

"Um ..." I don't want to go home yet—or I want to go home, but I want them to come with me.

"My place?" Lucky asks, and bless him and his unending confidence.

"I'll meet you." Sterling walks over to a monster of a Ducati, retrieving a helmet and jacket before straddling it.

I didn't think Sterling could get hotter, but apparently, he can. Leather looks good on him. More than good.

Fucking delicious.

"Damn, that's hot."

See? Lucky agrees.

"Always need a quick getaway, don't you?"

Sterling gives him a reproachful look. "Are you ever going to let that go?"

"And give up my leverage?" Lucky asks, and, jeez, I can hear the glee in his voice. "When did you start riding one of these then?"

"Right after I almost died in your passenger seat." He turns to me. "Don't let him fool you; his road rage is legendary."

"Wouldn't be a problem if more people followed the road rules."

Sterling waves a hand, as if to say, *Do you see my point?* "Meanwhile, the record still stands."

"Bullshit," Lucky counters.

"Not a single ticket."

"Smug looks awful on you."

Sterling's smile deepens. "I don't believe you. I think you love it."

"Oh, yeah?"

Without a word, Sterling catches him with a hand on his neck, pulling him in for a rough kiss. "Yes."

I'm close enough to catch the slide of their tongues against each other, and, *fuck,* we need to leave now.

"Okay, Mia," Sterling says, pulling his helmet on, "settle this for us. Bike or cab—who are you going with?"

Both. I want both.

"Don't make me choose."

"It's temporary, I promise you. Once we get to Lucky's, you'll have your fill of both of us."

I'm going to hold him to that because all I can think about is being full of them in every possible way.

"In that case ..." I jump onto the bike behind him, taking the helmet he offers me and throwing Lucky an apologetic look. "You'd better drive as fast as he says you do."

"Yes, ma'am."

He revs the engine over Lucky's laughter, who doesn't look disappointed in the least. All I know is, if I'm dreaming, nobody had better wake me up.

THE END

87

THE TENSION IS thick as I follow them into the office. I can still feel where Lucky trailed his fingers down my sides and the pressure of his thigh between my legs.

Now Sterling is looking at both of us like we're a feast he's ready to devour, and I'm more than willing.

Lucky's voice drips with the same fire that's burning through me. "So, Mac, how can we help you? Or did you come to talk about the weather?"

I know what I'm expecting when we walk in, but it still takes me by surprise when Lucky closes the door and Sterling is on him, pressing him into the wood and kissing him hard enough that I hear their teeth click together over the bar's music.

"You know what I want."

"Yeah, I do."

They trade kisses like blows, grabbing at each other's clothes, and fuck if it's not the hottest thing I've ever seen.

Lucky grabs Sterling's wrist, holding it up to stare at the tattoo there—a four-leaf clover. "When?"

The back of Lucky's neck goes white under Sterling's grip. "The year after I left. I had to. I needed a way to keep you with me."

"Fuck, Mac." Lucky surges forward, their mouths meeting with force.

Sterling catches me watching while his tongue is still in

Lucky's mouth, his eyes so dark that they're almost all black, and Lachlan moans loudly. There's no hesitation as he grips Lucky's hair and pulls his head back for a kiss that is deep and filthy and immediately sets my skin aflame.

Fuck.

Sterling pulls back, his gaze never leaving mine as he stands tall and licks his lips. "Mia."

That's it. Just my name, rough, and my heart is pounding.

I move, called to him like a magnet.

I'm expecting the same treatment, the same hard, insistent pressure charging at me, and I want it; I'm ready.

Instead, he goes slow. Brushes my lips with his so lightly that I might be imagining it. I need more. With his hands cupping my cheeks, Sterling keeps me still and pulls back. I ache to follow him and lean forward, testing how far he'll let me push.

"Wait," he says, holding me in place.

His breath ghosts my cheek, and I feel his lips just out of reach, but he doesn't move.

Why won't he kiss me already?

"Be patient, Mia."

A soft sound escapes my throat, but I stay still.

Slow enough that I can count the beats of my heart under each breath, Sterling presses closer, kissing my top lip, then my lower, the pressure dizzyingly gentle. I fist my hands at my sides, silently urging him for more.

He doesn't obey.

No, he knows how much I want him, and he's making me wait for it.

Anticipation stretches out, to the point of breaking; I'm shaking with the need to get his mouth on me. Just when I can't take it anymore, when I'm gearing up to stop following orders and fucking *move,* he finally kisses me.

His mouth is perfect, soft, insistent, and—oh God, his

tongue. Eager. Demanding. I already want to do it again, and we haven't even stopped yet.

"I want …"

He drags his lips along my cheek. "What do you want? Tell me."

Both of them. Everything.

"I want to watch," I whisper.

Sterling follows my gaze to Lucky and reaches up to gather his hair in his hand. "Is this what you want?" He dives back in, kissing him roughly, and Lucky groans into it.

Yes.

Sterling nips at his ear. "She likes those sounds you're making."

"I can see that," Lucky says, his head tipped back from the grip Sterling has on his hair.

"Let's show her what you're really good at."

"Fuck yes," he answers, his voice ragged, then groans when Sterling bites a mark on his neck.

"On your knees," he commands, already pushing Lachlan to the ground, never loosening his tight hold.

Lucky drops. The muscles in his neck strain as his head is tipped back, his eyes dark and hungry. He licks his lips.

"Good. Now open that gorgeous mouth for me," Sterling growls, and the answering moan rumbles through my bones.

Fuck, all my dreams will look like this.

There's no teasing, no preamble, just Lucky pulling Sterling's cock free from his pants and leaning in. He doesn't stop until he's taken it all.

"Fuck, Lucky, just like that," Sterling moans. "You're as perfect as I remember."

Lucky pulls back until just the thick red tip is sitting on his tongue. "Missed this taste, love." He laps at the head, teasing it before sinking back down.

Sterling's grip is tight in his hair. "Ten years, I've been dreaming of these lips." He holds Lucky still as he thrusts into the heat of his mouth.

With his free hand, Sterling pulls me back in, kissing me. "Is this what you wanted?"

I nod.

"Yeah?" Sterling nips at my ear, and it goes straight to my clit. "I bet you're dripping. You like watching me fuck his face, don't you?"

"Yes," I whimper.

"I know." Sterling licks deep into my mouth as he pumps his hips. "He likes it too. Don't you, Lucky?"

Lucky moans.

When I look down, I see how right Sterling was—Lucky is beautiful like this. His lips stretch around Sterling's long, hard cock, slick with saliva and pre-cum. Tears coat Lucky's lashes. And the sounds he's making ... my God. Moaning like he's getting paid to. Choking a little every time Sterling hits the back of his throat and then taking him deeper.

Sparks fly through me when Lucky curls his hand around my ankle, each stroke of his fingers going straight to my pussy.

I don't think I've ever been this wet.

Sterling swears again, then drags me into a filthy kiss. "Show us how much you're enjoying this, Mia. Touch yourself for me."

I do as told, pulling my skirt up and snaking my fingers under my soaked underwear to rub at my throbbing clit. *Oh my God.*

"That's it." Sterling sucks on my bottom lip. "Fuck, I'm gonna—"

He grunts when he comes, kissing me so hard that I almost come too.

Lucky blinks up at us as he wipes his mouth, his eyes blown wide. His cock is straining his pants, mouthwateringly hard.

Sterling drops his hands to dress himself. "Get back up here, Lucky."

Lucky wipes his mouth and stands, pressing a brutal kiss to Sterling's lips. There's a scramble at his belt, and Sterling is pulling him out, pulling him in tight, fast strokes.

"Mia, give me your hand."

Oh, yes, please. It almost kills me to stop touching myself, but I do, and it's worth it when Sterling captures my wrist and sucks my fingers into his mouth, licking me clean before wrapping my hand around Lucky's dick.

It's rock hard and scorchingly hot. Lucky surges down to kiss me as I stroke him, and Sterling swears under his breath as he kisses my neck.

"That's it—nice and tight, Mia. Let him fuck your fist." As he talks, Sterling slides his hand up under my skirt, and I widen my legs to help him out. I need his hands on me. "Is this where you need me?" he asks, teasing the seam of my pussy through my underwear.

"Yes," I breathe. "Please."

He slides his fingers in, and then there's a second set. Lucky is kissing me again, groaning as he bucks into my hand, pre-cum spilling out readily now, coating my palm, slicking the way. I know how he feels, and the filthy slide of their fingers inside me, circling my clit, has me on the verge of coming already.

Sterling must sense it because he's pumping his fingers in faster now, the wet sound of each thrust loud in my ears. "Fuck," he growls, "listen to you."

It's hot, but it's Lucky who has my attention. Oh God, the noises he makes, groans and moans when he likes something, and it just makes me want more.

"Are you going to come for her, Lucky? She's waiting for it. She wants you to."

I do.

Lucky grunts when he comes, and his cock is still pulsing in my hand when Sterling bites my neck and slips another finger into my pussy.

"Now you, Mia."

It pulses through me in great, rolling waves, and all I can do is grab on to both of them and hold on as I ride it out, my whole body throbbing like a fresh bruise, filled with a gorgeous satisfaction and an ache for more.

Fuck, we need to do that again. Immediately.

Do you think they need a fourth? Asking for a friend.

cool down. let them have a happily ever after (**turn to page 362**)

88

THE KNUCKLES on his right hand are bandaged now, and that's two wounds he got today because of me.

"I'm sorry."

"No, you're not going to do that. You're not going to apologize. I'd do it again if I had to, if it meant knowing you were okay."

"You were amazing today."

"No, you were."

Sterling's kisses are ... indescribable. As soon as he touches me, everything else falls away, and I wait to follow his lead. He's patient, then impassioned, gentle, then overwhelming, but always in control. If Lucky's kisses are collaborations, Sterling's are a journey, where he's in the driver's seat.

"I almost abandoned you in there with him."

"But you didn't. You stayed."

"I'm not going anywhere. Do you understand?"

How did this happen? It must be a dream.

It has to be.

"Yes."

"Good."

Sterling is ... smiling. *At me.* It's beautiful. Shit, did I know he had dimples? They're beautiful. He's beautiful. I can't believe I've never seen him really smile before.

I never expected this—to be here. I don't know what to do

with my hands, and so they hover aimlessly. Sterling doesn't have the same problem; he touches everywhere, gripping my hips, my ass, running his fingers down my spine, pressing harder as I gasp into his mouth.

"Please tell me this is real." I've wished for this too many times to believe it.

He picks me up like I weigh nothing. "It's real. I couldn't dream of anyone as perfect as you."

Just to be sure, I keep kissing him. His lips are real. His hands are real … real and strong, carrying me to the bedroom, holding me tight as he sits on the edge. His hair is real, and I slide both of my hands into it to make sure.

God, all this time spent staring at it, trying to stop, wondering how it would feel in my fingers. It's glorious. Curling around me like it's trying to hook me, keep me close.

He's hard in his jeans, a noticeable bulge I want to rub against. I'm getting wet, just thinking about it. The way he's straining the zip, he's big. I need him inside of me.

Sterling maps a slow path up my back, searching for my bra and unhooking it, stripping it and my shirt off with one insistent tug. It hits the floor, somewhere—I don't care—and he pulls back, his breath exploding out of him, cupping my breasts in both hands.

"Oh," I moan, my pulse hammering in my throat while he teases both of my nipples to hardness with his thumbs. Each stroke is a straight shot of pleasure down my spine.

He licks his lips. "Fuck, Mia, you're incredible."

Then he ducks down, takes one in his mouth, sucking as I arch back.

I grind down, but our pants are in the way, and I can't get close enough, can't get the friction I need. I reach between us, getting both of our zips undone before I'm thwarted.

I whine into his mouth, and he flips us over.

I can't wait anymore, and I push insistently at his jeans until he takes over, hooking his thumbs under his boxers and taking it all off. I try to catch a glimpse of him, but he's already back, taking care of my pants as well.

Then it's nothing but skin on fantastic skin.

All the while, Sterling keeps kissing me—as he strips off my underwear, as he rolls on the condom, as he pushes inside.

His hands find mine, fingers slip between mine, raising my hands above my head as he leans down and kisses down my neck. The scratch of the bandage reminds me how close I came to something awful happening.

"I can't believe you fought him. What were you thinking?"

"He went after you. I wasn't thinking." He presses a hard kiss to my mouth. "I'd rather it be me than you."

"Don't say that."

His cock is hard and hot against my stomach, and I rock up into it, into him, loving the trail of pre-cum he leaves on my skin. Marking me. I want to be covered in it.

I circle my thumb through a pearl of pre-cum, rubbing it around the head.

He moans, low, his hips twitching. "I mean it; you're not alone anymore, and I care what happens to you, okay? If you care about me—"

"You know I do." And, yes, I do know now.

"Then you have to keep yourself safe too."

It's not only Hal I see threatening him; it's the leader, his crew, every gun pointed at Sterling's face while he stared back, cold and determined.

"Being a hero is only sexy if you survive."

"I'm here, aren't I?"

"Yes, you are. Now prove it. I need you to fuck me."

With a growl so deep that I feel it vibrate in my bones, he

grasps at my hips and pulls me back onto his cock. Over and over, hard and deep. Moans spill from my lips, punched-out little sounds I can't control, and I hook my ankles behind his back, urging him on. Neither of us can get close enough.

Fuck, he's so deep, and I still want more.

"That's it, Mia. Let me hear you."

I scream as I come, the sound ripped out of me, and I don't think I've ever come this hard without doing it myself, so of course, it was Sterling who made it happen. My orgasm is answered with his own, and I hate my heart for stuttering when he pulls away, putting distance between us to get rid of the condom.

He'll leave now, right? We both finished, and now he's—oh, slipping under the covers, pulling me close. My nerves settle.

Sterling props himself up on one elbow, looking down at me. A damp curl falls over his temple, but I don't dare touch it. It's beautiful. He's beautiful.

"I don't do this lightly, you know. I've wanted you for a long time. I tried to stop—you were with someone, and we work together—but you have to be honest with me; you have to tell me if this isn't serious for you because I ..."

I brush my lips against his. "That's not something you ever have to worry about. I ... I tried too. Tried everything I could to not want you. I told myself it was just a crush, that it would fade over time, but it hasn't. I can't be anything but serious about this because it's all I've wanted since I met you."

"Good," he says, kissing me. "Because I want to be here when you wake up tomorrow, and I'm going to keep wanting to be with you until you tell me to stop."

"You'll be waiting a while," I say, smiling.

"I was hoping you'd say that."

AND THEY LIVED HAPPILY EVER AFTER.

But what about Lucky? (**turn to page 372**)

89

THREE MONTHS LATER

I WAKE to the sound of Sterling's monster of a coffee machine. A fancy monster. It has a touch screen. It also grinds beans with the decibels of a jet engine.

Anytime I sleep here—three times already this week—I wake up to two things: Sterling or coffee. Sometimes both. Any and all combinations are great, although as I roll over onto his side of the bed, it would be nice to get a cuddle in before he leaves.

He might like to run at four a.m., but I don't need to see what the world looks like before the sun rises. I don't even need to open my eyes to find him in the kitchen.

He hums as I plaster myself to his back.

"What day is it?"

"Sunday."

Oh good. Not a workday then. It's hard to keep track, especially this week—I've been chasing a hospital administrator round in circles. Technically, they aren't refusing an interview, which would give credence to the wrongful death suit I'm investigating. No, they've agreed to be interviewed, but it might as well be set for August 41st because the rain checks, delays, postponements are endless.

I sigh and try to melt into Sterling.

"No working," I say.

"What isn't?"

"You. I don't care what you're working on. I'm not letting you go."

He shuffles in place, and I hear the beautiful sound of coffee being poured in to two mugs. He's so good to me.

Sterling and coffee—there's nothing better.

"Don't worry; work is the last thing on the agenda. I was hoping to take you out."

"Oh?"

Usually, our date nights consist of work and takeout. I'm not complaining—I love any time I spend with Sterling—but it'll be nice to try something new.

"It's a beautiful day," he says, tucking my hair behind my ear. "You're the one I want to share it with."

I let my forehead fall to his chest. It's too early for him to attack my heart like this; I haven't even had coffee yet. What hope do I have to respond? The best I've got is the lovesick sound that squeezes out of me, that I hope conveys the swell of *you're amazing*, and *every day I know you, I love you a little bit more*, and *I never knew I could feel so much for one person and not explode.*

"There's something else." He brings his hands to my cheeks, tilting my head back until our eyes meet. He's using the smile he knows makes me speechless. "I think I should let you know that I love you."

I close my eyes on a groan. "Obviously, I love you, too, but tell me again after coffee."

He's still smiling as he kisses me.

It is a beautiful day. It's the sort of day where anything might be possible.

It's also possible I'm talking out of my butt because my vision is completely fogged over with Sterling-itis.

We end up across town, and I'm two blocks into explaining exactly why Alice's cinnamon rolls have no equal when I hear music. A crowd has gathered up ahead, surrounding two guitarists—a guy with long legs and tattoos and a young woman with her hair in a fantastic braid. They're laughing and battling while the crowd cheers them on.

I recognize the guy as my neighbor Lucky.

He looks good. Scruff dusts his jaw, and his hair is half tied back. A sleeveless shirt and tight pants put his fantastic body on display. He's like a sexy pirate.

I'm so entranced by their playing that it takes me a second to realize Sterling's stopped moving. He's staring at Lucky with a look I recognize.

One I've seen directed at me.

One of the ways we differ is that Sterling prefers an organized attack. He's sly—don't get me wrong—but he never coddles, and he rarely softens the blow when it comes.

I prefer the softer approach. Less planned, more emotive. People are far more willing to open up than you expect, as long as you give them a chance. It just takes a little time.

For this though, I'm going to need to adopt Sterling's way.

"Tell me about him."

Learning to interpret Sterling's restraint gets a heck of a lot easier once you understand that he's hiding a tender, aching heart underneath all that grumpiness. So, it doesn't surprise me when that's where his story starts.

"I was at a loss after my parents died. Lucky was the first bright spot in a very angry darkness and a reminder of everything I wanted to fight for. Even after we lost touch, I would check in on him, saw his career grow and when he moved here."

That's a long time to miss someone, and knowing Sterling, I'm positive he's kept himself away on purpose.

"You should say hello. I'm sure he'd like to see you."

The battle finishes, and there's a loud cheer. Someone's decided as the winner, but I'm too focused on Sterling to see who. He isn't moving, and I make a decision.

"Come on."

I don't know what their history is, but it's obvious there is some, and it's confirmed for me when Lucky spots us, his gaze triangulating between us and everywhere we touch—especially where Sterling has his arm around my waist.

We never did have that date, but if he's sad or jealous, he's hiding it well. In fact, he's got the same glint in his eyes that he had when he asked me out, except this time, it's directed at ...

Oh, I see now.

Well, that's interesting. Very interesting ...

"You're pretty talented on that thing," I tell Lucky, who laughs. "Do you take requests?"

"Let's find out." He looks up from where he's packing his guitar away, his eyes bright. There's no mistaking who his next words are for. "It's good to see you."

"You too," Sterling replies.

"I heard about what happened at the bank. Good to know you haven't given up your habit of throwing yourself face-first into danger."

"It wasn't always danger I threw myself at. I did kiss you first."

"Yeah, I remember," Lucky says, standing. It brings him close. "It's kind of impossible to forget."

"Are you ..." Sterling gestures around us.

"Busy? No, you know I can always fit you in." The words are directed at Sterling, but the wink is sent to me.

"Teaching," Sterling finishes, his voice rougher.

Lucky laughs like he knew that, like he's testing the boundaries on purpose. "Nothing official."

It's a beautiful day, the kind of day where anything is possible, but sometimes, Fate needs a helping hand.

"Hey, Lucky," I say. "Maybe you can do something for me."

He slides his hands into his pockets, casual as anything. "Anything, love."

"Well, a few months ago, you asked me a question."

He followed up on our maybe date a few days later, and I had to tell him I was seeing someone. If I'd known the possibility for something more existed ... well, it's never too late to make up for lost time.

"Can you ask me again? Both of us this time."

The question is barely out of his mouth when Sterling is accepting—a short, sharp, "Yes," that must have been waiting there for years.

Yes, I think, *this is exactly where I'm meant to be.*

THE END

90

ONE YEAR LATER

STERLING PRESSES himself to my back, brushing my hair back and planting wet kisses at the top of my spine.

God, I love mornings like this. Getting out of bed is impossible, but, oh, is it worth it.

Lucky drags his lips along my neck. "Did she hear anything yet?"

"No."

His answering groan makes me smile. Lucky's the only person more invested in Alice's dating life than I am.

"Give me his number. I'll sort him out."

"It's not your business, Lachlan. Stay out of it."

He kisses along my shoulder, nipping at the juncture of my neck.

"She's already got another date for Friday," I say, petting Lucky's hair. "He's in construction."

"Good with his hands then." His own continue to lazily explore. "Tell her, if she has any trouble, call me, yeah?"

"She knows."

Of course, he'll tell her again himself when we video-chat later because he can never stop himself from saying hello, even when he's in the middle of his own work.

The morning floats in and out of focus, soaked in warm skin

and the fuzzy edge of sleep. We don't often get to indulge like this —Sterling is always in the middle of one project or another, and Lucky is lost to a composition or a comment section somewhere, and me? I snuggle under a blanket with my third coffee and bask in how happy I am.

I never have to guess what Lachlan is feeling; he wears everything on his sleeve and doubles it all down with words. It's lovely how freely he expresses his love and the flush that spreads along Sterling's neck when Lucky whispers sweet things in his ear.

And Sterling ... his feelings may be hard-won, but they're just as deep as Lucky's are, even if they need to be coaxed out on occasion. But if you know him, you see it plain as day. It's in his watchful eye, his loyalty, his deep-seated need to see you thrive and improve.

Deny it all he likes, but he likes to see the best in people too. He might not believe it exists in everyone—he's seen too much of the world—but when he does see it, he treats it like a precious resource. There's a gentleness in him that most people will never know or could ever believe.

But it's there, and it's all for me and Lucky.

THE END

www.ingramcontent.com/pod-product-compliance
Lightning Source LLC
Chambersburg PA
CBHW020342310726
48979CB00015B/2470/J
* 9 7 8 0 6 4 5 9 7 4 3 7 9 *